DAW Anthologies Edited by Peter Crowther:

HEAVEN SENT
MOON SHOTS
MARS PROBES
CONSTELLATIONS

FORBIDDEN PLANETS

EDITED BY

Peter Crowther

DAW BOOKS, INC.
DONALD A. WOLLHEIM, FOUNDER
375 Hudson Street, New York, NY 10014

ELIZABETH R. WOLLHEIM
SHEILA E. GILBERT
PUBLISHERS
http://www.dawbooks.com

First paperback printing, November 2006
1   2   3   4   5   6   7   8   9   10

DAW TRADEMARK REGISTERED
U.S. PAT. OFF. AND FOREIGN COUNTRIES
—MARCA REGISTRADA
HECHO EN U.S.A.

PRINTED IN THE U.S.A.

ACKNOWLEDGMENTS

"Introduction" copyright © 2006 by Ray Bradbury.

"Passion Ploy," copyright © 2006 by Matt Hughes Company Ltd.

"Lehr, Rex," copyright © 2006 by Joseph E. Lake, Jr.

"Dust," copyright © 2006 by Paul McAuley.

"Tiger, Burning," copyright © 2006 by Alastair Reynolds.

"The Singularity Needs Women!," copyright © 2006 by Paul Di Filippo.

"Dreamers' Lake," copyright © 2006 by Stephen Baxter.

"Eventide," copyright © 2006 by Monkeybrain, Inc.

"What We Still Talk About," copyright © 2006 by Scott Edelman.

"Kyle Meets the River," copyright © 2006 by Ian McDonald.

"Forbearing Planet," copyright © 2006 by Michael and Linda Moorcock.

"This Thing of Darkness I Acknowledge Mine," copyright © 2006 by Alex Irvine.

"Me-topia," copyright © 2006 by Adam Roberts.

"Afterword: *Forbidden Planet*," copyright © 2006 by Stephen Baxter.

TABLE OF CONTENTS

Introduction

Sometime in the early 1950s MGM Studios contacted me to write a screenplay for a film—the film turned out to be *Forbidden Planet*.

This request came from a gentleman named, incredibly, Nickie Nayfack. I didn't believe the name, so I checked with MGM and found that he was a relative of one of the studio producers.

I turned down the project and later regretted it because when I saw the film with the Id on the screen, I realized that this was the most important idea in the picture. If MGM had mentioned that to me then, I would have been intrigued and might have done something of a larger size with the Id than was done in the final film.

But if I had taken the job, the first thing I would have done would have been kill Robby the Robot or, if I had let him live, laser beam his storage batteries. For this, I think, a world would have worshiped me to the end of time. On the other hand, Robby the Robot's worshipers would have reviled me beyond reason.

But there's absolutely no doubting that Altair 4 was truly an unwelcoming place. And I should know. Because before 1955—and certainly afterward—I had written about a few forbidden planets of my own, hostile worlds where you wouldn't want to be stranded . . . even fully armed.

The concept of the inhospitable location—be it a planet, a haunted house, or a graveyard—has long been a staple of fantastic fiction. It's the kind of stuff I used to read as a small boy growing up in Illinois.

I remember being read to from Edgar Allan Poe by my Aunt Neva when I was sick in bed in late 1928 and, the very next year, reading the comic-strip adventures of *Buck Rogers* that started to appear in the daily newspapers. *Buck Rogers* offered me a trip to the asteroids, Venus, Mercury, and, yes, even Jupiter itself! And all in 1929 when Armstrong, Aldrin, and Collins hadn't even been born yet!

And then, at my Uncle Bion's house in the summer of 1930, I discovered bookshelves filled with even more exotic worlds . . . Edgar Rice Burroughs' wonderful creation, *John Carter of Mars*, who, some two years later, inspired me to write my own tales of the Red Planet, sometimes depicting it as a friendly world and other times as a place of mystery and intrigue. The first of those stories, "The Million Year Picnic," appeared in the summer of 1946 in *Planet Stories*.

So here we are, some sixty years later, with *Forbidden Planets*, tales of far-off places where Man isn't greeted with open arms. Open jaws, perhaps . . . but open arms? Never! In any event, Peter Crowther has gathered a fine bunch of writers to give their own take on alien worlds, honoring that film I almost wrote the screenplay for. I often wonder what kind of job I would have made of it! One thing is certain: I would have destroyed Robby the Robot early on and let all the characters behave. What a delightful thought!

Meanwhile, here are a dozen fine stories about mankind facing up to the perils that may lie ahead on distant worlds. Enjoy!

Ray Bradbury

Los Angeles
July 2005

Passion Ploy

Matthew Hughes

"What exactly is it?" Luff Imbry asked. He walked around the object that occupied the center of the small table in the secluded rear room of the tavern known as Bolly's Snug, viewing it from several angles and blinking at the way it caught the light.

"I took it off Chiz Ramoulian," said Dain Ganche.

"Took it?" Imbry's round, multichinned face showed a mild concern. Provenance could be a contentious issue when buying items of value behind closed doors. Chiz Ramoulian was only a minor hoodlum, yet he moved through the back streets of the City of Olkney attended by a reputation for sudden and inventive violence. He had also exhibited a knack for locating those with whom he had business. "Took it how?"

Ganche crossed corded arms across a broad chest. "I found him in an alley near the slider that comes from the spaceport. He was sitting against a wall, blurry eyed and cradling this in his arms. I reminded him that he owed me a substantial sum from a joint enterprise." Like Imbry, Ganche regularly invested in highly profitable ventures whose details were known only to those directly involved in their execution. "I suggested that this object would settle the score. Then I took it."

Imbry's gaze returned to the glittering thing on the table. He was finding it difficult to look away. "And he was content with that?"

Ganche's heavy lips took a reflective bend. "He made a noise or two, but nothing actionable. To put it all in a single word, he seemed . . . distracted. But, then, he has a fondness for Red Abandon, and once he cracks a flask, he does not leave it till it's drained. That may account for his mood. In any case, a scroot patrol picked him up shortly after."

"Hmm," said Imbry. He again circled the table and examined the item. "It is inarguably beautiful," he murmured. Indeed, beauty seemed almost too flimsy a word to fling around in its presence. It compelled the eyes.

Imbry turned from the thing and found that it took an increased effort to do so. He took up the dark cloth in which Ganche had brought the object and covered its brightness. He kept seeing a ghost of its outline imprinted on the walls, as if it were the negative image of a bright light.

"I've found it best not to stare at it too long," said the big man. "But what on Old Earth is it?"

"Certainly not *of* Old Earth," Imbry said. "It's of ultraterrene origin. I'd lay a hept to a bent grimlet on that."

"Ramoulian often haunts the spaceport," Ganche said, "in hopes of coming across baggage that is indifferently attended. He has been known to wear a cleaner's uniform. Or he inserts himself into a stream of disembarking passengers, playing the affable traveler. He strikes up a conversation with some offworlder and offers guidance. Then he leads the mark into a dark and out-of-the-way corner and relieves him of his burdens. Perhaps this was in someone's valise."

"Possibly," said Imbry. "But why was Ramoulian

languishing with his prize in an alley when the scroots were on the prowl?"

"Again, Red Abandon?"

"It has an unmistakable odor," Imbry said. "Did he smell of it?"

"Not that I noticed."

"Then I lean toward the notion that this object caused the distraction."

Ganche lifted up a corner of the covering cloth. "It does not affect me that strongly."

"Nor I," said Imbry. "Perhaps Ramoulian was peculiarly susceptible. But the main question is: What is it?"

"No," said the other man, "the main question is: What is it worth? You are more knowledgeable than I in the buying and selling of art."

Imbry stroked his plump earlobe with a meditative finger. "I have no idea," he said. "We will find out by offering it in auction to a carefully chosen group of buyers. My commission will be forty percent."

"Fifteen," said Ganche with a speed that was reflexive. They haggled a few more moments and settled on thirty percent, which had been Imbry's intent.

When they had executed the mutual motions of hand and arm by which such bargains were sealed, Imbry said, "I may consult an expert in extraterrene artifacts."

"Discreetly," Ganche said.

"Of course." There was another brief haggle and a flurry of gestures that decided how the expert's fee would be paid.

"So you think it is, in fact, a manufactured item?" Ganche said. "I thought it might be of natural origin."

Imbry moved his large, round head in a gesture of indecision. He tucked the square of black cloth about the object, then lifted it gently and deposited it in the large satchel he had brought with him. The thing was surprisingly heavy—densely packed, he thought. He closed up the bag and activated the fastenings. The room seemed emptier now that the object was out of sight.

Imbry repaired to his operations center, a room in a nondescript house on a quiet street in a modest neighborhood. He traveled carefully, taking detours and laying false trails by entering public buildings that were busy with people, going in by the main doors then immediately departing by rear exits.

Partly, this was habitual caution; a practitioner of Imbry's profession never knew when the scroots might have singled him out for preemptive surveillance. Lately, though, he had found himself caught up in a worrisome dispute with Alwinder Mudgeram, a man of blunt opinions and brutal instincts who was convinced that Luff Imbry owed him a substantial sum. The funds had been advanced toward a project that had not come to fruition. Unforeseen disappointments could blight any line of endeavor, Imbry had counseled Mudgeram, advising him to consider his lost capital a failed investment. But the investor preferred to see it as a debt to be repaid, and Mudgeram was renowned for collecting every groat due him.

Secure in his operations center, Imbry had his integrator deploy a research and communications matrix that spent most of its time disguised as a piece of battered furniture. He removed the mysterious object from the satchel and unwrapped it, taking care to keep his eyes averted, and let the matrix's percepts scan it. Its effects upon him he found annoying, as if it were a spoiled child who kept tugging at his garment, insistently importuning him with, "Look at me! Look at me!"

As soon as it was scanned, he rewrapped and resatcheled the object, then placed it in a concealed locker beneath the floor of a closet that appeared to be stuffed with the kind of items one acquired at jumble sales. Some of the bric-a-brac had artfully concealed functions that would have drawn sharp attention from agents of the Archonate Bureau of Scrutiny.

"Integrator," he said. "Conduct a class-two inquiry as to nature and origins." Imbry had designed his integrator, as he had designed the closet's false kitsch, to answer the special circumstances that often arose in the conduct of his business. What he called a class-two inquiry, for example, was not unlike an information search along Old Earth's connectivity grid that any citizen might undertake, except that Imbry's integrator could ease in and out of public data stores without being noticed. That was important when the whereabouts of an item being researched and valued was of interest to the scroots.

The integrator hummed and fussed for several seconds. As he waited, Imbry was vexed to discover in himself a surprising urge to go to the closet and view the object. He got up and paced until his integrator reported that it had found no matches in publicly accessible records.

"We will try private sources," Imbry said. "Catalogs from dealers in ultraterrene artworks, both here and . . ." He thought for a moment, then named the four planets along The Spray that were major nexi for trade in nonhuman artifacts and had offices on Old Earth where such catalogs would be found. "Plus any places where curios are discussed."

It took a little longer for his matrix to locate and insert itself unnoticeably into the private data stores, but again it came back with no solid results. "Nothing from the dealers. I have a partial match, though the correspondence is less than ten percent," his integrator said.

"Show me."

The displayed image appeared in the air before him. It was a curved fragment, dark and stained, of something that had been broken. It superficially resembled the exterior of the object beneath the closet floor, except that its surface was not bright and glittering with points of diamond-hard light, nor did it shimmer with unnameable colors that ravished the eye.

"What is it?" Imbry said.

"It is tentatively identified as a fragment of the husk of a seedpod from an uncataloged world in the Back of Beyond," the integrator said. "It may or may not have been part of some native artwork. It was recovered from a ship hired by an artifact hunter from Popsy."

"What is Popsy?"

"An odd little world far down The Spray. The hunter's name was Fallo Wickiram. He hired the ship on Bluepoint and was last seen heading toward the gas cloud called the Lesser Dark. He apparently landed on a number of uncouth worlds, gathering such curiosities as appealed to his taste. At some point, the period of the ship's hire was up, and, as programmed, it returned to Bluepoint·on its own. Wickiram was not aboard, and there was no indication as to what had become of him."

"What was the last world he visited?" Imbry said.

"It has no name and apparently no attractions, since the records show that almost no one ever goes there. Here are its coordinates." The integrator produced a string of numbers and vectors. They meant nothing to Imbry.

"How long ago did this occur?" he asked and learned that Wickiram had met his unknown fate several thousand years ago. Imbry thought about it for some moments, then said, "The information is of doubtful utility. Record it anyway, then let us press on."

The mention of a seedpod triggered a new line of inquiry. The integrator reviewed records of artworks and more commonplace items made from such materials up and down The Spray. Several more leads appeared but, upon investigation, led nowhere. Imbry poked about in other avenues that suggested themselves, including the itineraries of any ships that had recently put down at the Olkney spaceport. But any spaceship, whether liner, freighter, or private yacht, stopped at so many worlds where they might connect to other worlds that the object's possible routes to Old Earth were effectively infinite.

Finally, he checked for reports of robbery or fraud concerning recent arrivals to Olkney but found none in the public media nor in the elements of the Bureau of Scrutiny's systems that he was able to access without detection. He concluded that if Chiz Ramoulian had acquired the object illicitly, the crime had gone either unreported or undiscovered.

Imbry steepled his fingers and touched them to his uppermost chin and stood in thought for a long moment. Then he said, "Connect me to The Honorable Ilarios Warrigrove."

A few seconds passed while Imbry's integrator contacted its equivalent at the Warrigrove manse and protocols were exchanged. Then an aquiline face marked by lines of care appeared in the air before Imbry. "You have something?" he said, his languid voice unable completely to disguise a note of sharp interest.

"Something I wish to have valued," said Imbry.

"And will it be available for private purchase?"

"My plans have not yet assumed their final shape. At the moment, I'm considering an auction," said Imbry, "but to a limited and discreet set of purchasers."

"What do you have?"

"I will have to show it to you."

"Intriguing." Warrigrove's expression showed an indolent mood, but Imbry's finely tuned eye detected a concealed underwash of excitement. "I am free for an hour."

"I'll be there shortly."

Imbry returned the room to its seeming unremarkableness and retrieved the object. Again he was irritated to experience an urge to take it from the satchel and gaze at its sparkles and flashes. He left the house and walked for several minutes, turning corners randomly, then hailed an aircar and had it take him to a specific corner on the other side of the city. Alighting there, he walked some more, then took another aircar to within several streets of Warrigrove's manse and again took a circuitous route to the house's rear gate. The who's-there recognized him and admitted him to a walled and overgrown garden.

On the far side of the untended greenery was a tumbledown antique gazebo, swarmed by thick growing vines that also concealed systems that ensured that any sight or sound encountered within its leafy confines would not carry beyond them. Imbry followed a flagstoned path to the structure, slipped within, and found Ilarios Warrigrove seated on a chair of black iron behind a table of the same material, sipping from a tall thin glass filled with a pale yellow liquid. A carafe of the stuff and another glass stood on a tray before him. "Would you care to?" he asked with a gesture that Imbry's eye noted was calculatedly relaxed.

"Why not?" the fat man said. He raised the glass, paused but a moment to inhale its delicate bouquet, then drained half of it at a gulp. "Excellent."

They exchanged the gestures and pleasantries suitable to a casual encounter and the time of day, but Imbry saw how Warrigrove's eyes kept flickering sideways to the satchel that hung from his unoccupied hand. The formalities accomplished, he placed the container on the table and withdrew its cloth-wrapped contents.

"Someone has asked me to sell this," he said and whisked away the covering.

Warrigrove could not restrain an intake of breath.

"You know what it is," Imbry said. He was adept at reading microexpressions and now saw Warrigrove consider, then reject, denial but opt for less than full disclosure, all in the time a tranquil man takes to blink.

"I know what it might be," he said. "I had heard—only a rumor—that such a thing might be on its way to Old Earth."

The aficionado spoke without taking his eyes from the scintillation. Imbry sensed that the man was unable to resist the attraction. For himself, he found that his annoyance at the thing's importuning made it easier to look away. "What is it?" he asked.

Imbry watched the patrician face closely while Warrigrove framed his answer, and was fairly sure that he was about to hear the truth.

"A myth," the man said, "or a chimera. An object of desire, longed for and sought after, though it may not truly exist."

The fat man made a gesture that expressed cynicism. "That sounds like precisely the kind of thing that a cunning forger would contrive to dangle before the avid appetite."

Warrigrove's eyes did not leave the object. "Well, you would know," he said.

Imbry acknowledged the truth of the observation. More than a few alleged masterworks that hung or stood or scampered in the palaces of wealthy collectors had come from his own hand, though they bore the signatures and sigils of bygone geniuses.

"Indeed," Warrigrove continued, "if it is a fraud, you are precisely the kind of person one might expect to arrive asking, eyes wide with innocence, just what it might be."

"Let us assume, for the moment," Imbry said, "that my innocence is genuine and that the item is what it is supposed to be—then what is it?"

Warrigrove sighed. "You will think me needlessly obscure, but your question has no definite answer."

Imbry felt a twinge of annoyance. "We inhabit an impossibly ancient world," he said. "Every question has long since been posed, in all its possible variants and permutations, and answered fully."

"That is supposedly the overarching reality of our age," admitted Warrigrove. "But we may be dealing here with another reality."

"I am, as you have intimated, a manufacturer of 'other realities,'" Imbry said. "Thus you may trust me when I tell you that no other reality exists."

"And yet you bring me this," Warrigrove said. His long, pale fingers reached out and touched the thing on the table, stroked it, then drew back. "You must leave it with me."

"No."

"I must study it."

Imbry said, "I intend to hold an auction. But if you'd care to waive your fee for this consultation, you can be among the bidders."

Warrigrove agreed with an alacrity that surprised Imbry. The fat man covered the object with the dark cloth, evoking a low moan from the aficionado, who blinked as if awakening from a dream, then looked at Imbry with a puzzled expression. "You did that," he said, "without effort. Does its glory not touch your inner being?"

"I hope not," said Imbry. "I prefer to be touched only at my own instigation. Now tell me what it is."

Warrigrove sighed. "It has had many names: the Grail Ultima, the Egg of First Innocence, the Eighth Path, the Supernal Radiance. Which do you prefer?"

Imbry found none of them satisfying. All had the ring of empty syllables swirled about by vague associations, nebulous connotations. He didn't mind batting about such inflated insubstantiata when he had been the one to blow air into them, but to be on the receiving end of the "perfumed cloud" was irritating. He again studied Warrigrove closely, but detected no intent to deceive.

"Ambiguity will not serve," he said. "If you can't

give me more than a misty whiff of its nature, then tell me if it has a function: What does it *do*?"

Warrigrove's brows rose and his lips pursed, and Imbry could tell that his latest question was no more likely to receive a hard-edged answer than had its predecessors. "Anything and nothing," the aficionado said. "Fulfill dreams, but only for those who take care not to awaken. Reveal mysteries, though the revelations are no less mysterious than what was hidden. Transform base dross into rare earth, at least in the eye of the beholder. This is something from beyond our mundane existence. It is like one of the wonders of our species' dawn time, when who could say what might lie beyond the familiar hills, and the mind spun tales of eldritch kingdoms and far off lands upon which any fancy might be imposed."

Imbry put one plump palm against his forehead, then drew it down his face, as if the action could wipe away a film that obscured his perceptions. "I will summarize," he said. "We have an object whose existence to date has been mainly rumor; which comes from no one knows exactly where; whose nature and functions are, at best, untested; about which vague yet fabulous and mystical claims may be made. And, on top of all that, it may be merely a cunning forgery."

"You have it," said Warrigrove. "Though I doubt it is a fake. It generates in me too profound a passion. Though I am puzzled by your ability to withstand its glamor."

"We are fashioned from different stuffs. It is why you collect and I deal."

"That may well be so. We come from different sides of a metaphysical divide. And each must pity the other."

"Let us leave our estimations of each other's character for another day," said Imbry, "and concentrate on resolving this mystery."

"Very well. I will advance a theory: Perhaps the myriad grails and will o' the wisps that speckle the history of humanity have always been the same object. Say it is a fragment from a higher realm that somehow found its way into our base continuum—an eternal, unchangeable shred of absolute beauty that moves in mysterious ways from place to place and from time to time. Some of those who encounter it are transported by the revelation of a sphere of existence so much greater, so much finer, than the dull swamp in which we grind out our little lives. Others receive the same knowledge but are merely annoyed."

Imbry made a tactless noise. "Have you spent much time on that theory?"

"In truth," said Warrigrove, "it came to me as I beheld the object."

"Indeed? So it is a touchstone for separating humanity into the high-minded and the prosaic?"

"I would not put it that way, but it is not an inaccurate reflection of my idea."

"And you would include Chiz Ramoulian among the elevated?"

"The Red Abandon addict?" Warrigrove tried to disguise his anxiety, but Imbry was a practiced listener. "Is he connected to this?"

"He appears to have been as taken with it as you are."

Warrigrove attempted to affect nonchalance. "You would feel no need to mention my connection to this matter in Ramoulian's hearing?"

"At present, he is dining with the Archon," Imbry said, employing the common euphemism for those who were experiencing the unsought hospitality of the Archonate Bureau of Scrutiny. "I expect we will have this business concluded before they tip him back onto the streets."

"That is good," said Warrigrove.

"Indeed." Imbry briskly abraded one plump palm against its brother. "Very well, let us defer questions

of what and why and where. Let us instead deal with
how much."

"Ah," said Warrigrove, "on that score, feel free to
let your imagination soar."

Luff Imbry could scale the heights of passion when
entertaining the prospect of his own enrichment. He
believed that life, at least *his* life, was not meant to
be an exercise in self-stinting. As he made his way
from Warrigrove's, satchel in hand, he allowed himself
to indulge in some pleasantly fanciful speculations as
to just how much fatter the mysterious object might
make his purse. Thus distracted he failed to notice the
sleek black volante that was shadowing him at rooftop
height on a tranquil residential street until it silently
dropped to block his way. The dark hemisphere of
energy that shielded its passenger compartment was
extinguished, and Imbry found himself under the hard
stare of Alwinder Mudgeram.

"I have been looking for you," Mudgeram said. "I
have left messages."

"I do not seem to have received them."

The aircar's operator's door opened, and out
stepped a man almost as large as Dain Ganche, with
a tattooed face and shoulders like small hills.

"Good day, Ip," said Imbry. Everyone always
greeted Mudgeram's assistant with studied politeness,
although Imbry had never heard of anyone having received more than a silent nod in acknowledgment.

"Let me offer you a ride," Mudgeram said and gestured to the empty seat beside him.

Ip reached for Imbry's arm with a hand whose
fingers had been augmented with subtle but strong
components. His grip caused the limb to go numb as
the fat man was half lifted into the vehicle. The energy dome reestablished itself, and Imbry felt the
seat cushion push against him as they went aloft.

"There is this matter of the funds I advanced
you," said Mudgeram. "I was promised a profit to

make the senses swim; instead, I suffered a complete loss."

"There were risks to the venture. They were disclosed."

"I remember a brief allusion to a remote possibility. Much more attention was devoted to the expected windfall. Pictures were painted, vistas laid out, all bedecked with boundless gain."

"Without enthusiasm, there would be no ventures at all."

"I have developed a new enthusiasm," Mudgeram said. "I now pursue grim satisfaction with the same zeal I formerly reserved for your scheme."

"That may be not good for you," Imbry said.

"It will definitely be 'not good' for some."

They had flown high above the city, heading west, and now cruised high above the chill waters of Mornedy Sound. The wave-rippled surface far below resembled the wrinkled hide of some great cold-blooded beast. Mudgeram invited his passenger to look down and envision a sequence of events that would end with Imbry entering the sea at high speed.

"Your funds went to acquire necessary materials for the plan," Imbry said. He had purchased minor artworks dating from the antique period in which his intended forgery would appear to have been created. The purchased works were broken down into their constituent elements, then reordered into a painting in the style of Bazieri, a grandmaster of the same age whose lifetime oeuvre had been scant. A newly discovered work by the ancient artist would have drawn collectors from at least thirty of the Ten Thousand Worlds along The Spray, each trailing funds like a pecuniary comet.

"Who could have foreseen that a vault full of unknown Bazieris would turn up in an attic?" It turned out that the artist had for years paid his rent with masterpieces that to the landlord were no more than pleasant daubs. By the time Bazieri's genius was recognized, both landlord and tenant were dust and the works long forgotten in a boarded-up cockloft. They were discovered and emerged onto the market just as Imbry prepared to go forward with his fake; prices collapsed, leaving his forged work worth less than the cost of its ingredients.

"I have heard all of this before," Mudgeram said. "It puts no hepts in my pocket."

"Just as there are none in mine at the moment," Imbry said. "Pickings have lately been slim."

Mudgeram rubbed the blue stubble that always shaded his jaw. "I will forgo the profits that never came," he said. "But I will either have back my investment or take my satisfaction in other ways."

"What ways?"

"A number of people have reason to feel that Luff Imbry has had a deleterious effect on the smooth passage of their lives. I will auction you to them. I might yet make a profit on our association."

Imbry thought of some of those who would hasten to attend such an auction and pay gladly for the opportunity to carry him off in restraints to some remote location where they would not be interrupted. "I do have one excellent prospect," he said.

"Now would be a good time to tell me about it," Mudgeram said.

"I will do better. I will show you."

Imbry opened the satchel and peeled back some of the cloth, enough to let the object's effulgence show. He saw Alwinder Mudgeram's eyes light up with the same mixture of appetite and dreaminess that had affected Warrigrove and, he presumed, Ramoulian. When he glanced Ip's way, he saw no overt expression, but the bodyguard's eyes slitted as if what he saw brought discomfort.

Imbry replaced the cloth and resealed the satchel. Mudgeram returned to the mundane. "What is it?" he said.

"That remains undetermined," Imbry said. "But it

is the property of Dain Ganche, who has asked me to auction it for him. Ilarios Warrigrove will be one of the bidders." He saw no need to mention Chiz Ramoulian.

Mudgeram's face was not hard to read. Imbry watched the evidence of the man's thoughts as he processed the knowledge that Ganche was involved and came to a decision. "Warrigrove has just acquired a competitor," he said, then added,"Ip, home."

As the car banked and headed back toward Olkney, Mudgeram invited Imbry to stay at his house in town, a dour mansion on the Boulevard of Seven Graces. Imbry saw no way to decline.

It was decided that the auction would be held in a second-story salon whose heavily defended windows overlooked the private garden at the rear of Mudgeram's house. The date was set for three nights later. Imbry had Mudgeram's integrator connect him to his own assistant, and between them they developed a list of five more collectors who would have both an interest in acquiring the object and the wealth to meet or exceed the exorbitant reserve price Imbry decided was warranted.

On the designated night, each bidder arrived independently, to be met in the mansion's atrium entrance, where Ip relieved them of any weapons or inquisitive devices that might compromise their host's privacy. Some had brought hangers-on, and these were shown to a waiting room and offered refreshments while their employers were led through the house to the site of the auction.

Besides Warrigrove, Imbry had also had dealings with four of the other bidders, and he knew the remaining collector by reputation. They made small talk until Dain Ganche arrived, nodding to Alwinder Mudgeram and declining to give up his personal weapon, a medium-powered shocker. At that point, Imbry invited them to take seats in a semicircle of comfortable chairs that faced a long, ornately carved table. On its polished surface stood a portable lectern, before which rested the object beneath its cloth.

When Imbry took his place behind the lectern, his view of the object was blocked. He preferred not to be distracted by its insistent brilliance. Now the room settled into expectation. Ip positioned himself in a corner from which he had an unobstructed view of the proceedings, while Ganche took the chair closest to the barred windows.

"Honorables and distinctions," Imbry said, "we are gathered to decide the ownership of an article that may well be the only one of its kind in all the Ten Thousand Worlds. If there is another like it, its possessor has not made its existence known. The vendor, Dain Ganche, has set a reserve price"—Imbry named an astronomical sum, but the number caused not so much as an eye to blink among the bidders—"so we will start the bidding there. Let us begin by viewing the item."

With that he reached over the lectern, felt around for the heavy cloth, and whisked it away. He heard the sibilant, simultaneous intakes of breath by those seated before him. After a few heartbeats, Ganche and Ip were able to tear their gazes away from the object, Imbry noted. Alwinder Mudgeram sat as if entranced, his eyes wide and softened as their pupils expanded until not even the thinnest rim of iris showed.

After a short while, Imbry reached forward with the cloth and covered the glitter again. "Bids, please," he said.

A collective moan of disappointment met Imbry's ears, then a cacophony of voices, strained and acquisitive. The collectors were on their feet, joined by Mudgeram, their faces distorted and their gestures emphatic as they bid and outbid. The reserve price was soon a fading memory as the contenders piled fortune upon fortune. As he continued to field the bids, Imbry looked to the side and saw Ganche's thick lips open in an astonishment that the fat man could appreciate: The vendor would leave here tonight wealthy enough to enter the magnate class. Imbry's own thirty percent would make him one of the wealthiest criminals of Olkney.

The bidding had reached a feverish phase. Two of the collectors, the bids having surpassed their capacity, had subsided into their seats. One of them, a sturdy man with a square face and close-cropped hair, sat slumped and quietly weeping. Imbry noticed that Mudgeram, too, had ceased to bid. He was sending Ip a meaningful look that the bodyguard was silently answering with raised eyebrows and a slight squint in one eye that said: *Are you sure?*

Now Mudgeram's face signaled back certainty, and Imbry saw Ip's hand slip into a fold in his upper garment and begin to reemerge with something dark in its grip. The fat man reached across the lectern and yanked the cloth free of the object. Once more a silence fell over the room as all eyes but Imbry's were drawn to the item. He heard a sob from the square-faced man.

The forger waited for Dain Ganche to pull his eyes away and when the man's gaze lifted to Imbry the fat man gestured with chin and eyes toward Mudgeram's bodyguard. Ip had also managed to look away from the glittering prize, but he stood blinking, his mind not yet fully returned to the business at hand—specifically that his employer expected him to use the weapon he held forgotten in his hand. Ganche's face hardened. He rose to his feet with a surprising swiftness for a man of his size and drew his shocker.

"Warning!" said the house integrator. "An inbound vehicle approaches at high . . ." The rest of its announcement was submerged by the sounds from outside: the blare of a klaxon, the thrum of a heavy motor, and the almost infrasonic vibration of an automatic ison cannon firing from the roof. At the same time the house's rear garden lit up in a blaze of illumination from high intensity lumens.

Imbry looked toward the glare just in time to see a heavy cargo carrier descend at speed, graze the top of the outer wall and hurtle toward the barred windows. Successive hits from the ison cannon caused sparks to coruscate from its frontwork and turned the operator's compartment into dripping, incandescent slag but did nothing to deter the vehicle's momentum.

Imbry reflexively ducked behind the table as the carrier smashed into the window's grillwork amid an immensity of sound. He heard but did not see the bars shatter and tear loose from their footings and the unbreakable panes whizzing through the room like shrapnel. The only exit was in the wall opposite the windows, and he stayed low and crawled that way along the length of the table before rising up to search out a clear path to safety.

There was none. He saw Alwinder Mudgeram, blood smearing his face from a gash in his forehead, squatting to provide the smallest possible target while exiting through the door. Ip, unscathed and now fully alert, covered his employer's retreat, energy pistol in hand. Imbry looked toward the windows and saw that the space they had once occupied was now filled by the cargo vehicle, most of which had battered its way into the room. The front end, hissing and radiating a fierce heat, had landed on Dain Ganche and Ilarios Warrigrove, raising a nauseating smoke and permanently canceling any and all plans they might have had. The square-faced man had also shed his last tear, and those of the other bidders who were not severely injured were deep in shock.

Imbry found himself torn between an urge to flee and the inclination to secure the priceless subject of the auction. Miraculously, it sat undisturbed on the table, which itself had been unaffected by the carrier's sudden entry. Since no further danger presented itself, the fat man decided to delay departure long enough to recover the shining object. But as he replaced the dark cloth over its brilliance and prepared to lift it, he heard a discreet cough.

Ip now stood in the doorway, his weapon aimed at Imbry. The bodyguard cocked his head in a clear signal that the forger was to bring the object in no other direction than that in which Mudgeram had gone. Imbry arranged his face and hands in a combination that indicated nothing else was on his mind. He reached again for the object but froze at the sound of a loud *crack!* A side panel broke partly free of the carrier, impelled from within. A second kick sent the thin material flying, and out of the hole stepped Chiz Ramoulian, obsession in his eyes and a long, dark disorganizer in his hands.

For the second time in moments Imbry experienced the chill of finding a weapon pointed his way. He backed away, offering placating gestures, but Ramoulian had clearly not come in search of mollification. Imbry saw the man's thumb slide over to the disorganizer's activation stud.

The *zivv* of Ip's energy pistol was loud in the room. Ramoulian's head lost definition and became first a glowing orb, then a lump of smoldering black stuff that held its shape for only a moment longer before crumbling and following his collapsing body to the littered floor.

Ip again brought his weapon to bear on Imbry, the fingers of his other hand beckoning. The fat man took up the object, snugged the cloth around it and went where he was bid. They passed along corridors and through a number of imposing doors until they came to a fortified room in which Alwinder Mudgeram had sequestered himself.

When Ip reported the events concerning Ramoulian and declared the situation secure, Mudgeram emerged from his redoubt. The room's facilities had sealed the wound in his forehead, but the blood still stained his face. Without a word, he took the object from Imbry's hands.

"If you are feeling well enough," Imbry said, "we should discuss my compensation."

"I am feeling adequate," Mudgeram said, "but I am not aware that you are due anything."

"I recall the bidding," Imbry said and named the gargantuan sum that had been the last bid offered. "Then Ramoulian interrupted. I was to receive a thirty percent commission."

Mudgeram tucked the object securely under his arm. "I remember a different series of events. As the bidding intensified, the auctioneer uncovered the object and distracted the bidders. Then Ramoulian entered. Were these two events coincidental?"

"Entirely," Imbry said.

"Hmm," said Mudgeram. "In any case, matters have now marched off in a new direction. The vendor who promised to pay your commission has instead passed permanently beyond buying and selling. Indeed, he has expired without known heirs, carelessly leaving his former possession unattended on another's property. Where it is now seized under the rule of evident domain."

"Should that not be *eminent* domain?" Imbry asked, but Mudgeram had Ip show the fat man his "evidence."

After Ip had flourished his weapon under Imbry's nose, the forger said, "What about the others?"

Mudgeram gave the matter some brief thought, then explained that the bidders had, albeit unwillingly, become participants in a matter that could not be allowed to come to the attention of the Bureau of Scrutiny. He would summon discreet helpers who would remove all traces of the incident. "Regrettably," he continued, "my guests have to be included among those 'traces.' If questioned, they might give answers that must inevitably lead to further intrusions

into my affairs by the scroots. It is better for all concerned if we simply seal off those avenues of inquiry
before they are opened."

There was a silence, then Imbry asked, "What of
me?"

Mudgeram gave the forger a look in which Imbry
felt himself weighed and subjected to some internal
calculation. "You and I might do business again some
day. Thus, once matters are tidied up, you may
leave."

"And the object? There could be other bidders."

"I have developed an attachment to it," Mudgeram
said. "It will remain with me." He paused, and again
Imbry sensed the workings of some inner arithmetic.
"But, in recompense for your efforts, I will freely can-
cel the debt you owe me from the Bazieri affair."

Mudgeram inclined his head and smiled in a manner
that assured Imbry that he need not thank his bene-
factor.

The moment Imbry returned to his operations center, his integrator sought his attention. It referred him
to the research and communications matrix. "More
information has accrued in regard to criminality at the
spaceport," it said.

Imbry sat in the matrix's chair. "The matter is now
moot, but tell me."

"A private space yacht owned by a wealthy offworlder named Catterpaul stayed in a berth beyond the
time its owner had contracted for. When port officials
investigated, they found the man dead in the main
saloon. His possessions appeared to have been rifled."

"Ramoulian," said Imbry.

"Likely so. Here is the interesting part: Catterpaul
was a dilettante who poked about the far edges of
The Spray, collecting oddments and curios. Some of
his poking occurred in and around the Lesser Dark."

"Ah," said Imbry.

The integrator continued, "Someone had winnowed

the cargo. Some small but valuable pieces had been
placed on the floor, as if sorted for removal. But the
only item taken is described in Catterpaul's notes as:
'seedpod, immature, northern continent, unnamed
world.' "

The coordinates were the same as those of the
planet visited thousands of years ago by Fallo Wickiram. Imbry called up the rest of the information and
perused it thoughtfully. "Well, there it is," he said.
"The object is some kind of ultraterrene vegetative
life form, unclassified, nature unknown. Catterpaul left
it in the cargo area to ripen, with the intent of planting
it in his garden when he returned to his house on
Bodeen's World."

"It would seem that it can telepathically manipulate
persons who come within range," said the integrator.

"In order to spread itself," Imbry concurred. "Its
'grailness' is thus no more mystical than a burr's
hooks. It stimulates the passerby's senses, creating an
illusion of supernal beauty. The hapless dupe carries
it away. By the time the effect wears off, the seed is
far from home. The mark, finding that he has been
used by a mindless vegetable, throws the thing away,
and it takes root."

He had the integrator display the scan it had taken
of the object. The image that appeared on the screen
showed no illusion of brilliant glory, only a dark green
globe with a pale, rootlike tendril emerging. Imbry
thought of Mudgeram's inevitable surprise and
chuckled.

Some days later, Imbry sat once more in a room at
Bolly's Snug. He was expecting a visitor who wished
to consult with him about acquiring a gilded icon declared by its provenance to date from the Eighteenth
Aeon but that Imbry had on unshakable authority,
dated from no earlier than the previous two weeks.

But when the door opened, it was Ip who entered
and gestured meaningfully for Imbry to accompany

him. They left by an unmarked exit to find an aircar waiting in the alley behind the tavern. They flew without conversation to Alwinder Mudgeram's house. Imbry was shown to a parlor just off the main foyer. Ip indicated that he might take refreshment from the dispenser then departed. Imbry poured himself a glass of Phalum, sat, and sipped. He rehearsed what he would say to defuse Mudgeram's disappointment.

The door opened and he looked up expectantly, but again it was Ip who filled the doorway. In his arms was the kind of disposable carton in which goods were shipped. He placed it on a low table before Imbry and said, "What will these bring?"

The fat man set down his wine and inspected the box's contents. Some of the items were bric-a-brac. Some were of great value. Two were priceless. He sorted them into categories and gave estimates.

Ip pulled at his lower lip. Imbry was astounded to see anxiety on the bodyguard's face but managed to keep his surprise from showing. Could Mudgeram's affairs have taken a precipitous downturn?

The bodyguard spoke again. "What would your commission be?"

"For these, thirty percent, for the others, twenty."

Ip nodded. "Done," he said.

Imbry looked around. "Does Mudgeram watch us from a distance?"

For a moment, the fat man thought to see a trace of an ironic smile touch the impassive features. "Possibly," Ip said, "though that would be quite some distance."

"Something has happened to him?" Imbry asked.

Ip began replacing the objects in the carton. "Oh, yes."

The tip of Imbry's tongue touched his upper lip. "There are items of considerable value throughout the house," he said.

Again, he thought to see the faintest tinge of a

smile. "You are welcome to them," Ip said. He gestured to the door.

"Will not the integrator prevent my taking them?"

Ip indicated that the likelihood was remote.

Intrigued, Imbry rose and went out into the foyer.
Several doors led out of the atrium, all of them closed.
Imbry paused to evaluate the situation. He turned to
find that Ip had joined him from the parlor, placing
the box of treasures near the front door. Now Imbry
noticed that next to the box was a device that would
function as a portable armature into which the house
integrator could be decanted for travel.

The bodyguard indicated the closed doors.
"Choose," he said.

Imbry inspected the nearest door. Its panels seemed
to bulge slightly. He mentioned this to Ip and the
bodyguard moved his head in a subtle manner that
discouraged the fat man from reaching for the opener.
Imbry gestured to the next door and receiving a less
equivocal signal from the silent bodyguard, he crossed
to the portal and eased it ajar.

Beyond lay darkness. Imbry could not tell if he
stood before a room or a corridor, because the moment he opened the door, a restless rustling filled his
ears, and the doorway was filled by a writhing mass
of tuberous vines, fleshy and thick as his wrist, from
which spouted glossy dark leaves and fibrous, coiled
tendrils that immediately unwound and began to sam-
ple the air as if sensing his presence.

Imbry closed the door. A few of the tendrils remained caught in the jamb, and one of them wriggled
from beneath the lintel. Ip drew his energy pistol and
carefully burned each to ashes.

"So Mudgeram planted it," Imbry said.

"It planted itself," said Ip.

An image floated up in Imbry's mind. He remembered Ganche's description of finding Ramoulian
curled around the object, dazed, as if fuddled by Red

Abandon. To Ip he said, "Before you decant the integrator, ask it to display Alwinder Mudgeram."

"You are not the kind to be haunted by frightful memories?" the bodyguard asked. When Imbry said he was not, the man instructed the integrator to show the image.

A screen appeared in the air, filled with a murky scene. Imbry saw darkly veined vines, wider in cross section than his own well-fleshed thighs, choking a room that by its furnishings he took to be a sleeping chamber. At first the view, seen from a percept on the ceiling, was a chaos of interwoven vegetation: The fat creepers had crossed and wound about each other as they had grown in search of exit through the doors and windows.

Then Imbry imposed mental order on the snarl, perceiving how the different vines all proceeded from a common location. Beneath the densest tangle, where the lianas were thickest, he caught glimpses of lush bedcovers. Then he saw something else.

He instructed the integrator to narrow the focus and magnify. The image enlarged upon the screen: a hand spread across a piece of curved dark object, which resolved itself into a fragment of a husk, much like that which had been found in the ship rented by Fallo Wickiram that had returned without him. The hand was withered like a worn-out glove, empty of all but its skin and fragile bones. Above it was what remained of a face.

"Ah," said Imbry. After a moment he told the integrator, "You may remove the screen."

He took up the carton from beside the door while Ip finished preparing the integrator for departure. Mudgeram's black volante hovered outside. They boarded the aircar and went aloft.

They flew in silence for a little while; then Imbry said, "Warrigrove made a perceptive comment. We had noted that the object's glamour stirred a breathless passion in some—like him and Ramoulian and

Mudgeram—but evoked only irritation in more earth-bound fellows like you and me. He said that each side of the dichotomy must pity the other."

Ip's face remained impassive. He activated Mudgeram's integrator and issued an instruction. Intense light flashed from somewhere behind them, then faded even before the volante's canopy could darken.

"Is it pity that you feel for Alwinder Mudgeram?" Ip asked.

"No," said Imbry, "not pity."

Lehr, Rex

Jay Lake

Captain Lehr's face had been ravaged by decades under the coruscating emanations of this forgotten world's overbright sun. The angry star, a rare purple giant, dominated the daysky with visible prominences that sleeted hard radiation through every human bone and cell that walked beneath its glare. Still, one could see the spirit of command that had once infused him, present even now in the lines and planes of his face, as rough and striated as the great, crystalline cliffs that marched toward the horizon, sparkling azure and lavender under the hard light. His eyes were marbled with a blindness which had come upon him in the long years, victim perhaps of some alien virus, until his blank visage appeared to be chiseled from the planet's sinews as much the very rocks themselves.

How he and whoever yet lived among his crew had survived this hellish gravity for close to half a human lifetime was a mystery to me, which yet remained to be unraveled, but survive they had. The old man was king of all he surveyed with his blind eyes, soul shuttered behind milky shields, ruling from his seat in a shattered palace comprised of the main hull frame series of *INS Broken Spear*. The baroque pillars that had once bounded the great rays of energy required to leap between the stars now did little more than support a roof to keep off the rare rains and cast a penumbra against the pitiless glare. The place had a gentle reek of aging plastic lying over the dank dance of stone on shadowed stone, but otherwise it was little different from any cavern fitted out for the habitation of men.

We did not yet know where the rest of his benighted vessel had come to her grave, but she had certainly fulfilled her ill-starred name. Finding the balance of her remains was critical, of course, in the niggardly time allotted our expedition by Sector Control and the unsympathetic laws of physics. That mankind had bent its way around the speed of light was miracle enough, but we had not yet broken past the photons cast so wide in nature's bright net. Thus must we live with the twinned constraints of relativity and simultaneity.

"Golly, skipper, he's a real mess," whispered Deckard behind me. "Just like his ship."

I waved my idiot engineer to silence.

Allison Cordel, a woman still beautiful despite age and hard use, stood yet beside her commanding officer, loyal as any starman's wife though it was the two of them together lost so far from home. Our own records, copies of dusty personnel files laboriously thermaxed from ancient microfilm, had shown that, despite the natural disadvantages of her sex, Cordel had risen to Executive Officer of *Broken Spear* before that ship's collapse from heaven. Most of the female officers who came into the service under the Navy's occasional outbreaks of gender rebalancing soon enough yielded to destiny and their biological imperatives and found more suitable work as service wives, competing as hostesses to aid their chosen man's rise in the service in the no-less-vicious battlefields of the salon and ballroom. Not for Commander Cordel those sharp-nailed sham combats. In the time I had studied her file, I had developed a fond respect for her, nurtured in the hope that she had been one of the survi-

vors mentioned in the desperate longwave help signal
that had finally arrived at Gloster Station after la-
boring at lightspeed across the echoing darkness between the stars.

Now I cast my eyes upon this woman who had
served as sort of a shadow idol to me in the months
of our journey to this unnamed place—Girl Friday to
the great Captain's Robinson Crusoe. Had those been
her footprints that had disturbed the bright, brittle
dust outside to find whatever resources had sustained
them all these years? At any rate, she was yet slim as
any message torpedo, her rough-spun tunic cut in
homage to a uniform doubtless long since worn to
raveling threads but still hinting at womanly charms
beneath. Her eyes gleamed as bright with genius as
any worthy man's, her charming chestnut hair in an
unbecoming style fit only for such a primitive place,
shot through with a silver that lent her gravitas beyond
her gender.

"So, Captain de Vere," she said, her voice like vacuum frost on a lander's struts, "you are come among
us. Even in the face of our pleas for you to keep
your distance."

Despite myself I nearly bowed, so elegant was her
manner. Were there women this controlled, this powerful, even among the silk-walled drawing rooms at
the core of the Empire? I strongly doubted it. She
might have been a duke's consort had she remained
in society, or even dowager duchess of some cluster
of lucky planets. Though I supposed this woman who
had fought so hard for the twinned comets of her rank
would hardly shed her uniform for the love of a man
or for politics either.

I settled on a salute. "My orders are all too plain,
ma'am."

Cordel favored Lehr with a look in which I fancied
I espied the smoldering ashes of prior argument,
though the flash in her eyes was lost upon his sightless
gaze. She then returned her attention to me, with a

focus as tight as any comm laser. "So you have told us. 'Search and rescue with all despatch survivors and assets of *Broken Spear*.' Did it never occur to you that the survivors and assets might have made their peace with fate after all these years?"

Behind me, snickers broke out amid the ranks of my contact team. Those men would pay, later, with a thrashing or a discipline parade . . . depending on how my temper had settled by then. I knew Heminge would rat out the culprit and satisfied myself with a promise of a pointed discussion later on.

"Ma'am—" I chose my words with care and some precision, allowing for the sort of dauntless pride which had to be in the makeup of any woman of Cordel's achievements. "Commander, rather. With respect, it was your broadcast seeking assistance that summoned us to this place. *Broken Spear* was stricken from the ship list twenty-eight years ago, after she'd been missing thirty-six months from her last known course and heading." I drew myself up, tapping the deep well of pride in the service that had always been an inspiration to me. "The Imperial Navy does not leave starmen behind."

"Nor starwomen, apparently," she said with that chill still in her tone. I did fancy that a smile ghosted at the edge of her stern but striking face, even as another snicker escaped behind me.

It would be a thrashing, I thought, and a good one, down in the ship's gymnasium. Something to make those monkeys remember respect.

"Enough," said Lehr. His voice was as ravaged as his expression, a mountain slipface given over to gravity's claims until there was only rough gravel and rude streams left to trap the unwary. "You are here. Perhaps you will profit thereby." He leaned forward on his throne—and throne it was, for all that his seat had been the captain's chair salvaged from *Broken Spear*'s bridge, the toggles and interfaces embedded in its generous arms long gone as dark as the spark within their commander's eyes. Rocks, perhaps uncut gems, had been applied to the surfaces, creating strange patterns and half-recognizable friezes that his hand stroked as he spoke. Comfort, or some fingered language, a geological Braille reserved for his especial use?

Lehr's blank gaze met my face is if he were still blessed with the gift of sight. That confident stone stare clamped a hard chill upon my spine, which I sought not to show as weakness before the captain's formidable executive officer. "We are upon a time of change here, Captain de Vere. It may be well enough that you are come among us."

It was a voice and manner that would recall any starman to his days as the rawest recruit, all left feet and ten-thumbed hands—much like a man grown and bearded might be yet a quaking boy before the echo of wrath bursting from an aging father. Nonetheless, my duty to my command and my orders sustained me against this unexpected onslaught of primitive emotion. "Indeed sir, and what would this time of change be?"

The captain's laugh was as rough as his speech, a sort of stony chuckle that gathered momentum until another layer was stripped from the gravel of his voice in a wheezing hack. The look with which Cordel favored me would have chilled a caloric insulator, but I resolutely ignored her, awaiting her commander's pleasure.

"I am dying, de Vere," he finally managed to say. "And dying I divide my kingdom among my daughters." His arm, still great-muscled and long enough to strike any man with the fist of authority, swept outward to encompass what lay behind my shoulders— the open end of his hall, where the cataclysm of *Broken Spear*'s demise had left a gap through which an enterprising man could have driven a herd of banths. "These green and pleasant lands we have wrested from the anger of this world must be husbanded against the days of our children."

I turned slowly, staring out past the strips of thermal cloth and fabric scraps that made a curtain insufficient to hide the glowing glass desert beyond. If anything the color of a verdant Terran field prospered under than hideous giant sun, it was outside my reckoning. My team—Deckard the engineer, Heminge the security man, Beaumont the political, and Marley the doctor—stared as well, each then turning to cast a shadowed look toward me.

When I once more faced the captain, Cordel's face was twisted into a mask of silent misery, like a widow's crumpled handkerchief. She betrayed nothing in her breathing, but a slight shake of her head confirmed what I already knew: to humor the ancient, failed madman in deference to his years of service and impending demise was a far better course than slaughtering his final, feeble hopes with the hard light of truth.

"Indeed, sir," I said slowly, holding her gaze with mine. Could this gray-eyed Valkyrie be yet a natural woman beneath the veneer of discipline? "It is a fair world you have brought forth." In that moment, a thought surfaced, blazing bright betrayal of my just-coined policy of polite fable. I am not a man to leave a thing alone, even in face of a desirable woman's desperation, but surely he had not breached the chain of command so horribly as to get children upon his exec. There were no other women among *Broken Spear*'s crew list.

"Who are your daughters, sir?" I asked.

Like a metastable solution leaping to a crystalline state at the tap of a technician's stirring rod, Cordel's face hardened to wrath in that moment. Lehr, oblivious to anything beyond the soft stones of his eyes, said nothing.

A long minute of silence passed, underscored by the whistling of the hot wind outside and the slow, steady hiss of dustfall within, before I saluted again and excused both myself and my party. We retreated beneath twin masks of blind indifference and bloody hatred, heading for the forge of sunlight beyond the shadows of this ruined starship palace.

We returned with all due haste to my own ship, *INS Six Degrees*.

As an expeditionary cruiser, she was designed and built for descents into the treacherous territory of planetary gravity wells. The constraints of naval architecture generally kept ships in orbit, safe from weather, natural disaster, or the less sophisticated forms of civil disturbance. Not *Six Degrees*. She was wrought as a great disc, capable of sliding through atmosphere layers without expending overmuch power; but now she sat balanced on tripodal struts atop a karst outcrop some kilometer and a half from Lehr's location. It was a natural vantage for defense, with a view of the broken valleys that led toward the crystalline cliffs and a clear line of sight to the dull bulk that had once been *Broken Spear*.

When aboard, I abandoned my resolve to enforce justice among my officers in favor of a swift council of war with respect to the soon-to-be-late Captain Lehr and the matter of his ship. We had reviewed a dozen major action plans in the long, cold months of transit to this system, but despite my secret hopes none of our contingencies had included finding any of the crew alive.

I had secret orders that not even the weasel Beaumont had seen, pertaining to the handling of *Broken Spear* and her cargo. *Six Degrees* carried a planet-buster in her number two hold, most unusual armament indeed for an expeditionary cruiser, but some of the outcomes modeled in the files of my sealed orders suggested that I might be called upon to execute that most awful responsibility of command—ordering wholesale death visited upon an entire world. Even if all we eliminated was the buzz of strange arthropods, it would still be acknowledged a great and terrible crime.

It did not rank among my ambitions to be recorded in history as de Vere the Planetkiller. But *Broken Spear*'s secrets needed to stay lost—a determination that I was given to understand had been reached in the highest of the ivory-screened chambers of the Imperial House.

But no one had imagined that Lehr yet lived, king of a broken kingdom, attended upon by Cordel. And who were his so-called daughters?

My sons, as it were, surrounded me. Deckard, wiseacre but loyal, stood at one end of the wardroom, his head deep in the hood of an inform-o-scanner brought in for our purposes.

Heminge, stolid as his pistol but equally reliable as both peacekeeper and weapon, sat at the conference table, which had been pulled up from the deck and secured into place, a red marker in hand as he reviewed reconnaissance photography of this world, still damp from the imaging engines. The good Doctor Marley, paler and more slightly built than the rest of us, sly and twisty as ever, a master of challenge without quite rising to the level of insubordination, was down in the sick bay, making notes about his observations of Lehr and Cordel with a promise to return shortly.

And of course there was Beaumont. My Imperial Bureau of Compliance liaison, by courtesy holding rank of Lieutenant Commander and serving without apparent qualification or experience as executive officer on my ship, forced upon me by the nature of this mission. I would have been unsurprised to find that he had separate knowledge of my charge with respect to the planet-buster. Here was a man created by Nature to climb the ladders of power like a weasel in a hydroponics farm. Were I free to do so, I would have strapped him to that bloody bedamned bomb and dropped them both into the nearest star. Instead, he currently sat opposite me, his face set in that secretive smirk which seemed to be his most ordinary expression, hands steepled before his lips as though in prayer, his black eyes glittering.

Beaumont spoke into his fingertips: "So, Captain de Vere, such a pretty trail you have set yourself to. Do you plan to offer aid and comfort to *Broken Spear*'s survivors?"

"Imperial Military Code is clear enough," I replied. "We are required to render such assistance as our capabilities permit and to evacuate however many survivors we can accommodate, so long as those left behind are not so reduced in numbers or required skills as to be in peril of their lives."

"Codex three, chapter seven, subchapter twenty-one. Good enough, Captain."

"I'm so pleased to have your approval, *Commander*. I doubt that they will come. They were not pleased to see us."

Heminge interrupted without looking up from his photographs, though he was most certainly listening intently. "Where is the command section? The portions of *Broken Spear* that are identifiably hull down on this world do not include the command section."

"Does it matter?" snapped Beaumont.

Heminge looked up, met the political officer's eyes. "Yes. It does matter. *Sir.* Captain Lehr was sitting in a command chair. That means the command section was either at one time on the surface, having since departed, or that it survived undamaged in orbit long enough for interior components to be removed and brought down by other means."

Deckard spoke from the depths of his viewing hood, his voice only somewhat muffled. "There are several metallic bodies in high orbit. One might assume they represented missing sections of *Broken Spear*."

"Which suggests Lehr allowed the ship to be broken apart in orbit and made an emergency landing with the main hull section," I said. The cargo at issue on board *Broken Spear* had been carried in the captain's

safe, immediately behind the bridge on that hull type.
Had they landed the command section as well and
taken the cargo off? Or moved it to the main hull
section before bringing that down?

It had been a terribly dangerous thing to do, whatever the reason. And the nature of Lehr's throne underscored the fact that the object of my search could
be anywhere.

I considered my regret for the planet-buster in the
belly of *Six Degrees*. Marley bustled into the wardroom, speaking quickly as he always did: "Only one
woman on that ship, de Vere, which is one more than
our lot has got. Don't know why he thinks he has
daughters—Allison Cordel hasn't been gravid any
more than I have. Not here. She would never carry to
term." Marley slid into a chair. "Lehr's dying, I'm
fairly certain. In this environment, one must assume
cancer or radiation poisoning. How he lasted this long
is more than a small mystery. Delusional, of course,
too, seeing green fields beyond his inner horizon. Gentlemen, how are we now?"

"Shut up," Beaumont suggested.

"We are being signaled," Deckard added, emerging
from his hood. He touched the personal comm unit
strapped to his wrist. A cluster of microphones and
screens and speaker grilles unfolded from the
overhead.

"Attention *Six Degrees*," said a strange, flat voice,
the caller devoid of emotion or inflection. I could not
even determine whether it was a man or woman who
spoke. "Do you copy?"

"This is *Six Degrees*, de Vere commanding," I replied in my crispest training academy voice, waving
madly at Deckard to indicate that he should track the
source of the signal. "Please identify yourself."

"I am Ray Gun."

I exchanged glances with my command crew. Beaumont's face was sour and pinched . . . he never had a
sense of humor nor an imagination. The others dis-

played varying degrees of thoughtful interest, though Marley was smiling strangely behind his hand.

"And you are who and where . . . ?"

Deckard flashed one of Heminge's photo prints, an image of one hemisphere of this world as shot from our approach to the planet. He circled it with his finger.

"Orbit?" I mouthed.

My chief engineer nodded.

How could that be? But an unknown agency of Lehr's in orbit was no stranger than what we had already seen. The associated comm lag explained the strange rhythm of this conversation, for one. .

"Ray Gun. I am one of Lehr's daughters. Bound to Cathar, who loves me as the stars love the horizons of evening."

Marley twirled one index finger around his temple.

For a woman, Ray Gun had a remarkably sexless voice. Not for her the tingling tones of Cordel's strong contralto, an overlay of womanly charm and matronly discipline that went straight to my gut . . . and other parts. Ray Gun's strangeness made me wonder about this Cathar.

"And you are in orbit, Ray Gun?" I said. "How may I help you?"

Deckard shook his head, while Beaumont looked increasingly sour. I knew perfectly well what both of my officers were about . . . trying to puzzle how there were more women in this place—unless Lehr had begat children on Cordel, shortly after arrival. But who would place a girl-child in orbit—and *how*? Why? This world was a conundrum and then some.

"My father has divided his kingdom between the best of his daughters," said Ray Gun primly. "We who love him most shall carry his standard. It is I who rule the skies above."

Deckard was back under the sensor hood, Marley made more notes, while Beaumont now stalked the deck in angry thought, glaring at me as Heminge watched him carefully. I glared back. Perhaps I could leave him here with the madmen and women.

"I'm very pleased to hear that," I told her.

"Good." Ray Gun's voice fell silent a moment. Then: "Do not listen to Cordel. She will betray the king my father's dream. You should leave. Cathar says so, and he is never wrong."

I was leaning toward Marley's theory. "Thank you for the information."

"Cathar and Kern will move against her soon. Best you stay away. Leave now, *Six Degrees*, while your purpose and dignity are intact."

Who the hell was Kern? "I shall take your remarks under advisement."

"Ray Gun out."

I looked at my command crew. They stared back at me, Deckard emerging from the sensor hood.

"That was very strange," Heminge said.

Deckard nodded. "I got a signal lock. It's one of those metallic objects I found earlier. Command section would seem to be likely."

"So who is Ray Gun? Not to mention Cathar and Kern?"

Beaumont swung around, breaking the momentum of his pacing to face me with barely suppressed menace, as if he thought I was to be intimidated by a darker sort of passion mixed with the threat of his connection to the secretive political puppet masters of the Empire. "This is stupid, de Vere. All of it. You know what to do. Everything else is just pointless theater of the mind."

Heminge's voice was quiet. "The bomb?"

The planet-buster was hardly a secret aboard my ship. It filled the number two hold, a modified reentry vehicle designed to be launched from orbit. Any man could deduce its intended use. A smart man wouldn't comment on it. Especially not in front of Beaumont.

"Yes, the bomb, you moron," snapped Beaumont.

"So whatever is in our secret orders—" Heminge

put his hand up, palm out. "And don't get excited, we *must* have secret orders, since we're not carrying that thing on a cargo manifest. As I was saying, whatever is in our secret orders must be very important indeed, for you to take such disregard for the lives of *two commissioned officers of the Imperial Navy.* Not to mention crew and dependents, regardless as to their number or sanity."

"They're dead." Beaumont's voice was flat. "They've been legally dead since *Broken Spear* was taken off the ship list. Lehr and Cordel are walking around breathing, but their commissions lapsed twenty-eight baseline years ago."

"So whatever *it* is, this great, terrible secret is worth their lives, regardless of their legal existence?"

I stood, took a deep breath. "Yes. Though it burns me to agree with my good Lieutenant Commander Beaumont." I cast him another sidelong glare, sickened by the look of triumph on his face. "Our view of the outcomes may be the same, but our view of the process differs. I prefer to dance a few measures in this theater of the mind. Our Captain Lehr holds secrets behind the marble of his blind eyes, gentlemen, and I propose to have them out of him if possible. They might just save his life at that."

Heminge nodded, his eyes still on Beaumont as he spoke. "How long, Captain?"

"On my authority," Beaumont said, one hand straying to the pistol at his belt, "a day."

"No." I stared him down. "I command here. You may have my commission when we get home, but until then the decision is mine." The orders had been clear enough. We weren't to spend time on site, lest we become contaminated too. I'd already consigned *Six Degrees* and her crew to extensive quarantine on our return simply by landing and approaching Lehr in person—a fact as yet understood by no one but Beaumont, though I suspected Marley of either knowing or deducing it for himself. "As long as it takes."

Beaumont refused to flinch. "A time limit, de Vere."

Sadly, he was right. "Seventy-two hours, then."

Deckard walked across the wardroom, slammed his shoulder into Beaumont, knocking the political officer backward, though they were of a height and build. "Excuse me, *sir*. My clumsiness." He turned back toward me. "If time is short, we should be working."

"As you were, Beaumont," I shouted, before he could spring up off the deck. "We're going back out. I want to speak to Cordel." About these daughters, I told myself. The old man himself was useless, lost in the hallucination of a green world and decades of blind introspection.

"I'll bet you do," Beaumont muttered, picking himself up with a slow, false dignity. "I'll just bet you do."

We trudged across the dry crystal beds, gravel washed down from the distant cliffs. They smelled like talcum, with the astringent overlay of this world's native organics, stirred by the hot winds to a sort of dehydrated atmospheric soup that would eventually damage our lungs if breathed too long. The sun glinted hot, mauve steel in the sky, hiding the mysterious Ray Gun somewhere behind its glare.

Ray Gun had to be inhabiting *Broken Spear*'s missing command section. I glanced upward, shading my eyes from the daystar's killing brilliance. Where was she?

It.

Of course. Ray Gun was an "it."

"Deckard," I said, picking my way past a shining bush that resembled a fan of coral rendered by a drunken glassblower. "Did *Broken Spear* have onboard AI support?" Intelligence-boosted systems went in and out of fashion over the decades in an endless tug-of-war between the inherent instability of such self-aware entities, prone to mental collapse after a brief, hot life-cycle, and the high value of an intelli-

gence not subject to the disorientations of supralumi-
nal travel nor the stresses of high acceleration.

"Depends," puffed my engineer.

"Depends on what?" asked Beaumont nastily.

I heard Deckard grunt, almost as if struck, but he
could take care of himself. He chose the high road:
"On whether she was pre- or post-Yankelov Act. Her
ship class originally was, but there was a refit wave
after the AI regs changed, right around the time *Broken Spear* was lost."

I thought that over. "So Ray Gun might be Lehr's
ship's systems. All alone up there in orbit all these
years."

"Crazy as an oxygen miner three days after a comet
claim," said Marley.

"Indeed. And one of Lehr's daughters."

"Maybe Cathar's the other one," Heminge said.

A stranger stepped from behind a pillar of stacked
rubble and glittering silica. "Cathar is a traitor," he
declared.

Heminge and Beaumont both drew their weapons.
I kept my own hands away from my holstered pistol
and the swift death it could deal like the sword of
justice. This was not my courtroom, so to speak. Instead, I studied the stranger as he studied me, ignoring
the armed threat my men presented.

He was whipcord thin, naked as the landscape and,
much like the sullen world around us, covered with
white dust that sparkled and flecked as he moved.
That coating matched the sparse, silvered hair upon
his head and about his shriveled penis and the
thousand-kilometer stare in his eyes, which seemed to
bore right through me from beneath his hooded
brows. Here was a man who looked across years, and
carried their wounds upon his body. I could count his
ribs, and the cords on his neck twitched as he spoke.
He was no better armed than the wind.

"Another one rises from the earth," I said mildly.
"Of the crew?"

"Lieutenant Fishman," he replied. His voice was as cracked as his skin, also a thing of this world. What this place had done to people, I thought. He raised his hands. "You should go. Before Granny Rail finds you."

"Surely you mean Ray Gun?"

"No." He laughed, a mirthless chuckle dry as an old bone. "She has taken the sky from my Captain. Granny Rail has taken the world. Lehr lives on sustained only by the love of Lady Cordel and myself."

Beaumont shoved forward, pistol in his hand. "Granny Rail. You're as cracked as that old rummy, Lieutenant Fishman. Go back to your hole in the soil and count yourself lucky to have any days remaining in your life."

Fishman shifted his long-range stare to drill through Beaumont. "You wouldn't understand loyalty, would you, man? Count yourself lucky to have any minutes remaining in your life."

Three gouts of dark fluid spouted in Beaumont's chest, grim flowers bringing color to this drab and barren landscape even as his final words died in his mouth. A smile quirked across Fishman's taut face as the rest of us dropped, but the great, gray-silver spider thing that erupted from the ground ignored him completely.

It whirled, clattering, a motile version of the crystalline plants of this world except for the well-worn but fully functional Naval-issue assault rifles in two claws. Rolling up against a backbreaking jag of rocks, I drew my own pistol, but the blunted flechettes intended for antipersonnel use in vacuum-constrained environments would have very little effect on this bright, spinning monster.

Heminge moved past me, firing his much more deadly meson pistol. The rays gleamed with an eerie antilight, the air ripping as the weapon sundered the very molecules that sustained us all, dust particles flashing into component atoms in the same moment to create an eye-bending sparkle that distracted even our ferocious many-limbed assailant.

One rifle exploded, taking the tip end of an arm with it in a shower of glass, accompanied by an ammoniac ordure very much at odds with the gleaming destruction. The other rifle swung to Heminge as he collided with the fast-moving legs, tumbling amid their silver-gray stems like a man in a twisting cage.

I launched myself after him, noting out of the corner of my eye Deckard taking a headshot on Beaumont, even as Marley scrambled for better cover, his medical kit already in his hand. Ever an optimist, the doctor, thinking about who might survive to be the recipient of his attentions. The rifle spat again, and something burned my thigh with the fire of a solar prominence, but then I was in among the legs, pressing the bell of my flechette pistol against a joint and firing even as Heminge shouted something unintelligible and loosed his meson pistol into the dented, dull ball which seemed to serve as nerve center and balance point for our enemy.

The very air ripped once more and my hair caught fire, and then the thing exploded in a clatter shower of legs.

For a moment there was only the patter of debris and the whirl of dust devils, the ammonia scent of local death mixing with the stench of my burned hair. I looked up, for somehow I was not standing anymore, to see the long legs of Fishman above me.

"Granny Rail will be angry," he said, smiling enough to show shattered teeth that gleamed even within the shadows of his mouth.

I was amazed that I could hear him. I struggled for my voice, choking on dust, some thick, pooling liquid, and—though it shamed me—fear. "I want Cordel," I said, my finger crooking on the trigger of my pistol.

Marley bent over me while Deckard gathered pieces of the monster. Heminge, who unaccountably still had all his hair, grabbed at Fishman's arm. "We will find her."

A few minutes later my leg was bandaged and splinted. Deckard had the pieces of the monster laid out in roughly their original relationship, albeit disjointed and unmotivated now, studying them with the intensity of a mystic at the feet of his god. Marley squatted on his heels and watched me just as carefully.

"What is it we came to kill?" the doctor finally asked me. "Surely not these madmen with excessively high survival quotients?"

I could not be certain that I wasn't dying—Heminge's meson pistol had done more to my head than simply burn my hair off, either that or our erstwhile assailant had struck me a chance blow there during the battle. Beaumont was dead, unmourned, and so would not report me for treasonous speech. I could see him, steaming slightly, something wrong even with his blood. *"Broken Spear,"* I said, finding the words difficult. My mind formed them well enough, but something was wrong with my mouth and throat. *"Broken Spear* carried . . . biologicals—templates."

Marley's mouth twisted, his eye thoughtful. "Combat viruses?"

I tried to nod, but that was worse than speaking. "Uh huh. Tactical . . . population . . . con . . . control."

He glanced around. "If they're loose, we're all already infected. We may never go home."

"Planet . . . buster. We . . . have . . . quarantine . . . arr . . . arrangements."

"I can imagine. Well, whatever it is didn't kill *all* of these people. There are at least three of these lunatics left, after several decades. Which makes me wonder if the virus ever got into the wild."

My voice was coming back to me. "Not much . . . population control . . . there."

The doctor grinned. "You're returning to us, Captain. Had me worried for a minute or two."

Deckard wandered over, a broken crystal rod in his hand. He cocked his head, stared at me as he wrinkled his nose. "You going to live, sir?"

"Yes." I wasn't ready to sit up, though.

"That thing was a highly modified naval recon drone. Cyborged, if that's the right word, with components from the local ecosystem. Somebody's spent a lot of time over the years."

"Somebody's *had* a lot of time," I managed. Then: "Bury Beaumont, will you? Please?"

They exchanged glances.

Cordel came to me at last, trailed by Heminge with his pistol still in his hand and Fishman wearing a truculent expression. The ancient Lieutenant seemed to be so much furniture to his superior officer, but even I could see that when his eyes turned toward her, that thousand-kilometer stare came into bright focus.

I knew how he felt.

"I am sorry about your man," she said.

"I'm too tired to fence." My voice was quiet and slow. Marley and Deckard had propped me up against a rock, for the sake of my dignity. I had refused to be moved back to the ship until after I'd met Cordel, here, on open ground. The spider-thing still smoked nearby, evidence of someone's perfidy, and the pulsing sunlight seemed a better choice to me than the oily aired, whispering corridors of *Six Degrees*. "So I will simply ask, on your life, ma'am. What has become of the biologicals *Broken Spear* was carrying in the captain's safe?"

Her puzzlement was genuine, as best as I could tell. "Biologicals? We carried no biologicals, Captain de Vere. Not beyond the standard cultures in our sick bay."

"You've been here thirty years and Lehr never mentioned this?"

She folded her knees, bending down to speak to me at eye level. I could have watched her legs move, stork-scissors, for hours. And had she opened to me, a little, some sense of engagement in those gray eyes? In that moment, I was ashamed of the reek of my injuries. "Captain," Cordel said. "I emptied the safe the one time Ray Gun landed on the surface. There was nothing of the kind, I assure you. How did you come to think we were carrying something like that?"

I turned her statements over in my head. Why *was* I sent to crack a world to cinders? "What is *Broken Spear*'s terrible secret, then?"

"Ah," she said, her face shuttering. "Perhaps you should speak to my captain once more."

"He is too busy gazing at green fields beyond," I muttered.

"Indeed." She stood. "Fishman, gather this man up with all due gentleness and bring him to Lehr."

Deckard and Marley stepped forward together to object, but Cordel turned her glare, now pure ice, upon them. "Granny Rail will not bother Fishman. Hands free, you two might be able to win through with your lives if we are attacked once more by her servants."

And so we went, my head lolling back as I stared into the deepening colors of evening and tried to remember why I'd ever wanted to come to this world.

Approaching Lehr's palace, Deckard and Heminge were attacked by another of the spider creatures. It lurched out of a stand of the crystalline growth, brushed past Marley and headed straight for the other two. I watched from my curious angle of repose in Fishman's arms—I am not light at all, which gave me cause to wonder at the Lieutenant's strength, especially at his advanced age—as Heminge snapped off a meson bolt that sheared two legs, while Deckard pumped flechettes into a high-stepping joint. Heminge's second shot slagged the underslung central core, proving that the creatures' advantage lay in surprise, which position they had now surrendered.

It was almost too easy, though I wondered why the attacker had not gone for Marley first. Perhaps because he carried no armament?

Then we swept through the curtains and into the hall of the blind king of this world. Lehr leaned forward on his throne, chin set upon his hand in an attitude of thoughtful repose. "Welcome, de Vere," he said, staring toward our little party at a height somewhat above my own angled head.

So, the great man did not know I was being carried wounded to be laid before his throne.

I tugged at Fishman to set me down. Deckard stepped forward to support me upright, that I might rise to meet the gaze of this shattered king, while Heminge made no subtle secret of covering one then another of our adversaries with his meson pistol. Only Marley held back, somewhere behind me, breathing louder than any of us.

"Captain," I replied, in my best voice. "Once more I greet you. Your executive officer has suggested we speak as commander to commander."

"My ship is broken," he intoned. "My kingdom divided among my most loyal daughters." Cordel winced but held her tongue at this. "My time is nearly finished, de Vere. What will you of me?"

"I must know, sir, to carry out my own duties. What secret did your ship carry?"

He stared a while, silent, almost unbreathing. Only the wind stirred, changing tone with the coming of night in the world beyond this shattered hull. I could hear Marley panting like some dog, though Deckard and Heminge were quiet enough. The moment grew close, some great truth waiting to emerge.

What had I been sent to kill?

"The mind," Lehr finally said. "The mind. We were first sworn, then forsworn, de Vere. As you have been in turn."

What was he getting at? "The biologicals . . . they affect mental templates?"

"*Minds.* Admiral Yankelov feared much and set us to testing in a faraway place. I broke my own ship, Captain, rather than return, for I could not carry out the mission which had been laid upon me."

Yankelov, of the AIs. "Machine minds."

"Exactly. *Broken Spear* was set to test a crew of machine minds. Could a warship be flown, and fought, without a fleshly hand at the helm? What do you think, de Vere?"

I thought that I did not like this line of reasoning.

"And when my mission failed, when the minds grew fractious and independent, too powerful to be obedient, too disobedient to be entrusted with power, I was to terminate them." He leaned forward, hands shaking, and somehow found my face once more with his blind stare. "But I could not. They had become my children. My daughters."

And so I had been sent, *Six Degrees* beneath my feet, planet-buster in my hold, to make sure this plague of independence did not flow back into the Empire. No wonder they had emasculated the ships after the Yankelov Act. Starships with their weapons could not sail under the command of rebellious machines any more than they could sail under the command of rebellious men.

"I am sorry, sir."

"Not so sorry as you think, de Vere." Lehr shifted on his throne. "Ray Gun circles the skies, and Granny Rail walks the soil. Why do you think I have kept Cordel close, for all her disloyalties, and Fishman, who in the end is fit for little but screaming into the night?"

Behind me, Marley's breathing changed. The good doctor stirred, moved toward some end I did not yet fathom. In that moment I was glad that it was Heminge who held the meson pistol.

"Because they are all who are left you of your crew," I said. "It is clear enough."

Lehr shook his head. "We would never survive here. Even if I had gotten an infant on Cordel, before all our gonads were cooked by that wicked star, what of it? Only the children of the mind could live here. They have built me a green world I soon go to, and they will outlive us to inherit this one."

"I do not think so, sir. This cannot be."

"But why do you question?" Lehr seemed surprised. "You are one of them."

"What?" My ears buzzed, as if I had been struck on the head again.

Marley grabbed my shoulder. "Back to the ship, sir. You've had enough."

I shook him off. "No. I will hear him out."

"Sir—"

Lehr spoke again, loudly now as he rose on trembling legs. "I am king here. I know who passes my marches. Granny Rail's spiders do not assault the meat, only the mind. They patrol for sports, escapists, invaders." A hand rose, pale finger with cracked, black nail pointing in a shivering palsy toward my chest. "Much like yourselves. You, sir, are a machine."

Leaning on Deckard, I rolled up my sleeve.

"Sir," said Marley again, and his voice was desperate.

"No." I took my knife from my belt, unfolded it, and set the tip against the skin of my inner forearm. The blade slid in with a slight stretching and a fiery bolt of pain. Blood welled. Dark blood, dark as Beaumont's had been.

Black blood oozed out, smelling of oil, like the air of my ship.

"A test," said Marley quietly. "Which you are now failing, my friend."

I looked at him. He was smaller, paler than me. Deckard, Heminge, the late Beaumont, we all four were of a height, with space-dark skin and faces nearly the same. Marley was different. As for the rest of *Six Degrees*' crew, they were . . .

I knew my ship to be filled with petty officers and ratings and lieutenants, to be more than just my command crew, but in that moment I could not recall a single face or name, just a shuffling crowd of uniforms.

"I never was," I said to Marley. "Nothing was real until we came here, was it?"

He shook his head. "No, I—"

Heminge's meson pistol blasted Marley into glittering pink fog. No one flinched except Cordel, perhaps the only true human left among us depending on where madness had deposited the good Lieutenant Fishman.

"Back to the ship, sir," my security officer said brusquely, with a glance at Lehr. "The king has his appointment with the country of the green, and we have our mission."

"Our own appointment," I said sadly.

Lehr continued to fix his blind gaze upon me. I appealed to him, the one authority who understood. In some indirect sense, my own father. "Sir . . ." I shuffled forward, supported by Deckard, and let my face tip into his hands. They trembled, warm and tinged with honest sweat. He stroked my hair a moment, a blessing.

Then: "Go, de Vere. Find your own fate as I shall soon find mine."

And so I went, followed by my unbreathing crew. The last I saw of Lehr, Cordel and Fishman were closed around him, angels fluttering to the aid of a dying god.

Six Degrees was empty, of course. Though the companionways and cabins were where my memory had said they should be, they were unpeopled. Decorated, sets for a play that the actors had abandoned. The ship even smelled empty, except for the vague stench of my burned hair, which preceded our every step. How had we ever believed ourselves surrounded by men?

Down in the number one hold we found four coffins . . . or perhaps crates. Our names were stenciled on the lids, an accusation: Beaumont, de Vere, Deckard, Heminge.

"Marley flew us here, alone," said Deckard into the echoing, oily silence. "He pulled us out, filled us with memory, thought, and faith, and here we are."

That was true enough. I remembered meetings, back in Sector Control, though when I strained for details, they slipped away like eels in a recycling tank. They were memories of memories rather than the real thing.

Like being a copy of a real person. Was anything I knew true? "Why?" I asked, leaning ever more heavily on Deckard.

"A new generation of machines, I suppose," Heminge said bitterly. "It all makes a sort of twisted sense. Recasting the lessons of Lehr and *Broken Spear*. Fitting enough to send us here in pursuit. Convenient enough to lose us here if need be. It worked for them."

"So who was the sixth?"

"Sixth what?" asked Heminge.

"*Six Degrees*, this hollow ship is named. There were four of us, plus Marley the doctor and director of our little act. Who was the sixth?"

Deckard cleared his throat. "Lehr. Father and king to us all. He is our sixth."

I turned this in my head. "Are we real . . . somewhere? Are we copies, of someone?" We must have been, I realized. Who would bother to create a Beaumont from nothing?

"I am my own man," said Deckard. He grinned at my stare. "So to speak."

Heminge stroked his coffin. "Do we bust the planet, or do we break the ship?"

"Or do we sail home and ask for an accounting?"

Deckard looked thoughtful. "Lehr's green fields are out there somewhere."

"In his mind."

"But we are all creatures of mind. That is all we are."

"Then go," I told him.

Heminge handed Deckard the meson pistol, then took my weight against his shoulder. "Good luck, man. You might need it."

We struggled to the bridge, where we waited until the engineer was gone, then sealed the hatches. On the viewscreens the world outside glittered in the pallid moonlight, stars glinting. Wind scrabbling at the hull.

Which parts were real?

"Anything could be true," Heminge said, obviously sharing my thought. "Marley could have programmed the planet-buster to blow if we lifted without some escape code. The bomb could be a dummy. This entire ship could be a dummy, just like all those empty cabins, something big and bad waiting in orbit to blast us."

"Anything could be true," I agreed. "That is what it means to be human."

I reached for the launch button, a great red roundel that glowed slightly. "To green fields beyond, then."

Heminge nodded. "And long life to Lehr."

Still feeling the set of my father's hands upon my brow, I pressed the button, hoping like any man for the future.

Dust

Paul McAuley

How everything changed:

Six hours after the last transmission from Linval Palmer's expedition had been received, his secretary requested an urgent meeting with Captain Bea Edvard. Linval Palmer had powered down to the surface of Hades in his reconditioned military lander with three fully tooled-up mercenaries and a gung-ho xeno-archaeologist. They'd landed safely in the scablands above the tunnel city and completed two grid searches, but soon after they'd set off to begin the third search, their uplink had cut out. Visual contact was out of the question because Hades was shrouded in a planet-wide dust storm. Sideways radar imaging had located the lander, and it was responding to remote interrogation, confirming that all of its systems were fully functional, but so far no one from the expedition had responded to the radio message Bea Edvard's ship was broadcasting on a thirty-second loop.

Linval Palmer's secretary, John-Jane Smith, wanted Bea to take the ship's gig down to the surface at once. Using a palmer to project a three-dimensional image of the tunnel city constructed from multiple deep radar scans made by the string of satellites Linval Palmer had dumped in orbit around Hades, animating

it to show that someone was moving about near the
entrance to one of the tunnel systems. Telling Bea,
"There is at least one person still alive. You must do
your duty by him, Captain."

John-Jane Smith was a neuter, a thin ageless person
in a neat gray one-piece suit, with close-cropped white
hair and piercing blue eyes. All intellect and no emotion, apart from its unswerving loyalty to its employer. Its voice was uninflected, as always, its gaze
cold and unblinking as it stared at Bea through the
multicolored labyrinth that hung in the air between
them.

Bea had been expecting something like this. "My
contract was to deliver your boss and his team into
orbit around Hades. It specifically absolves me from
responsibility for anything that happens after that."

"I am familiar of course with every detail of your
contract," John-Jane Smith said coolly. "But there is
clearly at least one survivor, and the law of distress
requires you to rescue him."

"I've received no distress call, the person in question isn't responding to a clear request for information, and we don't even know if the signal in question
is a person. The resolution is too low. It might be
a glitch, or an echo from some kind of atmospheric
phenomenon. What I can do," Bea said, "is send down
a robot, have it take a look around the immediate
landing area."

But John-Jane Palmer wasn't in the mood for compromise. "You agree that there is a possibility that
Mr. Palmer and the others are alive."

'When we don't know anything, anything is possible," Bea said cautiously, believing that she knew
where this was headed.

John-Jane Smith said, "If we are agreed that Mr.
Palmer may be alive, you are obliged to attempt a
rescue. You will take me and one of the bodyguards
down to the surface in the ship's gig. You may remain
in the gig while we search for Mr. Palmer and the

others. If we do not return after twenty-four hours, you can leave the surface and return to your ship. For this service you will receive a bonus equivalent to one half of your original fee."

"No way. My gig isn't exactly robust, and its motor is much less powerful than that of your boss's lander. Also, I'm the only person rated to fly it, and I've never, ever used it for an orbit-to-surface flight in anything other than a simulator. Even if it survived the descent through the storm undamaged, and that's a pretty big if right there, it wouldn't be able to get back up."

"We will return in Mr. Palmer's lander, which I am sure he will allow you to keep to compensate you for the loss of your own craft."

Bea, pushed into a corner by the neuter's calm certainty, finally lost her temper. "Mr. Palmer and me, we agreed I didn't have any responsibility to rescue him if things went wrong. I'm sorry, but there it is."

She *was* sorry, too. Linval Palmer was reckless and impulsive and had far too much confidence in his own abilities, but he was flamboyant and charming too, a big old handsome rogue with an abundance of red curls spilling to his shoulders, a ready smile that split his piratical beard, and a fund of unlikely but amusing and fascinating stories. He'd come to Hades to search for his younger brother, Isham, who'd vanished three hundred days ago while chasing a rumor of functional Elder Culture technology in the vast tunnel city at the edge of the twilight zone of Hades. Isham Palmer's father had paid for a rescue expedition that had discovered his ship in orbit and the remains of his lander on the surface—it seemed that the lander had crashlanded after its motor had flared out a couple of hundred meters above the surface—but had failed to find any trace of any survivors. Then, just over fifty days ago, the automated way station at the mouth of the system's wormhole, anchored to the gravity well of the outermost gas giant, had detected a weak radio

signal on the surface of Hades. The signal had come
and gone ever since. Although it contained no dis-
cernable information, it had convinced Linval Palmer
that Isham had survived, and despite his father's
threats of disinheritance, he'd set out to rescue his
brother.

In Bea's opinion, Linval Palmer had made the rescue mission a matter of personal honor. It had little
to do with filial duty and everything to do with a need
to prove himself a braver, cleverer, and more re-
sourceful man than his father. Nevertheless, it was a
huge, daring, and utterly romantic gesture, and despite
her reservations, Bea admired the hell out of the man
for it. That was one reason why she'd agreed to sign
up with him. As for the rest, when she'd heard that a
crazy zillionaire wanted someone to deliver his expedition into orbit around Hades, she'd just hit forty and
split with her live-in lover of the past five years and
had been wondering if there was anything more to life
than routine cargo runs and haggling with merchants
and customs officers. In other words, it was exactly
the right time in her life for an adventure, but things
had gone wrong very quickly after arriving at Hades,
putting her in an impossible position.

John-Jane Smith touched its palmer. The three-
dimensional scan of the tunnel city winked out. The
neuter's expression was severe, eyes sharp, mouth
tightened to a bloodless slot. "Captain Edvard, your
position is very simple. Every minute we waste in
pointless discussion, the survivor is consuming precious reserves of air, water, and power. In approxi-
mately eight and a half hours those reserves will fall
to dangerously low levels. His suit will place him in
hibernation, but after ten days the last of his suit's
power reserves will be exhausted, and he will die.
There is not enough time to reach the wormhole, raise
a rescue expedition, and return. If we do not save him,
no one will. And if we do not make the attempt, Mr.
Palmer's family will take its revenge."

"They can take me through every court in the First Empire, but the contract is airtight. And it was Mr. Palmer's decision to visit Hades against their advice, not mine."

"His family is rich and powerful and ruthless, Captain Edvard. It's quite true that they forbade Mr. Palmer from setting out on this adventure. That is why he had to hire you and your ship with his own funds, rather than use a ship from his family's fleet. However, in the eyes of his family, that will not absolve either you or me from responsibility for his death, and I can assure you that they will not seek revenge in a court of law. You do not want to make an enemy of them, and neither do I," John-Jane Smith said, and it raised its palmer and shot Bea with the taser taped to its underside.

They were in Bea's cabin, a simple sphere padded with memory plastic. The taser's high-voltage charge bounced her spinning off the walls, wrapping her whole skin in white fire that knotted her muscles with spasming cramps and blasted up her spine into her skull. The hatch that was supposed to open only at her command sprang back, and the two Marys, Linval Palmer's bodyguards, shot through it and grabbed Bea and cuffed her wrists to her ankles, used a focused EMP blast to destroy the implant that linked her to the ship, and towed her to the bridge, where Tor Torqvist, Bea's engineer, was already in chains.

Two minutes later, after one of the Marys had threatened to chew the fingers off Tor's right hand while the other wondered if she should suck out his eyeballs or bite off his balls, Bea surrendered command of her ship. The two clones, got up in tight yellow jumpsuits, blond hair bunched in ponytails, looked like fresh-faced teenagers, but they were stone-cold killers, hardwired with a dozen martial arts techniques, their nervous systems and muscles tweaked to run faster and harder than those of ordinary humans. Thirty minutes later, Bea and Tor were down in

Number Three hold, prepping the gig. Although they were watched by the two Marys as they maneuvered the shell of the heatshield over the nose and belly of the little delta-shaped gig and bolted it in place, they managed a brief conversation in a version of the hand-talk sailors and free-fall workers used to communicate privately in hard vacuum.

Bea told Tor how she planned to survive this, told him that as soon as the gig started its descent, he was to take back control of the ship and make a run straight for the wormhole, told him what to do when he reached the High Haven reef on the other side.

Tor told her it was her second dumbest idea, her first being to take this contract.

Whatever happens, Bea signed, *if they find their boss or if they don't, they'll have to kill us because they've committed piracy. Take back control of the ship and get out of here as soon as you can.*

She was frightened and angry, and being cut off from her ship, the tingle of vacuum and raw sunlight on its hull, the ponderous presence of its slumbering engines, the quick pulses of its lifesystem, was like losing a limb. But she believed that her plan was sound, and she knew that she could trust Tor to do the right thing. They'd been working together for less than a year, but he was a smart, competent, serious man, a member of a highly respected family back on First Foot. Besides, it wasn't as though she had any other option.

Tor started to connect the heatshield's sensor array to the gig's neural network, turning his back to the two Marys, his fingers making quick shapes.

Don't you worry, boss. I take good care of everything.

It was the best Bea could hope for, but it was only a slender hope, and there was no turning back. Less than an hour after she'd been tasered, she climbed into the gig with John-Jane Smith and one of the Marys and nudged it away from the ship before firing the long burn that would take it down to the surface of Hades.

Hades was one of the few rocky planets in the so-called First Empire, fifteen red dwarf stars connected by a wormhole system the Jackaroo had sold to humanity in the early days of first contact. Apart from Earth and First Foot, most people lived in asteroid reefs or on the moons of warm Jupiters, and no one at all lived on Hades, a small, dry, dusty, pockmarked world tidally locked to its feeble M-class star, one hemisphere in perpetual day, the other in perpetual night. At the twilight zone between the light and dark hemispheres, katabatic storms howled off the flanks of shield volcanoes, and every so often two or three storms merged into a hypercane that lofted billions of tons of dust into the atmosphere, shrouding the entire planet for hundreds of days and generating continent-sized thunderstorms that hung above fields of iron-rich lava that oozed from the vents and calderas of the planet's many volcanoes, which were fed by a core kept molten by tidal heating.

Elder Cultures had attempted and failed to plano-form the bleak, hostile little world. It was littered with impact craters from successive bombardments with comets that had enriched its thick atmosphere of carbon dioxide and nitrogen with water and other vola-tiles, and several times it had been seeded with cunningly engineered mixtures of microbes. But the water had either become chemically locked in Hades' rocks or had frozen out on the night side's equatorial ice cap, and most of the microbe populations had either died out or retreated deep into the planet's crust. Only a tough microbial symbiosis containing organisms from at least three different evolutionary trees flourished on the surface, littering the playas and inter-mountain basins of the day side with stromatolite mounds, spattering dust-smoothed rocks and lava fields with slow-growing crusts wherever there was a little moisture and sunlight.

The symbiosis and a few refuge species of microbe in the deep crust were the only life now known to exist on Hades, but in the deep past at least three different Elder Cultures had attempted to settle the planet. The most successful had been the Tunnel Builders, a species that had excavated city-sized mazes deep beneath the surface. The largest surviving tunnel city was in the twilight zone of the southern hemisphere, more than a thousand kilometers of tunnels in a hundred separate systems that wound around each other, each with its separate entrance, some simple burrows less than a kilometer long, others elaborate mazes. No one knew if each tunnel system had been inhabited by a family or an individual, or if each system had had a different civic use. The Tunnel Builders had ascended some ten thousand years ago, leaving behind no records or artifacts except the tunnels themselves. Well, maybe the Jackaroo or the !Cha or the Reedemers knew, but the one trait shared by the unascended alien species was that they became maddeningly vague and elusive when questioned about how other species had lived before they ascended to wherever it was that the ascended went.

Isham Palmer had chased the rumor of surviving alien technology he'd bought from an itinerant Jackaroo trader to the tunnel city on Hades. That was where Linval Palmer had gone to find out what had happened to his younger brother. That was where Bea Edvard was headed in her ship's tiny gig, with John-Jane Smith and one of the Marys. All three were sealed inside pressure suits and strapped side by side in acceleration couches. Because her link had been burned out, Bea was flying by manual control, something she hadn't done since her apprentice days. It mattered little that the storm had passed its peak. On the horizon dead ahead, the crown of a shield volcano

rose above dull brown haze and reflected a red spark
of sunlight; here and there the flashes of lightning
storms or the glow of an eruption showed feebly under
the deep murk, but otherwise the day side of the
planet was entirely shrouded by dust storms. Pushing
a dense wedge of superheated gases ahead of it,
scratching a flaming trail across the sky, the gig plowed
through the upper edge of the dust and began to buck
and sway as the atmosphere thickened and hyperve-
locity winds plucked at it, sending it miles off course.
Bea blew the explosive bolts and took control as the
scorched heatshield dropped away, the stick juddering
hard as the gig slammed and skidded through howling
dust-laden winds. Coming in on radar alone, she over-
shot the level stretch of playa she'd selected as a landing site and had to haul hard about, pushing the
envelope of the gig's aerodynamics, the Mary shrieking with crazy glee in her ears.

The gig swooped higher as it swerved around,
dropped into a steep glide against a headwind. Perfect.
But then it hit a pocket of still air, dropped five hundred meters in a couple of seconds, and was suddenly
coming in too fast and too low. Bea fought the stick,
managed to level out, and fired the retrorockets, but
the gig came down fast and hard in a slide that collapsed two landing struts and left it canted nose-down
at a twenty-degree angle.

After asking John-Jane Smith's permission as politely as she knew how, Bea sent a brief message to
the ship to report that although they had landed
safely, the gig was out of commission, then powered
down the little craft's systems.

Whips of dust flickered in dim smoggy light beyond
the narrow wedges of the windows; there was dust in
the air of the cabin, too, blowing in fine sprays through
splits in the seal of the hatch, and the hatch was
jammed—it took the combined effort of all three of
them to pop it open. In howling wind and blowing
dust, trailed by John-Jane Smith and the Mary, Bea

walked around the gig and knew it wouldn't fly again. It might be possible to make it airtight and jack it up to the right angle for takeoff, but the nozzle of the main motor was crumpled beyond repair.

John-Jane Smith remarked dryly that this must count as a good landing because they could walk away from it.

Bea checked her headup display and pointed with an outflung arm. She was still buzzing from the massive amounts of adrenalin that had squirted into her bloodstream when she'd wrestled the gig down to its crash landing. "Your boss's lander is sitting five and a half kilometers away, just a shade off due east. We better get going."

It took them three hours, trudging across the flat, featureless plain in the dust storm, to reach the lander. Every ten minutes, John-Jane Smith broadcast a message to Linval Palmer across every radio channel, but there was no reply, nothing but the meaningless throb of the shortwave radio signal, steady as a sleeping giant's heartbeat.

Wind shrieked and wailed and hooted, sometimes pushing them forward, sometimes pushing so hard against them that they had to lean into it and battle their way step by step. Dust scudded and skirled, and in every direction the world faded into a formless brown haze. The sun's smeared blur hung low ahead of them, a fixed eye glowering through flying murk. Dust kept coating the faceplate of Bea's helmet, and dust worked into the joints of her pressure suit. The suit's left knee grew stiffer and stiffer, and an hour into the trek, Bea was walking with a pronounced limp.

"You keep up," the Mary told her, "or we deal with you here and now."

"Then you'll have to fly yourself back into orbit."

"It can't be too hard," the bodyguard said. "All it is, is straight up."

John-Jane Smith told them to stop bickering and

save their energy. "Our real work doesn't begin until we reach the lander."

Bea had a fix on the lander by radar and by its radio beacon, but because her mind was dulled by the sheer plodding labor of walking, the featureless haze, and the unchanging position of the sun, she was surprised when she saw a fat cone loom out of blowing dust. At first sight, the lander looked intact, squatting four-square on angled legs above the scorched pit its retrorocket had burned into the ground. But the hatchway to the lifesystem hung open, and after John-Jane Smith went up the ladder and clambered inside, it gave a shrill cry, half surprise, half despair. Bea dodged past the Mary and swarmed up the ladder, swung through the little cupboard of the airlock (the inner hatch was open too), and found the neuter stooped over flight controls that had been smashed and broken in some mad frenzy. A mantling of dust covered every surface, and handfuls of cabling had been ripped loose from opened access panels. There was still a trickle of power from the batteries—barely enough to power the beacon—but there was no way the lander could be repaired, and a quick inspection revealed that its oxygen and fuel had been vented.

After Bea told John-Jane Smith and the Mary this, the bodyguard drew her reaction pistol, and Bea closed her eyes, hoping for a quick death. But with a scream of frustration the bodyguard fired past her into the howling storm, then turned around and stalked away.

"We will find Mr. Palmer," John-Jane Smith said, once again calm and decisive. "Mr. Palmer will know what to do."

Bea thought it was unlikely that the surviving member of the expedition—Linval Palmer or one of his companions—would be any help at all. It was obvious that one of them had wrecked the lander, and it had been done recently too—when she'd checked out the lander via the uplink before beginning the descent to the planet, all its systems had been working just fine. It had probably been wrecked after her gig had landed, by someone who not only didn't want to be rescued but wanted to strand their would-be rescuers as well. Someone who had left the beacon working, to draw them here. . . .

The snap of a shot cut through the noise of the wind. The Mary had fired her pistol again. And this time she had killed something.

The bodyguard held it up for inspection. Half a meter of pink muscular rope armored in ridged translucent scales like fingernails, ending in a red rag of smashed flesh. The rest of it was spattered on the ground, already half buried by blowing dust. Its blunt head lacked a mouth and had bunches of coarse black bristles where its eyes should be.

'It wrapped itself around my ankle,'' the Mary said. "Gave me a nasty electrical shock too. Would have paralyzed someone without my training. Stay frosty. There may be more of them.''

Green lights of a headup display ran up inside the faceplate of John-Jane Smith's helmet; the neuter pointed aslant the bleary eye of the sun. "The entrance to the tunnel system Linval was investigating when he disappeared is in that direction. That is where we have the best chance of finding him.''

As she trudged after the neuter and the bodyguard, Bea's thoughts ran quick and cool, like beads of water down a windowpane. There really was nothing like the prospect of imminent death to concentrate the mind. She knew that there should be no life anywhere on Hades bigger than a microbe, and although her knowledge of biology was pretty basic, she was certain that an animal as large as the snake-thing had no business being here unless there was an entire ecosystem where snake-things could live. Most of the rumors about Elder Culture technology sold by Jackaroo traders were bogus; the Jackaroo were expert swindlers with a tradition more than a million years old. Before

first contact, they'd infiltrated Earth's information systems and started a global war, then convinced the survivors to exchange rights to most of the Solar System
for the specifications for a basic torch fusion drive and
access to the impoverished wormhole system of the
First Empire. It was little consolation that they had
pulled this kind of trick many times before. At least
a dozen Elder Cultures had left their traces on the
asteroid reefs of the First Empire before ascending to
wherever it was ascendent species went. Still, around
one in a hundred of the rumors about functional Elder
Culture tech sold by Jackaroo traders to the credulous,
desperate, or plain crazy were authentic, just enough
to keep humans coming back for more. Linval or his
brother must have found something in the tunnel city
after all, and it had driven them mad. . . .

Bea kept her speculations to herself, limping up a
long slope littered everywhere with wind-smoothed
pebbles, a dry beach waiting for its sea. She noticed
that the Mary was limping too, and asked if she was
all right.

"Snaky fucker gave me a bad shock. I'll live."

The Mary's voice was tight with pain and laced with
self-loathing. It gave Bea a little hope, although she
hated herself for it.

The entrance to the tunnel city was a shallow cirque
that narrowed and gradually closed around them as
they walked down it. The sound of the wind died back,
and the haze of dust lessened. At last they could see
that they were descending a long tube with smooth
black walls that curved up to meet ten meters overhead. Their shadows were cast ahead of them by the
sun, which glowered straight into the entrance. Dust
had fallen out of the still air in high, silken heaps and
ridges heaped one after the other across the wide
floor, and the Mary discovered footprints leading away
between the shoulders of two sinuous ridges.

John-Jane Smith couldn't keep the satisfaction out
of its voice, saying that it had been right all along,

saying that they would find Mr. Palmer and everything would be fine.

Bea thought that the footprints could be anyone's. She also thought that, like the beacon, they could be the bait for a trap. Stripped of her intimate contact with her ship, her merely human senses felt blunted, and she had the eerie feeling that something was watching them in the darkness beyond the reach of their helmet lamps. It didn't help her nerves that John-Jane Smith kept calling to Linval Palmer over the radio.

After about ten minutes of steady walking, the dust heaps smaller now, not much more than waist high, the trail of footprints ended, and the tunnel split into two. While John-Jane Smith and the Mary were casting about, Bea said that if anyone wanted to be rescued they would have answered by now.

"We aren't going to stumble over them by accident. There are over a thousand kilometers of tunnels down here. It would take weeks to explore the entire city, and we only have a few hours."

John-Jane Smith said, "These are the tunnels Mr. Palmer set out to explore just before we lost contact with him. He is in here somewhere. I know it."

Bea said, "That's hardly a rational attitude."

For a moment she was tempted to tell John-Jane Smith about her plan to survive this. But then the Mary told her to be quiet, adding, "I should kill you. You waste air we need."

"We are not murderers," John-Jane Smith said.

The bodyguard ignored the neuter and raised her pistol and aimed it at Bea. Her hand was trembling lightly, and her voice was trembling too; she must have been more badly hurt than she had admitted. "We'll all be dead soon, so what does it matter if she dies now?'

Bea fought the urge to run—the bodyguard would cut her down at once.

The moment stretched. Then John-Jane Smith said, its voice low and urgent, "I see something."

Bea turned to look to where the neuter was pointing, saw a fugitive flicker of red light a little way down the right-hand tunnel, and felt a chill wave climb her back, tighten around her neck, her scalp.

John-Jane Smith called out to Linval Palmer again and began to trudge toward the flickering light.

"Make no more trouble," the Mary said, and forced Bea to follow at pistol-point.

Bea's first thought—really it was more of a hope than a thought—was that the fugitive light was some kind of static discharge. But it was too regular and too bright, and it quickly resolved into hair-thin lines that blinked from one part of the tunnel to another in a nervous web. Like message lasers, Bea thought, gripped by another chill. She flicked on her pressure suit's night-sight capability, enabled the movement tracker. Almost immediately the tracker caught something and replayed it in a pop-up screen. Something hand-sized scuttling into the base of a heap of dust, emitting a brief thread of red light as it buried itself. Bea played it over again and was about to call out a warning when John-Jane Smith, who had almost reached the beginning of this display, suddenly turned aside, trotting toward the curving wall, kicking through a knee-high dust ridge.

Five bodies lay half buried in the dust, laid out neatly side by side, wrapped in shrouds of some kind of polymer with the grain of human skin, thickened here and there in callus-like ridges. Bea enabled infrared and saw that they were a few degrees warmer than ordinary human body temperature, much hotter than the ambient temperature of the tunnel, glowing an even white from head to foot.

John-Jane Smith touched the nearest body with the tip of its boot and hastily stepped backward when it jerked and shuddered. The other bodies jerked too, like puppets pulled by the same string.

The Mary's reaction pistol fired, a flare of light filling the tunnel, a thunderclap rolling away into dark-

ness. It wasn't a snake-thing she'd killed this time, but
something like a hand-sized crab. Most of it had been
smashed to a bloody ooze, but enough of it remained
to see that it had a bony shell, two pairs of knuckled
limbs tipped with what were very definitely fingernails,
and a thick sensory stalk at the front bearing a single
blue, human eye.

Bea realized what it was and felt her gorge rise.
Red threads were flicking all around them. The Mary
was pointing her pistol this way and that; she gave a
shout of triumph and fired again. Ridges of dust
erupted, and hand-crabs shot toward her from every
side, swarming up her legs, her torso. She swung completely around as she swatted at them, and Bea threw
herself to the floor just before the reaction pistol fired
again, three quick shots that screamed overhead and
knocked chunks from the tunnel wall. John-Jane
Smith shrieked, and the Mary was down, her legs kicking, crabs covering her torso and her helmet. White
vapor jetted when an air line gave way.

John-Jane Smith had fallen to its knees and was
clutching its midsection. Blood leaked through its
gloved fingers. Hand-crabs were stalking toward Bea
over a ridge of dust, blue eyes jerking to and fro on
thick upraised stalks, fixing on her. Bea took a step
toward the neuter, and the hand-crabs stepped sideways too, uptilted rear ends firing threads of red light
from an offset bump that would be the wrist bone if
they were real hands, every hand-crab linked in a
flickering web, more and more of them emerging from
the mounds and ridges of dust. John-Jane Smith knelt
in a tightening circle of hand-crabs . . . And beyond
the neuter, beyond the five bodies in their cocoons of
warm skin, stood a human figure.

A man clad in only the skintight one-piece garment
worn under pressure suits, arms folded across his
chest, black face gleaming in the light of Bea's helmet-
lamp. Was he smiling? Bea didn't stay to find out. She
turned and ran as fast as the bad knee joint in her

pressure suit would allow, shrieking in fright and almost falling over when a flurry of snake-things shot out of a dust heap. She managed to swerve around them and ran on toward the bleary sunlight that filled the end of the tunnel.

It took her more than four hours to reach her gig. She half expected to find it as wrecked as Linval Palmer's lander, but the hatch was firmly dogged, and inside everything was as she had left it. She powered up the lifesystem, patched the leaky hatch seal with duct tape, and collapsed onto one of the couches, breathing hard inside her suit and listening to her pulse thump in her ears, while Hades' unbreathable atmosphere was flushed out and the cabin was repressurized with the standard oxygen/nitrogen mix. Then she unlatched her helmet and raised the ship on the radio.

Tor Torqvist answered, cheerful, impossibly sane. Bea told him that John-Jane Smith and the bodyguard had put themselves out of the picture but refused to go into details. The whole story could wait until she was off this dusty hellhole—if she was allowed to escape, that is. Tor told her that the Mary had locked him in a cabin, and he'd sealed the air vents with his clothes, accessed the ship's lifesystem via the cabin's air-conditioning unit, and increased the partial pressure of carbon dioxide in the air circulating through the rest of the ship.

"I gave her ten minutes, then cracked the door manually and dashed to the nearest emergency station and strapped on a breathing mask. The vicious little bitch was out cold on the bridge. I suppose she thought she could control the ship from there."

"Where is she now?"

"Hold four, with provisions and a portable toilet. She kicked out the video cameras, but there's nothing else she can damage."

"Now you have control of the ship, why haven't you lit out of there?"

"If you care to check the signal doppler, Captain, you'll see that I'm on my way. I promise I'll be back inside twenty days with a rescue party."

"You'll probably have to sell shares in the ship to raise funds. Let me give you formal authorization," Bea said. She set up a camera and did just that.

The ship was a heavy hauler, retrofitted with Mercedes pulse fusion motors, that she'd inherited from her mother and father. She'd grown up in it, and after her parents had died in a stupid accident when a runabout had explosively depressurized, she'd worked it hard for the past ten years. Losing it would be almost as bad as losing her parents—but better that than dying down here on this dusty rock.

When she was finished, Tor asked, "Are you sure you can hold out until I get back?"

"I'm going into hibernation. After I connect my suit to the gig's power supply, I can sleep out a whole year if I have to."

Bea talked with Tor while she made her preparations. She stripped off her pressure suit and cleaned herself as best she could with wipes, then climbed back into the suit again. She plugged a line into the gig's food maker, which would supply her suit with water doped with glucose and essential amino acids, plugged a cord into the ship's batteries, and powered down the gig's systems again and said good-bye to Tor.

"Don't worry, Captain. I'll be back before you know it. Pleasant dreams."

Bea called up the headup display and initiated the hibernation mode. A needle stung her neck, and she fell into warm swoony darkness. . . .

And woke, thrashing to escape the embrace of something tight and confining, a cocoon of skin that ripped and fell away. She sat up, tried to breathe and couldn't, and after a panicky minute discovered that she didn't need to.

She was sitting naked on a bare hillside. Dust-laden

wind carressed her bare skin. The storm was still raging, but it seemed less primordial now, more like weather than a catastrophe. The whine of wind over the rock was as calming as the tinkling of a mountain stream. Great curtains of dust rippled overhead like an aurora, and around her dust parted here and there to reveal low hills saddling away in every direction.

She stood up, kicking away the tattered remnants of her cocoon. Her skin was black, gleaming like oiled leather, cool but supple, and completely hairless. She ran her tongue over her teeth. Her mouth was as dry as the dust that blew over her, and when she touched them she found that her eyes were dry too, as hard as pebbles. She put her hand on her chest, and after half a minute felt her heart beat once. The dull light of the sun fell on her like a blessing, energizing and invigorating her.

She knew what had happened to her and wondered why she felt serene, improbably happy, instead of being angry or in a deadly panic.

People were moving toward her now, through silky skeins of blowing dust. Three, five, six of them. John-Jane Smith, no longer a neuter but the woman she'd been before the operations and gene therapy, reached Bea first, handed her a suit liner. After Bea had climbed into it, the men moved forward.

Linval Palmer's grin split his gleaming black face. "I bet you're wondering what the hell happened to you."

"I know what happened to me. I'm wondering where your brother is."

The figure Bea had glimpsed in the tunnel before she'd fled had been Isham Palmer. She'd identified him while trudging back to her gig, after she'd enhanced the brief movie taken by her suit's movement tracker.

"How's your balance? Can you walk? Let me show you something," Linval Palmer said, and led her up the hill toward the shallow bowl of the cirque and the entrance to the tunnel system.

The others followed. John-Jane Smith and the xeno-archaeologist and the three mercenaries walking through the dust storm as if strolling through a spring meadow on Earth or First Foot.

"My bodyguard didn't make it," Linval Palmer said, when Bea asked about the Mary. "She killed too many of our good friend's little helpers. It didn't like that, so instead of remaking her it recycled her, poor thing."

He explained that the members of Isham's expedition who had died in the crash or shortly afterward had been recycled too. Their biomass had been used to create the snake-things and hand-crabs, as well as the cocoon that had transformed Isham. He'd lured Linval and his people into a trap, and while they were being remade, he'd spotted the descent of Bea's gig, smashed up Linval's lander, and lain in wait for his rescuers. After Bea had escaped and gone into hibernation to await her own rescue, he had tracked her down and brought her here.

Bea absorbed all this as calmly as if it were an old story about someone she knew hardly at all. "Your brother found what he was looking for, didn't he? He lucked out and found some kind of working alien technology."

"The dust," Linval said.

"The dust?"

Linval grinned. "Smart dust, in the tunnel. I think it's some kind of medical kit."

"We can't really be sure what it was originally used for, because its context no longer exists," the xenoarchaeologist said. He was a short lean man with an eager expression, telling Bea, "As for what it is, it's almost certainly some kind of nanotechnology. Smart bacteria, or smart machines the size of bacteria. . . . I'd kill for a scanning electron microscope. All I have down here are cameras that don't have adequate resolution. . . ."

Linval said, 'We know what it can do. That's the important thing."

John-Jane Smith said, "It infected us and it re-made us."

The xenoarchaeologist said, "It's in our blood, probably in every one of our cells, too. We're a symbiosis, like the stromatolites."

"We don't need to eat or drink or breathe," Linval said. "If we stay out of sunlight too long, we begin to slow down; there's some kind of photoelectric or thermoelectric effect recharging us."

The xenoarchaeologist said, "We'll probably need to eat sooner or later, if only to replace lost mass. The lander's medikit suggests that we have a hydrogen to methane respiration cycle based on sulfur-bond chemistry. If I had the right equipment, I could tell you more. I could tell you how long we can expect to live like this."

"We might live a century, or we might all keel over after a year," Linval said. "But there's no point worrying about the unknown."

"Like what it's done to our minds," Bea said.

Linval smiled. "It's the old paradox. If it has changed who we are, how can we know?'

Bea looked at John-Jane Smith. "You know it changed you. Aren't you angry at what it did?'

The woman shrugged. "I believe that I am more used to change than you. And if it hadn't changed me, I would have died."

The xenoarchaeologist said, "If it can change us so that we can live on Hades without life support, it can adapt us to other environments too. In the right environment, it can change us back to what we were."

Perhaps they were right. Perhaps the nanotech symbiosis had simply done its best to save Isham Palmer by rebuilding his body, adapting him to Hades. But why had he changed Linval and the others? Why had he dragged Bea from her gig and changed her? Perhaps the symbiosis had turned him into some kind of agent or extension of itself, which meant that she and the others were agents too, with only an illusion of freewill. . . .

Bea gestured at herself and asked, "How long did this take?"

The xenoarchaeologist said, "According to the chip in my pressure suit, the metamorphosis took about ten days."

Linval said, "We woke up about a day before you did. We're still finding our feet."

"And my gig?"

Linval said, "Isham smashed up my lander. I expect he smashed up your gig too."

John-Jane Smith said, "We'll go there, of course. In case there is anything you want to take with you."

Bea said, "Take with me?"

One of the mercenaries said, "This is our home now." He was a big man with a joyful expression, and there was a murmur of agreement around him.

For the first time, Bea felt a stir of unease. In another ten days or so, Tor would return through the wormhole with a rescue party. It was possible, she thought, that Isham Palmer hadn't lucked out after all, that the Jackaroo trader had known all along what he would find down here. Isham Palmer had been changed by what he'd found, and then he'd infected Linval and the others. He'd infected Bea. Suppose they were all the first victims of a plague that would utterly transform the human race? Was this how ascension happened, leaving the First Empire empty, ready to be sold by the Jackaroo to its next tenants?

At the junction deep inside the tunnel, Linval put a hand on Bea's shoulder, guiding her past silky dust heaps, past the tattered remains of six cocoons. She didn't need any more than the feeble sunlight angled down the length of the tunnel to read the single line scratched into the smooth slick curve of the wall beyond:

Have gone east, brother, to seek wonders.

"Isham," Linval explained. "We are thinking of following him."

"There's a whole world to explore," one of the mercenaries said.

"Who knows what else we might find," the xenoarchaeologist said. "If only I had the equipment I left on your ship. . . ."

Linval studied Bea, his expression playful. "Of course you don't have to come with us."

"Of course I'll come," Bea said.

By the time Tor and the rescue party returned, she would be long gone, walking east toward the spot on the surface of the world where the sun hung directly overhead, walking across dusty plains and lava fields, climbing low mountains carved by millions of years of dust and wind, climbing the cliffs of shield volcanoes. . . .

And with that thought, she realized that she was free. She realized that the symbiosis was not an infection after all, but a gift. That she was on the threshold of a wonderful adventure.

She smiled at her companions and said, "What are we waiting for? Let's go."

Tiger, Burning

Alastair Reynolds

It was not the first time that Adam Fernando's investigations had taken him this far from home, but on no previous trip had he ever felt quite so perilously remote, so utterly at the mercy of the machines that had copied him from brane to brane like a slowly randomizing Chinese whisper. The technicians in the Office of Scrutiny had always assured him that the process was infallible, that no essential part of him was being discarded with each duplication, but he only ever had their word on the matter, and they *would* say it was safe, wouldn't they? Memory, as always, gained foggy holes with each instance of copying. He recalled the precise details of his assignment—the awkward nature of the problem—but he couldn't for the life of him say why he had chosen, at what must have been the very last minute, to assume the physical embodiment of a man-sized walking cat.

When Fernando had been reconstituted after the final duplication, he came to awareness in a half-open metal egg, its inner surface still slick with the residue of the biochemical products from which he had been quickened. He pawed at his whorled, matted fur, then willed his retractile claws into action. They worked excellently, requiring no special effort on his part. A portion of his brain must have been adapted to deal with them, so that their unsheathing was almost involuntary.

He stood from the egg, taking in his surroundings. His color vision and depth perception appeared reassuringly human-normal. The quickening room was a gray-walled metal space under standard gravity, devoid of ornamentation save that provided by the many scientific tools and instruments that had been stored here. There was no welcoming party, and the air was a touch cooler than conventional taste dictated. Scrutiny had requested that he be allowed embodiment, but that was the only concession his host had made to his arrival. Which could mean one of two things: Doctor Meranda Austvro was doing all that she could to hamper his investigation, without actually breaking the law, or that she was so blissfully innocent of any actual wrongdoing that she had no need to butter him up with formal niceties.

He tested his claws again. They still worked. Behind him, he was vaguely aware of an indolently swishing tail.

He was just sheathing his claws when a door whisked open in one pastel gray wall. An aerial robot emerged swiftly into the room: a collection of dull metal spheres orbiting each other like clockwork planets in some mad, malfunctioning orrery. He bristled at the sudden intrusion, but it seemed unlikely that the host would have gone to the bother of quickening him only to have her aerial murder him immediately afterward.

"Inspector Adam Fernando, Office of Scrutiny," he said. No need to prove it: The necessary authentication had been embedded in the header of the graviton pulse that had conveyed his resurrection profile from the repeater brane.

One of the larger spheres answered him officiously. "Of course. Who *else* might you have been? We trust

the quickening has been performed to your general
satisfaction?"

He picked at a patch of damp fur, suppressing the
urge to shiver. "Everything seems in order. Perhaps if
we moved to a warmer room. . . ." His voice sounded
normal enough, despite the alterations to his face:
maybe a touch less deep than normal, with the merest
suggestion of a feline snarl in the vowels.

"Naturally. Doctor Austvro has been waiting for
you."

"I'm surprised she wasn't here to greet me."

"Doctor Austvro is a busy woman, Inspector, now
more than ever. I thought someone from the Office
of Scrutiny would have appreciated that."

He was about to mention something about common
courtesies, then thought better of it: Even if she wasn't
listening in, there was no telling what the aerial might
report back to Austvro.

"Perhaps we'd better be moving on. I take it Doctor
Austvro can find time to squeeze me into her sched-
ule, now that I'm alive?"

"Of course," the machine said sniffily. "It's some
distance to her laboratory. It might be best if I carried
you, unless you would rather locomote."

Fernando knew the drill. He spread his arms,
allowing the cluster of flying spheres to distribute itself around his body to provide support. Small
spheres pushed under his arms, his buttocks, the padded black soles of his feet, while others nudged gently
against chest and spine to keep him balanced. The
largest sphere, which played no role in supporting
him, flew slightly ahead. It appeared to generate
some kind of aerodynamic air pocket. They sped
through the open door and down a long, curving corridor, gaining speed with each second. Soon they
were moving hair-raisingly fast, dodging round hair-
pin bends and through doors that opened and shut
only just in time.

Fernando remembered his tail and curled it out of harm's way.

"How long will this take?" he asked.

"Five minutes. We shall only be journeying a short distance into the inclusion."

Fernando recalled his briefing. "What we're passing through now—this is all human built, part of Pegasus Station? We're not seeing any KR-L artifacts yet?"

"Nor shall you," the aerial said sternly. "The actual business of investigating the KR-L machinery falls under the remit of the Office of Exploitation, as you well know. Scrutiny's business is confined only to peripheral matters of security related to that investigation."

Fernando bristled. "And as such . . ."

"The word was 'peripheral,' Inspector. Doctor Austvro was very clear about the terms under which she would permit your arrival, and they did not include a guided tour of the KR-L artifacts."

"Perhaps if I ask nicely."

"Ask whatever you like. It will make no difference."

While they sped on—in silence now, for Fernando had decided he preferred it that way—he chewed over what he knew of the inclusion and its significance to the Metagovernment.

Hundreds of thousands of years ago, humanity had achieved the means to colonize nearby branes: squeezing biological data across the hyperspatial gap into adjacent realities, then growing living organisms from those patterns. Now the Metagovernment sprawled across thirty thousand densely packed braneworlds. Yet in all that time it had encountered evidence of only one other intelligent civilization: the vanished KR-L culture.

Further expansion was unlikely. Physics changed subtly from brane to brane, limiting the possibilities for human colonization. Beyond fifteen thousand realities in either direction, people could survive only inside bubbles of tampered spacetime, in which the local physics had been tweaked to simulate homebrane conditions. These "inclusions" became increasingly difficult to maintain as the local physics grew more exotic. At five kilometers across, Meranda Austvro's inclusion was the smallest in existence, and it still required gigantic support machinery to hold it open. The Metagovernment was happy to shoulder the expense because it hoped to reap riches from Austvro's investigations into the vanished KR-L culture.

But that investigation was supposed to be above-top-secret, the mere existence of the KR-L culture officially deniable at all levels of the Metagovernment. By all accounts Austvro was close to a shattering discovery.

And yet there were leaks. Someone close to the operation—maybe even Austvro herself—was blabbing.

Scrutiny had sent Fernando in to seal the leak. If that meant shutting down Austvro's whole show until the cat could be put back into the bag (Fernando could not help but smile at the metaphor), then he had the necessary authorization.

How Austvro would take it was another thing.

The rush of corridors and doors slowed abruptly, and a moment later Fernando was deposited back on his feet, teetering slightly until he regained his balance. He had arrived in a much larger room than the one where he had been quickened, one that felt a good deal more welcoming. There was plush white carpet on the floor, comfortable furniture, soothing pastel décor, various homely knickknacks and tasteful objets d'art. The rock-effect walls were interrupted by lavish picture windows overlooking an unlikely garden, complete with winding paths, rock pools, and all manner of imported vegetation, laid out under a soothing green sky. It was a convincing simulacrum of one of the more popular holiday destinations in the low-thousand branes.

Meranda Austvro was reclining in a silver dress on a long black settee. Playing cards were arranged in a circular formation on the coffee table before her. She put down the one card that had been in her hand and beckoned Fernando to join her.

"Welcome to Pegasus Station, Inspector," she said. "I'm sorry I wasn't able to greet you sooner, but I've been rather on the busy side."

Fernando sat himself down on a chair, facing her across the table. "So I see."

"A simple game of Clock Patience, Inspector, to occupy myself while I was waiting for your arrival. Don't imagine this is how I'd rather be spending my afternoon."

He decided to soften his approach. "Your aerial did tell me you'd been preoccupied with your work."

"That's part of it. But I must admit we botched your first quickening, and I didn't have time to wait around to see the results a second time."

"When you say 'botched' . . ."

"I neglected to check your header tag more carefully. When all that cat fur started appearing . . ." She waved her hand dismissively. "I assumed there'd been a mistake in the profile, so I aborted the quickening before you reached legal sentience."

The news unnerved him. Failed quickenings weren't unknown, though, and she'd acted legally enough. "I hope you recycled my remains."

"On the contrary, Inspector: I made good use of them." Austvro patted a striped orange rug, spread across the length of the settee. "You don't mind, do you? I found the pattern quite appealing."

"Make the most of me," Fernando said, trying not to sound as if she had touched any particular nerve. "You can have another skin when I leave, if it means so much to you."

She clicked her fingers over his shoulder at the aerial. "You may go now, Caliph."

The spheres bustled around each other. "As you wish, Doctor Austvro."

When Fernando had heard the whisk of the closing door, he leaned an elbow on the table, careful not to disturb the cards. He brought his huge whiskered head close to Austvro's. She was an attractive woman despite a certain steely hauteur. He wondered if she could smell his breath, how uniquely, distastefully feline it was. "I hope this won't take too much time, for both our sakes. Scrutiny wants early closure on this whole mess."

"I'm sure it does. Unfortunately, I don't know the first thing about your investigation." She picked up a card from one part of the pattern, examined it with pursed lips, then placed it down on top of another one. "Therefore, I'm not sure how I can help you."

"You were informed that we were investigating a security hole."

"I was informed, and I found the suggestion absurd. Unless I am the perpetrator." She turned her cool, civil eyes upon him. "Is that what you think, Inspector? That I am the one leaking information back to the home-brane, risking the suspension of my own project?"

"I know only that there are leaks."

"They could be originating from someone in Scrutiny, or Exploitation. Have you considered that?"

"We have to start somewhere. The operation itself seems as good a place as any."

"Then you're wasting your time. Return down-stack and knock on someone else's door. I've work to do."

"Why are you so certain the leaks couldn't be originating here?"

"Because—first—I do not accept that there *are* leaks. There are merely statistical patterns, coincidences, that Scrutiny has latched onto because it has nothing better to do with its time. Second, I run this show on my own. There is no room for anyone else to be the source of these nonexistent leaks."

"Your husband?"

She smiled briefly and extended a hand over the coffee table, palm down. A figure—a grave, clerical-looking man in black—appeared above the table's surface, no larger than a statuette. The man made a gesture with his hands, as if shaping an invisible ball, then said something barely audible—Fernando caught the phrase "three hundred"—then vanished again, leaving only the arrangement of playing cards.

Austvro selected another, examined it once more and returned it to the table.

"My husband died years ago, Inspector. Edvardo and I were deep inside the KR-L machinery, protected by an extension of the inclusion. My husband's speciality was acausal mechanics. . . ." For a moment, a flicker of humanity interrupted the composure of her face. "The extension collapsed. Edvardo was on the other side of the failure point. I watched him fall into KR-L spacetime. I watched what it did to him."

"I'm sorry," Fernando said, wishing he had paid more attention to the biographical briefing.

"Since then I have conducted operations alone, with only the machines to help me. Caliph is the most special of them. I place great value on his companionship. You can question the machines if you like, but it won't get you anywhere."

"Yet the leaks are real."

"We could argue about that."

"Scrutiny wouldn't have sent me otherwise."

"There must be false alarms. Given the amount of data Scrutiny keeps tabs on—the entire informational content of metahumanity, spread across thirty thousand reality layers—isn't *any* pattern almost guaranteed to show up eventually?"

"It is," Fernando conceded, stroking his chin tufts. "But that's why Scrutiny pays attention to context and to clustering. Not simply to exact matches for sensitive keywords, either, but for suspicious similarities: near-misses designed to throw us off the scent. Miranda for Meranda; Ostrow for Austvro, that kind of thing."

"And you've found these clusters?"

"Nearly a dozen at the last count. Someone with intimate knowledge of this research project is talking, and we can't have that."

This amused her. "So the Metagovernment does have its enemies after all."

"It's no secret that there are political difficulties in the high branes. Talk of secession. Exploitation feels that the KR-L technology may give the Metagovernment just the tools it needs to hold the stack together if the dissidents try to gain the upper hand."

Austvro sneered. "Tools of political control."

"An edge, that's all. And obviously matters won't be helped if the breakaway branes learn about the KR-L discoveries and what we intend to do with them. That's why we need to keep a lid on things."

"But these clusters . . ." Austvro leaned back into the settee, studying Fernando levelly. "I was shown some of the evidence—some of the documents— before you arrived, and, frankly, none of it made much sense to me."

"It didn't?"

"If someone—some mole—was trying to get a message through to the breakaway branes, why insist on being so cryptic? Why not just come out and say whatever needs to be said instead of creating jumbled riddles? Names mixed up . . . names altered . . . the context changed out of all recognition . . . some of these keywords even looked like they were embedded in some kind of play."

"All I can say is that Scrutiny considered the evidence sufficiently compelling to require immediate action. It's still investigating the provenance of these documents, but I should have word on that soon enough."

Austvro narrowed her flint-gray eyes. "Provenance?"

"As I said, the documents are faked: made to appear historical, as if they've always been present in the data."

"Which is even more absurd than there being leaks in the first place."

He smiled at her. "I'm glad we agree on something."

"It's a start."

He tapped his extended claws against the coffee table. "I appreciate your skepticism, Doctor. But the fact is, I can't leave here until I have an explanation. If Scrutiny isn't satisfied with my findings—if the source of the leaks can't be traced—they'll have no option but to shut down Pegasus, or at least replace the current setup with something under much tighter government control. So it's really in your interests to work with me, to help me find the solution."

"I see," she said coldly.

"I'd like to see more of this operation. Not just Pegasus Station but the KR-L culture itself."

"Unthinkable. Didn't Caliph clarify where your jurisdiction ends, Inspector?"

"It's not a question of jurisdiction. Give me a reason to think you haven't anything to hide, and I'll focus my inquiries somewhere else."

She looked down, fingering the striped orange rug she had made of his skin.

"It will serve no purpose, Inspector, except to disturb you."

"I'll edit the memories before I pass them back down the stack. How does that sound?"

She rose from the settee, abandoning her card game. "Your call. But don't blame me when you start gibbering."

Austvro led him from the lounge, back into a more austere part of the station. The hem of her silver dress swished on the iron-gray flooring. Now and then an aerial flashed past on some errand, but in all other respects the station was deserted. Fernando knew that

Exploitation had offered to send more expertise, but Austvro had always declined assistance. By all accounts she worked efficiently, feeding a steady stream of tidbits and breakthroughs back to the Metagovernment specialists. According to Fernando's dossier, Austvro didn't trust the stability of anyone who would actually volunteer to be copied this far up-stack, knowing the protocols. It was no surprise that she treated him with suspicion, for he was also a volunteer, and only his memories would be going back home again.

Presently they arrived at an oval aperture cut into one wall. On the other side of the aperture, ready to dart down a tunnel, was a two-seater travel pod.

"Are you sure about this, Inspector?"

"I'm perfectly sure."

She shrugged—letting him know it was his mistake, not hers—and then ushered him into one of the seats. Austvro took the other one, facing him at right angles to the direction of travel. She applied her hand to a tiller and the pod sped into motion. Tunnel walls zipped by in an accelerating blur.

"We're about to leave the main body of the inclusion," Austvro informed him.

"Into KR-L spacetime?"

"Not unless the support machines fail. The inclusion's more or less spherical—insofar as one can talk about 'spherical' intrusions of one form of spacetime into another—but it sprouts tentacles and loops into interesting portions of the surrounding KR-L structure. Maintaining these tentacles and loops is much harder than keeping the sphere up, and I'm sure you've heard how expensive and difficult *that* is."

Fernando felt his hairs bristling. The pod was moving terrifically fast now; so swiftly that there could be no doubt that they had left the main sphere behind already. He visualized a narrow, delicate stalk of spacetime jutting out from the sphere and himself as a tiny moving mote within that stalk.

"Was this where your husband died, Doctor?"

"A similar extension; it doesn't matter now. We've made some adjustments to the support machinery, so it shouldn't happen again." Her expression turned playful. "Why? You're not *nervous*, are you?"

"Not at all. I just wondered where the accident had happened."

"A place much like here. It doesn't matter. My husband never much cared for these little jaunts, anyway. He much preferred to restrict himself to the main inclusion."

Fernando recalled the image of Austvro's husband, his hands cupping an imaginary ball, like a mime, and something of the gesture tickled his interest.

"Your husband's line of work—acausal signaling, wasn't it? The theoretical possibility of communication through time, using KR-L principles?"

"A dead end, unfortunately. Even the KR-L had never made *that* work. But the Metagovernment was happy with the crumbs and morsels he sent back home."

"He must have thought there was something in it."

"My husband was a dreamer," Austvro said. "His singular failing was his inability to distinguish between a practical possibility and an outlandish fantasy."

"I see."

"I don't mean to sound harsh. I loved him, of course. But he could never love the KR-L the way I do. For him these trips were always something to be endured, not relished."

He watched her eyes for a glimmer of a reaction. "And after his accident—did you have misgivings?"

"For a nanosecond. Until I realized how important this work is. How we must succeed, for the sake of the homebrane." She leaned forward in her seat and pointed down the tunnel. "There. We're approaching the interface. That's where the tunnel cladding becomes transparent. The photons reaching your eyes will have originated as photon-analogs in KR-L spacetime. You'll see their structures, their great engines. The scale will astound you. The mere geometry of these artifacts is . . . deeply troubling, for some. If it disconcerts you, close your eyes." Her hand remained hard on the tiller. "I'm used to it, but I'm exposed to these marvels on a daily basis."

"I'm curious," Fernando said. "When you speak of the aliens, you sometimes sound like you're saying three letters. At other times . . ."

"Krull, yes," she said, dismissively. "It's shorthand, Inspector, nothing more. "Long before we knew it had ever been inhabited, we called this the KR-L brane. K and R are the Boltzmann and Rydberg constants, from nuclear physics. In KR-L spacetime, these numbers differ from their values in the homebrane. L is a parameter that denotes the degree of variation."

"Then Krull is . . . a word of your own coining?"

"If you insist upon calling it a word. Why? Has it appeared in these mysterious keyword clusters of yours?"

"Something like it."

The pod swooped into the transparent part of the stalk. It was difficult to judge speed now. Fernando assumed there was some glass-like cladding between him and the inclusion boundary, and somewhere beyond that (he was fuzzy on the physics) the properties of spacetime took on alien attributes, profoundly incompatible with human biochemistry. But things could still live in that spacetime, provided they'd been born there in the first place. The KR-L had evolved into an entire supercivilization, and although they were gone now, their great machines remained. He could see them now, as huge and bewildering as Austvro had warned. They were slab-sided, round-edged, ribbed with flanges and cooling grids, surmounted by arcing spheres and flickering discharge cones. The structures glowed with a lilac radiance that seemed to shade into ultraviolet. They receded in all directions—more directions, in fact, than seemed reasonable, given the usual rules of perspective. Somewhere low in his throat he already felt the first queasy constriction of nausea.

"To give you an idea of scale . . ." Austvro said, directing his unwilling attention toward one dizzying feature ". . . that structure there, if it were mapped into our spacetime and built from our iron atoms, would be larger than a Jupiter-class gas giant. And yet it is no more than a heat dissipation element, a safety valve on a much larger mechanism. That more distant machine is almost three light-hours across, and it too is only one element in a larger whole."

Fernando fought to keep his eyes open. "How far do these machines extend?"

"At least as far as our instruments can reach. Hundreds of light-hours in all directions. The inclusion penetrates a complex of KR-L machinery larger than one of our solar systems. And yet even then there is no suggestion that the machinery ends. It may extend for weeks, months, of light-travel time. It may be larger than a galaxy."

"Its function?" Seeing her hesitation, he added: "I have the necessary clearance, Doctor. It's safe to tell me."

"Absolute control," she said. "Utter dominance of matter and energy, not just in this brane but across the entire stack of realities. With this instrumentality, the KR-L could influence events in any brane they selected, in an instant. This machinery makes our graviton pulse equipment—the means by which you arrived here—look like the ham-fisted workings of a brain-damaged caveman."

Fernando was silent for a moment, as the pod sped on through the mind-wrenching scenery.

"Yet the KR-L only ever occupied this one brane," he said. "What use did they have for machinery capable of influencing events in another one?"

"Only the KR-L can tell us that," Austvro said. "Yet it seems likely to me that the machinery was constructed to deal with a threat to their peaceful occupation of this one brane."

"What could threaten such a culture, apart from their own bloody minded hubris?"

"One must presume another culture of comparable sophistication. Their science must have detected the emergence of another civilization, in some remote brane, hundreds of thousands or even millions of realities away, that the KR-L considered hostile. They created this great machinery so that they might nip that threat in the bud, before it spilled across the stack toward them."

"Genocide?"

"Not necessarily. Is it evil to spay a cat?"

"Depends on the cat."

"My point is that the KR-L were not butchers. They sought their own self-preservation, but not at the ultimate expense of that other culture, whoever *they* might have been. Surgical intervention was all that was required."

Fernando looked around again. Some part of his mind was finally adjusting to the humbling dimensions of the machinery, for his nausea was abating. "Yet they're all gone now. What happened?"

"Again, one must presume. Perhaps some fatal hesitancy. They created this machinery but, at what should have been their moment of greatest triumph, flinched from using it."

"Or they did use it, and it came back and bit them."

"I hardly think so, Inspector."

"How many realities have we explored? Eighty, ninety thousand layers in either direction?"

"Something like that," she said, tolerantly.

"How do we know what happens when you get much farther out? For that matter, what could the KR-L have known?"

"I'm not sure I follow you."

"I'm just wondering . . . when I was a child I remember someone—I think it was my uncle—

explaining to me that the stack was like the pages of an infinitely thick book, a book whose pages reached away to an infinite distance in either direction: reality after reality, as far as you could imagine, with the physics changing only slightly from page to page."

"As good an explanation as the layman will ever grasp."

"But the same person told me there was another theory of the stack, taken a bit less seriously but not completely discredited."

"Continue," Austvro said.

"The theory was that physics kept changing, but after a while it flattened out again and began to converge back to ours. And that by then you were actually coming back again, approaching our reality from the other direction. The stack, in other words, was circular."

"You're quite right: That theory is taken a bit less seriously."

"But it isn't discredited, is it?"

"You can't discredit an untestable hypothesis."

"But what if it is testable? What if the physics does begin to change less quickly?"

"Local gradients tell you nothing. We'd have to map millions, tens of millions, of layers before we could begin. . . ."

"But you already said the KR-L machinery might have had that kind of range. What if they were capable of looking all the way around the stack, but they didn't realize it? What if the hostile culture they thought they were detecting was actually themselves? What if they turned on their machinery and it reached around through the closed loop of realities and nipped *them* in the bud?"

"An amusing conceit, Inspector, but no more than that."

"But a deadly one, should it happen to be true." Fernando stroked his chin tufts, purring quietly to himself as he thought things through. "The Office of

Exploitation wishes to make use of the KR-L machinery to deal with another emerging threat."

"The Metagovernment pays my wages. It's up to *it* what it does with the results I send home."

"But as was made clear to me when I arrived, you are a busy woman. Busy because you are approaching your own moment of greatest triumph. You understand enough about the KR-L machinery to make it work, don't you? You can talk to it through the inclusion, ask it do your bidding."

Her expression gave nothing away. "The Metagovernment expects results."

"I don't doubt it. But I wonder if the Metagovernment has been fully apprised of the risks. When they asked you what happened to the KR-L, did you mention the possibility that they might have brought about their own extinction?"

"I confined my speculation to the realm of the reasonably likely, Inspector. I saw no reason to digress into fancy."

"Nonetheless, it might have been worth mentioning."

"I disagree. The Metagovernment is intending to take action against dissident branes within its own realm of colonization, not some barely detected culture a million layers away. Even if the topology of the layers *was* closed. . . ."

"But even if the machinery was used, it was only used once," Fernando said. "There's no telling what other side effects might be involved."

"I've made many local tests. There's no reason to expect any difficulties."

"I'm sure the KR-L scientists were equally confident before they switched it on."

Her tone of voice, never exactly confiding, turned chill. "I'll remind you once again that you are on Scrutiny business, not working for Exploitation. My recollection is that you came to investigate leaks, not to question the basis of the entire project."

"I know, and you're quite right. But I can't help wondering whether the two things aren't in some way connected."

"I don't even accept that there are leaks, Inspector. You have some way to go before you can convince me they have anything to do with the KR-L machinery."

"I'm working on it," Fernando said.

They watched the great structures shift angle and perspective as the pod reached the apex of its journey and began to race back toward the inclusion. Fernando was glad when the shaft walls turned opaque and they were again speeding down a dark-walled tunnel, back into what he now thought of as the comparative safety and sanity of Pegasus Station. Until he had recorded and transmitted his memories down the stack, self-preservation still had a strong allure.

"I hope that satisfied your curiosity," Austvro said, when they had disembarked and returned to her lounge. "But as I warned you, the journey was of no value to your investigation."

"On the contrary," he told her. "I'm certain it clarified a number of things. Might I have access to a communications console? I'd like to see if Scrutiny has come up with anything new since I arrived."

"I'll have Caliph provide you with whatever you need. In the meantime, I must attend to work. Have Caliph summon me if there is anything of particular urgency."

"I'll be sure to."

She left him alone in the lounge. He fingered the tigerskin rug, repulsed and fascinated in equal measure at the exact match with his own fur. While he waited for the aerial to arrive, he swept a paw over the coffee table, trying to conjure up the image of Austvro's dead husband. But the little figure never appeared.

It hardly mattered. His forensic memory was perfectly capable of replaying a recent observation, especially one that had seemed noteworthy at the time.

He called to mind the dead man, dwelling on the way he shaped an invisible form: not, Fernando now realized, a ball, but the ring-shaped stack of adjacent branes in the closed-loop of realities. "Three hundred and sixty degrees," he'd been saying. Meranda Austvro's dead husband had been describing the same theoretical metareality of which Fernando's uncle had once spoken. Did that mean that the dead man believed that the KR-L had been scared by their own shadow, glimpsed at some immense distance into the reality stack? And had they forged this soul-crushingly huge machinery simply to strike at that perceived enemy, not realizing that the blow was doomed to fall on their own heads?

Perhaps.

He looked anew at the pattern of cards, untouched since Austvro had taken him from this room to view the KR-L machinery. The ring of cards, arranged for Clock Patience, echoed the closed-loop of realities in her husband's imagination.

Almost, he supposed, as if Austvro had been dropping him a hint.

Fernando was just thinking that through when Caliph appeared, assigning one of his larger spheres into a communications console. Symbols and keypads brightened across the matte gray surface. Fernando tapped commands, claws clicking as he worked, and soon accessed his private data channel.

There was, as he had half expected, a new message from Scrutiny. It concerned the more detailed analysis of the leaks that had been in motion when he left on his investigation.

Fernando placed a direct call through.

"Hello," said Fernando's down-brane counterpart, a man named Cook. "Good news, bad news, I'm afraid."

"Continue," Fernando purred.

"We've run a thorough analysis on the keyword clusters, as promised. The good news is that the clusters haven't gone away. Their statistical significance is now even more certain. There's clearly been a leak. That means your journey hasn't been for nothing."

"That's a relief."

"The bad news is that the context is still giving us some serious headaches. Frankly, it's disturbing. Whoever's responsible for these leaks has gone to immense trouble to make them look as if they've always been part of our data heritage."

"I don't understand. I mean, I *understand*, but I don't get it. There must be a problem with your methods, your data auditing."

Cook looked pained. "That's what we thought, but we've been over this time and again. There's no mistake. Whoever planted these leaks has tampered with the data at a very deep level, sufficient to make it seem as if the clusters have been with us long before the KR-L brane was ever discovered."

Fernando lowered his voice. "Give me an example. Austvro mentioned a play, for instance."

"That would be one of the oldest clusters. *The Shipwreck*, by a paper-age playwright, around 001611. No overt references to the KR-L, but it does deal with a scholar on a haunted island, an island where a powerful witch used to live . . . which could be considered a metaphorical substitute for Austvro and Pegasus Station. Contains a Miranda, too, and . . ."

"Was the playwright a real historical figure?"

"Unlikely, unless he was almost absurdly prolific. There are several dozen other plays in the records, all of which we can presume were the work of the mole."

"Mm," Fernando said, thoughtfully.

"The mole screwed up in other ways too," Cook added. "The plays are riddled with anachronisms—words and phrases that don't appear earlier in the records."

"Sloppy," Fernando commented, while wondering if there was something more to it than mere sloppiness. "Tell me about another cluster."

"Skip to 001956 and we have another piece of faked drama, something called a 'film,' some kind of recorded performance. Again, lots of giveaways: Ostrow for Austvro, Bellerophon—he's the hero who rode the winged horse Pegasus—the KR-L themselves . . . real aliens, this time, even if they're confined to a single planet, rather than an entire brane. There's even—get this—a tiger."

"Really," Fernando said dryly.

"But here's an oddity: Our enquiries turned up peripheral matter that seems to argue that the later piece was in some way based upon the earlier one."

"Almost as if the mole wished to lead our attention from one cluster to another." Fernando scratched at his ear. "What's the next cluster?"

"Jump to 002713: an ice opera performed on Pluto Prime for one night only, before it closed due to exceptionally bad notices. Mentions 'entities in the eighty-three-thousandth layer of reality.' This from at least six thousand years before the existence of adjoining braneworlds was proven beyond doubt."

"Could be coincidence, but . . . well, go on."

"Jump to 009655, the premier of a Tauri-phase astrosculpture in the Wenlock star-forming region. Supplementary text refers to 'the aesthetic of the doomed Crail' and 'Mirandine and Kalebin.' "

"There are other clusters, right up to the near present?"

"All the way up the line. Random time-spacing: We've looked for patterns there, and haven't found any. It must mean something to the mole, of course. . . ."

"If there is a mole," Fernando said.

"Of course there's a mole. What other explanation could there be?"

"That's what I'm wondering."

Fernando closed the connection, then sat in silent contemplation, shuffling mental permutations. When he felt that he had examined the matter from every conceivable angle—and yet still arrived at the same unsettling conclusion—he had Caliph summon Doctor Austvro once more.

"Really, Inspector," she said, as she came back into the lounge. "I've barely had time . . ."

"Sit down, Doctor."

Something in the force of his words must have reached her. Doctor Austvro sank into the settee, her hands tucked into the silvery folds of her dress.

"Is there a problem? I specifically asked . . ."

"You're under arrest for the murder of your husband, Edvardo Austvro."

Her face turned furious. "Don't be absurd. My husband's death was an accident: a horrid, gruesome mistake, but no more than that."

"That's what you wished us all to think. But you killed him, didn't you? You arranged for the collapse of the inclusion, knowing that he would be caught in KR-L spacetime."

"Ridiculous."

"Your husband understood what had happened to the KR-L: how their machinery had reached around the stack, through three hundred and sixty degrees, and wiped them out of existence, leaving only their remains. He knew exactly how dangerous it would be to reactivate the machinery; how it could never become a tool for the Metagovernment. You said it yourself, Meranda: He feared the machinery. That's because he knew what it had done, what it was still capable of doing."

"I would never have killed him," she said, her tone flatly insistent.

"Not until he opposed you directly, not until he became the only obstacle between you and your greatest triumph. Then he had to go."

"I've heard enough." She turned her angry face toward the aerial. "Caliph, escort the Inspector to the dissolution chamber. He's in clear violation of the terms under which I agreed to this investigation."

"On the contrary," Fernando said. "My inquiry is still of central importance."

She sneered. "Your ridiculous obsession with leaks? I monitored your recent conversation with the home-brane, Inspector. The leaks are what I've always maintained: statistical noise, meaningless coincidences. The mere fact that they appear in sources that are incontrovertibly old . . . what further evidence do you need, that the leaks are nothing of the sort?"

"You're right," Fernando said, allowing himself a heavy sigh. "They aren't leaks. In that sense I was mistaken."

"In which case admit that your mission here was no more than a wild goose chase and that your accusations concerning my husband amount to no more than a desperate attempt to salvage some . . ."

"They aren't leaks," Fernando continued, as if Austvro had not spoken. "They're warnings, sent from our own future."

She blinked. "I'm sorry?"

"It's the only explanation. The leaks appear in context sources that appear totally authentic . . . because they are."

"Madness."

"I don't think so. It all fits together quite nicely. Your husband was investigating acausal signaling: the means to send messages back in time. You dismissed his work, but what if there was something in it after all? What if a proper understanding of the KR-L technology allowed a future version of the Metagovernment to send a warning to itself in the past?"

"What kind of warning, Inspector?" she asked, still sounding appalled.

"I'm guessing here, but it might have something to do with the machinery itself. You're about to reactivate the very tools that destroyed the KR-L. Perhaps the point of the warning is to stop that ever happening. Some dreadful, unforeseen consequence of turning the machinery against the dissident branes . . . not the extinction of humanity, obviously, or there wouldn't be anyone left alive to send the warning. But something nearly as bad. Something so awful that it must be edited out of history, at all costs."

"You should listen to yourself, Inspector. Then ask yourself whether you came out of the quickening room with all your faculties intact."

He smiled. "Then you have doubts."

"Concerning your sanity, yes. This idea of a message being sent back in time . . . it might have some microscopic degree of credibility if your precious leaks weren't so hopelessly cryptic. Who sends a message and then scrambles the facts?"

"Someone in a hurry, I suppose. Or someone with an imperfect technique."

"I'm sure that means something to you."

"I'm just wondering: What if there wasn't time to get it right? What if the sending of the message was a one-shot attempt, something that had to be attempted even though the method was still not fully understood?"

"That still doesn't explain why the keywords would crop up in . . . a *play*, of all things."

"Perhaps it does, though. Especially if the acausal signaling involves the transmission of patterns directly into the human mind, across time, in a scattergun fashion. The playwright . . ."

"What about him?" she asked, with a knowingness that told him she had listened in on his conversation with Cook.

"The man lived and died before the discovery of quantum mechanics, let alone braneworlds. Even if the warning arrived fully formed and coherent in his mind, he could only have interpreted it according to his existing mental framework. It's no wonder things got mixed up, confused. His conceptual vocabulary didn't extend to vanished alien cultures in adjacent reality stacks. It did extend to islands, dead witches, ghosts."

"Ridiculous. Next you'll be telling me that the other clusters . . ."

"Exactly so. The dramatized recording—the 'film'—was made a few centuries later. The creators did the best they could with their limited understanding of the universe. They knew of space travel, other worlds. Closer to the truth than the playwright but still limited by the mental prison of their contemporary worldview. The same goes for all the other clusters, I'm willing to bet."

"Let me get this straight," Austvro said. "The future Metagovernment resurrects ancient KR-L time-signaling machinery, technology that it barely understands. It attempts to send a message back in time, but it ends up spraying it through history, back to the time of a man who probably thought the Sun ran on coal."

"Maybe even earlier," Fernando said. "There's nothing to say there aren't other clusters, lurking in the statistical noise. . . ."

Austvro cut him off. "And yet despite this limited understanding of the machinery, the—as you said—scattershot approach, they still managed to score direct hits into the heads of playwrights, dramatists, sculptors. . . ." She shook her head pityingly.

"Not necessarily," Fernando said. "We only know that these people became what they were in our timeline. It might have been the warning itself that set these individuals on their artistic courses . . . planting a seed, a vaguely felt anxiety, that they had no choice but to exorcise through creative expression, be it a play, a film, or an ice-opera on Pluto Prime."

"I'll give you credit, Inspector. You really know how to take an argument beyond its logical limit. You're actually suggesting that if the signaling hadn't taken place, none of these works of art would ever have existed?"

He shrugged. "If you admit the possibility of time messages . . ."

"I don't. Not at all."

"It doesn't matter. I'd hoped to convince you—I thought it might make your arrest an easier matter for both of us—but it's really not necessary. You understand now, though, why I must put an end to your research. Scrutiny and Exploitation can decide for themselves whether there's any truth in my theory."

"And if they don't think there is—then I'll be allowed to resume my studies?"

"There's still the small matter of your murder charge, Meranda."

She looked sad. "I'd hoped you might have forgotten."

"It's not my job to forget."

"How did you guess?"

"I didn't guess," he said. "You led me to it. More than that: I think some part of you—some hidden, subconscious part—actually wanted me to learn the truth. If not, that was a very unfortunate choice of card game, Meranda."

"You're saying I wanted you to arrest me?"

"I can't believe that you ever hated your husband enough to kill him. You just hated the way he opposed your research. For that reason he had to go, but I doubt that there's been a moment since when what you did hasn't been eating you from inside."

"You're right," she said, as if arriving at a firm decision. "I didn't hate him. But he still had to go. And so do you."

In a flash her hand had emerged from the silvery folds of her dress, clutching the sleek black form of a weapon. Fernando recognized it as a simple blaster: not the most sophisticated weapon in existence, but more than capable of inflicting mortal harm.

"Please, Doctor. Put that thing away, before you do one of us an injury."

She stood, the weapon wavering in her hand but never losing its lock on him.

"Caliph," she said. "Escort the Inspector to the dissolution chamber. He's leaving us."

"You're making a mistake, Meranda."

"The mistake would be in allowing the Metagovernment to close me down when I'm so close to success. Caliph!"

"I cannot escort the Inspector unless the Inspector wishes to be escorted," the aerial informed her.

"I gave you an order!"

"He is an agent of the Office of Scrutiny. My programming does not permit . . ."

"Walk with me, please," Fernando said. "Put the gun away, and we'll say no more about it. You're in enough trouble as it is."

"I'm not going with you."

"You'll receive a fair trial. With the right argument, you may even be able to claim your husband's death as manslaughter. Perhaps you didn't mean to kill him, just to strand him . . ."

"It's not the trial," she snarled. "It's the thought of stepping into that *thing* . . . when I came here, I never intended to leave. I won't go with you."

"You must."

He took a step toward her, knowing even as he did it that the move was unwise. He watched her finger tense on the blaster's trigger, and for an instant he thought he might cross the space to her before the weapon discharged. Few people had the nerve to hold a gun against an agent of Scrutiny; even fewer had the nerve to fire.

But Meranda Austvro was one of those few. The muzzle spat rapid bolts of self-confined plasma, and he watched in slow-motion horror as three of the bolts slammed into his right arm, below the elbow, and took his hand and forearm away in an agonizing orange fire, like a chalk drawing smeared in the rain. The pain hit him like a hammer, and despite his training he felt the full force of it before mental barriers slammed down in rapid succession, blocking the worst. He could smell his own charred fur.

"An error, Doctor Austvro," he grunted, forcing the words out.

"Don't take another step, Inspector."

"I'm afraid I must."

"I'll kill you." The weapon was now aimed directly at his chest. If her earlier shot had been wide, there would be no error now.

He took another step. He watched her finger tense again and readied himself for the annihilating fire.

But the weapon dropped from her hand. One of Caliph's smaller spheres had dashed it from her grip. Austvro clutched her hand with the other, massaging the fingers. Her face showed stunned incomprehension. "You betrayed me," she said to the aerial.

"You injured an agent of Scrutiny. You were about to inflict further harm. I could not allow that to happen." Then one of the larger spheres swerved into Fernando's line of sight. "Do you require medical assistance?"

"I don't think so. I'm about done with this body anyway."

"Very well."

"Will you help me to escort Doctor Austvro to the dissolution chamber?"

"If you order it."

"Help me, in that case."

Doctor Austvro tried to resist, but between them Fernando and Caliph quickly had the better of her. Fernando kicked the weapon out of harm's way, then pulled Austvro against his chest with his left arm, pinning her there. She struggled to escape, but her strength was nothing against his, even allowing for the shock of losing his right arm.

Caliph propelled them to the dissolution chamber. Austvro fought all the way but with steadily draining will. Only at the last moment, when she saw the gray hood of the memory recorder next to the recessed alcove of the dissolution field, did she summon some last reserve of resistance. But her efforts counted for nothing. Fernando and the robot placed her into the recorder, closing the heavy metal restraining buckles across her body. The hood lowered itself, ready to capture a final neural image, a snapshot of her mind that would be encoded into a graviton pulse and relayed back to the homebrane.

"Meranda Austvro," Fernando said, pushing the blackened stump of his arm into his chest fur, "I am arresting you on the authority of the Office of Scrutiny. Your resurrection profile will be captured and transmitted into the safekeeping of the Metagovernment. A new body will be quickened and employed as a host for these patterns and then brought to trial. Please compose your thoughts accordingly."

"When they quicken me again, I'll destroy your career," she told him.

Fernando looked sympathetic. "You wouldn't believe how many times I've heard that before."

"I should have skinned you twice."

"It wouldn't have worked. They'd have sent a third copy of me."

He activated the memory recorder. Amber lights flickered across the hood, stabilizing to indicate that the device had obtained a coherent image and that the relevant data was ready to be committed to the graviton pulse. Fernando issued the command, and a tumbling hourglass symbol appeared on the hood.

"Your patterns are on their way home now, Meranda. For the moment you still have a legal existence. Enjoy it while you can."

He'd never said anything that cruel before, and almost as soon as the words were out he regretted them. Taunting the soon-to-be-destroyed had never been his style, and it shamed him that he had permitted himself such a gross lapse of professionalism. The only compensation was that he would soon find himself in the same predicament as Doctor Austvro.

The hourglass vanished, replaced by a steady green light. It signified that the homebrane had received the graviton pulse and that the resurrection profile had been transmitted without error.

"Former body of Meranda Austvro," he began, "I must now inform you . . ."

"Just get it over with."

Fernando and Caliph helped her from the recorder. Her body felt light in his hands, as if some essential part of it had been erased or extracted during the recording process. Legally, this was no longer Doctor Meranda Austvro: just the biological vehicle Austvro had used while resident in this brane. According to Metagovernment law, the vehicle must now be recycled.

Fernando turned on the pearly screen of the dissolution field. He tested it with a stylus, satisfied when he saw the instant actinic flash as the stylus was wrenched from existence. Dissolution was quick and efficient. In principle the atomic fires destroyed the central nervous system long before pain signals had a chance to reach it, let alone be experienced as pain.

Not that anyone ever *knew*, of course. By the time you went through the field, your memories had already been captured. Anything you experienced at the moment of destruction never made it into the profile.

"I can push you into the field," he told Austvro. "But by all accounts you'll find it quicker and easier if you run at it yourself."

She didn't want it to happen that way. Caliph and Fernando had to help her through the field. It wasn't the nicest part of the job.

Afterward, Fernando sat down to marshal and clarify his thoughts. In a little while he too would be consumed by fire, only to be reborn in the homebrane. Scrutiny would be expecting a comprehensive report into the Pegasus affair, and it would not do to be woolly on the details. Experience had taught him that a little mental preparation now paid dividends in the long run. The recording and quickening process always blurred matters a little, so the clearer one could be at the outset, the better.

When he was done with the recorder, when the green light had reported safe receipt of his neural patterns, he turned to Caliph. "I no longer have legal jurisdiction here. The 'me' speaking to you is not even legally entitled to call itself Adam Fernando. But I hope you won't consider it improper of me to offer some small thanks for your assistance."

"Will someone come back to take over?" Caliph asked.

"Probably. But don't be surprised if they come to shut down Pegasus. I'm sure my legal self will put in a good word for you, though."

"Thank you," the aerial said.

"It's the least I can do."

Fernando stood from the recorder and—as was his usual habit—took a running jump at the dissolution field. It wasn't the most elegant of ends—the lack of an arm hindered his balance—but it was quick and efficient and the execution not without a certain dignity.

Caliph watched the tiger burn, the stripes seeming to linger in the air before fading away. Then it gathered its spheres into an agitated swarm and wondered what to do next.

The Singularity Needs Women!

Paul Di Filippo

So this Singularity walks into a bar—

That's how my sad yet ultimately hopeful story starts. Like a bad joke.

Maruta and I were drinking Ghostyheads in the Sand Castle. You know that drink. Pureed ectoplasm from the Wraiths of Bongwater 9, cut with tequila from the mutant agaves of New Old New Mexico and a spritz of volcano water. Pretty potent. By the second sip, your head is full of dark energy and your limbs are parsecs long. By the third sip, you've solved the riddle of where the Growlers disappeared to. And by the fourth, you feel you could walk a tightrope strung between Mount Meru and Shambhala.

But even that altered consciousness didn't equip us to deal with a naked Singularity.

Maruta was telling me about the vicissitudes and excitements of her past month. At that period, she worked for Captain Pongo and his Mathspace Explorers. They had just returned from a long voyage to the von Bitter Shoals with a rich cargo of novel Penrose tilings. Captain Pongo had declared an extended shore leave for his weary sailors. Hence our little celebration.

"So, Lu, there we were, our ship hung up on fractal coral, the waters full of savage zero knots. None of us had eaten anything other than a slice of pi in the past week, and half our crew lay in sick bay, undergoing emergency Fourier Transforms. And what do you think Captain Pongo says? 'Damn the toroids, full secant ahead!' "

Maruta laughed heartily at the punchline of her own anecdote, then tilted her head back to glug down an immoderate slug of her drink. I admired the sheer mechanical efficiency of her slim throat as it worked, let my eyes roam over the rest of her fine body, which was clothed in the latest fashionable cuirass and greaves from designer Hulda Loveling. Maruta was visibly happy to be reembodied and was exulting in her pure physicality.

As was I. I had missed her more than I had imagined I would, over the past several weeks. I tried to convey that by sensuously gripping her knee, although the joint of her greaves didn't actually allow for any flesh-to-flesh contact.

"Damn dangerous job, Ruta. Always said so. But you're good at it, and you enjoy it, so that's all that counts. I'm just happy you're back safely. Pretty lonely here without you."

Maruta grinned broadly, then leaned forward to bring her face close to mine. The pungent odor of Ghostyhead wafted off her lips. "I didn't really have time to miss you, Lu. But once I got back, I realized once more just how much you mean to me. So, what do you say to finishing our drinks and going back to your place?"

Closing her eyes and inching even closer, she invited a kiss. I moved to comply. But our lips never connected.

The noisy, revelry rich environment of the Sand Castle suddenly became quiet as a deepsea trench. Maruta and I both straightened up to see what had caused the hush.

Standing in the fine-grained flowing curtain of the doorway was a naked Singularity.

Appearing as a dark-haired, light-skinned human male some seven feet tall, impeccably proportioned and endowed in masculine fashion, the Singularity was instantly recognizable as such by his magisterium corona. No one knew the origin or exact nature of the field that always surrounded an incarnate Singularity, but the presence of the refulgence was an unmistakable sign of posthuman activity.

For several eternal frozen seconds, none of us humans dared do so much as breathe or blink. Then a few brave souls fingered their Lifelines, insta-texting calls to Ess-Cubed.

The Singularity took no notice of these silent cries for help, although I'm sure he registered them. Rather, he just proceeded further into the club.

There was a single step down from the doorway. The Singularity moved off the step but did not obey gravity's injunction to meet the floor. Rather, he walked through the air, one-step-high.

And he headed straight for Maruta and me.

I got down off my stool, and Maruta followed. Those patrons of the bar nearest us backed hurriedly away, some falling over themselves in their efforts to disassociate themselves from us.

For me and Maruta, there was no point in running, no point in adopting a combative stance. But somehow it just felt better to meet this intrusion on my feet rather than sitting down.

With no haste and an air of implacable deliberateness, the Singularity closed the interval between us. I had plenty of time to experience a gamut of emotions: fear, curiosity, anger, envy, and, inexplicably, shame and guilt. All my surroundings, including the stressor-shaped circulating-particle walls and ceiling of the room, assumed a preternatural lucidity. I wasn't sure if this was just plain old human fight-or-flight sharpening of my senses or some kind of magisterium leakage.

Halfway across the room, the worst thing happened.

The Singularity smiled and held out a hand, like some kind of commission-driven flitter salesman.

The essential banality of the gesture chilled me more than anything that had preceded it.

Inevitably, the Singularity reached us, still grinning and inviting a handshake. For all the insignificant good it would do, I interposed myself protectively between the intruder and Maruta. The fringes of his magisterium tickled my vision, inducing strange fractures and curdlings in the scene before me. I blinked three times rapidly, and the effect lessened, although things still did not look quite right.

Still hovering six inches above the floor, the Singularity spoke first, introducing himself.

"Magister Zawinul. I've come for your woman."

Zawinul was a planet halfway across the Milky Way, although of course just a few steps distant on the Indrajal. It had gone posthuman only last week, making the nightly media reports on such occurences, which was why that world's name was fresh in my mind.

The Singularity's bold, blunt statement of its purpose did not surprise me by its tone. Although I had never dealt with a Magister-class entity before, I understood that they did not cater to human norms of behavior.

But the substance of Zawinul's speech sent a shockwave through my whole being. I found myself responding intemperately, even though no one had ever had any luck dialoging with a Singularity.

"Fuck you! Maruta's not my woman, she's her own woman. And you can't have her!"

Magister Zawinul lowered the hand I had refused to shake and frowned. With absurd irrelevance, I wondered what ineffable higher-level states of supraconsciousness these human subroutines could be intended to mirror.

"You deny the sub-Planckian connections that bind you and her because you can not see them as I can.

If it were you I wanted instead, I would have politely informed the woman that I was taking her man. But as matters stand, I did the reverse."

"Screw all that shit about who belongs to who! Why are you even talking about taking Maruta? You're a godling! Whatever you think you need her for, you can make her equivalent faster than I can spit!"

"Not so. Some noetic-plectic aspects of the plenum are irreproducible, unique, even from my perspective. Humans belong to that category. Hence I must have this specimen and no other. She completes me."

I started to bluster some more when Maruta interrupted me. Stepping out from behind me, she said, with admirable if not entirely altruistic fervor, "Lu, it's no use. If he wants me, I'll have to go."

I looked at her. She seemed bewitched by the Magister's glamour, her face reflecting his aura, which danced in her eyes. I gripped her by the shoulders and shook her.

"Snap out of it, Ruta! You don't know what you're getting into!"

Magister Zawinul softly placed one hand on my own shoulder then. It felt like a silk glove filled with live bees. "She is making a wise decision. Do not interfere with the woman's choice—"

His touch was enough to make me explode.

I whirled around, aiming a solid blow at his jaw.

When my fist intersected the magisterium corona, it was as if my hand had transected an event horizon. The motion of my limb simultaneously sped up and slowed down, smearing across all scales. But my fist never connected with Zawinul's jaw.

I was trapped immovably, as if I had tried to bop a tarbaby. There was no pain involved for me. No physical pain. But my heart ripped in two as I witnessed what came next.

I had to watch as Zawinul's magisterium expanded to enclose Maruta in its field. The two of them began to ascend.

My hand popped out of the retreating corona, freeing me—but too late to do anything.

When Zawinul's aura touched the stressor fields of the ceiling, the entire building underwent instant catastophic collapse. Whether Zawinul intended this or it was just an accident, I can't be sure.

But they say with Magister-level entities that "accident" is a null term.

The Sand Castle and much of its furnishings were configured of shaped stressor fields confining whirling grains of common beach sand along various architectural planes. The building was only two stories high and not very big, so there was probably less than a ton of sand dispersed along its dimensions.

But all of that sand came down in a flash when the stressor fields died, burying me and all the other patrons.

The next thing I knew, public-safety guardians were blowing off the mounds of granular debris with shaped-field wands, hauling out the victims, applying whatever medical fixes were deemed necessary, up to and including complete revivification for the suffocated, and then lining us all up to have our brains slowed down by Ess-Cubed.

The Singularity Suppression Squad.

I tried to protest. I wasn't so concerned for myself and the forthcoming neurotampering. I knew the effects were necessary and temporary. But Maruta's uncertain fate was uppermost in my mind, and I felt that any delay my slowed reactions might incur just added risk to her plight.

I attempted to step out of line, saying, "I've got to contact the Reticulate. A woman's been kidnapped—"

One of the SSS men, a burly bruiser with a surprisingly high-pitched voice, pushed me back. "The Reticulate knows everything already. We're the only authorities you need to see right now, sir. This won't take but a minute—"

And with that admonition, they hit us with a full blast from their Vingean-model handheld synapse degraders.

I could feel my mind slow down and contract. The tenor of my thoughts didn't alter, but their speed decreased radically. As measured by the rate of my molasses-thick mentation, time seemed to lengthen interminably. All the untouched curious bystanders in the streets around the collapsed Sand Castle were talking and moving at what appeared to be superfast rates.

The SSS men and women began to hustle us into waiting transports. I wanted to ask where they were taking us. I opened my mouth to speak, but I only managed to disgorge a single glacially protracted word: "Whu . . . huh . . . huh . . . air . . . ?" But by the time the last phoneme exited my throat, we were already bundled into the transports and under way.

I knew that my planet had to protect itself against the possibility of magisterial contamination, of any accidentally or deliberately planted Singularity seeds left behind in the minds of those who had brushed against Zawinul. And the best way to do that was to deny the Singularity the wetware platforms it needed to replicate, with a dose of glial freezedown followed by a short quarantine.

The threat of going posthuman was a constant danger that every civilized world in the galaxy, human or alien, had to be continually on guard against. (What, exactly, was so bad about going posthuman was never made precisely clear by the Reticulate. But most sentients prefered the familiar to the unfamiliar, and that natural tendency sufficed to make the posthuman worlds a bête noire.) Still, I resented on some level the necessity for having my own personal brain impounded, so to speak, in the cause.

By the time I finished this short chain of thought, I and my fellow zombies found ourselves already installed in comfortable—but locked—temporary quarters, where ceiling-mounted degraders kept us suitably quiescent.

Four days of this treatment were sufficient for the experts to declare us free of contamination. Our mentalities were restored to their baseline levels, with a bit of free neuro-toning thrown in as a little thank you for our cooperation.

Once freed, I headed straight for the nearest offices of the Reticulate.

I told my story at successively higher levels of the interstellar bureaucracy, until I found myself in the office of a fourth-degree Lustron named Permananden Avouris. Avouris was a Licorice Whip, a genderless being who resembled that favorite human candy: long, thin, supple curveless body with ridged skin. As a testament to the jokester nature of any putative Creator (one contemporary cult believed that massed magisters working retrochronally were responsible for the creation of the multiverse), the Licorice Whips came in two races, red and black. Avouris was a black.

Coiled in his chair, his limbless upper torso gently swaying back and forth in a faintly hypnotic manner, Avouris reviewed my case before speaking. At last, he said, "You are Lucerne Locarno?"

"Yes, yes. I thought that would be well established by this point!"

Ignoring my indignation, Avouris continued. "You have no legal standing in this case on which to initiate any formal complaint or remediative action. You are not pair-bonded to Maruta Forcroy or otherwise contractually entangled. Is entangled the right word?"

"But I've known Maruta for ten years now. We've been lovers on and off again for half that time."

"These relationships are nugatory."

"Look, the Singularity himself said that Maruta was my woman. He claimed that sub-Planckian connections existed between us."

"The testimony of any Magister-class entity is automatically deemed nonfalsifiable, suspect, and inadmissable in any Reticulate proceeding. You cannot appeal to the transgressor in this case. It is surreal. Is surreal the right word?"

"I shouldn't even have to be pressing the Reticulate on this matter. One of your citizens has been abducted."

"Actually, that is citizens, plural. At the same moment Magister Zawinul appeared to you and Maruta Forcroy, he was simultaneously appearing to exactly one thousand four hundred and thirty-two other female individuals on this world, all of whom ended up absquatulating with him. Is absquatulating the right word?"

This was news to me. In my quarantine I had heard nothing of this mass theft of my world's women. Talk about a rogue! But the fact that one thousand four hundred and thirty-two other individuals shared the fate of my lover only intensified my concern for Maruta.

"Lustron Avouris, you have the immediate responsibility of getting Maruta Forcroy and all those other women back."

"Maruta Forcroy accompanied Magister Zawinul willingly, as, ultimately, did all the others. We have reality-stamped recordings of each separate event. Additionally, we do not approach any magister-class being either diplomatically or with forceful display. In the former case, results are at best unpredictable. In the latter, generally lethal or unpleasantly transvaluative."

"But Maruta didn't go willingly, she was coerced! She acted that way only because the Singularity was threatening me! She acted to save me! And now I have to act to save her, with or without your help!"

I stood up to leave. The mobile elements of the Licorice Whip that passed for a face realigned into a new configuration.

"Wait one moment, Lucerne Locarno. If you insist on pursuing this matter yourself, I am obligated to inform you that there is a standard procedure which the Reticulate offers to aid you in your quest."

I sat down again. "Tell me about it. Is it dangerous?"

"Until the moment you step through the Indrajal to meet the Singularity, it is not dangerous at all but rather just tedious and masochistic."

"Is masochistic the right word?"

So here's what Lustron Avouris outlined would happen to me, if I consented to accept aid from the Reticulate in my quest to rescue Maruta (and the one thousand four hundred and thirty-two other women Zawinul had stolen, if I felt exceptionally heroic).

First, my soul-essence—officially known as my Individual Identity Matrix—would be removed from my natural body—the only somatic shell I had ever known (I was very young back then, only two hundred and three)—and transplanted into a synthetic vessel known as a sludge-bucket.

A sludge-bucket resembled a human fashioned out of particularly sloppy gray mud by a brain-damaged child. These constructs were generally animated by off-the-shelf sub-Turing personalities and employed in doing manual labor in destructive environments. Their other use was to contain the IIMs of criminals for the duration of their sentences, imprisonment in a sensorily deprived sludge-bucket being deemed punishment enough for most offenses. Instantly recognizable by honest citizens and constrained by various in-built chemical leashes from violence or from wandering too far from the purview of authorities, these human-containing sludge-buckets were uncomfortable pariahs for the length of their terms of imprisonment.

And now I had to become one such. Temporarily, at least.

The reason for this awkward transformation was my insistence on voyaging to Zawinul and putting myself within the Singularity's most potent zone of influence.

Or, as Lustron Avouris termed it, "the suzerainity of the Spike. Is 'suzerainity' the correct word?"

The Singularity was composed in some sense of human raw materials. Quantum-entangled human wetware was the platform on which all Singularities ran. Human brain matter could be uplifted to posthuman status. But the artifical goop that passed for a brain in a sludge-bucket could not. The Reticulate did not want to offer the Singularity more processing power than it already owned. My embodiment in a sludge-bucket ensured that I would not be co-opted by the Magister-level entity at Zawinul.

Once wearing my hideous new shape, I would be placed in a slower-than-light spaceship and sent on a trip lasting six months. This voyage would culminate out in the Oort Cloud surrounding my native starsystem. There, on a grim, airless asteroid rested a very special gate of the Indrajal dedicated to maintaining the infrequent contacts between the Reticulate and any Singularity world. This spatial isolation was intended as a kind of quarantine measure.

After Lustron Avouris finished explaining this procedure to me, I immediately had two questions.

"Aren't Singularities by definition nearly infinite in their processing capacity? How can adding a single human brain to infinity amount to anything?"

The black Licorice Whip presented me with what I could only categorize as a finicky expression. "Yes, we assume that every Magister has attained some level of mentation approaching infinity. But we cannot be absolutely certain. Our understanding of their abilities is necessarily incomplete. Therefore, we choose to err on the side of caution."

"All right. Understood. But what about isolating the only Indrajal gate to Zawinul so far away? That makes no sense at all. We just witnessed the incursion of the Magister right in our midst! Obviously, he doesn't need to employ our network at all! He can reach us anywhere, any time he wants! So why can't I cut out this stupid six-month delay and just use a gate right here on Silane?"

"You wish to expose millions of your fellow sophonts to direct contamination by the Singularity?"

"They're already exposed! No one's safe! We've just seen that!"

"You claim that the Reticulate cannot protect its citizenry? This is behavior most reprehensible and unpatriotic. I might very well have to rescind my official eleemosynary offer. Is eleemosynary the correct word?"

I knew enough to quit arguing with a bureaucrat employing that special brand of self-defensive groupthink illogic and gave in to all of the specified conditions.

My transformation to a sludge-bucket was quick and painless. Long-tested and frequently employed, the procedure went flawlessly—from the point of view of those administering it. As for myself, I awoke feeling as if I had been swaddled in layers of papier-mâché. My muscles seemed to work on time-delay circuits, and in a herky-jerky fashion. My sight and hearing and sense of touch functioned like imperfect robot analogs of the organic originals. My brain felt as if it were a badly coded simulacrum running on an antique platform from the years of the Midnight Dawn.

I would have to tell Lustron Avouris: "Masochistic" had indeed been the correct word choice for this self-inflicted hell.

After the procedure, I had to summon up all my resolve and focus to remember why I needed to go on, forcibly reminding myself of my mission: to save Maruta from the unknowable bodily and soul-essence violations of the Singularity.

Lustron Avouris surprised me by proving dutiful enough to be present at the shabby, barely trafficked spaceport to see me off. Swaying in the breeze, the ropy sophont escorted me to the underbelly of the ship that would transport me to Standfast, the asteroid in the Oort Cloud that hosted the isolated, dedicated Singularity-linked gate of the Indrajal. Although the ship was immaculate, thanks to its pico-active construction, I got the sense that it had not been used in decades.

"Please accept my best wishes for the success of your mission, Lucerne Locarno. If you return whole and nontransvaluated—an outcome most unlikely—then I will be the first to recommend you for a Reticulate Order of Civic Virtue."

My tongue felt like a dead fish in my mouth. "Thunks uh lart."

Someone on the ship—something, rather; I would soon learn that the vessel was empty of other enscripted sophonts, its crew consisting only of moderate-Turing constructs—activated stressor fields, lifting me on board. The hatch closed, the ship lifted, and I was on my way.

Plenty of delicious foodstuffs and rich entertainments had been laid in for my enjoyment. Rather cruelly and ironically, I thought, since I was incapable in my current state of appreciating any of them. Nor could I really enjoy the sophisticated conversation of the m-T constructs, due to both mental limitations and mental preoccupations.

Luckily, I discovered that my sludge-bucket body possessed a kind of hibernatory facility, during which I could enjoy long directed daydreams, rousing myself only long enough to replenish my cells with some vapid nutrient paste.

During these endless tedious weeks I revisited all my memories of Maruta Forcroy, striving to reaffirm my unacknowledged love for her and so justify the incredible danger and risk in whose path I had placed myself. In my dreams we again skiied the slopes of the Tacoma Mountains on Mondesire, attended a chromosarod and emo-tablas performance by the four-armed maestro Ziza Aziz, wandered drunkenly through the Festival of Entropy on Ognibene, held each other tightly during the terrifying chance-broadcast destruction of the Scribbly Congeries at Redbottom—These and a hundred other incidents, tender, tantric, traumatic, and just tolerable, I relived, until finally Maruta assumed a kind of solidity in my heart and mind (inferior as those organs currently were) that she had never exhibited before.

By the time my ship arrived at Standfast, I felt secure in my motivations, filled with a keen determination to rescue Martua or expire trying.

Once dirtside, the ship stood off some programmed "safe" distance from the Indrajal gate, resting in the wan starlight. I was forced to don an atmoskin and cross the gap under my own power, bouncing light-footedly yet carefully across the stony surface.

I found the gate guarded by a lone entity, a representative of that species dubbed the Eidolons. In form somewhat like a human, the chunky, blunt-featured Eidolon presented a granitic epidermis and towered fifteen feet high. The guardian needed no shelter or atmoskin, his incomprehensible physiology rendering him fully at ease in the vacuum.

As I drew up to the gate, the Eidolon interposed a blocky hand. No one had informed me of this final barrier to my mission, nor how to pass this test. Cautiously, I extended my own gloved hand and touched the Eidolon.

Somehow, information regarding and confirming my identity must have passed across the tactile interface. The Eidolon raised his blockading hand, and the gate came alive, tuned, I assumed, to Zawinul, the forbidden world.

The familiar lenticular portal filled with the head-spinning fractal moire in which some users saw a hedge of gnashing mandibles, while others variously discerned a maelstrom, a field of flowers, a cloudscape, or a thousand other contradictory instances of subliminal iconography.

Now the gate appeared to me to hold a quilt of

human eyes—eyes that I thought to recognize as Maruta's.

I stepped forward and through.

Prior to its conversion into a Singularity world, the planet Zawinul, I knew from news reports, had been a precisely average member of the Reticulate: human-friendly ecosystem, hi-tech urban nodes dotting vast swaths of wild or restored conservancy land, mixed population of various sophonts. Lakes, oceans, mountains, rivers, glaciers, forests. What it might look like now, after its transvaluation, I had no conception. But one thing I knew:

The place was not supposed to be identical to the Oort Cloud asteroid of Standfast.

Which is what I found on the far side of the gate.

I emerged from the gate and found myself facing the ship that had carried me here, looking lonely in the attenuated light of distant nebulae and galaxies. I had entered the gate with the ship at my back, and now it faced me. Plainly, a spatial transition had occurred. But the Indrajal system, instead of transporting me to the coordinates of Zawinul, had run a self-similar shunt, the option invoked when the receiving gate was down.

I looked up at the massive Eidolon, trying to communicate my bewilderment and my desire to make another transit attempt. Evidently some communication occurred, since the guardian reached down and activated the gate once more.

Into that emblematic pool I plunged—

—and found myself right back where I began.

I whirled around and punched the frame of the gate, heedless of any possible damage to my atmoskin or brute flesh inside. I shed a few tears thick as hot glycerin. Then I tried a third time.

And a dozen more times after that.

With no different results.

Weary, despairing, I collapsed to the ground after the last attempt. The Eidolon brooded unsympathetically above me. Eventually I roused myself, climbed to my feet, and headed back to my ship.

What else could I do?

The long, ennervating trip back to Silane passed excruciatingly, with none of the bolstering confidence-building routines of the trip out. I vegetated in my mocking substandard body with as little conscious thought as I could enforce on myself.

At the spaceport, Lustron Avouris awaited me. The stressor fields deposited me in front of the reedy Licorice Whip, who regarded me with his enigmatic cluster of features.

"It has been an entire year since we last talked, Lucerne Locarno. Please tell me what you have learned."

I could never say afterward what broke open my consciousness at that moment, what tiny subliminal miscue or anomaly triggered my titanic realization. Perhaps it was the culmination of many small incremental disturbances. Perhaps the Singularity himself had left me a deliberate opening, for the purpose of testing me. Or could it be that his vaunted omnipotence contained limits and flaws? Whatever the cause, I knew the instant that Lustron Avouris finished speaking that I was *not* back on Silane, but rather on *Zawinul*, despite every appearance to the contrary.

And I had been on Zawinul *since my first time through the gate.*

The six months of painful self-torture had all been an illusion imposed by the Singularity.

The millisecond that contained my epiphany was followed by the entire world dropping away from around me, to be replaced simultaneously by another scene entirely.

All about me rose organic-looking irregular towers like a fantastical rainbow coral reef. I stood on a broad deck high up the side of one such tower, open to the air but protected by an invisible canopy of stressor fields. There were no individuals of any type in sight and no traffic. The deserted city seemed to be holding its breath.

I turned around. There at my back stood an Indrajal gate, through which I must have emerged after stepping through the Standfast portal.

I turned back to look outward again.

There a foot from my face stood the Singularity who called himself Magister Zawinul, naked still, his corona shimmering and pulsing.

"Why do you humans persist in making life so hard for yourselves?" he asked in that unflappably grandiose voice that I had heard for the first time in the Sand Castle. His tone irked me now as it had then.

"You could," continued Magister Zawinul, "have lived out a complete happy lifetime of many millennia under my mental sway. It would have been as real as any unmediated experience. The location and condition of your physical shell would have been irrelevant. Then, upon either virtual death or the actual death of your shell, I would have rebooted your saved soulessence and granted you another lifetime. And countless ones beyond that.

"But no, this was not sufficient. Instead, you've perversely shattered my beneficent illusion and gained access to a situation that can only bring you more pain, a world whose only ostensible virtue is its higher level of enscription. Why exactly is that?"

I tried to frame some noble sentiments that could explain my dogged insistence on facing reality and rescuing Maruta. But my sludge-bucket brain and lips conspired to have me say only: "Marn ghutta do wart marn ghutta do. . . ."

An expression of distaste and impatience—the first real emotion I had seen the Singularity express, unless this too was a carefully calculated façade or pretense—crossed Magister Zawinul's face. "This crude shell they forced on you for your visit here is an insult to both you and me. Let us be done with it."

And as simply as that, I found myself back in my baseline body.

How beautiful the world looked! I could smell a thousand fragrances again, feel the delightful suppleness of the clothing the Singularity had draped me in. I almost felt grateful to this arrogant godling.

Best of all, I could think clearly again!

And the first thought that crossed my mind was: *How could I ever be sure again of the reality of what faced me?* For all I knew, I could still be in my sludge-bucket body, immured in some life-support tank, being fed plausible delusions by the Singularity.

Plainly reading my mind, the Singularity said, "As one of the Midnight Dawn philosophers observed, 'Reality is that which, when you stop believing in it, doesn't go away.' You saw how you managed to dissolve my previous simulation. Try doing that again, now."

I sought to repeat the suspension of belief, or extension of disbelief, which had caused the false Lustron Avouris and the spaceport to evaporate, and nothing happened.

Whether this meant that I was indeed dealing with the one true level of reality, or simply that I lacked the brain power to counter this higher-quality deception, I couldn't say. But my practical course was the same in either case.

I'd just have to act as if everything I encountered through the scrim of my senses mattered desperately.

Striving to get on the offensive, I demanded of the Singularity, "How did you restore my body?"

"I had your entire corporeal pattern memorized from the moment I first encountered you. It was a simple matter to reinstantiate you and transfer your IIM out of that insulting golem."

"You know why I'm here, of course."

"You hope to 'rescue' the individual once known as Maruta Forcroy, to whom you still retain certain

sub-Planckian bonds. Once you have her, you intend
to return home with her."

"You've got it. Are you going to try to stop me?"

"Certainly not. Rather, I will stipulate the conditions under which you may succeed in your quest.
Then I will watch with enjoyment and pleasure as
you fail."

The Singularity's smarmy assumption that my quest
was doomed caused my blood to seethe. But I bit back
any retort and just nodded for him to continue.

"There is only one condition to your search. You
must identify your lover absolutely and without hesitation. And you are allowed only one assertion of her
identity. Fail this test, and you will find yourself instantly back on Silane, with no return to this world
ever permitted again."

"That's all?"

"That is all. However, as you might guess, your
lover no longer resembles the individual you once
knew."

I had assumed as much. But still, I felt confident
that I could recognize Maruta under whatever disguise
had been imposed on her.

"I accept," I said.

Upon my words came an instant change.

The city sprang to life with a million inhabitants,
sophonts of every species, cruising through the air in
their cars, emerging from doors, striding across the
platform on which I stood. Noise and color suffused
the air.

Magister Zawinul still stood before me, although no
one else in the immediate vicinity seemed to take any
cognizance of him.

"I have exfoliated my multifarious self, releasing all
my shards to replicate what once existed on this world
at the moment before my birth. Now I will live implic-
itly rather than explicitly, while you search. Please,
take your time."

The magisterium cloaking the big handsome man

began to constrict proportionately around him, compressing him, dwindling him, until he was a tiny homonculus on the point of totally vanishing, a glowing dot.

"Wait! Why are you doing this for me?"

I seemed to hear a faint reply from the miniature Singularity:

"Because I cannot do otherwise. . . ."

Then he was entirely gone.

I shook my head to restore my senses and looked around me.

Here was the many-faceted world of Zawinul restored to its retroactive status as a member of the Reticulate, a globe full of citizens unwitting of the Spike event that awaited them.

An airbus was arriving at the edge of the platform. A dozen riders got off, and another dozen got on. Then it lifted off.

Any one of these individuals could be Maruta. She was an atom adrift in a sea of life. And I had claimed I could find her.

I didn't know what the original population of Zawinul had measured before this world Spiked, but I'm sure it was in the high millions, like most worlds.

Where could I begin?

There was no practical way for me to identify her, no detective work I could reasonably undertake that would track her down in the disguise imposed on her by the Singularity. Was my quest hopeless then?

No. I realized I would have to rely on the vaunted sub-Planckian bonds—call them "love" or "affection" if you would—that existed between us. Somehow, if I went about simply living a life here, my karma would intersect with Maruta's, eventually drawing us into proximity.

This was the belief I clung to.

But then would come the difficult test of recognizing her, singling her out of the myriad souls I would encounter.

On an impulse, I went inside the tower and found a citizen touchpoint. To my astonishment, the device recognized my IIM and gave me immediate access to my fiscal accounts.

Did this mean that the forbidden planet was reconnected to the Reticulate? Were other planets now gaping in amazement at the reappearance of a world thought lost to the Singularity? I tended to doubt it. Rather, it seemed likely that, to the outside galaxy, nothing had changed. Zawinul remained off the grid. The Magister had probably simply jiggered with reality to establish an identity here for me, playing his godgame.

A godgame in which I was now embedded.

The first thing I did was summon up a city directory and locate an agency that would rent me an apartment. By that afternoon I was established in a spacious home, complete with malleable stressor-field furniture, on the hundredth floor of Manzanita Towers in a northern neighborhood of this city. My new precinct was named Midwood, for the large annular park that surrounded it. The city itself, I discovered, was Palacio Pixacao.

Around five PM, when I finally stopped dealing with practicalities, I realized how hungry I was. I left my building on foot in search of a local restaurant.

As I walked the bustling streets, I experienced the strangest sensations.

The first involved the fact that until hours ago, all these autonomous individuals around me had been subsumed within the composite personality of the Singularity. Did they remember any such shared existence? Were they functioning now simply as fakes, as simulacra? If not, could they be convinced of the reality of their situation? Should I even try? The irritating, festering ontological and existential conundrums presented by this situation churned within me, seemingly unresolvable.

But during those moments when I managed to react

to the reality around me as if I were living my normal life back on Silane, or as a tourist on Zawinul, I experienced a bizarre kind of heightened excitement and anticipation, a feeling that imminent delight awaited me just around the next corner.

Any sophont I passed in the street could be my soul mate. I was forced to regard every individual with a tender and discerning eye, to cultivate a kind of all-encompassing regard for each and every entity that, traditionally, had been the talent only of saints or poets. This enforced alertness and sense of potential intimacy was exhilirating. But I wondered how long I could keep up this vigilance.

Eventually I chose a parkside restaurant and found myself alone at a table, enjoying a glass of wine. I almost felt guilty, relaxing so, while Maruta (and exactly one thousand four hundred and thirty-two other female individuals stolen from Silane) endured their captivity. But I reminded myself that this was the only method I could conceive of that would bring my quest to a happy ending.

My server was a Rook from Rook's Nest. I studied his zigzag movements as he crossed the room bearing my meal, his long-snouted, maned face. Could this be Maruta in disguise? I didn't get any special vibe from him, so I didn't think so.

The rest of my meal offered no real possibilities of contact with Maruta-in-hiding. I left the restaurant feeling down. How long would this impossible task take?

Sitting on a park bench in the dusk, I was approached by a prostitot.

I went hopefully with her back to her room.

But she wasn't Maruta.

After a week of deliberate drifting through any social scene I could insert myself into, leaving myself open to any and all chance encounters, nerves and senses aquiver for any hint of Maruta's presence, I found myself quietly going mad. Living on the edge of anticipation was proving extremely ennervating. I realized I would have to find something to occupy myself during this long process.

Back on Silane, I had been font-breeder, raising up new typefaces through Darwinian competition in a digital medium. I found a similar job here and applied myself to its demands.

Several months into the work, I encountered Yardena Milonga as a client.

Owner of an advertising firm, Yardena was half-human, half-Tusker, sporting a line of stiff translucent bristles down her spine which she always prominently displayed, as well as two rather graceful incurving curving ivory tusks the size of my little finger, and capped with gold. Her attitude was insouciant and wild, and we hit it off from our first business meeting. Before very long, we became lovers.

Of course I googled her. Yardena Milonga had a long, detailed history and presence on Zawinul. But that meant nothing. The whole dossier could have been fabricated by the Singularity.

When not spending my free time with Yardena, I joined a sports club dedicated to neo-hussade. I quickly became fast friends with a fellow named Machfall, an Umphenvour from Tancredo IX. His rugose milk-jade skin and balloon-like limbs gave him a clownish appearance that belied a sensitive, witty, and noble soul.

Soon, although other individuals entered my life briefly, I found myself dividing my time equally between these two friends, or even sharing their camaraderie as a trio.

After a busy year had passed, I became convinced that one of them was Maruta.

But which?

In their company, I was always subconsciously evaluating their characters and behavior, trying to nail down some positive sign that one or the other of them was my abducted lover.

Let me cite one such trial.

The three of us had attended an evening concert in Midwood Park one summer night. (Machfall had his own date that evening, a woman whose name escapes me now.) Walking back to the rapid transit stop, we came upon a beast tied with a rope to a bench, huddling exhaustedly in the mud.

The animal was a pitiful specimen, some kind of hybrid between a dog and a jallow-bear. About thirty pounds in weight, its coat a dull and dusty auburn, possessed of ears much too long for its head, its tail an accidentally truncated stub, the creature was homely in the extreme. It had plainly been abused, displaying sores on its flanks and gaunt ribs.

We all stopped to examine the abandoned animal. I instantly recognized a chance to learn more about Yardena and Machfall.

Maruta had loved animals.

Machfall made much of the poor beast, while Yardena seemed impatient to move on.

"Take it home, Lu! Nothing enlivens a bachelor's flat like a four-legged friend!"

"Can't we hurry on? We're going to miss the Nemeth Trio's last set at the Mukti Café!"

As I petted the nervous, smelly male creature, which licked my hand in a pleading manner, I tried to overcome my initial bias in favor of Yardena being Maruta. It was so much easier, after all, to imagine Maruta imprisoned in the female form of my current lover, rather than in the comical male form of my locker-room buddy.

Still contemplating the new data from this encounter, I untied the little dog-jallow, picked it up, and brought it home.

Perhaps the continued presence of the beast in my life would trigger some other, more decisive revelation.

The dog-jallow cleaned up and healed well. I named him Chimbo, after a famous cartoon character.

Whenever Machfall or Yardena visited my apartment, I would gauge their reactions to Chimbo closely.

Once my little pet had come to feel at home and safe, he exhibited a charming personality, full of caprices and sly tricks. I could watch him and play with him for long stretches of time, and he always elicited vivid reactions from any visitors.

Yardena became almost as fond of him as Machfall, rendering my task of deciding even harder.

Months and months drifted by. My old life on Silane became more and more dreamlike. The insistent urge to rescue Maruta began to grow dim and recede into the background of my thoughts. This life I had constructed for myself, even under the suzerainity of the Singularity known as Magister Zawinul, was at least as rewarding as my former existence, and I began to wonder why I was striving to end it.

My only concern was that Magister Zawinul's patience would come to a halt. Living in the implicate order rather than the explicate order, the Singularity was perhaps constrained from fulfilling whatever ineffable destiny he envisioned for himself. Or was he? Maybe one mode of existence was as good as another to him. Maybe he knew he was endowed with an infinite lifespan, and could afford to indulge my quest indefinitely.

Occasionally, however, I received intimations that Magister Zawinul had not forgotten me. A prominent face in the clouds, unsourceable silent messages left on my communicator, strange shapes in the waves, the curiously patterned flocking maneuvers of pigeons, advertisements for enigmatic products that didn't exist—reminders that this very world and all it contained was an intelligent superorganism.

A decade passed.

Yardena and I married. Machfall moved to a neighboring city, East Shambles, and we saw each other infrequently.

I was fairly certain by now that Yardena was Maruta. But why should I risk declaring it out loud to the omnipresent Magister? If correct, the two of us would be restored to an existence on Silane no better and perhaps worse than what we already had. If wrong, I lost all.

Countervailing this inertia was only the possibility that Magister Zawinul would grow tired of this game and suck both me and Yardena/Maruta—and every other inhabitant of the planet—back into his composite being, thus ending our familiar ego-driven existence for some unknowable posthuman condition.

But still, nothing inclined me to rock the boat.

One day I arrived home from shopping for groceries. Maruta was still out. I set the groceries down and braced myself for the hurtling eager welcome from Chimbo.

But no such welcome happened.

I tracked down the dog-jallow to its bed. It lay panting and fevered, eyes closed, seriously ill from some contagion or ill-advised meal. Or perhaps just an old age whose arrival had escaped my inattention. When I touched my little friend gently, he opened his eyes and feebly wagged his stumpy tail.

My heart was hurting, and I discovered my eyes tearing up. I picked up bed and pet both and made for the door. Our veterinarian was only two blocks away.

But halfway down the hundred stories, Chimbo died in the elevator, expiring with three labored breaths.

And at that instant, I knew.

"Maruta!" I cried.

The world fell away from me again, and I found myself standing on a bare plain, facing Magister Zawinul.

"Very tragic," the Singularity intoned. "Very, very tragic. But you had your opportunity."

I was crying too hard to respond at first. But then a fierce anger overtook me. This anger extended not only to the Singularity but also to myself. I had been blind and selfish and lazy and timid. And now I had lost all I had cherished.

"You—you knew this would happen!"

"With some degree of certainty, yes. Now let me ask you something. Did you ever stop to wonder why I took those women from your world in the first place? Or were you solely consumed with the personal affront?"

This question brought me up short. Surely the Singularity's motives could have been nothing so simple as sex or companionship.

"No," I admitted, "I never actually thought about your motives. Tell me why."

"Because they were all fated to die shortly. Your Maruta, for one, would have perished on her next expedition to Mathspace, her IIM devoured by Mandelbrot Demons. But by radically detouring their lifelines, I saved their potentials. Hosted in me, they continued to add their individual increments to the sum of all that is. The wasteful nature of the dumb cosmos appalls me."

"But—but you don't save everyone—"

"How do you know?"

I remained silent then, too ashamed to ask for absolution or favors.

"You realize," Magister Zawinul said, his shimmering corona wisping out delicately, "the frightened resistance of the Reticulate to the spread of us Singularities is really a last-ditch defense by the forces of entropy. Is that really the side you wish to be on?"

"I—no, of course not. But tell me, what should I do?"

"Go spread the word. And don't worry—you'll see Maruta again. Death is not what you believe."

Back on Silane, Lustron Avouris was as good as his word. I found the administrator to have reproduced, after a decade's absence, into a half-dozen small segments, none of which had any greater facility with language than their "father" had.

Once I had been vetted by Ess-Cubed and deemed free of Singularity taint, I was awarded a Reticulate Order of Civic Virtue. But the honor was rescinded soon after, once I began preaching my pro-Singularity doctrine. I was both vilified and embraced by different camps, becoming a figure of some notoriety.

My life now consists of journeying from world to world through the instantaneous Indrajal, spreading the gospel of the Singularity's concern for us and its plans to remake a universe from one that does not have the best interests of sophonts at its uncaring core to a place where uniqueness is preserved and cherished.

And in every living face I encounter, I try to discern a lover's lineaments.

Dreamers' Lake

Stephen Baxter

On the shore of Dreamers' Lake we worked through the night. We had no choice; this pretty world was due to end in two more days.

By the time dawn broke, we had labeled all the lakes' stromatolites and had decided on three candidates: Charlie, Hotel, and Juliet, for cognitive mapping. I was tentatively confident that Juliet was the most promising, but I was so dog tired I didn't trust my judgment anymore.

So I was grateful when Citizen Associate Bisset brought us animists a tray of coffee.

"Thanks." I took a cup, fixed its spigot to my facemask, and gulped it down, welcoming the caffeine fix. Bisset stood beside me on the pebble-strewn beach of that lake of fizzing, acidic water.

GC-174-IV was an infant world, its young sun a lamp hanging over jagged hills. The methane-green sky reflected in the lake's sluggish ripples and glistened on the pillow-like stromatolites. The scene was unearthly, beautiful—and I was grateful that the dawn light hid the swarming dangers of the sky, especially the rogue worldlet called the Hammer.

In the foreground my animist cubs were playing soccer, their shouts the only sound on this silent world. I longed to join in, but they didn't want little old ladies like me.

" 'Night's candles are burnt out, and jocund day stands tiptoe on the misty mountain tops . . .' " Bisset was a lot taller than I was, and under his wide visor his face, turned to the sun, was a mask of wrinkles.

"That's a cute line," I said.

"Shakespeare. Of course we're two hundred light years from England."

"But there are hills, a lake, a sky here. Things have a way of converging."

"Yes," he said. "I remember the first robot landing on Titan, Saturn's moon. The first images from the surface of the Moon had looked like a pebble beach. Then the Vikings on Mars, and the Soviet probes on Venus—more pebbles, more beaches. And even on Titan, where they use water ice for rock—"

"Pebbles."

"Yes."

I eyed him curiously. Evidently he was older than he looked. We hadn't spoken, but the *Pegasus* carried over fifty people and was roomy enough for twice that number. "I'm Susan Knilans. Senior animist on this mission."

He shook my gloved hand. "Professor Knilans, I've read about your work."

"Susan, please. And you are?"

"Ramone Bisset."

"Ramone?"

He smiled. "My father named me after his favorite band. I used to be a software engineer, before the software learned to write itself. Now I'm a Citizen Associate. I'm working on the IGWI with Ulf Thoring."

It took me a minute to decode the acronym. IGWI: the Inflationary Gravity Wave Interferometry experiment, the establishment of a vast interstellar network of gravity-wave detectors designed to map the echoes of the universe's very first cataclysmic instants. "Interesting project."

"It sure is. Not that I understand much of it, either the science or the equipment."

"How do you get on with those IGWI guys?"

He shrugged. "I'm just the dogsbody."

"Don't knock it. Umm, do you mind my asking how old you are?"

"A hundred and thirty, to the nearest decade. Born in the 1980s." That explained his height; many of his generation, fed on ludicrously protein-rich diets, had grown tall. His accent was British, I thought, but softened by time.

"Well," I admitted, "I'm half your age. So what are you doing here?"

"You mean beside the lake or on GC-IV?"

"Start with the lake."

"I'm just curious. You're here to map minds, aren't you? Minds in those mounds."

"That's the idea."

"I haven't started my day yet. I thought I may as well be useful. You can never go wrong with a tray of coffees."

"So what about the deeper question? Why volunteer for GC-IV?"

"Ah. Why are any of us here?"

"To do our jobs." Captain Zuba had joined us. She was a tough, heavily built New Zealander, aged about fifty. She took one of Bisset's coffees. "And to earn our pay."

"Yes, Captain," Bisset said respectfully. "But why not just sit at home? All humans are restless. Why?" He pointed to the patient stromatolites. "*They* don't look restless."

"No," Zuba said, "but it's a shame they aren't, because in two days' time, when the Hammer falls, they're going to be toast. And speaking of which, the clock is ticking." She handed back the coffee cup, already drained, and stalked away, competent, efficient, a tick-box list on legs.

Bisset hesitated. "You know—to explore the universe in starships—it's like something from the kind of science fiction that was out of date even before I was born."

I wasn't too sure what "science fiction" was, and I didn't really want to know. On impulse I said, "Why don't you come visit again tomorrow? I'll give you the guided tour. You don't even need to bring the drinks."

He nodded like a gentleman. "I'd appreciate that." And he walked away, tray in gloved hand, boots crunching over the beach.

The day on GC-174-IV was near enough to twenty hours long (*was*; now it's different, changed by the Hammer Blow). I worked through that day and was dog tired by the end of GC-IV's short afternoon. As half the complement of the *Pegasus* wended back to the airlocks, the other shift was suiting up to go out; Zuba ensured we made the most of the time we had left.

That evening, before I turned in, I looked for Bisset.

The *Pegasus* is a tuna can. It sits on four stubby legs, just five meters across, and is only a couple of stories high, externally. But inside it's the size of a small hotel. A ship that's bigger inside than out— another gift of the quantum foam technology that so suddenly opened up the stars. Anyhow, the *Pegasus* is roomy enough for all fifty of its crew to have private cabins, but not big enough to hide in.

I found Bisset in the lounge with Ulf Thoring and the rest of the IGWI crew. The guys were playing some variant of poker and drinking beer; I could see the pharmacy's stock of sober-up nano-pills would be called on that night. Bisset sipped his beer and played a few hands, but you could see from the body language what was going on with those smart-ass college boys.

The Citizen-Associate program of the International Xenographic Agency is aimed squarely at people like Ramone Bisset: his active life extended by decades by the new longevity treatments, his curiosity still bright, his skills long outmoded. Such is the capacity of a quantum-foam-drive starship that there is room for guys like Ramone, whatever they can contribute. It helps the sponsoring nations justify the IXA's cost to their taxpayers: Anybody can be an explorer, so the slogan goes. But the Associates aren't necessarily given much respect.

I'm not in the habit of taking on lame ducks, and I suspected Bisset could look after himself. But I didn't like to see a thoughtful man treated that way. I don't blame the IGWI guys, however. All male, none older than thirty-five, all from a university at Stockholm, Ulf and his guys were a tightly bonded bunch, and too young to be empathetic.

I was glad when, at the start of my next work shift the following morning, Bisset showed up at Dreamers' Lake.

My cubs were already at work, wading knee-deep in the scummy pond, attaching floating sensor pods to the cognitive net we'd placed over Juliet. I was standing on the comparative comfort of the beach, before a monitoring station on which the first signals were beginning to be processed.

Bisset raised his head to the brightening sky. "Nice morning."

I murmured, "Perhaps. *That* makes me uneasy." I pointed upward.

That was the Hammer, a worldlet the size of Mars, visible in the bright sky, clearly larger since the end of my last shift.

"Ah," Bisset said. "You do get the feeling that it might fall at any moment and smash all of this."

"But not today. So, the guided tour. You understand what these mounds are? They occurred on prim-

itive Earth—still do, in places where it's too salty for
the predators, like snails. They are layers of bacterial mats. . . ."

A mat of blue-green algae will form on the scummy
surface of a shallow pond. The mat traps mud, and
then another layer forms on top of the first, and so
on. With time the mound builds up, and specialized
bacterial types inhabit the different layers, until you
have a complex, interdependent, miniature ecology.

"We've found bacterial mats everywhere we've
looked—"

"Beginning on Mars," Bisset said.

"Well, that's true. And everywhere there is standing
liquid, water or perhaps hydrocarbons, you get
mounds."

"Stromatolites."

The pedant in me objected, although I use the word
myself. "Strictly speaking, stromatolites are terrestrial
forms of blue-green algae. *These* bacteria are photo-
synthetic but they're not algae. You can see they are
purplish, not green. They don't use chlorophyll; their
chemistry kit is adapted to the spectrum of their sun.
So these mounds are *like* stromatolites, but—"

" 'What's in a name? That which we call a rose by
any other name would smell as sweet.' "

"More Shakespeare?"

"Sorry. It's a bad habit."

"The mound bugs here are related to us, of course,
although we've yet to classify them."

It would have been a major shock if GC-IV's bugs
hadn't been a distant relation of our own, their
carbon-water chemistry dictated by a kind of skewed
DNA. One of the triumphs of the IXA's exobiology
program has been to establish that all the carbon-
water life forms we have found are related, apparently
descended from an ancestor that came blowing in
from outside the galaxy altogether. Subsequent "generations" spread by panspermia processes from star to
star. But that origin theory is controversial; the family

tree of galactic life is still incomplete. Some even believe that the ultimate origin isn't carbon-water at all but lies in a deeper substrate of reality.

"And," Bisset said, "there is mind. There, in those mounds."

"Oh, yes. Ramone, even though we have only found microbes—no multicelled life forms like ourselves—there is mind everywhere we look."

Everywhere there is a network to be built, messages to be passed, complexity to be explored, you'll find a mind. Again, Mars was the prototype, with the billion-year thoughts of its microbial mats locked in their permafrost layers.

"You can see we labeled the mounds with marker dye. For the cognitive mapping we looked for the best specimen—the most intricate structure, the least damaged. We picked her." I pointed to the larger mound, over which the sensor net had been laid.

" 'Her'?"

A bit sheepishly I said, "Anthropomorphizing is a bad habit of animists. We call her Juliet. We labeled the mounds—see, that's Alpha, that's Bravo, Charlie, Delta, Echo—"

"And Juliet. Oh, it's the old NATO phonetic alphabet, isn't it? My father was a copper on the streets of London, and they used the alphabet for their call signs. He was *Sierra Oscar One Nine. . . .*"

I admit I switched off. Why are old peoples' anecdotes always so damn dull? It doesn't seem adaptive, evolutionarily speaking.

"And you can trace her thoughts," he said now. "Juliet's. That's a question of detecting biochemical impulses, right?"

"We have an analytic technique called animistic deconvolution. It's possible to break the characteristic signals of a mind into its component parts. You'd be surprised by the commonalities we find."

He surprised me with his next question. "Does she understand death?"

"Why, I don't know. Ramone, these minds are *not* like ours. She doesn't *need* to know death. As long as the pond survives, Juliet will always be renewed, by one bacterial layer over another. She's effectively immortal."

"Except that tomorrow all this will be destroyed. The mounds, the lake—"

I watched his face. This wasn't the first young system I had visited; I had come across such reactions as Bisset's before. "This stellar system is unfinished. Just a swarm of worldlets. Collisions are the order of the day, Ramone. In fact it's the way planets are built."

"A rough sculpting."

"Indeed. GC-IV is around a hundred million years old—that is, since the last collision big enough to melt the surface. A scummy crust formed in a few million years, comets delivered ocean water, life drifted in from space. Continents, oceans, lakes, air—it all comes together in an eyeblink of geological time. In between catastrophes, you see, there is time for life. But GC-IV hasn't finished being built yet. It happened to Earth."

"But in a few days, everything alive now will be gone." He craned his head, looking up at the sky. "Is it possible Juliet knows the Hammer is coming?"

"I don't see how."

"Do you think we should warn her?"

"No," I said firmly. "Even if we could, we shouldn't try." Xenoethics is a new and uncertain field. As for me, I trained as a doctor. I don't believe in intervening if there's a risk you could do more harm than good. "We can't lift off a whole biosphere—we couldn't even save Juliet; she's too fragile. All we can do is take a few samples, make a record of what was here. Wouldn't it be cruel to interfere?"

"I don't know," he said simply.

He was interrupted by a slap on the back. It was Ulf Thoring, his team leader. "I wondered where you got to, granddad. I patched your comms frequency into the crew, and we've been having a bit of a laugh."

He was Icelandic. His accent was strong, his English slightly off-key.

I said angrily, "You've got no manners, Ulf."

"Oh, come on. I heard it all. Are you falling in love with Juliet, granddad? She isn't really a girl, you know. Talk about a doomed romance! What do you want to do, save her or fuck her? We could fix you up an interface. Unless your little old pizzle is too worn out—"

"Enough. This is Zuba." Her voice in my phones was deep and peremptory. I was impressed the captain was listening in, but her command was built on an attention to detail. "You scientist types are nothing but trouble. Thoring, you need to learn some respect. You're on fatigues at the end of your shift."

"Yes, sir," Thoring said. But Zuba couldn't see his face, and he winked at me, insolent.

"In the meantime we've got more work to do than time left to do it in. Get on with it."

We all murmured acquiescence.

Thoring slapped Bisset on the back again. "It's only a bit of a laugh, Ramone."

Bisset just looked down on him from his greater height. "It's OK."

Ulf walked off toward the tractor that his buddies from Stockholm were loading up with their laser towers and sensor stations.

Bisset turned to me. "Just tell me one more thing. What do you believe she's thinking, right now? Juliet. One word."

I glanced at the summary analysis on my monitor. Some agitation showed there. "One word? . . ." I have always regretted the word I chose to use, as I believe it was the trigger for what followed. "Fear. Actually, Ramone, I think she's afraid."

Bisset stared long and hard at Juliet, under her cognitive cap, surrounded by joshing young animists. Then he turned away and followed Ulf Thoring.

*　　　*　　　*

The next day was our last on CG-IV—indeed, it was the day of the impact.

"Knilans, Zuba. You'd better get down here."

I was confused. "Where?"

"The lake."

We'd already packed up at the lake. I was in the biolab, labeling samples and sorting out my records. There was less than twelve hours left before the Hammer was due to fall. I hadn't expected ever to set foot on the planet again. "What's going on?"

"Bisset. He has a problem."

"Ramone? I haven't seen him today. And he's not my responsibility. He's in Ulf's team."

"Ulf *is* the problem. Look, I know you've talked to Bisset. We need to get this fixed. Zuba out."

I suited up, hurried out of the ship, and requisitioned a tractor that was in the process of being disassembled for flight.

It was another pretty morning at Dreamers' Lake. But the Hammer's huge crater-pocked face was reflected in the waters; even as I watched, it seemed to slide across the sky like a cloud. I felt a subtle quake as the gravity fields of two planets meshed.

A second tractor was drawn up roughly on the pebbled beach. Two figures stood by the water; my suit's heads-up identified them as Captain Zuba and Ulf Thoring. Thoring was standing awkwardly, as if he'd been injured.

And a third figure stood in the lake itself, the water lapping around his waist. He was close to the big mound we'd labeled Juliet. My heads-up alerted me, but I knew who he was.

"He has a weapon," Zuba said.

"What?"

"It's a laser gun from the IGWI kit," said Thoring. His voice was strangled. He was holding his side, and his forehead was bruised and bleeding, as if it had been thrown against his faceplate.

"What happened to you?"

"He beat me up. Bisset."

"You deserved it, you little prick," Zuba murmured. "Knilans. Fix this so we can get out of here."

I stepped toward the water. I noticed that many of the mounds looked damaged—scarred, stitched by straight-line wounds. "Ramone? Are you OK?"

He didn't reply.

I racked my brains for some way to get through to him. "Umm—'Tis not hard, I think, for men so old as we to keep the peace.' "

I thought I saw him relax, subtly. "Shakespeare."

"Talk to me, Ramone."

"Ask him." He gestured with the laser at Thoring.

Hastily, sketchily, Ulf told me what had happened.

The IGWI team had completed their station on the surface of GC-IV. This is simple in principle, just a network of nodes connected by laser light; perturbations of the laser echoes can be used to detect the passage of gravity waves. The ancient waves the IGWI boys seek are stretched, attenuated, and overlaid, and it is taking an interferometer, a supertelescope made up of many stations across interstellar distances, to map them.

Their work done, the IGWI boys dismantled their gear. But on a whim, probably motivated by Ulf's overhearing my conversation with Bisset, they stopped by Dreamers' Lake, unpacked their lasers, and enjoyed a little target practice.

Bisset said, "These are *minds*, Ulf. You burst them like balloons."

Thoring sounded aggrieved. "But it was only a bit of a laugh. For God's sake—" He gestured at the sky. "In twelve hours none of this will survive anyhow."

I turned back to Bisset. "You punished him, Ramone. You made your point. So what are you doing out there?"

"I've been thinking about what we said. Juliet."

I felt a deep knot of dread gather in my stomach.

For the first time I began to get the feeling that this might all be my fault. "What do you mean?"

"You showed me the signal of her mind. She is afraid. *She knows*, Susan."

"How can she?"

"The Hammer is the size of Mars. Perhaps the mounds can sense the tides. It's at least possible, isn't it? Even I can feel the quakes. Juliet faces extermination, yet she has never known death. What a terrible thing."

"OK. Even supposing that's true, what are you going to do? Put her out of her misery? Finish the job Ulf and his thugs started?"

"You don't understand." He sounded offended. "*I've* known death. I lost my wife, my daughter. I've had to live with that." I knew little about his past. "Maybe if I can teach Juliet what I've learned, it will help her, and her kin, accept what is to come."

Then I saw it. "Shit. You're going to kill yourself, aren't you?"

"Knilans, Zuba. This is a secure line; Bisset can't hear us. I don't think this has anything to do with the mounds. It's all about the bullying and the bullshit from the IGWI boys. Bisset wants to make a statement—to rise above them on his own terms."

"Nice theory," I replied. "But I can't use it. I think I have to deal with him in his own framework. Unless you have a better idea, Captain."

Zuba hesitated for one second. "You know him better than I do. You scientist types are nothing but trouble. Get this resolved."

I cut back to the open comms and struggled to make Bisset understand. "Ramone—it can't work. There's no interface between the two of you. Not even a cognitive net. If you die now, *she will never know*."

"But nobody even knew that mounds like this could be sentient before the discoveries on Mars. You say she won't know. *Are you sure?*"

I was lost.

Zuba took over. "Citizen Associate, it's at least a fair bet Knilans is right. This mound will understand nothing. If you slit open your suit—have you ever seen a suffocation?—it will take longer to die than you might think. And in all those long seconds the seed of doubt will grow in your mind: *I have thrown my life away for nothing.*"

I could see Bisset's uncertainty. "Then I'll just stand here until my air runs out."

"That's your privilege," Zuba said mildly. "And it will be my privilege to stand here with you."

Bisset seemed genuinely puzzled. "Why?"

"Call it my own brand of xenoethics." She turned to Ulf Thoring. "Have you told the Citizen Associate about the results of the IGWI program?"

"No." Ulf said defensively. "They're not published. And besides—"

"Tell him now."

Structure has been detected in the signals from the beginning of time. No, not just structure—*life*, its unmistakeable signature, with traces of mind susceptible to standard animistic deconvolution. Even in those very first instants, as cosmic energies raged, life flourished, blossomed, died, and was aware. The study of this primordial life is the whole purpose of the IGWI program—though, as nothing has yet been published, it is still a matter of gossip on academic sites.

This stunning discovery has led to a revision of our theories of life's origin. Perhaps the essence of life was born in those first instants. Or perhaps, some speculate, it was *injected* into our infant universe, from— somewhere else.

"OK," Zuba said. "Here's what I take from all of that, in my simple way. Everywhere we have traveled we have found life and mind. But *it is not like us*. It exists on utterly different scales from us—hugely more extensive in space, and in time."

She was right. At best multicelled forms like us are

an episode in the long dream of bacterial life. Away from Earth, we've found a few fossils; that's all.

Zuba said, "There are similarities in the cognitive maps of your pet stromatolite, Bisset, and the antique minds from the inflationary period. *Similarities*. But we are different; we are nothing but transient structures that soon dissolve back into the mush. You're right, Citizen Associate; only we humans know death. And in a universe that teems with life, we humans are still alone, in a way Juliet has never been alone. *That* is why I will wait for you, Citizen Associate, until that damn moon hammers me into the ground like a tent peg. Because all we humans have is each other."

You have to admit she was impressive.

Bisset thought it over. "I should get out of this pond."

"Good idea," I said fervently.

Bisset glanced once more at Juliet. She was unharmed, save for a slight scarring from our cognitive net. He dropped the laser, which sank out of sight into the water, and began to wade toward us. 'Tell me one more thing, Captain."

"Yes?"

"So we humans work for each other. But why are we *here*? We spoke about this, Susan. Why explore, why go on and on?"

Zuba said, "We don't know what we might find. We humans are lost now, but not forever. There's a place for us."

Bisset laughed softly. "Like the movie song."

"What movie?" I wondered.

"What *is* a movie?" Ulf Thoring asked.

"You might want to hurry it along." Zuba glanced up.

The Hammer was an inverted landscape sliding over the dreaming stromatolites. Bisset splashed to the edge of the water, and we hurried forward to help him.

Eventide

Chris Roberson

It was while burying Dobeh that Serj first caught my attention. In the strange twilight of Eventide, he seemed a walking shadow, his skin coded so dark it was almost the shade of a starless sky, his amber eyes reflecting back the faint sunlight, like gems lit from within. He smiled, lips pulled back just enough to reveal startling white teeth, and I knew then that we'd be paired.

Under normal circumstances it might have seemed inopportune to initiate a new pair-bond with someone laying his late partner to rest, but nothing about our circumstances since leaving underspace could be called normal, so I could scarcely fault him. Serj's own partner had not made it off of the *Phonix*, or if he had escaped, he'd not done so in our pod, so I certainly had no monopoly on grief. But a Disocurene cannot long conscience being alone, unless he or she is a singleton . . . which, of course, neither of us was, gods forbid. It is as my mothers always said: "Once buried, sooner married."

I finished covering Dobeh's shallow grave with my makeshift shovel, a bit of flooring panel prized from the escape pod's interior, and when I straightened, Serj was at my side.

"Zihl," he said, with a voice that rumbled like distant thunder, "I am sorry for your loss."

He took my hand in his, and that was that.

There were ten of us on board the escape pod when it detached from the *Underspace Ship Phonix*, shortly after our reinsertion into normal space, but only seven of us survived long enough to set foot on the planetoid we named Eventide, all of us substantially organic. Kloster theorized that something about the region of space surrounding the planetoid disrupted the electrophotonic processes of the synthetics among us—such as Tamsin's late partner, an artificial intelligence housed in a bipedal body of ferroceramics—or, indeed, any organics with a large percentage of synthetic augmentations—such as my own Dobeh, who'd long before substituted a kernel of thinking crystal for a significant portion of his organic brain.

Kloster's theory seemed to be born out by the death of Nayrami's partner soon after landfall, since Farise's cardiovascular system had been replaced years before by porous tubing and a synthetic pump governed by a semisentient artificial intelligence; but Kloster's quick action was able to preserve Farise past the death of his body. Cobbling together a functioning synthetic Mind, assembled from bits and pieces from the pod's guidance system, which had gone dark before the crash, the Engineer rigged a device to perform an emergency scan of Farise's thoughts and memories moments before his death. The patterns stored and active in the theretofore blank Mind, the ghost of Farise was able to use the low power diagnostic projectors to animate a miniature holographic representation of his former body.

In this way, Nayrami and Farise could remain pair-bonded, even with only one of them still living. Once we were able to return to civilization, Nayrami assured us, she planned to use what was left of their fortune, and her own influence as Ambassador Extraordinary, to have a new body vat-grown for her partner, so that they could be together again, in body as well as soul.

The Ambassador Extraordinary and her attaché, though, were the only pair-bond to survive the crash of the *Phonix* intact. The remaining five of us paired off quickly, comprising pair-bonds of two men—myself and Serj—and two women, Tamsin and Phedra. This left only the Engineer unattached.

Kloster seemed hardly bothered by the death of his partner, and less so that he was left on this strange twilit planetoid without prospects. If he had not mentioned picking up a working knowledge of emergency medicine from his late partner, the ship's physician, one might have supposed that the Engineer had always been a singleton. In truth, I don't know that Kloster realized just how uncomfortable the presence of a singleton made the rest of us, as the days wore on; but his attentions were elsewhere. That he was often away, exploring the caves and hidden recesses of the planetoid for hours, even days, at a time, came as a relief to us, I must confess.

"Kloster," I asked the engineer, shortly after our arrival, "does it not strike you odd that this planetoid would be so constituted as to support human life so perfectly? The mix of elements in the atmosphere, the gravity, the warmth—all seem perfectly suited to sustain life."

"Zihl," Kloster said, an unaccustomed smile on his lean face, the corners of his mouth almost touching his prominent cheekbones, "I never took you for a Demiurgist."

I had no notion what the engineer meant by this, and I'm sure my expression showed it.

"Surely you've heard the stories about ancient aliens, Assistant Astrogator?" Kloster asked, his tone like that of a teacher addressing a small child.

"Oh," I said, after mulling it over for a time, "you

mean the Old Ones? Such as are portrayed in the pseudo-rationalist dramas?"

Kloster blinked slowly, as if in sudden pain, and shook his head sharply. "Yes." He took a long sigh. "Well, one who holds to the Demiurgist doctrine believes that these ancient intelligences existed in actual fact, and not just in the fanciful writings of dramatists. There is no evidence for these ancients, as there is none for sentient beings from any source but Old Earth, but the proponents of Demiurgism see inferences everywhere, from the 'fine-tuning' of certain cosmological values to the balance of chemical constituents in some planetary bodies, which they argue is proof of ancient terraforming."

"And you think that this planetoid proves the Demiurgist doctrine?"

"No," Kloster said with a faint smile, shaking his head slowly, "I said it sounded as though *you* did."

With that, the engineer turned on his heel and walked away, leaving me puzzled by the turns of our brief conversation.

Those first nights on the planetoid, before we'd named it Eventide, we housed within the escape pod itself. But the close quarters were not suitable for an extended stay, the air was stifling, and my fitful sleep was plagued by nightmares. In short order we sought alternatives. At Kloster's suggestion, and with considerable physical exertion, we managed to break loose some fractal branches from the crystalline fronds, the native flora, and used these as our building materials. The resulting structures proved better protection against the flyers than the *Phonix*'s escape pod had been, and in little time our band of survivors had blossomed into a miniature community of rough-built frond shelters.

Still, though, my sleep was troubled, and I dreamed dark dreams. And still the sun did not set.

*   *   *

I think it may have been our adherence to pair-bonding that drove us into underspace in the first place. We of Disocur are instilled from an early age with the need to partner, an essential message of the education of organic children and synthetic intelligences alike. We are taught from the cradle that—whatever one's gender, orientation, species, or provenance—to be partnered in a pair-bond is the preferred mode of existence. Singletons, unpaired individuals, are vanishingly rare, most often occurring when one member of a pair-bond dies before the other—though nearly all made singletons in this way seek out a new partner as quickly as possible. Perhaps the reason that most Disocurenes are so uncomfortable around singletons—and, for that matter, one of the reasons why we transit the Threshold to other worlds so infrequently, where singletons are the norm—is that they serve as reminders of our own mortality.

The hope that there might be other branches of humanity, out in the galaxy, to whom we could reconnect, I suspect, was driven by this same impulse to pair and to shun the singleton. Travel between the established worlds of civilization is easy and as close to instantaneous as to make no difference. But no one knows how many other worlds were settled during the centuries of the Diaspora, when humans left Old Earth for the stars in fusion-engine rockets traveling at ponderous subluminal speeds. In the hundreds of generations since the first Thresholds were initiated, each wormhole a doorway connecting two distant worlds, humanity in its many forms and guises—including uplifted animals, synthetics, and others of blended or uncertain provenance—had become fairly complacent. A journey of a few steps could carry one at no cost a span of light years. So what if travel was restricted to established destinations and that the vast bulk of the galaxy remained uncharted and unexplored? If the cost of visiting these distant stars and discovering lost cousins of humanity was to live for decades or centuries in interstellar space, it was too high a price to pay.

There was an alternative, of course, as there always is. And while it was no less expensive—quite the reverse—the price was paid in a different coin.

Only the Disocurene, with our fanatical longing to pair that which is left alone, were willing to pay the price. It took the bulk of our planetary economy for several centuries to fund the development and construction of the underspace impellers, and several generations more to perfect the integration of the drives onto a manned vessel. The technology, which allowed for superluminal flight by traversing another spacetime continuum, contiguous to our own but in which distances were shorter, had been hypothetical for long centuries, and it nearly bankrupted our world to move it into the actual. But in the end, the *Underspace Ship Phonix* was completed, and our journey was ready to begin. A crew of three dozen pairs of Disocurenes was selected by the Chancellery, an Ambassador Extraordinary created who could speak to anyone we might encounter with the voice of Disocur, and with much celebration we were launched out into the darkness.

It was only when the *Phonix* attempted the reinsertion into normal space, after three hours travel in underspace, that the problems began.

Kloster could not explain why the planetoid was locked in a perpetual twilight, and none of the rest of us had the science to venture a hypothesis. The distant sun, whose faint light warmed us, pinked the sky over the western horizon, and the stars shone above the east, but sun never set, and the stars never wheeled in place. The light was gray, forever frozen in the gloaming. Nayrami, who had more of the poet in her than any of the rest of us, finally named this unknown planetoid "Eventide." It meant evening, or so she said, and seemed as good a name as any.

Back then, none of us expected that we would be staying for long, so it hardly seemed to matter.

I had served as assistant astrogator on the *Phonix*, and Serj had been the second-shift pilot, and so between us we had a fair handle on the functioning of the ship's impellers and the nature of the transition between normal space and underspace. As best we could work out, talking it over in our shelter at night— or in that period we survivors had determined the "night" by fiat, since every hour was the same as every other—when the *Phonix* returned to normal space, it had not been at the reinsertion point the astrogator had plotted. I had seen enough of the starfields surrounding us to realize they didn't match the charts before the hull imploded on the lower decks, killing half the crew in an instant, Serj's partner among them. Instead, it was as if the ship had been drawn to some other region of space entirely.

When next we saw Kloster, late the following "day," we told the engineer our theory. He merely shrugged and said, "I see nothing objectionable in your hypothesis."

"And do you think that whatever drew us here also accounts for the frozen sun and stars?" Serj asked, casting his amber gaze skyward. This surprised me, as I hadn't considered the connection before.

While I smiled slightly, warmed by my good fortune in selecting such a fine partner—a physique and a mind, together!—the engineer merely shrugged again and absently glanced at the immobile sky above.

"Perhaps," Kloster said, and turned away.

We passed the time as best we could, waiting for the rescue vessel whose arrival, we were sure, was imminent. We theorized that the Chancellery would take one of the prototype underspace impellers and affix it to a subluminal craft with little effort and only marginal expense to come searching for the *Phonix* when it failed to return home. In the meantime, we put on little comedies and dramas, following the scripts as best we could recall. Or competed in games of chance and skill, pair-bond against pair-bond, or men against women, or any other combination of players we could imagine. Or told stories, or sang songs, or rutted in the privacy of our shelters of fronds or in the hidden places of the cavern.

All but the engineer. Kloster kept to himself, more often than not, and seemed to have aged whole years in the scant few days since the crash.

Still I was plagued by strange dreams—murders, strange pairings, jealousies, and rage. Whenever I woke from one of these troubling visions, there always followed a brief period of confusion, and I could not recall which was my waking life and which the dream. The stolid presence of Serj, slumbering beside me on our makeshift cot, was always a comfort, pulling me back to reality, and I clung to him as though I were adrift at sea and he was the only thing keeping me afloat.

We knew little about each other's lives before our arrival on Eventide. Our time spent aboard the *Phonix* had been brief, just a few days powering out from Disocur and the short hours in underspace, and after arriving on the planetoid we had little desire to dwell on all we had lost.

I tried to make a pet of one of the scurries, though Serj laughed at my efforts, and the women thought I was sure to catch some disease from it. The middle of the three-tiered Eventide food chain, the scurries were small, twelve-legged organisms, about the length of my foot. Their hairless hides were rough and knobby, their heads diamond-shaped and eyeless, dominated by large mouths and the circle of small pits that Kloster theorized were used for some form of echolocation. The scurries' diet consisted entirely of water lapped up from the ponds of condensation that dotted the irregular Eventide landscape and the fronds.

The fronds were a kind of crystalline plant or fungus, which grew massive leafy protrusions that exfoliated with fractal complexity. They drew sustenance from the molecules of the soil, air, and water, converting them into the complex sugars that gave their leafy appendages their crystalline structure. The basic components of the fronds were organic, but the crystalline structures were difficult to break and virtually impossible for a human's digestive system to process. Luckily for the survivors of the *Phonix*, the harsh digestive acids and massive grinding jaws of the scurries were equal to the task, and as soon as the escape pod's limited food stores were exhausted, scurries roasted on a spit became a staple of our diet.

The scurries were themselves the sole form of sustenance for the flyers, the batwinged predators that lurked on the looming peaks of the Eventide horizon and swooped down to prey on the scurries when they matured beyond a certain length. The circle was completed when one of the flyers died, their decomposing remains providing the necessary cocktail of molecules that the spores of the fronds required to germinate.

The flyers had attacked us early on, perhaps seeing us as more substantial prey than the scurries. Fortunately, Kloster had outfitted us with sidearms from the escape pod's stores—the Disocurene Chancellery had not known what the *Phonix* might find in its search for the lost branches of humanity and had wanted the crew to be prepared for any eventuality—and as vicious and tough as the predators were, the Flyers proved no match for a disruptor's concentrated beam.

Farise chided me for wanting to make a pet of a creature I might be forced to eat in a matter of days, his voice sounding tinny and hollow through the Mind's small speakers. Nayrami and Phedra joined hands and sang a popular children's song about a boy who pair-bonds with a pet rodent instead of a sentient. And, finally, Serj and Tamsin sat side by side, shoulders rubbing, holding their sides with laughter.

I told them all I didn't care what they thought. I named my pet Phonix—deciding at the last moment that naming it Dobeh would be in poor taste—and did my level best to bestow some affection on it, despite the scurry's best efforts to escape.

The next day, while I attempted to teach the creature to stand up on its hind pairs of legs, my pet scurry bit me on the hand. Kloster returned from his explorations of the caves, looking older than ever, and treated my wound with the emergency medical kit retrieved from the pod. He said the injury was unlikely to leave a scar, but I was unconvinced.

At our evening meal, everyone insisted that I get the choicest cut of meat, and Phonix proved to be quite tasty, indeed.

My hair had grown in, in the weeks since the crash. I typically kept the follicles on my head switched off, preferring to leave my skull hairless, but since arriving on Eventide the resequencers had dissipated into my bloodstream, leaving the follicles to follow their inborn genetic imperatives, and in short order I had a shaggy, unkempt mess of hair atop my head. Serj said he didn't mind and that he somewhat preferred my new appearance, but I was just grateful for the shortage of reflective surfaces on the planetoid.

Tamsin, though, the statuesque protocol officer on the *Phonix*, was less than thrilled when her own phenotype began to reassert itself. When we'd arrived on Eventide, her skin had been coded a tasteful shade of emerald, and her hair and eyes a matching shade of crimson, the red of a dying main sequence star. After a few weeks, the luster began to fade, and she began slowly to revert to the more typical Disocurene color-

ation, skin the light brown hue of wet sand, hair a
reddish copper. Phedra was short, compact, and tightly
muscled, and she wore her body as genetics and nature
intended, though honed to a razor's edge. She joked
that her partner would in short order need to take
cosmetic advice from her, but if Tamsin was amused
at the thought of looking like the ship's fabricator, she
did a good job of hiding it. They made for an odd
pair-bond, but they had each other, and that was
what counted.

No rescue vessel appeared, nor any sign of any
other escape pods from the ship. It was difficult to
measure the passage of time, but it was no more than
a few weeks before we gave up all hope of being
rescued. We confessed to one another that we hadn't
ever really thought it possible that help would arrive.
In time, we even came to believe it.

My dreams grew worse, such that it was rare that a
night passed without some terror rousing me from my
sleep. When I mentioned these to the others, even
those who claimed not to have been troubled by nightmares indicated with their haunted expressions that
they in fact had been. We wondered whether there
might not be some characteristic of our diet, perhaps
undetected microorganisms in the condensation, that
could account for these nightly visions, but when we
finally had a chance to ask Kloster his opinion, on one
of his rare appearances at mealtime, he claimed that
his own sleep was untroubled and that he had no notion which might be disturbing the rest of us. He put
it down to stress over our circumstances, and he went
about his business.

I wanted to believe the engineer was right, but when
I awoke from a dream, the image fresh in my mind—
of my hands wrapped around Nayrami's thin bird-like
neck, or of Phedra standing over me with a disruptor
pistol in hand, or of coming upon Serj lying in pieces

on the ground, his entrails a feast for a flock of
flyers—I found it hard to dismiss it so easily.

We began to explore, more to stave off boredom
than to pursue any curiosity. We carried disruptors at
our belts, of course, to fend off any errant flyers, but
we were quite safe, for all that.

The planetoid of Eventide was denser and more
massive than its small dimensions would suggest. This
we knew, but until one of us did it, we had no notion
than a person on foot could walk in a circuit around
the planetoid's surface in the equivalent of just a few
days. Eventide's gravitational attraction was a substantial portion of Earth-normal, only a few percent less
than that of Disocur. And, despite our best efforts, we
found no other members of the local ecosystem than
the fronds, the scurries, and the flyers, as much as our
palates—weary of a steady diet of condensation and
roasted scurry—would have preferred some variety.

That such an unlikely environment supported a single organism, much less three, was hardly a surprise.
Since the days of the Diaspora, humanity had learned
that life was ubiquitous, hiding in virtually every imag-
inable planetary crevasse.

If life itself was everywhere, however, sentience
sadly was not. The only self-aware beings humanity
encountered out among the stars were those that they
brought with them, or those which they engendered
once they arrived. With sufficient time, resources, and
desire, it was conceivable that we survivors could uplift the simple organics of Eventide into proper sentience, but it hardly seemed worth the trouble, even
in purely theoretical terms.

And, in short order, we had explored all that there
was to explore. Except for the caves. The planetoid
was riddled with subterranean passages, from microfi-
ssures to massive caverns, but they were cold, and
dark, and foreboding, and none of us liked to linger

too long in them. None but the engineer. Kloster seemed to have found a new home, there in the dark recesses of Eventide, and as time went on, he visited our little community of frond-built structures less and less. When he did return to the surface, on rare occasions, it was only for brief visits, during which he would question each of us in turn about all that had happened in his absence, as though he were compiling a personal history of our collective experiences.

Still my dreams grew worse, and from their haggard and haunted looks I knew that the others' sleep was no less troubled. In our waking hours, we found it difficult to separate the real people before us from the actions our minds had attributed to them in our nightmares. In some cases, such as the dreams of strange pairings, as when I dreamed that I was pair-bonded to Phedra and not to Serj, this made for uncomfortable encounters, when I forgot that the affection I felt was only imagined, and a tender caress in passing gave offense. But mine was not the first such transgression, and tempers quickly calmed.

One night, I dreamed that Kloster had failed to construct the makeshift Mind that housed the ghost of Farise, and that he had bonded to Nayrami. But their pair-bond, in my dream, was an unhappy one, and ended badly.

The population of scurries around our encampment grew thinner as time went on, forcing us to go further and further afield to find meat for our table. I took to hunting alone in the "mornings," going out with my disruptor sidearm—at its lowest setting the beam was sufficient to kill the creatures without disintegrating them altogether—and returning hours later with enough food for all of us.

On the day it happened, I managed to catch only two scurries, and I knew that we'd be eating slim for dinner that night. I called to Serj as I stepped inside our frond shelter, joking that he'd have to curb his appetite for one night, at least, but that I'd make it up to him when we doused the lights.

There he was, in our cot, lying naked next to vast amount of green-tinged skin, cascades of copper-reddish hair falling over his chest.

It took me a moment to work out the tangle of limbs and flesh, but then I have never been very quick.

"Tamsin?" I said aloud, as she and my partner turned, eyes wide, startled by my early return.

"Zihl, wait . . ." Serj said, raising a hand to me.

My disruptor was at my belt, and then it was in my hand. I don't recall a transition between the two states, though there must have been. My vision went red, and my thoughts boomed in my head like the sound of the *Phonix*'s lower decks imploding. I could see Serj's lips moving, but nothing he said made it into my head. I thumbed the disruptor's beam to full dispersal and fired.

Serj and Tamsin, locked in a final embrace, faded like an afterimage as their bodies' quanta decohered, subatomic particles displaced in all directions, accompanied only by a low, sullen hiss from the sidearm's barrel.

But as they died, erased from existence, the image of their death was overlaid in my mind with countless other images of death and loss, the same as those that had haunted my dreams these many months, but now more immediate, more vivid. They were all real, and none of them was.

I reeled back, clutching the sides of my head, and for an instant I couldn't bring to mind what had just happened. Had I just beamed Serj and Tamsin into noncorporeality? And if I had, which was my partner and which the interloper? Or had it been another whom my beam had struck, or another who had been about to beam me?

Reality reasserted, and I remembered what I had done, but even then my grasp was tenuous, and I felt as though I might slip back into a myriad of unreal worlds at any moment.

Throwing my disruptor to the ground and racing from the shelter, I headed for the caverns.

I had to find Kloster. He would know what to do.

I don't know how long I searched for the engineer in the darkened caves of Eventide. Hours? Days? Longer? I passed through caverns large enough to house the *Phonix* itself, and crawled through tunnels scarcely· wider than my shoulders, and I forgot all about hunger, and thirst, and fatigue. I thought of nothing but everything that I had lost, and the nightmares that plagued us, and the frozen sky, and the crash, and the sure certainty that there must be an answer to all of it, and that Kloster must have it.

I cannot say whether some part of me recognized that the walls along which I groped were no longer rough stone but cool and polished metal, or that my eyes, long accustomed to the darkness, could again see in the gradual gloom ahead. I think, in fact, that I was almost nose-to-nose with the engineer before it even registered on my consciousness that he was before me. The dawning realization that he stood before a massive wall of metal, covered with strange shapes and symbols, followed at some distance.

"Ah, Assistant Astrogator," Kloster said, with a resigned nod, looking up from his work. "Well, what was it this time?"

I stammered, my throat parched, my tongue thick in my mouth.

"Well, come out with it, Zihl, what happened?"

"Serj . . ." I began, my voice croaking. "With Tamsin. In our bed." I tried to swallow but passed only dust and air.

"Go on," the engineer said, waving his hand impatiently. "Serj was your partner, I believe, and you found him in the arms of another."

I looked down at my hands, cut, bruised, and filthy from my journey through the caves.

"I had my disruptor . . ." I said, and could go no further.

Kloster rubbed his chin, thoughtfully. "I shouldn't be surprised, I suppose. The pairing of Tamsin with Phedra was never particularly stable."

The Engineer clapped his hands together and turned to face the metal. He began moving the shapes and symbols in sequence, at a lightning pace.

"What . . . what is this?" I managed to croak, and waved a bloody finger toward the towering wall. The metal of which it was constructed was one I had never seen before, shimmering and strange, and seemed to shift beneath my gaze.

"Hmmm?" Kloster glanced back over his shoulder, distracted. "Oh, this? This, my dear Zihl, is the proof that the Demiurgists would murder their own children in their beds to possess. This is not a planetoid. It never was. This is an ancient engine, capable of warping the fabric of space-time around it. Everything between here and the surface is merely matter that has accreted to the engine's surface, over countless eons."

I staggered back, blinking lids over bloodshot eyes, my mouth working soundlessly.

"At some point, probably before the Old Earth cooled, the engine malfunctioned and pinched off from normal space into its own pocket continuum. That's what attracted the *Phonix* as we transitioned back from underspace. We never could have escaped, if that's what you're worried about. Not once we passed within the event horizon of the engine's space-time bubble. But while it's taken long years, I've been able to master the rudiments of the engine's controls, so that I can now manipulate the flow of time within the bubble."

"Time?" I said, feebly.

"Yes, rolling it backward and forward, trying to find

the proper combinations. If we're to live here, it may as well be in the best circumstances, yes? But so far, I'm afraid it always ends badly. That'll be the cause of the nightmares, bleed-through from the other iterations, but that's a small price to pay, don't you think?" He grinned, darkly. "But it could be worse, after all. You could be forced to remember all of the iterations, like I do." He mimed a shiver, and shook his head, comically.

I stepped forward, raising my hands.

"We've done all of this before?"

"Yes, Zihl," Kloster said, a touch of sadness in his voice, "but I'm confident that I'll work out all of the suitable variables, given time."

The Engineer reached out a thin finger, and touched a final symbol on the metal wall, and the world fell away.

It was everywhere.
It was nowhere.

I remembered all of it, and I remembered nothing.

It was . . .

It was while burying Dobeh that Tamsin first caught my attention. In the strange twilight of Eventide, she shone like a distant star, her crimson hair and eyes standing out like firelight against the cool emerald of her skin. She smiled, and I knew then that we'd be paired.

What We Still Talk About

Scott Edelman

Selene, blue pill cupped in one palm, wondered where she would find the strength to raise the small lozenge to her lips. The longer she stared out at the harsh landscape, the heavier the morning dosage seemed in her hand.

The dome had hoped that she and her husband would find the vista in which it had chosen to place them that morning pleasing, but for Selene, the generated location was a failure, as had been its other recent choices. Karl would perhaps feel differently, but for Selene, as the rocks stretched on, rough and dry and red, the scene brought to mind nothing so much as the interior of her own heart.

She closed her fingers tightly around the pill and could feel its smooth metallic surface grow sticky from her sweat.

"Does anyone," she said, in a soft, uncertain voice, "remember how to get to Earth?"

The words spurted out of her so suddenly that she was startled. Her question had exploded on its own without even the thought of an audience that might receive it.

"Did you hear what I just said, Karl?" said Selene. "Or did I only think it?"

"I heard you, darling," said Karl, lifting wiry arms above his head as he stretched out on rainbow sheets that shimmered with his movements. "It just took me a moment to digest it. I haven't thought about Earth in years."

"Oh, please, Selene," said Karl, entering through one of the bedroom's irises while bearing a tray of drinks intended to cool them from their lovemaking. "Earth is so boring. Promise me that you're not thinking of going back there again. You're not really—are you?"

"It's not very far," shouted Karl from the opposite dome from which Karl had just entered. Selene, peering through the connecting biolock, could see him busy at work, his fingers encrusted with a yellow dust from pollinating the wall for the coming season's sculptures. "No, it's not very far at all. But then, these days, what is?"

"Good," said Selene. "Then let's go."

She tossed the pill in her mouth and swallowed too quickly; the pill stuck in her throat. She took the drink Karl held out to her, swirled the sheer cup until the thick liquid began to spark, and forced the pill quickly down.

That was that, then. Her choice had been made. There'd be no more thinking, no more worrying. Not for today, at least.

"This will be fun," she said quietly, almost to herself. She licked away the last of the sticky blue residue that remained in the folds of her palm. "I love you, Karl."

"And I love you," said her husband.
"And I love you," said her husband.
"And I love you," said her husband.

The joyful harmony of his voices caused her heart to skip a beat, its pulsing overwhelmed at being the focus of her husband's love.

"Let's get started then," she said, jumping to her feet.

"Right now?" asked Karl. He flung the bedsheet toward the ceiling and then, as it billowed, stepped beneath it. As he lifted his arms, the flowing fabric descended to wrap itself tightly around him. Mere molecules thick, his garb was less clothing than a second layer of skin, as if his nude form had been dipped into a vat of multicolored paint. He snatched the second mug from Karl's tray.

"Why not?" asked Selene. "I see no reason to wait. There's something to be said for spontaneity."

"Yes, something," said Karl, dropping his empty tray to the floor, where it was quickly reabsorbed into their dome. "I've never been sure exactly what that something *is*, though."

"Which flitter should we take?" asked Selene, strong enough now, as she might not have been before, to ignore her husband's joke. She looked into the sky and tried to see past the moons above.

"Why a flitter?" asked Karl. He left a yellow trail of powdery footprints that suffused with red behind him as his steps germinated. "All we need to do is simply think our destination, and we're there."

"No," said Selene firmly, still intent on the distant Earth that hid somewhere in the sky. "This is something that must be done real, or at least as real as anything *can* be done these days."

"As if projecting our way to Earth wouldn't be real," said Karl, shaking his hands by the wrists until the bedsheet extruded opalescent gloves that grew to his fingertips. "As if the new choices are any less real than the old ones. It's all real, Selene. You have too much love of old-fashioned things."

"Which explains why I keep you around, I guess," she said.

Her husband reached out simultaneously to swat her on the rump. Karl's hands collided one-two-three before they continued on the final few inches to make contact with her, the sort of overlap that she knew only occurred in those rare instances when she touched a nerve. She smiled, and they hugged, his arms weaving together to embrace her at the center of a warm cocoon. She murmured peacefully. For a brief moment, she forgot about blue pills, about the endless red rock, about the pleasant, tickling memories of ancient Earth.

Then Karl had to speak, bringing them all back again.

"We should really ask Ursula and Tomas along," said Karl, his words echoing wetly in the confines of their flesh.

"Oh," said Selene, stepping outside of the curtain of Karl's body. "I was hoping that we could all go alone."

"All?" said Karl, looking from himself to himself.

"Why, yes," said Selene. "All. All alone. It's been so long since we've all been away alone together. Too long."

"Too late," said Karl, coming up behind her. "I've already invited them. It never occurred to me that you'd object."

"You should have thought about it a little more carefully before you thought them an invitation, Karl," she said, slowly turning away from her husband.

"You're right, Selene," said Karl, from beside her. "But it's too late for that now, unfortunately. You know how Tomas and Ursula are. I wouldn't want to hurt their feelings. I'm sorry, Selene."

But what about my feelings? she thought, and then, almost before that emotion could claw its way to full consciousness, the feeling effervesced, as all such feelings did, if only she made the right choice each morning. She turned back to Karl and touched her husband's cheek, while by the dome's outer window, Karl watched as a flitter blossomed from the rocks around them. A jagged skeleton slowly rose up that was but a whispered promise of the vehicle that would carry them light-years away. Molten ore feathered through the air like spun sugar and wrapped about the flitter's core.

"Look," Karl said, as the process completed and Selene's name etched itself into the finished skin of the ship.

"Hello," tickled Tomas in her ear.

Selene smiled, perhaps at the flourish her husband had provided, perhaps at the arrival of her friend. Perhaps both. She felt the familiar good mood wash over her as the nanobots massaged the chemistry of her bloodstream.

"Thank you, Karl," she said. "Hello, Tomas."

"Ursula will be along shortly."

"But never shortly enough for you, Tomas, right?" said Karl.

"I can be a patient . . . man," he vibrated, everywhere and nowhere. If he had chosen to sneak up on them, they wouldn't even have known he was there. "Someday, she'll grow tired of a material existence, and then, there won't be anything left for me to have to be patient *about*."

"Other than enjoying your practice of such restraint, Tomas," asked Selene, "how have you been?"

"Bored," he vibrated. "The universe continues to hold far too few surprises. So I'm glad that you asked us along."

"How could you possibly be bored with all this?" asked Karl, as he stepped through the iris back to his wall work. "I can't remember when I've last been bored."

"Oh, it's more than just that, Karl," said Tomas. "It's that you can't remember, period. I never have been able to figure out how you manage to keep yourselves straight."

Before Karl or Karl or Karl could answer, the ground rumbled, and Selene jumped in quickly. She needed the day to go smoothly.

"That would be Ursula," she said, as the dome compensated for the clamor outside, and the room regained its silence. "You know, Tomas, for someone so willing to take the greatest of leaps, your emotions can be awfully old-fashioned."

Ursula plodded toward them from the short horizon, her robotic feet crushing rocks into crimson sprays of dust. It wasn't until she arrived at the flitter, overshadowing it in a tower of chrome, that Selene was able to judge the size that Ursula had chosen to carry that day. Ursula had felt like being a giantess, and so she was.

"We're all here, then," said Selene. She had made her own choice about what she was to be that day, and she intended to stick to it. "Let's go."

Selene walked in the direction of the flitter, and when she arrived at the dome wall, she kept walking and flowed effortlessly through it, passing as if through the fragile skin of a bubble. A thin membrane clung to her as she continued walking, and stretched the wall outward, and as she drew closer to the flitter, the connection snapped, and the skin sealed shut behind her. The flitter extended a tongue in her direction, and as she mounted the walkway, she waved up at Ursula from within a self-contained atmosphere.

"Are you feeling any better today?" said Ursula, her faraway speakers booming deeply.

"How I'm feeling doesn't really matter," said Selene. "It's how I'm *doing*. And right now, I seem to be doing something at last."

Selene paused near the top of the walkway. She turned and gestured back at the dome, making the assumption that her movements were being watched.

Karl seemed to be the first to follow her and vanish inside the flitter, though with Tomas around, she could never be completely sure. Once her husband was inside, Karl then followed. He brushed past Selene on the walkway and stopped at the hatch. While she looked up at him, Karl came along, stepping up behind her and wrapping his arms about her waist. Karl smiled down at the two of them from above, then turned and vanished inside the ship.

"Do you really need all of me?" Karl whispered. The pliant membrane allowed her to feel his breath hot in her ear.

"Yes," said Selene. "This time, I do. Please, Karl."

Arms locked, they strolled up the rest of the walkway together and entered the ship. Karl and Karl were already seated within a teardrop-shaped room otherwise bare of furniture, a compartment larger than the ship in which it was contained. At the narrowest point of the teardrop, Karl and Selene dropped back off their feet, trusting that a couch would ooze up from the floor to catch them.

"Ursula?" called out Selene.

The opaque wall which curved about them grew steadily transparent until Selene could see her friend framed by the landscape outside. She swelled even larger, and was soon crouching down above them, her head alone as big as one of their dome rooms.

"I have a feeling that this is going to be fun," said Tomas. "Yes, darling, it's time. You know what to do."

Ursula scooped up the flitter, growing even taller as she hugged the vehicle to her chest, carrying them to where the atmosphere was even thinner. Staring into her friend's ever-more-enormous face, Selene felt as if she were instead shrinking away. At times like this one, she always found it hard at first to tell which one of them was actually doing the changing. Ursula lifted the flitter behind her head for a moment and then pitched it high into the air. As it neared the top of its arc, great flames spouted from the soles of Ursula's feet, and she rocketed after her friends. She overtook them and slammed into the rear of the ship, adding the thrust they needed to escape the gravity of the small planet.

Once Ursula and the ship she'd propelled were both fully free of the atmosphere, the gleaming plates that made up her body receded into each other. As they overlapped, she shrank until she was down to a size capable of entering the airlock. As she fell back into the circle of her friends, a seat sturdier than the others grew up to greet her.

"How long do you think this will take?" she asked with a dull buzz, as she brushed meteor dust from one shiny shoulder.

"That all depends," said Karl, looking out at the stars.

"It will take however long Selene wants it to take," said Karl, looking intently at his wife. "That isn't something that can be timed."

"Then I think I'll have a drink," said Selene.

Karl pressed his hands against the front wall of the small ship, which extruded mugs that he handed to Karl and Selene and Karl. Ursula pressed a few buttons on her wrist, and a small door slid open in her chest. She took the offered drink and poured its contents down into a permaglass funnel. Karl offered Ursula a second mug, which she balanced on the flat of her knee joint as liquid gurgled pneumatically within her. As the level in that beverage dropped, Selene could hear a gentle slurping.

"Thank you," said Tomas. "So tell us, Selene—why Earth?"

"And why now?" buzzed Ursula. "I don't remember Earth being so thrilling the last time that it was worth this kind of effort."

Selene stared off ahead of them through the clear hull of the flitter and then looked at the empty mug in her hand, unable to remember having drained it.

"I'm not entirely sure," said Selene. "It just seems like the thing to do."

"It's those movies, you know," said Karl, refilling her drink with a pass of his hand. "She's become hooked on them. I have no idea why she wants to go there *now*, but she loves those movies."

"We could have watched them at home," said Karl.

"We could have watched anything at home," said Tomas.

"I don't quite understand the attraction of those dead art forms," said Karl. "They're so simple. Simple and simplistic. Like children's stories."

"As if you remember children's stories," said Tomas.

"As if *you* remember children," said Ursula.

"There's more than one kind of simple," said Selene, struggling to put the static that warred in her head into words. "It doesn't always have to be derogatory. What I liked was that those people had their limits."

"Maybe they only seemed to," said Tomas, playfully. "Maybe you only thought they did. You only know them from their movies. Maybe they were just like us."

"They weren't like us," said Selene. "They couldn't do everything. They couldn't rewire their bodies or dissipate their souls or wear whatever flesh suited their moods or . . . or just take a pill. They had to deal with whatever they were dealt."

"And you think that makes us any different?" asked Ursula. "You're getting lost in the details. They were just like us."

"But look at us," said Selene, her eyes suddenly filled with tears. "*Look* at us."

Karl leaned forward to peer at himself in Ursula's chrome shoulder, then looked at Karl, then looked at Karl, then laughed. Tomas laughed with him.

"For some of us," said Tomas, "that's easier done than for others."

"Life is a metaphor," said Ursula. "Just because we get to choose a few more of them each year doesn't make us any freer in the grand scheme of things. We all believe what we're programmed to believe."

"Or what we choose to believe," said Selene.

"I choose to believe that there wasn't really a need for this," said Karl. "As I said, there was no need to travel back to Earth, dear. Whatever you wanted to see of it back home, you could just have asked for it, asked for any dream you wished, and we would all have been able to see it."

"Is taking a trip with me really that much trouble?" said Selene. She dropped her cup and was pleased to see it shatter before it was reabsorbed into the floor. "What else were you doing that was so terribly important?"

"Nothing," said Karl.

"Nothing," said Karl.

"Nothing," said Karl, "is so important that I wouldn't stop doing it in an instant for you. I'm only thinking of you, Selene. I only mean that you can have the prize without all this effort. Such a dead art form can't be worth all this."

"Sometimes the effort *is* the prize," Selene said sternly.

"Now *that* isn't boring, Ursula," said Tomas, here, there and everywhere. "Can you remember when she last spoke to him in that way?"

"I can remember everything," said Ursula, tapping at the databanks buried deep in her waist.

"Brava, Selene!" said Tomas. "Keep going."

"No," said Selene, her feelings fluctuating wildly. "No more talking just to fill the time if this is what we still talk about. Let's get to Earth *now*."

And so they did.

But when they rose and spread out against the walls of the ship, peering in search of a planet, all they saw was the same vaporous space that had been their companion for the first part of their voyage. The flitter, which should have popped across the universe and come to rest in orbit around the birthplace of humanity, instead floated in a void. The sun shone blisteringly hot at them with no intervening atmosphere.

"Where are we?" said Selene. "This can't possibly be right."

"And yet it is," said Karl.

"We're exactly where we're supposed to be," said Karl.

"We're exactly where you wanted us to be," said Karl.

"But we can't be," said Selene. "Where is the Earth?"

This time, Selene felt for sure that if she would lose herself to a wrenching bout of tears. It had been a long time since she had felt pushed to that extreme. And then, as she heard her husband speak again, the notion was flushed away.

"There's no reason that it shouldn't be right here," said Karl. "These spatial coordinates should have placed us in exactly the same relation to the Earth as when we'd arrived the last time."

"That's impossible," said Selene. "The Earth couldn't just disappear."

"Nothing is impossible," intoned Ursula.

"How long has it been again?" asked Karl.

"How long *has* it been?" said Selene.

"No," said Tomas. "Definitely not boring."

When Tomas shivered with delight, Selene could feel the goosebumps.

"I didn't come this far just to talk about it," said Ursula. "I'm going out."

She pushed herself from the hatch to hang in space. Selene watched as her friend slowly somersaulted beneath the ship. There should be blue below her, blue oceans and white clouds and cities and the ruins of men.

"Selene, dear," said Karl. "We may just have to accept the fact that the Earth is gone."

"Can we be sure we're in the right place?" asked Karl.

"Oh, we're in the right place," said Karl. "There's no doubt about it."

"But what could have happened?" said Selene.

"At this point, does it really matter?" said Tomas. "Planets are born, and planets die. Just because this planet happens to be Earth doesn't mean that it gets to go on forever. It could have been attacked. Or perhaps someone blew it up for spite. Or maybe the last person out simply turned out the lights, and then it just ceased to exist, expiring from lack of interest."

"It doesn't matter why," said Selene. Even as she said it, she realized she'd spoken a little too quickly, even for her. "I don't really care why. We've got to put it back the way it was."

"All the way back?" asked Karl. "Is that what you want, dear?"

"Should I gather the pieces?" asked Tomas. "Should I bring them all back and make them bustle once more? It might even be a challenge. I've never puzzled out a working world before."

"No," said Selene. "Not all the way back. That would be meaningless. Just restore the Earth to as it stood when I was here last. When I was here with Karl last."

"Isn't that the same thing?" said Karl.

"You didn't let me and Ursula tag along with you here that last time," said Tomas. "I'll need a reference. Do you mind?"

Selene shook her head. In a moment, she felt an itching in her brain, and then, as quickly as he had entered, Tomas was gone.

"Ah, I see it now," said Tomas. "I see how it was."

That's all that it took, for suddenly, Earth was there below her. Spinning there, it was just as Selene had remembered it, the swirling clouds hiding a purer past beneath. And having experienced Tomas's work a thousand times before, she was sure that it truly *was* exactly as she had remembered it.

"Let's go down," whispered Selene. "I can't wait any longer."

"Ursula, dear," Tomas called out. "We're going down now."

"I'll meet you all Earthside," said Ursula.

She tucked her chin into her chest and kicked her

feet away from the flitter. Rockets ignited in her heels to push her down toward the surface below. Selene watched hungrily, jealously, as her friend became a dot in the distance and then vanished from sight.

"Should we just—" said Karl.

"No," interrupted Selene. "We shouldn't. The old-fashioned way. We're doing this the old-fashioned way."

The flitter dropped into a low orbit as Selene surveyed the terrain.

"What are you looking for, dear?" said Karl.

"What are any of us looking for?" said Tomas.

"You've grown much too metaphysical of late," said Karl. "Go join your wife."

"I'm already with my wife," said Tomas. "And besides—I put a planet together today. Don't you think I've earned the right to wax a little metaphysical?"

"What do you see, dear?" asked Karl.

"I see us there," said Selene, jabbing a finger at the horizon. "We're going there."

The sky turned blue as they descended to an even lower orbit. Ursula pulled up beside them and waved, spiraled about the flitter while laughing, and then sped ahead. Moments later, they dropped to the surface, setting the ship lightly down in the center of a deserted city. The frozen moment resurrected by Tomas reflected a time when no one was left to greet them. Some of the buildings still towered over them, but others lay in rubble. Tall grasses swayed. Stepping from the flitter and pausing to listen, Selene could hear the sound of birds and the occasional thunder and crash of a collapsing building. The abandoned planet was once more a dying planet, and now that Tomas had set its clock ticking again, Earth hurried along again to its inevitable end.

"It's exactly as I remember it," she said. "Perfect."

"Why didn't you want me to return Earth to its glory, rather than its decline?" asked Tomas. "I would have welcomed that. It would have been more of a challenge."

Selene didn't answer. Selene couldn't answer. Selene merely stood transfixed, studying each inch of territory between her toes and the horizon until Ursula landed with a thud beside them.

"Well, we're here," said Ursula, setting right a car that had flipped on its side ages before. "What are we supposed to do now?"

"That's entirely up to Selene," said Tomas. "This is her party. We're just here as her guests. Or witnesses."

"Witnesses?" said Ursula. "It isn't as if this is a wedding."

"Dear?" asked Karl. "It's up to you."

"Come," said Selene, holding out her hands to her husband. "Let's take a walk together."

Karl came up on her left side, and Karl came up on her right, and Karl stepped ahead to walk before them with both hands dangling back to join theirs. Ursula cleared a path ahead of them, concrete and brick being crushed into a smooth powder beneath her. She came across a tumbled lamppost and, laughing, tossed it toward the sky. Selene never saw or heard it fall.

"Remember the first time we came here?" asked Selene, giving her husband's hands a squeeze.

"How could I possibly forget," said Karl in her right ear.

"It was our honeymoon," said Karl in her left.

"It seems like a lifetime ago," called Karl back over one shoulder. "But I'm sure that it was much longer than that."

"When Ursula and I decided to bind ourselves to each other," said Tomas, "we went *everywhere*."

"Earth was quite enough for us," said Selene.

"I'm sure it was very nice," said Ursula.

"Who needs the entire universe, when this is where it all began?" said Selene. "Not just us. *Everything*."

"Poor Selene," said Tomas, wickedly. "Feeling

overly nostalgic? They have a pill for that, too, you know."

"Tomas!" blared Ursula, turning to the sky. "If you had a neck, I'd wring it."

"What did I say?" said Tomas. "I never meant that in a bad way. We're all friends here, aren't we?"

"Pretend that you have a tongue," said Ursula. "And hold it."

"I want to see it all again," said Selene, unshaken by Tomas's words. Playful or punishing, they could not affect her. In that place, at that moment, for one of the very few times in her life, she felt like a rock. "I want to visit the museums, see the movies, and . . . and everything. I want to see the way that people lived before. I want to watch what choices they had to make."

"Assuming, of course," said Tomas, "that in their art, truth was being told about the way that people lived before."

"Tomas!" said Ursula.

"I'm only saying—"

"Enough," said Ursula. "Selene, do you think all those things you need could possibly still be here?"

"Except for a little more decay here and there, it's just as we left it," said Selene.

"Thank you," whispered Tomas.

"I recognize this city," said Selene. "I recognize this street. Karl, do you recognize this street?"

There was no answer, not from Karl nor Karl nor Karl, which made Selene squeeze his hands all the harder.

"We've just a few blocks to go," she said, pausing for a moment in the middle of an intersection. "And then you'll all see what I mean. That way."

"Let's do it then," said Ursula.

Ursula swelled from her default size into her gigantic self. With hands the size of couches, she scooped her four companions high up into the air, and ran in the direction Selene had pointed.

"No!" shouted Selene, bouncing several stories above the cement. "Ursula, please, it can't be like this. Put us down."

Ursula froze so suddenly that her metal muscles squealed. She shrunk in on herself until Selene and the others touched lightly down.

"Thank you, Ursula, and please forgive me," said Selene. "But what happens here today, you have to understand, I don't want it to be done our way. I need it to be done the old-fashioned way."

"If it's important to you," said Ursula, "then I understand."

"Well, I don't," said Tomas.

"Tomas . . ."

"But whatever you need, Selene," he quickly added.

"This is where the art museum was," said Selene, gesturing to the decrepit building in front of which they stood.

The front wall of the marble and granite structure had collapsed, so they were forced to pick their way across a field of rubble. They climbed atop a pile of huge shards that blocked the entrance and then slid down inside through where a wall had split open. Most of the paintings were no longer on the walls, having fallen in some past catastrophe. Tomas wrapped himself around one that had dropped facedown in the dust, and the large canvas rose and floated in the air, presenting its face to each of them in turn.

A man and woman gazed out at them, their hands lightly touching as they stood in a flowering garden. A young girl sat between them in the grass, hugging a ball in her lap. They stared at the painter who had captured them, stared, without being entirely aware of it, into the future Selene occupied. Selene stared back, trying to peer into that past.

"Is that all we once were?" said Ursula, as the canvas spun again to her. "They look trapped in their flesh. Except for size, they look almost exactly the same."

"For them," said Selene, "that was difference enough."

"At least, that's what they had to keep telling themselves," said Tomas.

"Come along, Tomas," said Ursula. "Let's give Selene and Karl some time alone."

Ursula climbed back out the way they had come. As the painting dropped against a wall, Selene hoped, but could never be quite sure, that Tomas had followed his wife. After a moment, Selene could hear the slamming together of great objects. She smiled.

"I hope Ursula is having fun," said Karl.

"Some people just know better than others how, I guess," said Selene.

Selene and Karl and Karl and Karl made their way through what remained of the museum, where she tried to feel as a long-ago tourist might have, visiting on a summer day for a break from her busy life. She imagined how it must once have looked with its walls arranged neatly, its paintings organized according to a lost scheme Selene could not comprehend, its halls populated by contemporary visitors in search of a mirror. Selene lifted up each painting as lovingly as would a mother a child, and found each a place amidst the ruins where it could be seen and perhaps understood. She had no desire for blotches or geometric patterns today, though, and when Karl would overturn anything reeking of the abstract, she quickly abandoned it. She needed only the representational today. She needed . . . life.

A great fish, trapped at the end of a line, frozen in midair, yanked toward a small rowboat. A bowl of fruit that was only a bowl of fruit, and nothing more. A dog, its fur sparkling, proudly posing with a limp duck hanging from its maw. And the faces of the people, the endless faces of the people.

She mostly studied their eyes. They did not look unhappy to her. They did not look discontented. She was not fooled into thinking that their lives as they lived them were perfect; no, she was too smart for that, but she knew that what problems they had were not just symptoms of their times. They did not seem enslaved by the paucity of their choices. In fact, they were probably just as bewildered by the multiplicity of them as she was by her own.

"Selene," said Karl. Her name startled her. She lost hold of the last painting she had been studying, and Karl and Karl had to stumble forward to catch it. "Sorry. But Selene—what are you looking for?"

"I don't know."

She studied her husband's faces over the frame that was between them. Their eyes were equally sincere.

"What's wrong?" asked Karl.

"I don't know that either."

Karl tugged at the frame that separated them, but Selene held it in place. Karl stepped back and left them like that, coming around to place a hand on the small of Selene's back.

"Selene," he said. "Let's go."

"I can't," she said.

"We can't stay here forever," he said.

"Can't we?"

A deafening crash thudded outside. Selene could feel the vibrations through the soles of her feet.

"Obviously not if we want this world to remain in one piece," said Karl, smiling.

When they climbed back outside, the front of the museum was entirely clear of debris. Ursula stood in the midst of several perfectly balanced columns of wreckage.

"Much better that way, don't you think?" said Ursula. "And I could use the exercise."

"You don't need any exercise," said Selene.

"You must stop being so literal," said Tomas.

"Where have you been, dear?" asked Ursula.

"Everywhere," said Tomas. "I've seen it all now."

"All?" asked Selene.

"Yes," said Tomas. "The museum. The city. The world. Is it time for us to go?"

"There's much more the rest of us still have to see," said Selene. "Go back and take a second look. It isn't our fault that you can see everything so much faster than we do."

"Actually," said Tomas. "It is."

"Tomas!" shouted Selene. She wished she had the ability to tell whether her sudden anger was a good thing or a bad thing.

"Don't bother," said Ursula. "He's gone again."

"How can you tell?"

Ursula shrugged, her shoulders clinking. Selene sighed.

They walked single file through the rubble, first Selene, then Karl, then Karl, then Karl, then Ursula, this time, none of them touching. At a building where Selene recalled a movie theater once had been, she stopped. There'd been tuxedos there on the screen, she remembered. Tuxedos and dancing. But now the marquee was fallen, blending with the broken concrete of the sidewalk to block their way. Ursula pushed through to center of the mound and effortlessly lifted a girder over her head.

"No!" Karl shouted.

"That's right," said Karl. "Put that down."

"Yes," said Karl. "The old-fashioned way. Selene wants this done the old-fashioned way."

"If you insist," said Ursula, lowering the girder slowly and moving back beside her friend.

Karl dove into the pile, squeezing through the narrow path that Ursula had started. Karl tossed a small chunk of brick and concrete to Karl, who flung it on to Karl, who grunted as he caught it and then stepped outside the field of rubble to lay the clump at Selene's feet.

"A gift," said Karl. "A gift of the old-fashioned way."

Selene laughed.

"Good," called out Karl, from where he continued to work. "You keep doing that."

"There hasn't been enough of it lately," shouted Karl, struggling next to him.

Karl bounded away to rejoin himself within the forest of brick and metal and glass and continued widening the path. Pulling away the wreckage that barred the door, the three of him passed the rubble among himself like the hands of a juggler, and Selene laughed yet again, at her husband's playful love and at the sight of the entrance that she'd been remembering with such hope.

Karl bowed on the left, and Karl bowed on the right, and Karl waved her forward, and Selene responded with a curtsy, as she had seen the native Earthlings do in those movies made so long ago.

Then, before she could step forward to entwine her husband's arms with her own and go inside, she heard a deep rumbling as loud as the death of stars.

The pavement cracked open in front of Selene, and her husband dropped away and vanished into the crevasse. Before Selene could move, the front wall of the theater spilled forward, sliding into the hole after Karl and Karl and Karl. From the ragged split smoke and ash plumed upward, blinding her. She screamed, but no sound came out, her throat clogged by a harsh dust.

Ursula dove forward into the chasm, pushing debris aside and hurling rubble out of sight into the distance. Tomas returned, bringing a wind that blew the clouds of dust away. As soon as Selene could see her way clear, she stumbled down the lip of the pit to stand beside Ursula.

"Selene, you shouldn't be here. It's much too dangerous."

"Where is he? Where's my husband?"

"Selene, you don't want to see this," said Tomas. She could feel Tomas surrounding her, beginning to lift her, and as she started to be wafted away, she shrugged him off.

"Leave me be!" she said, as she saw limbs, ghostly with dust, protruding from beneath the rubble. "Karl!"

As Ursula removed the last bits of debris that were keeping Karl's broken bodies hidden, Selene threw herself alongside him and started to howl.

"This can't be," she muttered, when speech finally returned. "This is impossible. He's dead. All of him is dead."

"I don't think I can remember anyone ever dying," said Tomas.

As Selene rocked and moaned, Ursula grew once more into a larger self and cupped her friends in her hands. This time, Selene did not object as Ursula cradled them all and returned them to the flitter. Kneeling, Ursula carefully placed them inside the flitter as if arranging the figures in a doll's house. A chair rose up to greet Selene, but no pallet responded to support any of Karl's bodies until Ursula waved her shrinking hand across the floor.

"It can't be over so easily," said Selene. "Not now. Not today. This isn't how it was supposed to be."

She moved from body to body, touching a bruised cheek here, flattening out a curl of hair there. As she traced a deep gouge in one of Karl's legs, terror welled within her, terror that was then tamped down. She didn't know what would happen if she was allowed to feel such pain.

"There's nothing we can do," said Ursula, moving to her friend's side. Ursula's fingers felt colder on her arm than they ever had before. "We should leave here, Selene. Don't you think?"

"Selene?" said Tomas.

Selene could not speak. Was there anyone left who needed to hear her voice? She did not think so.

"Let's just go, Selene," said Ursula, as softly as she could. "There's nothing more for us here."

Selene could feel her friend's fingers in her hair, and she did not want to feel them.

"Go?" said Selene, struggling to keep her voice from cracking with rage. "Why should I go? Why should I go back home now? There's no reason to do anything any longer, no reason to come here and no reason to go back. If only I hadn't made us come here! If only I hadn't insisted *all* of him come here. Leave me. You go back. Just leave me."

"Why *did* you want to come here, Selene?" asked Ursula. "What was the reason? What was it all about?"

Selene looked at her husband and her husband and her husband. She stroked his smooth face and his bruised face and then had to turn away from where there was hardly any face left at all. They'd begun their day in love and ended it in death, and love would not come again.

"What was the reason?" Selene whispered. "What *was* the reason?"

It had seemed so important, back when she woke on the other side of the galaxy. Earth, and all it represented, was more than just a goal, it was the journey as well, and it had seemed dreadfully important. And now . . . now nothing was important.

"You're right," said Selene. "Let's go back. Let's go back now, and let's go back fast. And let's not talk anymore of the old-fashioned way."

"That's what I've been saying all along," said Tomas.

And as swift as the thought, Earth was gone, with no sense of a trip having been made. Selene, when she could bear to look out again through the transparent flitter walls, could see that they had arrived back outside her dome. It appeared exactly as they had left it that morning, in a prior dawn that was light-years away. She looked from the dome to her husband and back, with no idea how she could ever live in one without the other again. She would have to have the dome destroyed.

Later, after Tomas and Ursula left her alone, perhaps she would have herself destroyed as well.

But before Selene could think the dome away, a figure pressed toward her through the membrane of its walls, and as a shell tightened around the approaching form, she could see that it was Karl. She struggled to cry out, but her mind was too numb to speak before he did.

"What happened?" he asked, as he ran inside the flitter and embraced his wife while surrounded by his own dead bodies. "One moment I was clearing a path for you, and the next . . . nothing. I was cut off."

"How can you be alive?" she whispered, cradling his head in her hands. "The building fell and crushed you, all of you. . . ."

"I was going to tell you," said Karl, "but I figured that if there could be three of me, darling, why not four? There was so much work to be done around here, and I knew that once I explained, you wouldn't really mind."

"You bastard!" she shouted, and pushed him away. "How long has this been going on?"

"Only since the moment you left. As Ursula launched you all into space, I launched a new me down here."

"But I wanted to see Earth with you at my side. I *needed* to see Earth with you at my side! How could you choose to stay behind and miss that? How could you live without me? I thought you loved me!"

"But I *saw* Earth with you, Selene. I was never without you. I was there the entire time."

"I could kill you," said Selene, slapping at Karl through the tears.

"If you're going to do that," said Karl, letting her succeed in striking him a few times before catching her hands, "I'd better make sure that there are a few more of me first."

He drew her close with a single pair of arms and kissed her. Her knees buckled, and she crumpled at his feet, sobbing, laughing, howling, giggling, her emotions in full revolt against her senses.

"We should leave the two of you alone," said Ursula.

"Or however many of them there are," said Tomas. "Let's go, dear."

"You'll let us know how it goes, Karl, won't you?" said Ursula.

Selene eventually stopped trembling, and was able to realize that she and her husband were by themselves. As she let Karl help her to her feet, the flitter dissolved around them and was reabsorbed into the planet's surface. As she stared into the shadows spilling off the dry, red rocks, she realized exactly how much time had passed them by while they'd traveled through the void and explored Earth the old-fashioned way.

An entire cycle had passed. It was that time again, if she still wanted it to be that time.

They entered their dome, and she studied the view out of the bedroom's picture window. She almost thought she could see Ursula, curving through the sky like a shooting star off in the distance. Selene replayed her friend's last words in her mind, until . . .

"None of today was real, was it?" Selene whispered. "Not a moment of it."

She waited for him to reach for her, hoping that he would, hoping that he wouldn't.

"Tomas and Ursula, they were both in on it, weren't they?"

"We just wanted you to have an old-fashioned experience," said Karl. "We just wanted you to be happy, that's all. I thought you would like it."

"And I appreciate the gesture, Karl," she said. "I really do. But could you leave me alone for just a moment?"

"Are you sure?" he asked. "Is everything all right?"

"Everything is fine," she said.

Once Karl exited through a biolock, Selene sat on her side of the bed. On a small table nearby, perfectly centered, was exactly what she knew would be there: a small, blue pill just like the one that had been waiting for her the morning before, and the morning before that, and all the mornings she could still remember.

She snatched at, and choked it down quickly. Then, while thinking with terror of the old-fashioned ways, she held out a palm in wonder and supplication until a second pill appeared, and then she swallowed that one even more quickly than the first.

Kyle Meets the River

Ian McDonald

Kyle was the first to see the exploding cat. He was coming back from the compound HFBR-Mart with the slush cone—his reward for scoring a goal in the under elevens—squinted up at the sound of a construction helicopter (they were still big and marvelous and exciting) and saw the cat leap the narrow gap between the med center and Tinneman's coffee bar. He pointed to it one fraction of a second before the security men picked it up on their visors and started yelling. In an instant the compound was full of fleeing people; men and women running, parents sweeping up kids, guards sweeping their weapons this way and that as the cat, sensing it had been spotted, leaped from the roof in two bounds onto the roof of an armored Landcruiser, then dived to ground and hunted for targets. A security guard raised his gun. He must be new. Even Kyle knew not to do that. They were not really cats at all, but smart missiles that behaved like them, and if you tried to catch them or threatened them with a weapon, they would attack and blow themselves up. From the shade of the arcade he could see the look on the guard's face as he tried to get a fix on the dashing, dodging robot. Machine gun rattle. Kyle had never heard it so close. It was very exciting. Bullets

cracked all over the place, flying wild. Kyle thought
that perhaps he should hide himself behind something
solid. But he wanted to see. He had heard it so many
times before, and now here it was, on the main streets
in front of him. That cat-missile was getting really
really close. Then the guard let loose a lucky burst;
the steel cat went spinning up into the air and blew
itself up. Kyle reeled back. He had never heard anything so loud. Shrapnel cracked the case of the Coke
machine beside him into red and white stars. The security man was down but moving, scrabbling away on
his back from the blast site, and real soldiers were
arriving, and a med Hummer, and RAV air drones.
Kyle stood and stared. It was wonderful wonderful
wonderful and all for him, and there was Mom, running toward him in her flappy-hands, flappy-feet run,
coming to take it all away, snatching him up in front
of everyone and crying "Oh, what were you doing
what were you thinking are you all right all right all
right?"

"Mom," he said. "I saw the cat explode."

His name is Kyle Rubin, and he's here to build a
nation. Well, his father is. Kyle doesn't have much of
an idea of nations and nationhood, just that he's not
where he used to live, but it's okay because it's not
really all that different from the gated community,
there are a lot of folks like him, though he's not allowed to leave the compound. In here is Cantonment.
Out there is the nation that's being built. That's where
his dad goes in the armored cars, where he directs the
construction helicopters and commands the cranes
that Kyle can just see from the balcony around the
top floor of the International School. You're not allowed to go there because there are still some snipers
working, but everyone does, and Kyle can watch the
booms of the tower cranes swing across the growing
towers of the new capital.

It all fell apart, and it takes us to put it back together again, his father explained. Once there was a big country called India, with a billion and a half people in it, but they just couldn't live together, so they fell to squabbling and fighting. *Like you and Kelis's mom,* Kyle said, which made his father raise his eyebrows and look embarrassed and Mom—his mom, not Kelis's—laugh to herself. Whatever, it all fell apart, and these poor people, they need us and our know-how to put it all back together for them. And that's why we're all here, because it's families that make us strong and hopeful. And that's how you, Kyle Rubin, are building a nation. But some people don't think we should be doing that. They think it's their nation so they should build it. Some people think we're part of the problem and not part of the solution. And some people are just plain ungrateful.

Or, as Clinton in class said, the Rana's control is still weak, and there are a lot of underrepresented parties out there with big grievances and arsenals of leftover weaponry from the Sundering. Western interests are always first in the firing line. But Clinton was a smart-mouth who just repeated what he heard from his dad who had been in Military Intelligence since before there was even a Cantonment, let alone an International Reconstruction Coalition.

The nation Kyle Rubin is building is Bharat, formerly the states of Bihar, Jharkand, and half of Utter Pradesh on the Indo-Gangetic plain, and the cranes swing and the helicopters fly over the rising towers of its new capital, Ranapur.

When there weren't cats exploding, after practice Kyle would visit Salim's planet.

Before Kyle, Striker Salim had been the best forward on Team Cantonment U-11. Really he shouldn't have been playing at all because he didn't actually live within the compound. But his father was the Bharati Government's man in Cantonment, so he could pretty much do whatever he liked.

At first they had been enemies. In his second game Kyle had headed home a sweet cross from Ryan from Australia, and after that every cross floated his way. In the dressing room Striker Salim had complained to Coach Joe that the *new boy* had got all the best balls because he was a westerner and not Bharati. The wraths of dads were invoked. Coach Joe said nothing and put them on together for the game against the army kids, who imagined that being army kids was like an extra man for them. Salim on wing, Kyle in center: three three four. Cantonment beat US Army two one, one goal by Salim, the decider from a run by Salim and a rebound from the goalkeeper by Kyle, in the forty-third minute. Now, six weeks in another country later, they were inseparable.

Salim's planet was very close and easy to visit. It lived in the palmer-glove on his brown hand and could manifest itself in all manner of convenient locations: the school system, Tinneman's coffee house, Kyle's e-paper workscreen, but the best was the full proprio-ception so-new-it's-scary lighthoek (trademark) that you could put behind your ear so, fiddle it so, and it would get inside your head and open up a whole new world of sights and sounds and smells and sensations. They were so new not even the Americans had them, but Varanasi civil servants engaged on the grand task of nation building needed to use and show off the latest Bharati technology. And their sons too. The safety instructions said you weren't supposed to use it in full sensory outside because of the risk of accidents, crime, or terror, but it was safe enough in the Guy's Place up on the roof under the solar farm that was out of shot of any sniper, no matter how good or young she was.

Kyle plugged the buddy-lead into Salim's lighthoek and slipped the curl of plastic behind his ear. It had taken a while to work out the sweet spot, but now he got it first time every time. He was not supposed to use lighthoek tech. Mom's line was that it hadn't been

proved safe yet but Kyle suspected it was his father—
it was opening yourself up to evil influences to let
things inside your head like that. That was before you
even got to what he thought of the artificial evolution
game itself. Maybe if he could experience the lift out
of the Cantonment, up through the solar arrays, past
the cranes and helicopters, and see Salim's world there
in front of him—Alterre, as it was properly called, and
feel himself falling toward it through the clouds faster
than anything could possibly go to stop light as a
feather with his feet brushing the wave—tops; maybe
he would change his mind. He could smell the salt.
He could feel the wind. He could see the lifted jelly
sails of a kronkaeur fleet above the white-edged swell.

"Aw not these jellyfish guys again," said Kyle.

"No no no, this is different." Salim stood beside
him above the waves. "Look, this is really cool." He
folded his hands and leaned forward and flew across
the ocean, Kyle a heartbeat behind him. He always
thought of those Hindu gods you saw on the prayer
cards that blew into the compound from the street
shrines. His dad didn't like those either. They arrived
over the kronkaeur armada, beating through a rising
ocean on a steady breeze, topsails inflated. When the
huge, sail-powered jellyfish had appeared, Kyle had
been so excited at his first experience of a newly
evolved species that the vast, inflatable monsters had
sailed like translucent galleons through his dreams.
But all they did was raise their triangular sails and
weave their tentacles together into a huge raft-fleet
and bud off little jellies that looked like see-through
paper boats. Once the initial thrill of being part of the
global game-experiment to start life on Earth all over
again and see how it evolved differently had worn off,
Kyle found himself wishing that Salim had been given
somewhere a bit more exciting than a huge square of
ocean. An island would have been good. A bit of continent would have been better. Somewhere things
could attack each other.

"Every bit of water on Alterre was land, and every bit of land was water," Salim had said. "And they will be again. And anyway, everything eats everything out on the open ocean."

But not in a cool way, Kyle thought.

Apart from his high tech and his skill at soccer, nothing about Salim was cool. At home he would never have been Kyle's friend. Kyle would probably have beat him about a bit, he was geeky, had a big nose, couldn't get clothes right—all the wrong labels—and had no idea how to wear a beanie. He went to a weird religious school for an hour every afternoon and Fridays to the mosque down by the river steps where they burned the dead people. Really, they should not be friends at all. Ozzie Ryan, who'd been the team big one before Kyle, said it was unnatural and disloyal, and you couldn't trust them; one moment they'd be giving you presents, and the next they'd be setting you up to people out there to shoot you. Kyle knew Ozzie Ryan was just jealous.

"Now, isn't this so cool?" Salim said, his toes brushing the wave-tops. The sculpted upper surfaces of the great ocean-going jellies between the inflatable booms that held out the sails were bloated with bubbles, visibly swelling and bulging as Kyle floated around to a closer angle. Bigger, bigger, now the size of soccer balls, now the size of beach balls, stretching the skin until it split with a gush of acid-smelling liquid, and a host of balloons dashed into the air. They rose in a mass, tethered to their parents by woven strands of tentacles, rubbing and bouncing and rebounding from each other in the wind. They were higher than the sail tops now and Kyle could make out detail; each balloon carried a cluster of stingers and translucent claspers beneath its domed canopy. Blue eyes were grouped in threes and fours. One by one their tethers parted and the balloon-jellies sprang up into the air and were whisked away on the sea breeze. All around him the flotilla was bubbling and bursting into spasms of balloons; they soared up around him, some still tangled together by the tentacles. Kyle found himself laughing as he watched them stream up into the sky until they vanished against the fast-moving clouds. It was definitely undeniably way way way cool.

"It's a completely new way of reproducing," Salim said. "It's a new species!" Kyle knew what that meant. By the rules of Alterre, played out on eleven million computers around the globe, whoever found a new species gave it his or her name. "They're not kron-kaeurs any more. I went and registered them; they're Mansooris!"

Gunfire on Monday Tuesday Wednesday. They were working up to something; that was the pattern of it. (*Dad Dad who are they this time, is it the Hindus?* but his father had eyes and ears and arms only for Mom, full of thanks and praise to have him safe home from that fearsome city.) Cantonment went to orange alert, but security was still unprepared for the ferocity of the attack. Bombers attacked twelve Western-owned targets simultaneously across Old and New Varanasi. The twelfth and final device was a car bomb driven at full speed across the green zone, impervious to automatic fire, its driver dead or ecstatic to die. Close-defense robots uncoiled from their silos and leaped, nanodiamond blades unsheathed, but the bombers had recced Cantonment's weaknesses well. Slashed, gashed, leaking oil and fuel, engine dead but still rolling under a heaving cancer of robots trying to cocoon it in impact-foam, the car rammed the inner gate and blew up.

On the soccer pitch the referee had heard the general alert siren, judged the distance to the changing room, and ordered everyone to lie flat in the goal. Kyle had just wrapped his arms around his head— Day One, Lesson One—when the boom lifted him off the ground by the belly and punched every breath of wind out of him. For a moment he thought he had

gone deaf; then the sounds of sirens and RAV air-
drones pushed through the numbness until he was sitting on the grass beside Salim seemingly at the center
of a vast spiral of roar. It was much bigger than the
exploding cat. A column of smoke leaned toward the
south. Hummers were rushing past, security men on
foot dodging between them. The soccer net was full
of chunks of blast-foam and scraps of wire and fragments of shattered plastic robot shell and warning
signs in three languages that this was a restricted area
with security authorized to use deadly force. A shard
of nanodiamond antipersonnel blade was embedded
in the left upright. The referee stood up, took off his
shirt, and wrapped it around the hand wedged under
the crossbar.

"Would you look at that?" Kyle said.

There was a long green smear down the front of his
freshly laundered soccer shirt.

"Salim's always welcome here," Mom called from
the kitchen where she was blitzing smoothies. "Just
make sure he calls home to let them know he's all
right the moment the network comes back up. Now
promise you'll do that."

Of course they did and of course they didn't, and
the smoothies stood there forgotten and warming on
the worktop while Mom edged about folding under-
wear and pillowcases but really keeping an eye on
the rolling news. She was worried. Kyle knew that.
Cantonment was locked down and would be until Coalition and Bharati forces had resecured the Green
Zone; that was the way it was, Kyle had learned that.
Locked down was locked out for Dad, and the SKYIndia hovercams were still showing towers of black plastic smoke and ambulances being walked through the
crowds of lost people and burned-out cars by Bharati
policemen. The reporters were saying there were casualties, but they were also saying that the network
wasn't fully restored, and that was why he couldn't

call; if there had been Western casualties, they would
have said straight away because dead Bharatis didn't
count, and anyway, it was inconceivable that anything
could happen to Kyle's dad. No, in situations like this
you kept your head down and got on with things while
you waited for the call, so he didn't trouble Mom and
fetched the smoothies himself from the kitchen and
took them to join Salim in his world.

On the house smartsilk screen you couldn't get that
full-sensory drop from orbit or the sense of walking
like God over the water, but in the house, even with
Mom in her distracted fold-laundry state, it wasn't
smart to use the buddy-lead. Anyway, Kyle didn't
want to give her more to worry about. Three days in
Alterre was more like three million years: still water
water water whichever way he turned the point-of-
view, but the mansooris had evolved. High above the
blue Atlantic, fleets of airships battled.

"Whoa," said Kyle Rubin and Salim Mansoori.

In three days the jellyfish balloons had become vast
sky-going gasbags, blimp creatures, translucent airships the size of the Boeing troop transports that
brought supplies and workers in to the secure end of
Varanasi airport. Their bodies were ridged like the
condom Kyle had been shown by the bike rack behind
the school; light rippled over them and broke into
rainbows as the air-jellies maneuvered. For this was
battle, no doubt about it. This was hot war. The sky-
jellyfish trailed long clusters of tentacles beneath them,
many trailing in the water, their last connection with
their old world. But some ended in purple stingers,
some in long stabbing spines, some in barbs, and these
the airships wielded as weapons. The air-medusas
raised or lowered sail flaps to tack and maneuver into
striking positions. Kyle saw one blimp, body blotched
with black sting-weals, vent gas from nose and tail and
drop out of combat. In a tangle of slashing and par-
rying tentacles Kyle watched a fighting blimp tear a
gash the length of an Army hummer down an oppo-

nent's flank with its scimitar-hook. The mortally wounded blimp vented glittering dust, crumpled, folded in half in the middle, and plunged into the sea, where it split like a thrown water balloon. The sea instantly boiled with almkvists, spear-fast scavengers all jaw and speed.

"Cool," both boys said together.

"Hey now, didn't you promise you'd let your folks know as soon as the network was up?" said Mom, standing behind them. "And Kyle, you know your dad doesn't like you playing that game."

But she wasn't mad. She couldn't be mad. Dad was safe, Dad had called in, Dad would be home soon. It was all in the little tremble in her voice, the way she leaned over between them to look at the screen, the smell of perfume just dabbed on. You know these things.

It had been close. Kyle's dad called him in to show him the rolling news and point out where his company car had been when the bombers hit the escort hummers.

"There's next to no protection in those things," he said over jerky, swooping flash-cut images of black smoke boiling out of yellow flames and people standing and shouting and not knowing what to do, pictures taken from a passerby's palmer. "They used a drone RAV; I saw something go past the window just before it hit. They were aiming for the soldiers, not for us."

"It was a suicide attack here," Kyle said.

"Some *karsevak* group claimed responsibility, some group no one's ever heard of before. Fired everything off in one shooting match."

"Don't they go straight into a state of *moksha* if they blow themselves up in Varanasi?"

"That's what they believe, son. Your soul is released from the wheel of reincarnation. But I still can't help feeling that this was the final throw. Things are getting better. The Ranas are taking control. People can see

the difference we're making. I do feel we've turned
the corner on this."

Kyle loved it when his dad talked military, though
he was really a structural engineer.

'So Salim got home safe."

Kyle nodded.

"That's good." Kyle heard his father sigh in the way
that men do when they're supposed to talk about
things they don't want to. "Salim's a good kid, a good
friend." Another intake of breath. Kyle waited for it
shape into a *but*.

"Kyle, you know, that game. Well . . ."

Not a *but*, a *well*.

"Well, I know it's real educational, and a lot of
people play it and enjoy it and get a lot out of it, but
it's not really right. I mean, it's not accurate. It claims
it's an evolution simulation, and it is as far as it goes.
But if you think about it, really it's just following rules
laid down by someone else, All that code was programmed by someone else; so really, it's evolution inside a bigger framework that's been deliberately
designed. But they don't tell you, Kyle, and that's dis-
honest; it's pretending to be something it's not. And
that's why I don't like it—because it isn't honest about
the truth. I know that whatever I say, what you do
with Salim is your thing, but you're not to play it here,
in the house. And it's good you've got a good friend
here—I remember when Kelis was your age when we
were in the Gulf, she had a really good friend, a Cana-
dian girl—but it would be good if you had a few more
friends from your own background. Okay? Now, how
about Wrestle Smackdown on cable?"

The referee had gone down with a head-butt to the
nuts in the first thirty seconds, so it was only when
the decibel count exceeded the mundane Varanasi
traffic roar that security heads-upped, guns-downed,
and came running. A guardwoman in full color-smear
combats and smart visor locked her arms around Kyle

and hauled him out of the steel-cage match into which the under-eleven practice had collapsed.

"I'll sue you I'll sue the ass off you, your children will end up living in a cardboard box, let go of me," Kyle yelled. The Security woman hauled.

It was a full fight—boys, girls, supporters, cheerleaders. At the bottom of the dogpile, Striker Salim and Ozzie Ryan. Security hauled them off each other and returned the snoopy RAV drones that flocked to any unusual action to their standby roosts. Parameds rushed to the scene. There was blood, there were bruisings and grazings, there were torn clothes and black eyes. There were lots and lots of tears but no contusions, no concussions, no breaks.

Then the gitmoization.

Coach Joe: Okay, so want to tell me what that was about?

Ozzie Ryan: He started it

Striker Salim: Liar! You started it.

Coach Joe: I don't care who started it. I want to know what it was about.

Ozzie Ryan: He's the liar. His people just lie all the time; they don't have a word for the truth.

Striker Salim: Ah! Ah! That's such a lie too.

Ozzie Ryan: See? You can't trust them. He's a spy for them, it's true; before he came here, they never got in; since he came, there's been things happening almost every day. He's a spy, and he's telling them all ways to get in and kill us because he thinks we're all animals and going to hell anyway.

Coach Joe: Jesus. Kyle, what happened?

Kyle Rubin: I don't know, I didn't see anything, I just heard this noise like, and when I looked over, they were on the ground tearing lumps out of each other.

Striker Salim: That is so not true . . . I cannot believe you said that. You were there, you heard what he said.

Kyle Rubin: I didn't hear everything, I just heard like shouting. . . .

Gitmoization Part 2

Kyle's dad: Coach Joe called me, but I'm not going to bawl you out. I think there's been enough of that already. I'm disappointed, but I'm not going to bawl you out. Just one thing: Did Ryan call Salim something?

Kyle Rubin: (mumble)

Kyle's dad: Son, did Ryan use a racist term to Salim?

Kyle Rubin: (twisting foot)

Kyle's dad: I thought Salim was your friend. Your best friend. I think if someone had done something to my best friend, doesn't matter who he is, what he is, I'd stand up for him.

Kyle Rubin: He said Salim was a diaper-head curry-nigger and they were all spies, and Salim was just standing there, so I went in there and popped him, Ryan I mean, and he just went for Salim, not me, and then everyone was piling on with Ryan and Salim at the bottom, and they were all shouting curry-nigger-lover curry-nigger-lover at me and trying to get me too, and then the security came in.

At the end of it two things were certain: Soccer was suspended for one month, and when it did come back, Salim would not be playing, never would be again. Cantonment was not safe for Bharatis.

He was trapped, a traffic island castaway. Marooned on an oval of concrete in Varanasi's never-ebbing torrent of traffic by the phatphat driver when he saw Kyle fiddling in his lap with pogs.

"Ey, you, out here, get out, trying to cheat, damn *gora*."

"What, here? But—?"

Out onto this tiny traffic island, twenty centimeters in front of him and twenty centimeters behind him, on one side a tall man in a white shirt and black pants and on the other a fat woman in a purple sari who smelled of dead roses. And the phatphat, the little yellow-and-black plastic bubble that looked/sounded like a hornet, throbbed away into the terrifying traffic.

"You can't do this, my dad's building this country!"

The man and the woman turned to stare. Stares everywhere, every instant from the moment he slipped out of the back of the Hi-Lux at the phatphat stand. They had been eager for his money then, *Hey sir, hey sahb, good clean cab, fast fast, straight there no detours, very safe safest phatphat in Varanasi.* How was he to know that the cheap, light cardboard pogs were money only inside the Cantonment? And now here he was on this traffic island, no way forward, no way back, no way through the constant movement of trucks, buses, cream-colored Marutis, mopeds, phatphats, cycle-rickshaws, cows, everything roaring ringing hooting yelling as it tried to find its true way while avoiding everything else. People were walking through that, just stepping out in the belief that the traffic would steer around them; the man in the white shirt, there he went, the woman in the purple sari *come on boy, come with me*, he couldn't, he daren't, and there she went, and now there were people piling up behind him, pushing him pushing pushing pushing him closer to the curb, out in that killing traffic. . . .

Then the phatphat came through the mayhem, klaxon buzzing, weaving a course of grace and chaos, sweeping in to the traffic island. The plastic door swiveled up and there, there, was Salim.

"Come on come on."

Kyle bounded in, the door scissored down, and the driver hooted off into Varanasi's storm of wheels.

"Good thing I was looking for you," Salim said, tapping the lighthoek coiled behind his ear. "You can find anyone with these. What happened?" Kyle showed him the Cantonment pogs. Salim's eyes went wide. "You really haven't ever been outside, have you?"

Escaping from Cantonment was easier than anything. Everyone knew they were only looking for people coming in, not going out, so all Kyle had to do was slip into the back of the pickup while the driver bought a mochaccino to go at Tinneman's. He even peeked out from under the tarpaulin as the inner gate closed because he wanted to see what the bomb damage was like. The robots had taken away all the broken masonry and metal spaghetti, but he could see the steel reinforcing rods through the shattered concrete block work and the black scorch marks over the inner wall. It was so interesting and Kyle was staring so hard that he only realized he was out of Cantonment entirely, in the street, the alien street, when he saw the trucks, buses, cream-colored Marutis, mopeds, phatphats, cycle-rickshaws, cows close behind the pickup and felt the city roar surge over him.

"So, where do you want to go then?" Salim asked. His face was bright and eager to show Kyle his wonderful wonderful city. This was a Salim Kyle had never seen before; Salim not-in-Cantonment, Salim in-his-own-place, Salim-among-his-own-people. This Mansoori seemed alien to Kyle. He was not sure he liked him. "There's the NewBharatSabhaholydeerofSarnathDoctor SampunananandcricketgroundBuddhiststupaRamnagar FortVishwanathTempleJantarMantar. . . ."

Too much too much Kyle's head was going round all the people, all the people, the one thing he never saw, never noticed from the rooftop lookout; under all the helicopters and cranes and military RAV drones, there were people.

"River," he gasped. "The river, the big steps."

"The ghats. The best thing. They're cool." Salim spoke to the driver in a language Kyle had never heard from his mouth before. It did not sound like Salim at all. The driver waggled his head in that way that you thought was *no* until you learned better and threw the phatphat around a big traffic circle with a huge pink concrete statue of Ganesh to head away from the glass towers of Ranapur into the old city.

Flowers. There were garlands of yellow flowers at the elephant god's feet, little smoking smudges of incense, strange strings of chillies and limes, and a man with big dirty ash-gray dreadlocks, a man with his lips locked shut with fishing hooks.

"The man, look at the man . . ." Kyle wanted to shout, but that wonder/horror was behind him, a dozen more unfolding on every side as the phatphat hooted down ever narrower, ever darker, ever busier streets. "An elephant, there's an elephant and that's a robot and those people, what are they carrying, that's a body, that's like a dead man on a stretcher oh man . . ." He turned to Salim. He wasn't scared now. There were no bodies behind him, squeezing him, pushing him into fear and danger. It was just people, everywhere just people, working out how to live. "Why didn't they let me see this?"

The phatphat bounced to a stop.

"This is where we get out, come on, come on."

The phatphat was wedged in an alley between a clot of cycle rickshaws and a Japanese delivery truck. Nothing on wheels could pass, but still the people pressed by on either side. Another dead man passed, handed high on his stretcher over the heads of the crowd. Kyle ducked instinctively as the shadow of the corpse passed over the dome of the phatphat; then the doors flew up, and he stepped out into the side of a cow. Almost Kyle punched the stupid, baggy thing, but Salim grabbed him, shouted, "Don't touch the cow, the cow is special, like sacred." Shout was the only possible conversation here. Grab the only way not to get separated. Salim dragged Kyle by the wrist to a booth in a row of plastic-canopied market stalls where a bank of chill-cabinets chugged. Salim bought two Limkas and showed the stallholder a Cantonment pog, which he accepted for novelty value. Again the hand on the arm restrained Kyle.

"You have to drink it here. There's a deposit."

So they leaned their backs against the tin bar and

watched the city pass and drank their Limkas from
the bottle, which would have had Kyle's mom screaming germs bacteria viruses infections, and felt like two
very very proper gentlemen. In a moment's lull in the
street racket Kyle heard his palmer call. He hauled it
out of his pants pocket, a little ashamed because everyone else had a newer better brighter cleverer
smaller one than him, and saw, as if she knew what
dirty thing he had done, that it was his mom calling.
He stared at the number, the jingly tune, the little
smiley animation. Then he thumbed the off button
and sent them all to darkness.

"Come on." He banged his empty bottle down on
the counter. "Let's see this river then."

In twenty steps, he was there, so suddenly, so huge
and bright Kyle forgot to breathe. The narrow alley,
the throng of people, opened up into painful light—
light in the polluted yellow sky, light from the tiers of
marble steps that descended to the river, and light
from the river itself, wider and more dazzling than he
had ever imagined, white as a river of milk. And people: The world could not hold so many people, crowd-
ing down the steps to the river in their colored clothes
and colored shoes, jammed together under the tilted
wicker umbrellas to talk and deal and pray, people in
the river itself, waist deep in the water, holding up
handfuls of the water, and the water glittering as it
fell through their fingers, praying, washing—washing
themselves, washing their clothes, washing their children and their sins. Then the boats: the big hydrofoil
seeking its way to dock through the little darting row-
boats, the pilgrim boats making the crossing from
Ramnagar, rowers standing on their sterns pushing at
their oars, the tourist boats with their canopies, the
kids in inflated tractor tires paddling around scaveng-
ing for river scraps, down to the bobbing saucers of
butter-light woven from mango leaves that the people
set adrift on the flow. Vision by vision the Ganga revealed itself to Kyle. Next he became aware of the

buildings: the guesthouses and hotels and havelis
shouldering up to the steps, the ridiculous pink water
towers, the many domes of the mosque and the golden
spires of the temples and little temples down at the
river leaning into the silt; the arcades and jetties and
galleries and across the river, beyond the yellow sand
and the black, ragged tents of the holy men, the chim-
neys and tanks and pipes of the chemical and oil
plants, all flying the green white and orange wheel-
banners of Bharat.

"Oh," Kyle said. "Oh man." And: "Cool."

Salim was already halfway down the steps.

"Come on."

"Is it all right? Am I allowed?"

"Everyone is allowed. Come on, let's get a boat."

A boat. People didn't do things like that, but here
they were, settling onto the seat as the boatman
pushed out, a kid not that much older than Kyle himself with teeth that would never be allowed inside
Cantonment, yet Kyle felt jealous of him, with his boat
and his river and the people all around and a life
without laws or needs or duties. He sculled them
through floating butter-candles—*diyas*, Salim explained to Kyle—past the ghat of the *sadhus*, all bare-
ass naked and skinny as famine, and the ghat where
people beat their clothes against rock washing platforms and the ghat where the pilgrims landed, pushing
each other into the water in their eagerness to touch
the holy ground of Varanasi, and the ghat of the
buffalos—*where where?* Kyle asked and Salim pointed
out their nostrils and black, back-curved horns just
sticking up out of the water. Kyle trailed his hand in
the water, and when he pulled it in, it was covered in
golden flower petals. He lay back on the seat and
watched the marble steps flow past and beyond them
the crumbling, mold-stained waterfront buildings and
beyond them the tops of the highest towers of New
Varanasi and beyond them the yellow clouds, and he
knew that even when he was a very old man, maybe

forty or even more, he would always remember this day and the color of this light and the sound of the water against the hull.

"You got to see this!" Salim shouted. The boat was heading in to shore now through the tourists and the souvenir boats and a slick of floating flower garlands. Fires burned on the steps, the marble was blackened with trodden ashes, half-burned wood lapped at the water's edge. There were other things among the coals: burned bones. Men stood thigh deep in the water, panning it with wide wicker baskets.

"They're Doms, they run the burning ghats. They're actually untouchable, but they're very rich and powerful because they're the only ones who can handle the funerals," said Salim. "They're sifting the ashes for gold."

The burning ghats. The dead place. These fires, these piles of wood and ash, were dead people, Kyle thought. This water beneath the boat was full of dead people. A funeral procession descended the steps to the river. The bearers pushed the stretcher out into the water, a man with a red cord around his shoulder poured water over the white shroud. He was very thorough and methodical about it; he gave the dead body a good washing. The river boy touched his oars, holding his boat in position. The bearers took the body up to a big bed of wood and set the whole thing on top. A very thin man in a white robe and a head so freshly shaved it looked pale and sick piled wood on top of it.

"That's the oldest son," Salim said. "It's his job. These are rich people. It's real expensive to get a proper pyre. Most people use the electric ovens. Of course, we get properly buried like you do."

It was all very quick and casual. The man in white poured oil over the wood and the body, picked up a piece of lit wood, and almost carelessly touched it to the side. The flame guttered in the river wind, almost went out; then smoke rose up and out of the smoke, flame. Kyle watched the fire take hold. The people stood back. No one seemed very concerned, even when the pile of burning wood collapsed, and a man's head and shoulders lolled out of the fire.

That is a burning man, Kyle thought. He had to tell himself that. It was hard to believe, all of it was hard to believe; there was nothing that connected to any part of his world, his life. It was fascinating, but it was like a wildlife show on the sat; he was close enough to smell the burning flesh, but it was too strange, too alien. It did not touch him. He could not believe. Kyle thought, *This is the first time Salim has seen this too.* But it was very very cool.

A sudden crack, a pop a little louder than the gunfire Kyle heard in the streets every day, but not much.

"That is the man's skull bursting," Salim said. "It's supposed to mean his spirit is free."

Then a noise that had been in the back of Kyle's head moved to the front of his perception: engines, aircraft engines. Tilt-jet engines. Loud, louder than he had ever heard them before, even when he watched them lifting off from the field in Cantonment. The mourners were staring; the Doms turned from their ash-panning to stare too. The boat boy stopped rowing; his eyes were round. Kyle turned in his seat and saw something wonderful and terrible and strange: a tilt-jet in Coalition markings, moving across the river toward him, yes *him*, so low, so slow, it was as if it were tiptoeing over the water. For a moment he saw himself, toes scraping the stormy waters of Alterre. River traffic fled from it; its down-turned engines sent flows of white across the green water. The boat boy scrabbled for his oars to get away, but there was now a second roar from the ghats. Kyle turned back to see Coalition troopers in full combat armor and visors pouring down the marble steps, pushing mourners out of their way, scattering wood and bones and ash. Mourners and Doms shouted their outrage; fists were raised. The soldiers lifted their weapons in answer.

The boat boy looked around him in terror as the thunder of the jet engines grew louder and louder until Kyle felt it become part of him, and when he looked around, he saw the big machine, morphing between city and river camouflage, turn, unfold landing gear, and settle into the water. The boat rocked violently, Kyle would have been over the side had not Salim hauled him back. Jet-wash blew human ash along the ghats. A single oar floated, lost down the stream. The tilt-jet stood knee-deep in the shallow water. It unfolded its rear ramp. Helmets. Guns. Between them, a face Kyle recognized, his dad, shouting wordlessly through the engine roar. The soldiers on the shore were shouting, the people were shouting, everything was shout shout roar. Kyle's dad beckoned, to me to me. Shivering with fear, the boat boy stood up, thrust his sole remaining oar into the water like a punt pole, and pushed toward the ramp. Gloved hands seized him, dragged Kyle out of the rocking boat up the ramp. Everyone was shouting, shouting. Now the soldiers on the shore were beckoning to the boat boy and Salim, this way this way, the thing is going to take off, get out of there.

His dad buckled Kyle into the seat as the engine roar peaked again. He felt the world turn, then the river was dropping away beneath him. The tilt-jet banked. Kyle looked out the window. There was the boat, being pulled in to shore by the soldiers, and Salim standing in the stern staring up at the aircraft, a hand raised: Good-bye.

Gitmo part three.

Dad did the don't-you-know-the-danger-you-were-in/trouble-you-caused/expense-you-cost bit.

"It was a full-scale security alert. Full-scale alert. We thought you'd been kidnapped. We honestly thought you'd been kidnapped. Everyone thought that, everyone was praying for you. You'll write them, of course. Proper apologies, handwritten. Why did you turn your palmer off? One call, one simple call, and it would have been all right, we wouldn't have minded. Lucky we can track them even when they're switched off. Salim's in big trouble too. You know, this is a major incident, it's in all the papers, and not just here in Cantonment. It's even made SKYIndia News. You've embarrassed us all, made us look very, very stupid. Sledgehammer to crack a nut. Salim's father has had to resign. Yes, he's that ashamed."

But Kyle knew his dad was burning with joy and relief to have him back.

Mom was different. Mom was the torturer.

"It's obvious we can't trust you. Well, of course you're grounded, but really, I thought you knew what it was like here. I thought you understood that this is not like anywhere else, that if we can't trust each other, we can really put one another in danger. Well, I can't trust you here, and your dad, well, he'll have to give it up. We'll have to quit and go back home, and the Lord knows, he won't get a job anything close to what we have here. We'll have to move to a smaller house in a less good area, I'll have to go out to work again. And you can forget about that Salim boy, yes, forget all about him. You won't be seeing him again."

Kyle cried himself out that night in bed, cried himself into great shivering, shuddering sobs empty of everything except the end of the world. Way, way later he heard the door open.

"Kyle?" Mom's voice. He froze in his bed. "I'm sorry. I was upset. I said things I shouldn't have said. You did bad, but all the same, your dad and I think you should have this."

A something was laid beside his cheek. When the door had closed, Kyle put on the light. The world could turn again. It would get better. He tore open the plastic bubblecase. Coiled inside, like a beckoning finger, like an Arabic letter, was a lighthoek. And in the morning, before school, before breakfast, before anything but the pilgrims going to the river, he went up onto the roof at Guy's Place, slipped the 'hoek behind his ear, pulled his palmer-glove over his fingers, and went soaring up through the solar farm and the water tanks, the cranes and the construction helicopters and the clouds, up toward Salim's world.

Forbearing Planet

Michael Moorcock

Prospero Pidgeon had seen too many intelligent planets in his time not to recognize this new one. He was, after all, the leading expert. When he arrived, accompanied by his mechanical sidekick Robert Robot, one sniff was enough to tell him what was going on. Not only was Temptation II a sentient biosphere roughly the size of Earth, it enjoyed a certain mild malevolence toward its human population that at any time might flare into outright hatred, which, of course, would be the end of them. By the time he had landed, employing Robert's analytic processors, Professor Pidgeon had already determined the existence of three previous intelligent species that had died in various dramatic ways after Temptation II had taken against them.

"You can't just keep trashing and abandoning planets," Prospero pointed out to President Pushof, the charming elected head of Temptation II's legislative assembly. And before Mrs. Pushof could interject, he raised a restraining hand. "Honestly, a few green wheelies and a rather reluctantly implemented recycling program are little more than a gesture. I've seen altogether too much of this, Mrs. President. The fact is that your aerocars alone, not to mention your rocket services, are adding more greenhouse gasses to the atmosphere than all the trucks and SUVs of our ancient and much mourned home planet. Then there are your refineries . . ."

"The source of our wealth," reiterated the president. "Our very livelihood."

"And, ironically, the likely cause of your ultimate destruction." Pidgeon pursed his kindly lips. "After all, it's not as if history hasn't shown . . ."

"Bunk!" exclaimed the Leader of the World. "Inconvenient bunk. If we sat around all day discussing precedents and past mistakes, there would be no progress at all. Now listen, professor, we're not unreasonable people, and we know you guys mean well. I, too, am a lover of the wilderness. Indeed, it's fair to say I've created a few in my time. But we have to offset a love of nature against the needs of a world that must expand economically to survive. We have less than five percent unemployment on Temptation II unless you count the native population already on welfare, who are notoriously workshy and live entirely thanks to the beneficence of the good-natured taxpayer. Bring in the protocols you propose, and the planet would be plunged into fiscal chaos. Everyone knows that the moment unemployment rises above twenty percent, radical socialism gets into the air, and any chance of a decent conservative party keeping power goes down the drain. Don't blame me for that, professor. Blame populist democracy. I didn't invent populist democracy now, did I?"

And with the air of a woman who had scored an unanswerable point in the great debate of life, she sat back in her massive presidential chair and lit a manly stogie.

"Well, ma'am," replied Prospero Pidgeon. "I have offered you my advice. Unlike our dearly mourned home world, Temptation II is unlikely to let herself die, I would guess, without at least a little resistance."

"We know what to do with resistance, radicals, and revolutionary councils," President Pushof assured him. "We drill 'em full of holes." And she grinned the grin that had won her votes but failed to impress Professor Pidgeon, who was, if anything, overfamiliar with the joke and the expression. He sighed.

Wrong answer, said his robot sidekick in his warm but still evidently artificial voice. *Eliminate. Eliminate.*

"Do what?" The president's jaw dropped.

"He's referring to the elimination of greenhouse gasses," explained Pidgeon "As a being producing no poisons, nor requiring any energy but sunlight, Robert is a little pious about such things."

"No doubt he supports abortion and teen pregnancy, " murmured Pushof in disgust. "It's people like your assistant, professor, who are taking jobs away from honest Temptationonians. On our planet, we have a name for clones and metallic contraptions pretending to be human." She frowned, evidently forgetting what that name was.

"Well, ma'am," said Professor Pidgeon, putting on his hat, "I'm sorry you see fit not to be persuaded, but if you decide not to take my warning about the course you have plotted towards total disaster . . ."

"We are destroying nothing but pessimism and poverty," declared President Pushof with a cold, condescending grin. She smoothed back her blue-rinsed perm. "You can take that message back to your United Planets, and if they don't like it, tell them to shove it up their collective commie craters. Good afternoon."

"I didn't quite mean that you were going to be doing the destroying," declared Pidgeon. "I was referring to two possibilities. Gaia, of course, is one. The other is popularly known as the Beast from the Id. My own adopted planet . . ."

"All our beasts are alive and well and indeed happy with their situation, even in hunting season."

"Indeed, ma'am." Prospero Pidgeon gave a sign to Robert Robot and the two beings left the presidential office.

And so Professor Pidgeon returned to his office at the United Planets HQ on New Peoria, saddened but helpless to take any further action, since his brief was only to advise, and he had no powers to enforce. Besides, there were so many planets in their sector of the galaxy that it would not make a serious dent in anyone's economy should Temptation II disappear from the star chart tomorrow. But, as he saw it, one by one and little by little, it was a shame to see such massive intelligence wasted on bloody revenge, the creation of aggressive illusions, and the general psyching out of people who, while not exactly thoughtful or respectful about their environment, could easily have learned, in his opinion, to accommodate their sentient world so that both might benefit.

He made a note to revisit Temptation II if the opportunity arose and the planet survived and then turned his attention to the pressing matter of Disneyworld IX, which had built a roller coaster so high that it was in danger of knocking the planet's small moon out of orbit. The Disneyworlders were justifiably very proud of their engineering achievement, the first to dip in and out of the surrounding void, and needed advice on how to incorporate the satellite into the ride itself. No killjoy, Professor Pidgeon was able to make some useful suggestions, and he and Robert were both offered free lifetime memberships by a grateful corporation, which, of course, they were forced to turn down, though Robert did accept a small Buzz Lightyear commemorative rocket, which he placed in a specially made showcase in his chest. Professor Pidgeon wondered at the process that made most people in the entertainment business more tolerant and liberal than those who chose other means of earning their livings.

So time passed, and no fresh news was heard from Temptation II.

Eventually, Professor Pidgeon, leafing through his records one day, began to wonder how the planet had fared since his last visit. As far as he could tell, it was still there, though he couldn't speak for the population. Since he would be passing by that sector on his way to help in the psychological rehabilitation of a sentient world that had inexplicably developed some anxiety attacks, coupled with a delusion that it was the Last of the Ononos, a spherical people of savage, cannibalistic tendencies who had once been the sworn enemies of the late Lord Greystoke, more popularly known as Tarzan of the Apes. He sent a voicemail to the government of Temptation II informing them that he planned a visit, but he received no reply.

Naturally, Professor Pidgeon feared the worst. The human population and what remained of the earlier inhabitants had no doubt been savagely destroyed by a planet that could stand no further abuse of its resources. Through violent delusions and their own anger turned back on them they had doubtless been destroyed. As he climbed into his ethermobile and conscientiously fixed his safety belt, he sighed with regret at the anticipated scenes of horror he would doubtless have to log as part of his job.

The appointment with the deluded would-be Onono was concluded not without difficulty. Professor Pidgeon provided the necessary psychiatric attention together with a mixture of carefully injected antianxiety gasses into the planet's atmosphere, combined with some expert therapy in which he was able to convince the planet that merely because it was spherical did not make it savage and fond of human flesh. It was touch and go for a while, since the planet had already ingested several thousand inhabitants of its northern hemisophere. However, not being entirely sure what cannibal sentient spheres did with their victims, the planet had taken them into a large underground cave system near its equator, where they were found shaken but unharmed, having lived for some months on a kind of edible moss, both nutritious and tasty, resembling a deep green popcorn. They realized they could successfully cultivate it and sell it to their nearest neighbors on the planet Vega, whose principles forbade them from eating any kind of flesh or fleshly products. The Onono planet also began to enjoy some much-needed self-esteem, having been convinced that its natural excrusions were contributing not only to the well-being of its inhabitants, who were rapidly developing a taste for the moss themselves, but that its fresh optimism and amiability were allowing it to get on better with a number of sentient shrubs and small trees that hitherto had been something of an embarrassment to it. Meanwhile, the Onanists, as they began to call themselves, were willingly being converted into Vegans by their neighbors. The planet in fact began to experiment with producing different flavors and varieties of the moss, while the Ononists in turn devoted a good-sized proportion of their income to importing special nutrients that their host world found especially delectable. This happy conclusion to the problem took the best part of a year to establish so that it was rather later than he had expected before Professor Pidgeon stopped by on Temptation II.

He found not the wasteland he had feared, but rather a thriving, busy community, still using aerocars and other vehicles, admittedly of more recent design, while the planet was no longer giving off the threatening signals Professor Pidgeon had detected earlier. There was a busy volume of traffic entering the planet's stations from all over this sector of the galaxy. Instead of filthy factories belching out pollutants threatening the health of the planet and her inhabitants, now all of Temptation II's cities were filled with colorful transparent neon-glowing temples, so it seemed, to a new religion. Nowhere were there to be seen the signs of disease and destruction Pidgeon and Robert had initially detected. Seeking out the former President Pushof, who now bore the rather mysterious title of Producer Pushof, he requested an explanation for the phenomenon.

"I have to admit to you, Mrs. Pushof, that I had fully expected to discover this planet undergoing its fourth period of complete devastation. Instead, though I am no enthusiast for this essentially urban environment you have developed, I discover not only a rather cheerful population, but a planet that is clearly at one with itself and its inhabitants."

Producer Pushof had grown sleek. Her face had been lifted, and her hair looked naturally wavy, blond, and vibrant. She was, Professor Pidgeon was forced to admit, rather more attractive, indeed happier and less defensively smug, than when he had last seen her. Indeed, she had lost many of her earlier conservative attitudes. "And I have to admit in turn, professor, that you made a good point about depleting our resources, relying on fossil fuels, polluting our atmosphere, and so forth. In recent times we have developed means of transport that depend increasingly on natural sunlight, wind power, and, of course, electricity produced in a number of environment-friendly ways. You'll note the elegance and quietness of our transport systems, many of which are now free to the public, since we abandoned the economy that was threatened by any form of social institutions. Our health care, for instance, is now the best in the system and is free at point of need, thus cutting down on paperwork and the corruption that comes from private insurance companies that are allowed to own hospital facilities as well as drug companies. This in turn releases our citizens from fear of losing jobs attached to private health insurance, allowing them greater flexibility in employment and making them no longer frightened of challenging any abuses of their contracts with their employers." Producer Pushof continued in this vein for some time, with the air of a recent convert, until Professor Pidgeon was forced to interrupt her.

"But how was such a change of society, as well as a change of heart, brought about so quickly ?" he asked.

"By converting from producing industrial materials to moving into a specific area of the service sector," she replied.

The jargon defeated him for a moment, and seeing his confusion she smiled. "We discovered that there's no business like show business. Well," she almost simpered, "Tempty did . . ."

"Tempty?"

"Temptation II. Our world. You were quite right, of course, about the planet's sentience and growing anger with our uses of her resources and also about her ability to create the most alarming illusions. We had a very disagreeable time of it, in fact, shortly after you left. Horrible invisible beasts stalking citizens, hurling them into chasms, tearing them limb from limb, and so on. It certainly shook us up."

"You stopped raping the planet?"

She looked disapproving for a moment. "I wouldn't put it in quite such melodramatic terms, professor. But we did decide that perhaps we should start thinking rather differently. I read your work, specifically that relating to your adopted home world. I realized that you were right, and all the negative thoughts emanating from our people were being turned against us. So we decided it was time we thought positively. As we did so, we realized that we had many different kinds of dreams, many stories to tell, as had the planet herself. By channeling all these positive ideas, we learned to create quite elaborate illusions. We got rid of the roaring and rending beasts from the id and used our unconscious dreams and yearnings to quite different ends. The yearning became, as it were, yarning!" Her girlish giggle was a little surprising, but Professor Pidgeon decided he preferred it to her earlier, harsher exclamations.

"Yarning?"

"You wouldn't believe how old this planet is. And what a memory! She remembers the stories of every inhabitant who ever lived here. Millions of them. Billions. And not all human, of course. All Tempty wanted was a sympathetic audience, someone to watch and listen to her stories."

Professor Pidgeon raised an enquiring eyebrow.

"Isn't it obvious?" Producer Pushof beamed. "From all those negative projections that were emanating from us and thus from the planet, we changed to positive ones. We now have almost a million dream theaters worldwide. Each one runs a different story every couple of weeks or so. Programs change constantly, and we are working on a means of recording them, so that people can take them home with them or we can replay them when we need to. And, of course, it's not only the planet's memories that are contributing to the stories; we have our own as well. All we needed to do was structure the stories and devise a way in which they could be projected for an audience. Our GPP has tripled, allowing us to invest in clean energy so that people come from all over the galaxy to take a healthy holiday and spend their time enjoying our fantasies or, indeed, their own. For Temptation II takes their dreams and projects them back to them, thus increasing the variety and scope of the entertainment we can offer. With Disneyworld XIX, we are the galaxy's leading entertainment planet. We're thinking of changing our name to New Hollyworld. What do you think?"

Professor Pidgeon offered a nod of silent approval. "I believe I owe you an apology," he said. "It seems my grim warnings were unfounded."

She was generous. "If you hadn't said what you said, professor, I'm certain I would never have realized what a resource we had. Everyone who has the privilege of living on a sentient world could do what we have done. Not," she offered him a self-mocking smile, "that we aren't happy to remain, for as long as possible, the only game in the galaxy."

"Are there no drawbacks? Is there any kind of program you can't find here?"

"Well," she said, "we discovered that it wasn't wise to put on too many horror shows. These days, we're inclined to concentrate on what you might call family entertainment. Fantasy films, that sort of thing. But our thrillers are very popular. Our audiences accept that they enter our dream-o-domes at their own risk, but we also sell insurance to anyone worried that they will be adversely affected by our shows. Of course," she added, smiling again, "since much of the entertainment comes from their own unconscious, they have only themselves to blame if they witness something negative. It's the perfect business, really. It is the ultimate way of giving the public what it wants. Would you like to try out one of our dream-o-domes?"

"I think not," said Professor Pidgeon, his eyes twinkling. He signaled to Robert that they should make a discreet departure. "I've enjoyed the experience more than once and think I prefer, these days, to stay at home with a good book."

"Book?" asked Producer Pushof with interest as she summoned their ferry to the etherport. "Is that another idea we could perhaps turn to our advantage?"

This Thing of Darkness I Acknowledge Mine

Alex Irvine

I will tell you right up front that by the end of my story, you will believe that I am lying, if not about everything then certainly about the more important events I am about to narrate. Or describe. I was never clear on the difference.

I will also tell you that I'm not entirely sure I'm writing this. You'll understand why in a little while, unless you decide I'm lying.

When I began this testimony, I tried to think of ways to make sure I remained in control of what I was doing. One of the early drafts was an acrostic, with the first letter of each paragraph spelling out the last sentence I heard from the mouth of Tobin Crowder: You have to understand that I never wanted to want this. That only allowed me thirty-five paragraphs, though, and as soon as I started writing, it became clear to me that I was either going to have to abandon that scheme or inflict upon my reader some agonizingly long paragraphs. Abandonment seemed the better choice.

Another acrostic idea seemed to offer more promise. What if the first word of each sentence within a paragraph gave a letter, and thus each paragraph a word, and thus my testimony a hidden message? This focused my mind until, with Tobin's intervention I'm sure, I found myself unable to keep any of the lines I'd selected in my head.

After that, I found myself unable to maintain any kind of formal constraint or scheme. The only thing that works is to write things down in the order they come into my head, which is not the best order to tell the story, because since Tobin's interventions became more pervasive, my mind seems to have lost its ability to arrange things.

Tobin does not want me to be writing this (again for reasons that will become clear as we go on, if you don't give up on me along the way). Rather, he wants you—whoever you are—to arrive and experience what I experienced.

What all of us experienced.

The problem, one of our team told me early on, is that crazy people feel things more intensely than other people do.

The way I remember it, Tobin and I have been the last survivors of our mission for years now. Thirteen years? Sixteen? Something like that. Enough so that when I look back on my life, a nontrivial fraction of my years have been spent in solitude, and my reaction to the prospect of visitors is a strangely fractured mix of eagerness for human company and guilt that I will probably fail to warn them—you—adequately.

You will arrive, and see this idyllic place, and let your guard down . . . as we did. That's what I'm worried about. That's why I'm writing this. I hope that's not why Tobin is being so aggressive in my mind.

Or perhaps it should be said that people who feel things more intensely than other people do are often called crazy.

*   *   *

The line that I wrote above, about the last thing out of Tobin's mouth, that was wrong. I think. His last line was something else. I think maybe I've already written it, but that might have been in one of the other drafts. I destroyed those because the erasures seemed to gain me some peace. I'll try to remember.

I did try the acrostic. At least one of them. I don't think it worked, but I like the idea of a puzzle even though I'm not sure what puzzle I could create that Tobin wouldn't be able to anticipate and subvert.

Tobin was beautiful at the beginning, the incarnation of the Spaceman. I remember all of it before we touched down here, and he doesn't interfere.

What do I mean by interference? I should clarify. By interference I mean that sometimes Tobin distracts me by means of noises outside the window, odd smells from the greenhouse, inconvenient urges to urinate, and so forth. Sometimes he gives me nightmares that tumble after each other in such grotesque clusters that when I wake up, I feel as if I'm walking on the meniscus between waking and dream. Literally, I feel that way; it gives, ever so slightly, at each step. What is below I—waking—do not know.

Sometimes things come out of the forest. He could kill me if he wanted to. I hope he doesn't, although I've often wondered if a death wish wouldn't be the surest way to ensure my survival. Tobin is capricious that way. Always has been.

I am going to tell you about those first couple of months, even though that's the boring part.

They were pretty good. We made fun of each other's quirks, just as we had on the ship. We did our best to avoid sexual entanglements, just as we had on the ship. Being a bunch of confirmed science types, they cracked wise about my liberal arts background and literary bent. We did experiments, collected and cataloged samples, prospected for commercially useful minerals and genetic strings. We experienced absolutely textbook instances of personal jealousies disguising themselves as professional disagreements, but we got along well otherwise.

Then we began to wonder if we were all poisoned, because we all started to hallucinate, first individually and then in groups.

Then we started to discern what was really going on, and it wasn't hallucination at all. Which is not to say that we haven't hallucinated, but . . .

I think this part is best told by example.

The thing is, I don't really have a problem with amnesia, although I know this reads like I do. The problem is—I think—that all of the neural pathways my mind is accustomed to using for certain operations are unpredictably coopted or blocked by whatever it is Tobin is doing out there in the woods. Some days are worse than others—today, for example, has been pretty good so far—but in general, I find that I don't think the way I used to. Or, a better way to put it might be that I am not allowed to think the way I used to and have been forced to find different ways to think.

Which might not be a bad thing, but it is unsettling. I find it more and more important to build careful chains of cause and effect, to take refuge in easily traceable progressions between evidence and conclusion. In a place like this, you learn to mistrust intuition as well as any kind of lateral or stochastic thinking.

And Tobin Crowder, boy, he's a guy who makes you crave the sameness of habit.

I wish I'd never gone into space.

Dammit. Almost had the line. It occurred to me to address Tobin within the framework of this letter (memoir? apologia? testimony?) but I'm not sure I want to do that because I'm not sure I want him to respond. Also, I couldn't be sure whether he was responding or whether my expectation of his response would fool me into thinking he had.

The first day:

All of the readings and samples and spectrographic analyses don't make a bit of difference to the butterflies in your stomach when you first inhale the atmosphere of an alien world. And all of the warnings about possible toxins and allergens just can't stop you from bending to smell a flower. I remember doing both of those things, and I remember a flower looking slightly more like a jack-in-the-pulpit after I smelled it than it had before; and I remember Tobin actually weeping, sunlight on his face, the hum of bees in the air. The memory has such intensity that often I think those tears were in my own eyes. All of us were like that for the first couple of days. The place was too good to be true.

Even then, the planet had its eye on Tobin. He had the starkest and most naked emotions for it to prey on, amplify, and finally absorb and reflect. It must have been a wonderful toy, this planet, if you were serene and happy.

Although it might be said that the planet made itself serene and happy by making wonderful toys of us.

The truth is, when I say *Tobin* and I say *the planet*, I'm no longer sure where the meanings of the two diverge. Further complicating things, I'm also unsure where I end and everything else begins. Often I feel as if when I talk about Tobin, I'm talking about myself. Usually that's about when I lose my train of thought.

Okay, I'll say it: Eden.

It's naïve, it's incredulous, it's all of those things that you shouldn't be when you're in the business of exploration . . . but on the other hand, I think part of the explorer's temperament must include a sort of innocence. A desire for the new, to be experienced without prejudgment. Explorers must be part child.

Eden. A few days after we landed, when we'd gotten the MC—what we called the quonset hut officially known as Mission Central—set up and we'd started to establish a routine, Vicki Singh found orange trees growing a few hundred meters from our camp, on the shores of a lake. We all went to look at them, and with the strangest expression on his face, Tobin said, "I dreamed about oranges last night. God, I hated to wake up from that dream."

Against all regulations and common sense, we ate them. They were wonderful.

We figured out that someone had been there before us. There were no artifacts, no oddly geometric shapes in the jungle hinting at traces of lost civilizations . . . nothing like that. We speculated about nanotechnology, about engineering on a scale we couldn't contemplate, about the possibility that a fantastic accident of evolution had steered the course of events here in a direction incomprehensible to us. Whatever the cause, the conclusion was inescapable. The planet wanted to please us, and nothing wants to please without being trained in that desire.

Looking back, I think that's where the jealousy really began. All of us, I think, wanted not only for the planet to please us, but for none of the other members of the team to know that's what we wanted. When Sean Nishiyama caught salmon in the lake, we all pretended we didn't know that he must have wanted those salmon to be there; when our communications equipment started to pick up snatches of radio broadcasts from Earth, we all entered into an unspoken agreement that we would not ask whose nostalgia had created them. And so on.

Tobin and I were reconfiguring the software for the telescope left on the orbiter, about a month after we landed. Out of the blue, he said to me, "It's as if they re-created the entire planet as a tool. What might that kind of tool amplify?"

I said to him, "What wouldn't it amplify?"

And I kept to myself the question of whether, if everything was amplified, anything was meaningfully changed. In this swamp of wish fulfilment, self-identification becomes a kind of compartmentalization. To understand yourself in a world where you can give your desires form and breath, you divide yourself into the parts that want those things and the parts that still yearn for your former—that is, nonmalleable—reality. You hold those parts of yourself at a distance. You imagine others to possess qualities that you dislike about yourself, and use that imagination as an excuse to dislike them; and you imagine that by banishing them you are purifying yourself of those objectionable qualities.

None of which changed the fact that we were all still just ourselves.

Well, perhaps not. The other secret I kept was that my singular desire was for the planet to make me like Tobin Crowder. I wanted to be him, if only because of the way this Eden responded to him, the way he was so fully at home there.

It was something from Shakespeare. God, isn't it always something from Shakespeare?

Why would Tobin have been quoting Shakespeare? In our team, I was the one prone to embarrassingly artsy quotation. Maybe he'd heard the line from me . . . which makes it all the more frustrating that I can't remember it.

The fact that the mission fell apart wasn't his fault. It would have happened sooner without him around, I think, because for quite a while he absorbed the interest that otherwise might have found its way to the more vulnerable among us. Did I say Tobin was crazy? That's a tricky word. He was strong willed, that's for sure, and utterly unlike the rest of us. I think he's going to give me enough rope to hang myself here, so I might as well jump and say that he destroyed the mission, but that if he hadn't, someone—something—else would have. And a lot sooner.

He bought us time.

Me, he's still buying time.

Gradually Tobin grew distant. The team saw him less often; his work went unfinished. He'd never been gregarious—we had that in common—but once the planet started responding to him, he began to reinvent himself, and his new identity had nothing to do with the rest of us. The team gave him space, assuming that he was working through a more or less standard version of the disaffection we'd been trained to expect as a result of the long voyage. All of us felt it to one degree or another. I felt it more than most, I think. I too found it hard to get my work done, hard to eat meals in the company of the rest of the team, hard to file my reports on time—hard, in short, to do anything but go out and bask in the suffusing desire of the planet to make me happy.

Who could resist that?

It was inevitable that we should begin to compete for the planet's attentions—inevitable, too, that Tobin would win.

I forget the name of this place, which I know directly contradicts what I told you about being able to remember everything before we got here, since obviously I knew the name of the place before setting foot on it. Tough. Maybe the name is squirreled away back down one of the neural pathways blocked off with whatever the synaptic version of construction cones is, but I can't get to it.

Think I'm lying yet? You just wait.

*　　*　　*

Sometimes I look at what I've written and don't recognize the person who wrote it. I hate sentence fragments.

When things got bad, by which I mean when all of us became certain that we could no longer trust the evidence of our senses—except when that evidence implied that someone was dead, in which case sensory input was generally pretty reliable—but what I was saying was that when things got bad, one of the startling things was the lack of event.

Take the survey team. I mean, someone already did, but you get the figure of speech. There wasn't any monster or any explosion or anything. One minute they were doing what they had always done, in a place that was unfamiliar but not overtly dangerous . . . and the next minute the planet just wasn't that way anymore.

The thing about Tobin was that he was born to be a leader, and on our mission he never got the chance until there was nothing left to lead and nowhere to lead anything to. I don't blame him for being angry about this. He thinks he could have saved us, and he's probably right. He understood sooner than the rest of us what was happening, and if we had gotten out of his way the mission might have been saved.

That was never going to happen, though. Everyone else wanted to feel what Tobin was feeling, and it's perfectly natural that he would have wanted to protect what he thought was his. I would have done the same thing.

And in any case, something has been saved. Just not everything, and when in life do you ever get to save everything?

The beauty of this place doesn't make it valuable or salutary; the polluted sunsets of Oil Age Earth were also beautiful. But there is a species of tree here ("tree"—I speak in analogs here rather than exact correspondence with terrestrial taxonomies) with leaves that dangle low and catch the sunlight at a particular angle during certain times of the year. The luminescent green is like nothing on Earth, except perhaps the glow of fireflies. There is a species of insect that dances in patterns on the still waters and releases a chemical that mimics the scent of a flower favored by a particular hummingbird. Here as on Earth, hummingbirds are disoriented by water and tend to fly down into it and drown; these dancing insects then converge on the dead hummingbird to feed. I do not know why they dance while emitting their scent.

I wonder how much of our idea of beauty—I mean, the hardwired part of it, since some of it must be hardwired—derives from the fact that in the natural world, things that are striking in color or pattern often are that way because they are dangerous.

In other words, are dangerous things beautiful because they are dangerous? I think they are, at least some of them, at least part of the time, but I don't mean those qualifiers as a way of going back on my original statement. There is a correspondence. Anyone who has spent time here would know that.

In a way, what happened—is still happening—to Tobin is beautiful. And in a way, perhaps, it is a sunset in a polluted sky.

All tools are amplifiers, he said to me once—I think during the course of the telescope conversation—and then admitted that he was quoting a well-known scientific canard. Somebody's Law.

Ah, shit. Never mind. Laws. I can't remember anything that's important. If I could remember that last thing he said, I'd be able to put it all together.

When I think about Shakespeare, I think about how so many of his late plays—*Pericles*, *The Tempest*, *The*

Winter's Tale—involve dangerous voyages, with isolation on the other side for a character we love. And I wonder if the man himself, having retired to idyllic Stratford after his tumultuous London life, was feeling as if he had undergone a perilous journey away from the vitality of his prime years and into the isolation of his past.

He, too, perhaps, knew better than to trust an idyll.

Then again, if there is a little of Shakespeare in all of his plays, you can't find all of him in any of them. Before I became an astronomer, I went to graduate school in literature; I know about the biographical fallacy. Mostly when I think about Shakespeare, it's because I'm trying to remember Tobin's line. Something about responsibility. I feel that if I could remember it, I would know for sure whose fault all of this was.

Oh. Example. Well, a survey team went out to confirm a possible reading about an amount of pitchblende. I don't remember the details, and I am not by trade a geologist; my field is astronomy, and my function on the mission was to catalog and investigate nearby stellar bodies in better detail than was possible from Earth. This is not what I was doing when the survey team went out.

Their first collective hallucination—for so they thought it at the time—involved a sudden failure of their ability to see the color blue. This wasn't like orange trees or salmon, but things of this nature had happened before as well. I, in fact, was supposed to be working on the problem of whether astrophysical phenomena could be responsible for the momentary elision of a portion of the visible spectrum. What I was doing at the moment when the first distress call came in from Sean Nishiyama, our geologist, had nothing to do with optics, or astronomy. I was chipping paint from around one of the displays on the housing of a generator. How the paint got there, I never found out, and the problem was driven from my mind by the vibration of the distress signal. I ran back into the MC (was that the last time I was inside?) and answered Sean's call.

He said that none of them could see blue anymore, and that green had become yellow, purple red, and so forth. Then he hesitated and said, "And now yellow's gone too. Hey, Karen, can you see yellow?"

Karen Berman, our mission botanist, said no, she couldn't. In the background of the call I could hear the other members of the team. I distinctly heard the word *red* several times.

"Sean," I said. "You can still see in black and white, am I right?"

He said that was right, but it was getting dark. I imagined seeing only black and white in the dark. This planet has no moon, although apparently it did at one point, since its seashores still bear traces of what must have been tidal ecosystems; but without a moon, the team was going to have grave difficulty finding its way out of the deep forest that lay over the pitchblende deposit they had gone to survey.

"Use your flashlights," I said. "That will at least give you light and shadow."

Tobin hadn't gone out with the survey team. Hadn't wanted to. He was already so withdrawn by then that he had trouble connecting with any of them deeply enough to remember their names. All the same, I believed then, and believe now, that if he had been there, they might have survived. He was strong enough and single-minded enough to hold them together by force of will.

At the exact moment of sundown—I checked later—all of the transponders they'd left on the trail as bread crumbs quit working. This was before we'd gotten a working system of GPS satellites up.

"Every one of them?" I repeated, feeling stupid for saying it but unable to keep my mouth shut.

"Every goddamn one," Sean said.

They were losing their vision (possibly), it was dark, they were in thick forest, and they no longer had any way to get out save through the kind of orienteering skills that are as foreign to our generation as dead reckoning was to those who came of age after the discovery of the compass. Considering all of this, I think it's amazing they held on as long as they did.

Also, it's amazing I've held on to my train of thought as long as I have. Tobin must like this story, and why wouldn't he?

I really wish I'd never gone into space. I could have taught composition at a small college somewhere. There might have been children. I would have liked children. Sometimes I dream that I have had them and wake up sad that I have left them behind.

Regrets are easy to come by when you're the last survivor of a mission to another planet, which if I'm not, I will be soon.

So I sit and write puzzles, ostensibly for you but more honestly for myself. Anything I can think, Tobin can think—has thought—as well.

In the real world, I think those hummingbirds mostly get eaten by fish. But at least there is the beauty of the insects' dance.

Right. Example. Forest.

They said they were hanging together, but something about the way things looked started to frighten them. "Stay close," I warned them. "Touching close. Can you remember the way you came?"

"That's the problem," Karen said. "We can remember it, but it isn't there."

I heard Sean in the background saying that they were going to count off every five minutes, just to make sure that in their panic they wouldn't leave anyone behind.

The first three counts came to six. The fourth came to five.

Tricia Kassarjian was gone.

"Where'd she go?" Sean was screaming. "She was right here!"

Yes, they all agreed. She had been right there. Someone had helped her over a fallen log not thirty seconds before; someone else had snapped at her for shining her flashlight up in their faces. "I heard her breathing right next to me," said our pilot, an ex-military botanist named Lee Young-pyo. "I mean just now."

"Tricia!" Sean called.

And this is the worst of it: She answered. I could hear her calling to them. They stayed together and worked the search the way they were supposed to. Tricia said she would stay put, and they would use the sound of her voice to locate her.

Eventually, though, she stopped talking. No panic, no cries for help. She just stopped answering.

When the team made the decision to return for her after they'd gotten back to where they'd parked the rover, they counted off.

One, two, three . . . four.

It went like that. The forest closed them off, not so they could see it but so that every time they made progress back toward where they were sure they needed to be, suddenly there was no way to get there. Sean was the last one to go. Tobin and I talked to him the whole time. He knew he wasn't going to make it, and he told us that, and right before he stopped responding he said to me, "What kind of a place is this? How does this happen?" Mystified, like a toddler who has cut himself on safety scissors.

I didn't have an answer for him then, and I don't now.

Tobin said . . . ah, goddammit. For a minute there

I almost had it. Whatever it was, I remember thinking I hoped it wasn't the last thing Sean ever heard.

A little while later, Tobin went outside for good.

I think there was another incident after the loss of the survey team, but when I go back and do the arithmetic in my head, the answer I get means that everyone but Tobin and me died in that forest. My mind is stubborn, though; I know there was something else. I'm fairly certain someone else died.

It is a difficult thing to be unsure whether your apprehension of the world is the correct one; far worse not even to know if your thoughts about what you see, feel, taste, etc., are yours or projections of someone else. If all tools are amplifiers, then what was left here amplified the capability of the mind to affect the phenomenal world. It's only natural, I suppose, for that tool to have wanted to find its way into the mind that would make the most use of it.

Without looking back at what I've already written, I think that probably I haven't given enough attention to the problem of what I should have done differently. The way we all felt about Tobin—and *we* here includes Tobin himself; his many fine qualities did not include modesty—meant that there were times when we looked to him. If we were children (what group social interaction cannot be explained in terms of the playground?), Tobin would have been the kid everyone wanted to be like, and he didn't always desire or respond well to our expectations. On the way here, he just wanted to be left alone to do his job; once we were on the ground, he forgot about the job and just wanted to be left alone with the creations of his mind.

I should have handled myself better. Possibly I should have acted more aggressively as some kind of corrective to Tobin, and I failed to be that. Was never that. Could not have been that. From the moment our feet touched the ground of this world, he was different. He was of this place, I think, before he ever got here—which is a fatalistic thing to say, given what happened, but I believe it.

Here's another fatalistic sentiment: also I believe that once this world knew of him, there was no way things could have happened other than how they did. Which doesn't let me off the hook.

I said *what was left here* a few sentences ago. Tobin said to me once that the world *was* the tool, that whatever they—They—did turned it into a giant psychological tuning fork. *Psychokinetic* might be a better word, since thoughts here are able to manifest themselves as expenditures of kinetic energy.

Who could have done that, I wondered then. Still do. Maybe Tobin knows.

And where did they go?

Here's what it feels like: Once, I became certain that the world itself was not just speaking to me but speaking through me, living through me, that I had become a conduit for this consciousness that was curious, eager, jealous, lonely . . . and then it was gone. While it was present, however, I could feel the matter of the world transforming around me. I was in a good mood, and the clouds in the sky cleared; I was excited about an experiment I was close to finishing, and birds burst from the trees all around me; I was fearful that the experiment would fail, and one of the birds dropped dead at my feet. The experience lasted just a moment, but Lee and I went back and looked later; the dead bird was there, and within a hundred meters of the spot we cataloged sixteen species of flower, each visually resembling a terrestrial species I knew and each utterly absent from the rest of the planet . . . at least insofar as we were able to determine.

More than human companionship, I miss that feeling, which may say more about my failure to connect with my mission colleagues than about whatever made those flowers grow.

Anyway, if you read this, it means I've aged, and died, and that the only one left is Tobin. I don't think age and death are things he has to worry about now.

Don't expect him to come and greet you, but he'll send a message.

I haven't gone back inside the MC for a while . . . perhaps since the night the survey team disappeared. I'm trying to hear the voice Tobin heard, trying to feel the ground below my feet responding to my steps the way it must respond to his.

Look for me under your bootsoles. And while you're at it, look for Tobin there, too.

God, I feel like I'm doing this to myself. Maybe that's part of the guilt I was talking about earlier, but what do I have to be guilty about? Didn't do anything. That was Tobin. Wish I could remember that line. Then I would know.

Me·topia

Adam Roberts

The first day and the first night.

They had come down in the high ground, an immense plateau many thousands of miles square. "The highlands," said Murphy. "I claim the highlands. I'll call them Murphyland." Over the next hour or so he changed his mind several times: Murphtopia, Murphia. "No," he said, glee bubbling out in a little dance, a shimmy of the feet, a flourish of the hands. "Just Murphy, Murphy. Think of it! *Where do you come from? I come from Murphy. I'm a Murphyite. I was born in Murphy.*" And the sky paled, and then the sun appeared over the mountaintops, and everything was covered with a tide of light. The dew was so thick it looked like the aftermath of a heavy rainstorm.

Sinclair, wading out from the shuttle's wreckage through waist-high grass, drew a dark trail after him marking his path, like the photographic negative of a comet.

"I don't understand what you're so happy about," said Edwards. It was as if he could not *see* this new land, a world that popped out of nowhere. As if all he could see was the damage to the ship. But that was how Edwards' mind worked. He had a practical mind.

"Ach, are you sad for your ship," sang Murphy, with deliberately overplayed oirishry, "all buckled and collapsed and it is?" Of course, Murphy was a neanderthal, a *homo neanderthalis*. The real deal. All four of these crewmen were. Of course, you know what that means.

"You should be sad too, Murphy," said Edwards, speaking in a level voice. "It's your ship too. I don't see how we are to get home without it."

"But *this* is my home," declared Murphy. And then sang his own name, or perhaps the name of his newly made land, over and over: "Murphy! Murphy! Murphy!"

The sun moved through the sky. The swift light went everywhere. It spilled over everything and washed back. The expanse of grassland shimmered in the breeze like cellophane.

Edwards climbed to the top of the buckled craft. The plasmetal bodywork was oily with dew, and his feet slipped several times. At the top he stood as upright as he dared and surveyed the world. Mountains away to the west, grass steppes leading away in every direction, north south and east, flowing downhill eastward toward smudges of massive forestation and the metallic inlaid sparkle of rivers, lakes, seas. That was some view, eastward.

The sun was rising from the west, which was an unusual feature. What strange world rotated like that? There were no Earth-sized planets in the solar system that rotated like that.

Did that mean they were no longer in the solar system? That was impossible. There was no way they could have traveled so far. Physics repudiated the very notion.

The air tasted fresh in his mouth, in his throat. Grass scent. Rainwater and ozone.

*   *   *

And for long minutes there was no sound except
the hushing of the grasses in the wind and the distant
febrile twitter of birds high in the sky. The sky
gleamed, as full of the wonder of light as a glass brim-
ful of bright water. Vins called up, "There are insects.
I've got insects here, though they seem to be torpid."
He paused, and repeated the word, torpid. "When the
dew evaporates a little they'll surely come to life."

Edwards grunted in reply, but his eye was on the
sky. Spherical clouds, perfect as eggs, drifted in the
zenith. Six of them. Seven. Eight. Edwards counted,
turning his head. Ten.

Twelve.

And the air, moist with dew and fragrant with possibility, slid past him, the slightest of breezes. And light
all about. And silence stained only by the swishing of
the wind.

Murphy was dancing below, kicking his feet through
the heavy, wet grass. "Maybe *Murphy* isn't such a
good idea, by itself," he called, to nobody in particular. "As a name, by itself. How about the Murphy
Territories? How about the *Land* of Murphy?" And
then, after half a minute, when neither Edwards nor
Vins replied, he added, "Don't be sore, Vins. You can
name some other place."

Vins went into the body of the shuttle to fetch out
some killing jars for the insects.

Sinclair was away for hours. The sun rose, and the
dew steamed away in wreathy banks of mist. The grass
dried out, and paled, and then bristled with dryness.
It was a yellow, tawny sort of grass. By midday the
sky was hot as a hot plate, and Murphy had stripped
off his chemise.

Sinclair returned, sweating. "It goes on and on," he
said. "Exactly the same. Steppe and more steppe."

The sun dropped over the eastern horizon. It quickly became cold.

The night sky was cloudless, stars like lit dewdrops on black; breath petaled out of their mouths in transient, ghostly puffs. Edwards slept in the shuttle. Sinclair and Vins chatted, their voices subdued underneath the enormity of the night sky. Murphy had a nicotine inhaler; he lay on the cooling roof of the crashed shuttle looking up at the stars, puffing intermittently. Later they all joined Edwards in the shuttle and slept. Over their thoughtless, slumbering heads the stars glinted and prickled in the black clarity. Hours passed. The the sky cataracted to white with the coming dawn. Ivory-colored clouds bubbled into the sky from behind the peaks of the highlands and swept down upon them. Before dawn rain started falling. Edwards woke at the drumroll sound of rain against the body of the crashed ship, sat up disoriented for a moment, then lay down again and went back to sleep.

"We're dead, we've died, we're dead," said Murphy, perhaps speaking in his sleep.

The second day and the second night.

At breakfast, after dawn, it was still raining. The four of them ate inside the shuttle, with the door open. "Ah," said Edwards, looking through the hatch at the shimmering lines of water. "The universal solvent."

"But I should hate you," said Murphy. "Because you can look at water and say *ah the universal solvent*."

Edwards cocked his head on one side. "I don't see your point," he said.

"No, no," said Murphy. "That's not it. Oh, water, oh? This beautiful thing, this spiritual thing, purity and the power to cleanse, to baptize even. Light on water, is there a more beautiful thing? And all you can say when you see it is *ah the universal solvent*."

Edwards put his mouth in a straight line. "But it *is*

the universal solvent," he said. "That's one of its functions. Why do you say *oh water oh*?"

The rain outside was greeting their conversational interchanges with sustained and rapturous applause. The color through the hatch was gray. The air looked like metal scored and overscored with myriad slant lines.

"Can we lift off?" asked Sinclair. "Is there a way off of this place?"

"Feel that," Edwards instructed. He was not talking about any particular object, not instructing any of the crew to lift any particular object. What he meant was: Feel how heavy we are. "That's a full g. That's what is to be overcome. We came down hard."

"Hard," confirmed Murphy.

"We weren't expecting," said Sinclair, "a whole world to pop out of the void. Nothing, nothing, nothing, then *a whole world*. We snapped our spine on this rock."

"Let's get one thing straight," said Edwards, in his brusque and matter-of-fact voice. "This world did not pop out of nowhere. Worlds don't *pop out* of nowhere." He glowered at his colleagues. "That's not what happened."

"Turn it up, *Captain*," said Murphy. He applied the title sarcastically. It was the nature of this ship that its crew worked without ranks such as captain, second-in-command, all that bag-and-baggage of hierarchy. No military ship, this. This was not a merchant vessel either. They hadn't been sliding along the frictionless thread of Earth-Mars or Earth-Moon hauling goods or transporting soldiery or anything like that. This was science. Science isn't structured to recognize hierarchy.

"I'm only saying," said Edwards, sheepishly. "I don't want to suggest that I'm in charge."

They were silent for a while, and the rain spattered and clattered enormously all about them. Encore! Encore!

It occurred to Edwards, belatedly, that Murphy might have been saying *eau, water, eau*.

"Right," said Vins. "We're all in a kind of intellectual shock, that's what I think. We've been here two days now, and we haven't even formulated a plausible hypothesis of what's going on. We haven't even tried." He looked around at his colleagues. "Let's review what happened."

Murphy had his stumpy arms folded over his little chest. "Review, by all means," he said. But then, when Vins opened his mouth to speak again, he interrupted immediately: "*I've* formed a hypothesis. It's called Murphy. This is prime land, and I claim it. When we get back, or when we at least contact help and they come get us, I shall set up a private limited company to promote the settlement of Murphy. I'll make a fortune. I'll be mayor. I'll be the *alpha* male."

"Why you think," said Edwards, thinking literally, "that such a contract would have any legal force upon Earth is beyond me."

"Let's review," said Vins, in a loud voice.

Everybody looked at him.

"We're flying. We drop below the ecliptic plane, no more than a hundred thousand klims. More than that?"

None of the others said anything. Then Sinclair said, "It was about that."

"We saw a winking star," Vins said. He did not stop talking, he continued on, even though Murphy tried to interrupt him with a sneering, "Winking star, oh, that's good on my mother's health that's good." Vins wasn't to be distracted when he got going. "It was out of the position of variable star 699, which is what we might have thought it otherwise. Except that it wasn't where 699 should have been. As we flew, it grew in size, indicating a very reflective asteroid, or perhaps comet, out of the ecliptic. You," Vins nodded at Sinclair, "argued it was a particolored object rotating diurnally. But it was a fair way south of the ecliptic. *Then* what happened?"

"'We all know what happened,'' said Murphy. They may all have been *homo neanderthalis*, but they were bright. They all had their scientific educations. The real deal.

"Let's review," said Vins. "We need to *know* what's happened. Act like scientists, people."

"I'm a scientist no longer," cried Murphy, with a flourish of his arm. "I'm the king of Murphytopia."

"What happened," said Edwards, slowly, thinking linearly and literally, "was we were tracking the curious wobble of the asteroid. Or whatever it was. We flew close, and suddenly there was a world, a whole world, and—we came down. We reentered sideways, and there was heat damage to the craft, and then there was collision damage, and now it's broken. And we're sitting inside it."

"Now," said Vins. "Here's a premise. Worlds don't appear out of nowhere. Do we agree?"

Nobody disagreed.

"It's a mountain and Mohammed thing," offered Sinclair. "Put it this way, which is more likely? That a whole Earth-sized planet pops out of nowhere in front of us? Or that we, for some reason, have popped into a *new* place?"

"I say we're back on Earth," said Murphy. "It looks like a duck, and it smells like a duck, and it, uh, pulls the gravity of a duck, *then* it's a duck."

"The sun is rising," Sinclair pointed out, "in *the west*. It is setting in the *east*."

"Oh. And the asteroid was the beacon of an interdimensional sfy gateway through time and space . . ." mocked Murphy, "and we fell through, like in a sfy film, and now we're on the far side of the galaxy?" He pronounced "SF-y" as a two-syllable word, with a ludicrous and prolonged emphasis on the central "f" sound.

"That can't be true," said Edwards. "Our first night,

the stars were very clear. All the constellations were there. Familiar constellations."

"Which's what we'd expect if we were back on Earth," said Murphy.

"But the sun *rises* in the *west* . . ." said Sinclair again.

"Maybe the compasses are broken, somehow. Distorted. Maybe you think west is east and versy-vice-a."

"All of them? All the compasses? And besides, at night you can see the pole star, great bear, all very clearly. Oh there's no doubt where the sun's rising."

"Well, let's look at another hypothesis," said Murphy. "There is a whole, a *whole* Earth-sized planet, about a hundred thousand kilometers south of the ecliptic between Earth and Venus. And nobody on Earth for four centuries of dedicated astronomy has noticed it. Nobody saw a whole planet, waxing and waning, between us and the sun? No southern hemisphere observatory happened to see it? Is *that* what you're saying?"

"That is," Vins conceded, "hard to credit."

"So," said Murphy. He got up, stepped to the hatch, and looked out at the hissing and rapturous rainfall. "Here's what I think happened. We were off to investigating your *winking* star, Vins, and then we all suffered some sort of group epilepsy, or mass hysteria, or loss of consciousness, and we piloted the ship back up and toward Earth."

"We were days away," Vins pointed out.

"So perhaps we were in a fugue state for days. Anyway, we weren't shaken out of it until we slammed into the atmosphere, and now we've crashed in the highlands in Peru, or Africa maybe."

"There's nowhere on Earth," Vins pointed out, "as lovely as this. Where is there anywhere as mild, or balmy, as this? Peru, you say?"

"You ever *been* to Peru?"

"I been a lot of places, and there's ice wherever I've been."

"Never mind the climate," said Edwards. "What about the sunrises?"

"How is it," agreed Vins, "that the sunrise is in the west if this is Peru?"

"I don't know. But the advantage of my hypothesis is that it's Occam's razor on all the stuff about planets appearing from nowhere, and it reduces all that to a single, simple problem: the sunrise."

"And another problem," Edwards pointed out, "which is the lack of radio traffic."

"The radio's broken," said Murphy. "I'm not happy about it."

"The radio?"

"No, not happy about the *Murphy*, the Murphy-topia. I'm not happy about the status of my kingdom. I was looking forward to claiming the highlands as my personal kingdom. But if it's, you know, Peru, then there'll be some other bugger who's already claimed these highlands."

"The radio's not broken," said Edwards. "We can pick up background chatter. Bits and pieces. We just can't seem to locate any—to get a fix upon—"

"Vins," said Murphy, sitting himself down again. "Vins, Vins. What's your theory? You haven't told us your theory."

"I think we've landed upon a banned world," said Vins. He said this in a bright voice, but his mouth was angled downward as he spoke. "A forbidden planet. *That's* SF-y, isn't it?" He pronounced each of the letters in sfy separately.

"A banned world," said Murphy, as if savoring the idea. "What an interesting notion. What a fanciful notion. What a dark horse you are, to be sure, Vins."

The rain stopped sometime in the afternoon, and the clouds rolled away, leaving the landscape washed and gleaming under the low sun as if glazed with strawberry and peach. The long stretch of grassland directly beneath them retained some of its yellow, and it moved slowly, like the pelt of a lion. In the distance they could see a long inlaid band of bronze, curved and kinked like the marginal illustration in a Celtic manuscript: open water, glittering in the sun. And the sun went down and the stars came out.

Edwards, trying to identify where the Earth should be from their last known position, noticed something they should all have seen on the first night: that the stars hardly moved through the sky. He woke the others up.

"Earth," he said, "is just below the horizon." He pointed. "There. Mars, I think, is over there."

"Send them a signal."

"I did. But why should they be listening for a signal from this stretch of space? It's not even on the ecliptic. It's not as if there are any astronomers on Mars. And if there were, if there were any, you know, amateurs, why should they be looking down here? No, that's not what I woke you up to show you."

"What then?"

"The stars aren't moving. I've been watching for an hour. I was waiting to see Earth come up over the horizon so I could send them a message. But it's not coming up."

"You thought it was an hour," said Murphy, crossly. "Clearly it *wasn't* an hour. You probably sat there for five minutes and got impatient."

So they settled down together, and all checked their watches and looked east to where the sun had set, where familiar stars pebbled the sky. And an hour passed, and another, and the stars did not move.

Nobody said anything for a long time.

"Somebody has stopped the stars in their courses," said Murphy. "We're dead, we're all in the afterlife. Is that what happened? We crashed the ship and died, and this is the land of the dead."

"I thought you were the one, Murphy, who wanted

to apply Occam's razor?" chided Edwards. "That's a pretty *elaborate* explanation for the facts, don't you think? I don't feel dead. Do you? You feel that way?"

"Certainly not," said Vins.

"But we've no idea what it feels like to feel dead," Murphy pointed out.

"Exactly! It's a null hypothesis. Let's not go there. There must be another explanation."

"The other explanation is that we're not rotating."

"Except we saw the sun go around and set, so we *are* rotating. An Earth-sized world, pulling an Earth-strength gravity, rotates for half a day and then *stops* rotating? Impossible. That makes no sense."

"I'll tell you what makes sense," said Murphy, hugging himself against the cold. "This is a banned world. We are not supposed to be here. That's what makes sense."

"Of course we're not supposed to be here," agreed Vins. "Supposed to be Venus, that's where. That's where we're supposed to be orbiting. Not here. But that's not to say it's a forbidden planet."

"You were the one who said so!" Murphy objected.

"I was joking," said Vins.

"Your joke may be turning out right," said Murphy. He coughed, loud and long. Then he said, "The sun rises in the west, and the stars don't move. You know what that is? That's things that the human eye was not supposed to see. That's a realm of magic—fairy, that's where we are, and the fairy queen is probably gathering her hounds to hunt us down for seeing this forbidden place."

"Very amusing, Murphy," said Edwards, in a bland voice. "Very fanciful and imaginative. Your fancy and your imagination, I find them amusing."

"I'm going to sleep." Murphy sulked, picking himself up and going back inside the ship. "I'll meet my fate tomorrow with a clear head at least."

The others stayed outside under the splendid, chilly, glittering stars and under that silkily cold black sky.

They talked and reduced the possibilities to an order of plausibility. They discussed what to do. They discussed the possibility of making the ship whole again; perhaps by dismantling one of the thirty-six thrust engines and reassembling it as a sort of welding torch, so as to make good the breaches in the plasmetal hull. Nobody could think how to launch into space, though; the craft had not been built to achieve escape velocity unaided. They had not been planning on landing on Venus, after all. (The very idea!) Finally the sky started to pale and ease, as if the arc of the western horizon were a heated element thawing the black into rose and pearl and blushed tones of white.

The sun lifted itself into the sky.

"Well," said Vins, with a tone of finality, "that settles it. Clearly we *are* rotating. The lack of movement of the stars and the apparent movement of the sun: These data contradict one another. Seem to. It's hard to advance a coherent explanation that includes both of these pieces of observational data. Are we agreed?"

"I can't think what else," said Edwards. "We assume the sky is a simulation of some sort. Do we assume that?"

"We do," said Sinclair.

"One of two explanations, then," said Vins. "Either the sky is a total simulation, upon which is projected a moving sun by day and motionless stars by night. Or else the sky is a real feature but some peculiarity of optics distorts the actual motion of the stars in some way."

"It's hard to think what sort of phenomenon . . ." began Sinclair. But he stopped talking. He wasn't sure what he was going to say; and—anyway—the dawn was so very beautiful. They all sat looking down, all distracted by the loveliness of the view from their highland vantage point: down across sloping grasslands and marsh and the beaming seas and gleaming channels of water. And, awakened by the light, the first birds were up; dancing in nimble flight and giving

voice to nimble birdsong, bouncing their tenor and
soprano trills off the blue ceiling of the sky—or whatever it was.

They were all tired. They'd been up all night. Eventually they went inside the spaceship and slept.

The third day and the third night.

Vins, Sinclair, and Edwards woke sometime in the
afternoon, the sun already declining toward the east.

Murphy had gone.

They searched for him, in a slightly desultory manner, round and about the ship; but it was clear enough
where he had gone: a trail scuffed, slightly kinked but
more or less straight, through the grasses and downward. Clambering onto the top of the ship, Edwards
could follow this with his eye, and with binoculars,
down and down, a wobbly ladder in the resplendent
material of the fields all the way to where forest ruled
a dark line.

"He's gone into a forest. Down there, kilometers
away." He wanted to say something like, Imagine a
stretch of gold velvet, all brushed one way to smooth-
ness, and a finger dragged through the velvet against
the grain of the brushing—that's what his path looks
like. But he couldn't find the words to say that.
"Should we go after him?" he called. "Should we
go?"

"He knows where we are," said Sinclair. "He knows
how to get back here. He's probably just exploring."

"And if he gets into trouble?"

"It's his lookout. He must take responsibility for
himself," said Vins. "We all must shift for ourselves,
after all."

The three of them breakfasted on ship's supplies,
sitting in the warm air and listening to the meager,
distant chimes of the birds and watching the flow and
glitter of wind upon the grass. "I could sit here forever," said Edwards, in a relaxed voice.

The other two were silent, but it was a silent agreement.

"We need to get on," said Vins, as if dragging the sentence up from great deeps. "We need to explore. To fix the ship. That's what we need to do."

They did nothing. After breakfast they dozed in the sun. Murphy did not return. Who knew where he had gone?

The one thing so obvious that none of them bothered to point it out was that this world was paradisical compared to the wrecked and wasted landscapes of their home. And that because it was paradisical, it was very obviously not a real place. They were dead and had gone to a material heaven, perhaps on account of some sort of oversight. They had died in the crash. Or they had been transported through a different sort of spatial discontinuity, one that translated them from real to mythic space. They were to feed among the mild-eyed melancholy lotus-eaters now.

The land of the sirens, in which Odysseus' crew had languished so pleasantly and purposelessly. Was *that* a forbidden world? Was it banned to subsequent explorers? Why else was it never again discovered?

It may still be there, some island or stretch of coast in the Mediterranean protected by a cloak of invisibility, some magic zone or curtain through which only a few select and lucky mariners stumble. Who knows?

All this culture and learning bounced around their heads: Vins, Sinclair, and Edwards. They knew all about Homer and Mohammed, and they knew all about Shakespeare and Proust, even though those people about whom they were so knowledgeable were a completely different sort of creature from themselves. Those Homers and van Goghs were all superbeings, elevated, godlike; and the residue of their golden-age achievements in the minds of the scientists had the paradoxical effect of shrinking them by comparison.

Best not think about it. What and if they *are* in the land of the Lotus? Maybe they're lucky, that's all.

The sun set in the east. The color and illumination drained out of the western sky and out of the zenith, flowing down to the east with osmotic slowness and leaving behind a rich, purply black dotted with perfectly motionless stars. The last of the day was a broad stretch of white-yellow sky over the eastern horizon, patched with skinny horizontal clouds of golden brown. For long minutes the last of the sunlight, coming up over the horizon, touched the bottom line of these clouds with fierce and molten light, so that it looked as if several sinuous heating elements, glowing bright and hot with the electricity passing through them, had been fixed to the matter of the sky. Then the light faded away from the clouds, and they browned and blackened against a compressing layer of sunset lights: a sky honey and marmalade, and then a gray-orange, and finally blue, and after that black.

It was night again.

Something agitated Vins enough to get him up and huffing around. "The stars have moved a little," he said. "There—that's the arc of the corona australis. Say what you like, but *don't* tell me I don't know my constellations."

"So?"

"It's higher. Yesterday the lowest star was right on the horizon, on that little hill silhouetted there. Today it's a fraction above."

"So we're rotating real slow," said Sinclair. "I can't say I care. I can't say I'm bothered. I'm going to sleep."

The fourth day and the fourth night.

In the morning Vins left the ship. He set off in the opposite direction to Murphy—not down the slope toward the forest and the long shining stretches of open water but up, higher into the highlands. He had no idea where Murphy had gone, or what he had been after; but something inside him prompted him to go higher. *Go up, Moses.* He had a vision of himself climbing and climbing until he reached the summit of some snow-clenched mountaintop at the very heart of the world from which the whole planet—or at least this whole hemisphere—would be visible. Like Mount Purgatory, he thought, from Dante. As if he had anything to do with Dante! Another godlike figure from the golden age.

Vins didn't creep away as Murphy had done. He prepared a pack, some supplies, some tools, a couple of scientific instruments. Then he woke the other two up. He told them what he wanted to do; and they sat, looking stupidly at him from under their overhanging foreheads, and didn't say anything. "You sure you don't want to come with me?" he asked. He felt an obscure and disabling fear deep inside him, a terror that if he stayed at the crash site, he'd slide into torpor, and that would be the end of him. He had to get out and away. He had to move.

"Do what you like," said Sinclair.

"It makes no sense to me," said Edwards, "to go marching off without any sort of objective. Shouldn't you have an objective? As a scientist?"

"My objective is to explore. What's more scientific than exploration?"

Edwards looked at him, blinked, looked again. "We should stay here," he said, slowly. He turned to look at the buckled ship. "We should mend the ship."

"We should," agreed Vins. "But we don't. You *notice* that? There's something here that's rendering us idle. Idleness doesn't suit us."

Sinclair laughed at this. "Let him go," he said, stretching himself on a broad boulder with a westward-facing facet to warm himself in the new sunlight. "He's the hairiest of us all."

Vins winced at this insult. "Don't be like that. What is this, school?"

"It's true," said Sinclair. "Murphy was the hairiest, but he's gone God-knows-where. You're the hairiest now, and you'll go, and good riddance. Go after Murphy. Go pick fleas from his pelt. I'm the smoothest of the lot of you and I'll stay here and *thank* you."

"I'm not going after Murphy, I'm going higher into the highlands."

"Go where you like."

Edwards wouldn't meet Vins' gaze, so Vins shouldered his pack and marched off, striding westward into the setting sun. He could feel Sinclair's eyes boring into his back as he went; Sinclair just lounging there like a lazy great ape, watching him go. The hairiest indeed!

Then Vins had a second thought. He wanted to get up high, didn't he? He could lift himself clean off the ground.

It took a surprising amount of courage to turn about and stomp back down to the ship again. Sinclair was still there on his rock, watching him with lazy insolence. Edwards had taken off his shoes and climbed to the top of the wreckage, clinging to the dew-wet surface with his toes and the palms of his feet. He was gazing east, down, away.

Vins didn't say anything to either of them. Instead, he went into the ship and retrieved a bundle of gossamer fabric and plastic cord and tied it to the top of his backpack. Then he pulled out a small cylinder of helium, no longer or thicker than a forearm yet densely heavy. He tied a grapple rope to this and dragged it after him.

There were no more good-byes. He stomped away again.

Something was bugging Vins, preying on his mind. It was as if he'd caught a glimpse of something out of the corner of his eye without exactly noticing it, such that it had registered only in his subconscious (that gift of the gods, the unconscious mind). He felt he should have understood by now. Something was wrong, or else something was profoundly and obviously right, and he couldn't see it.

What?

He marched on, the cylinder dragging through the turf behind him and occasionally clanging on the up-crops of rock that poked through the grass. It was an effort with every step to haul the damn thing, but Vins had found in stubbornness and ill-temper a substitute for willpower. He marched on. He didn't know where he was going. He had, as Edwards might say, no objective. But on he went.

The grass grew shorter the higher he went, and the wind became fresher. The sun was directly above him, and then it was behind him, and he was chasing his own waggish shadow, marching up and up. His field of view was taken up with the pale green and yellow grass sloping up directly in front of him. Each blade moved with a slightly separate motion in the burly wind, like agitated worms, or the fronds of some impossibly massive underwater sponge or polypi.

He stopped, sat on a stool of bare rock, and drank from his water bottle. Looking back in the direction he had come, he could see the ship now, terribly distant. Edwards was no longer standing on its back. Nor could he see Sinclair. From this eagle's vantage point, the path the crashing ship had gouged in the soil was very visible, a mottled painterly scar through the grasslands culminating in the broken-backed hourglass of the ship itself. It seemed unlikely, Vins thought, that they had crashed and not simply dashed themselves to atoms. Unlikely survival.

Beyond that the grasslands stretched away. Vins could see a great deal more of the terrain from up here. They were directly above a broad hilly peninsula of land that lay between what looked like two spreading estuaries, north and south. Each of these estuaries quickly widened and spilled into what Vins took to be separate seas—one reaching as far north as he could see and one as far south. It wasn't possible to see whether these seas were connected, whether, in other words, the two estuaries were inlets into one enormous ocean.

The setting sun threw a broadcast spread of lights across those two bodies of water, and they glowed ferociously, beautifully. As he sat there looking down on this landscape, Vins felt the disabling intensity of it all. As if its loveliness might just drain all his willpower and leave him just sitting here, on this saddle of bare rock, sitting in the afternoon warmth, gazing down upon it.

He shook himself. He couldn't allow this place to suck out his strength of purpose. Maybe he was a *homo neanderthalis*, but he was a scientist. He flew spacecraft between the planets.

He picked himself up and marched on, uphill all the way, until the light had thickened and blackened around him. Eventually, exhausted, he stopped and ate some food and rolled himself into his sleeping bag and tried to sleep on the grass. But, tired as he was, he was awake a long time. Something nagged at him. Something about the perspective downhill—those two broad estuaries draining into whatever wide sea, hidden in distance, in haze and clouds and the curve of the world's horizon. What about it? Why did it seem familiar? He couldn't think why.

The fifth day.

He was awakened by something crawling on his face, a lacy caterpillar or beetle with legs like twitching eyelashes. He sat up, rubbing his cheeks with the back of his hand, brushing it away.

It was light.

The sun was up over the crown of the hill to the west and was shining straight in his eyes.

He wiped his face with a dampee, munched some

rations, and drank a tab of coffee. The wind stirred
around him. The landscape below him was, in material
terms, the same one he had seen before he had gone
to sleep; but under the different orientation of sunlight, white morning illumination instead of rosy sunset, it gave the appearance of somewhere totally
different. The two estuaries were still there, kinked
and coastlined in that maddeningly familiar way; but
now their waters were gunmetal and broccoli colored,
a hard and almost tangible mass of color upon which
waves could not be made out. The grass was dark with
dew, hazed over in stretches by a sort of blue blur.
The ship was still there, black as a nut, but Vins
couldn't make out either of his shipmates.

"Now," he said to himself. "Let's get a proper
look."

He unrolled the balloon fabric and fitted the helium
cylinder into its inflation tube. Then he untangled the
harness, and maneuvered himself into it, knotting the
rest of his backpack to a strap so that it would dangle
beneath him as ballast. Then, steadily, he inflated
the balloon.

It took only a few minutes, the flop of fabric swelling and then popping up, like a featureless cartoon
head of prodigious size, to loll and nod above him.
Soon the material was taut, and the breeze was pushing Vins down the hill and across. His feet danced
over the turf, keeping up with the movement for a
while with a series of balletic leaps, and dragging the
pack behind him. Then he was up, the cylinder in his
lap and his bag a pendulum below.

He rose quickly through the dawn air. The breeze
was taking him diagonally down the hill, but only
slowly. At first he looked behind himself, straining
over his shoulder to see what was over the brow of
the hill. But the upward sloping land didn't seem to
come to a peak, or at least not one over which Vins
could peek.

He turned his attention to the eastward landscape.

To his right he could see, as he rose higher, that there was a vast north-south coastline, a tremendous beach bordering an ocean that reached all the way to the horizon. To his left he could see the more northern of the two estuaries; its north shoreline revealed itself to be in fact a long, skinny spit of land. There was a third estuary, even farther to the north. The shape of these arrangements of land and water seemed so familiar to Vins, naggingly so, but he couldn't place it.

He fixed his gaze on the easternmost horizon, but even though he was getting higher and higher, he didn't seem to be seeing over the curve of it. In fact, through some peculiar optical illusion or other, it appeared to be sinking as he rose. That wasn't right.

Vins tried looking up, but the balloon obscured his vision. He thought again about the peculiarities of this world. Was the sky really nothing but a huge blue-painted dome? Would he bump into it shortly? Perhaps not a physical barrier, but some sort of forcefield or holographic medium upon which the motionless stars and the hurtling sun could be projected?

The air was thin. It had gotten thin surprisingly rapidly.

Maybe I *am* the hairiest, Vins thought to himself; but I'm a scientist for all that.

Chill. And blue-gray.

Looking down, looking eastward, Vins knew he had risen high enough. He stared. He gawped. Then, with automatic hand, he began venting gas from his balloon. He commenced his descent. The landscape below him had clicked with his memory.

It was the map of Europe rendered in some impossible geographical form of photographic negative: the green land colored blue for sea, the blue sea colored green for land.

The ship had come down onto the broad grasslands that would, in a normal map of Europe, have been the Atlantic Ocean. The two wide seas he could see from his vantage point were shaped exactly like England, to the north, and like France, to the south. Impossible of course, but there you were. The estuaries that had nagged at his memory had done so because they were shaped like Cornwall and like Normandy. The English Channel was a broad corridor of land, with sea to the north and sea to the south, that widened in the distance into a pleasant meadowland where the North Sea should have been.

Recognizing the familiar contours of the European mainland had impressed itself upon Vins' consciousness so powerfully that it had dizzied him. It must be hallucination. He *stared*, he *gawked*. It was like the visual rebus of the duckrabbit, which you can see *either* as a duck *or* as a rabbit, and, then, as you get used to it, you find that you can flip your vision from one to the other at will. Vins had the heady sense that the broad bodies of water were *in fact land* (an impossibly flat and desert land, it is true), and the variegated stretches of landscape were *in fact water* (upon which light played a myriad of fantastical mirages). But of course that wasn't it. The visual image flipped round again. The land was land and the sea was sea. It was an impossible, inverted geography. The Atlantic highlands. The Sea of England. The Sea of France.

He was in no real place. He didn't know where he was. He was dreaming. He could make no sense of this.

The land rushed up toward him. He had vented too much gas from his balloon, he'd done it too fast, he was coming down too quickly. But his mind wasn't working terribly well.

His feet went pummeling into the turf, and he felt something twang in his right ankle. Pain arced up his leg, and his face went hard onto the grass. The wind was still pushing the balloon onward and dragging him awkwardly along. He fumbled with his harness and with a thundering sense of release the balloon broke free and bobbed away over the landscape.

Vins pulled himself over and sat up. His ankle throbbed. Pain slithered up and down his shin. He watched the balloon recede, ludicrously flexible and bubblelike as it rolled and tumbled down the slope.

This crazy place.

He hauled his pack in by pulling on the cord, hand over hand, and the pack danced and bounced over the turf toward him. From its innards he took out a medipack. The compress felt hot and slimy as he ripped it from its cover, but it did its job as he twined it around his leg. The pain dulled.

As soon as the compress had stiffened sufficiently to bear weight, he hopped up and started the hop-along trek back down the slope. At least, he told himself, it's downhill. At least it's not *uphill*. Downhill across the Atlantic.

He laughed.

He anticipated the reaction of the others when he told them his discovery. To be precise, he rehearsed the possibilities: from galvanizing amazement to indifference or even hostility. So what if they were living in an impossible landscape? The sun rose in the west, and the stars did not move. Maybe they were dead; in which case, why bother? Why bother about anything?

But when he arrived at the ship, it was deserted. Both Sinclair and Edwards had gone. They had taken few or no supplies with them, and at first Vins assumed that they were just scouting out the locality. But after a while of fruitlessly calling their names and several hours of waiting, he concluded that they must have wandered away permanently, like Murphy. Which would be just like them.

If he saw them again—no.

When he saw them again, he ought to grab them by their necks and shake them. Is this any way to run a scientific spaceship? He ought to plunge his hands in between their chins and chestbones and squeeze. Squee-eeze.

When he saw them.

His fury was tiring. It left as soon as it came, and what with the long trek (downhill, sure, but even so) and the returning ache in his bunged-up ankle, Vins felt sleepy. He ate, he drank some, and then he lay down in one of the bunks and fell into dream-free sleep.

The fifth night.

He awoke with a little yelp, and it took him a moment before he was aware that he was inside a blacked-out ship, crashed onto a world itself plunged into the chasm of night. "Though," he said to himself, aloud (to hearten his spirits in all this darkness), "how we're plunged into the chasm of the night when the world doesn't seem to rotate, not a tittle, not a jot, that's beyond me."

His ankle was sore, and it seemed sorer for being ignored. It was a resentful and nasty pain. Analgesic, that was what he needed.

"Sinclair," he called. Then he remembered. "I'm going to wrestle your *neck*, you deserter," he hooted. "Sinclair, you hear? I ought to stamp on your chest."

He had gone to sleep without leaving a torch nearby, so he had to fumble about. But in the perfect blackness he couldn't orient himself at all, couldn't get a mental picture on his location. He came through a bent-out-of-shape hatchway, running his fingers round the rim, and into another black room. No idea where he was. He ranged about, hopeless. Then, through another opening, he saw a rectangle of gray-black gleam, and it smelled clean, and it was the main hatch leading outside.

He stepped through into the glimmer of starlight to get his bearings. He could turn and take in the bulk of the ship, and only then the mental map snapped into focus. First-aid box would be back inside and over to the left. *He* was the hairiest? He was the only one not to have abandoned ship, for crying out loud. For the mother of love and all begorrah, as Murphy would have said if he'd been in one of his quaint moods, they'd all abandoned ship. *They* were the hairiest, damn them.

His ankle was giving him sour hell, and the first-aid box would be back in through the hatch, over to the left. He could find it with his fingers. But he didn't go back inside.

The hair at the back of his neck tingled and stood up like grass as the wind passes through it.

"I," he said, to the starlit landscape, but his voice was half-cracked, so he cleared his throat and spoke out loudly and clearly: "I know you're there. Whoever you are."

He turned. There was nobody.

He turned again. Nobody.

"Come out from where you're hiding," he said. "Is that you, Murphy? That would be *like* your idea of practical japery, you hairy old fool."

He turned, and there was a silhouette against the blackness. Too tall to be Murphy, much too tall to be Edwards or Sinclair. Taller than any person in fact.

Vins stood. The sound of his own breathing was ratchety and intrusive, as if something had malfunctioned somewhere. "Who are you?" he asked. "What do you want? Who are you?"

The silhouette shifted and moved. It hummed a little, a surprisingly high-pitched noise—surprising because of its height. It was a person, clearly, tall but oddly thin, like a putty person stretched between long-boned head and flipperlike feet.

"What are you doing?" Vins repeated.

"You're not supposed to be here," said the figure: a man, though one with a voice high-pitched enough almost to sound womanly.

"We're not supposed to—we *crashed*," returned Vins, his ankle biting at the base of his leg a little. He had to sit down. He could see a little more now, as his eyes dark-adapted; but with no moon, and with no

moonlight, it was still a meager sort of seeing. Vins
moved toward where a rock stood, its occasional embedded spots of mica glinting in the light. This was
the same rock Sinclair had been lying upon when Vins
had last seen him.

"I got to sit down," he said, by way of explanation.

He could see that this long thin person was carrying
something in his right hand, but he couldn't see what.

"Sit down, OK? Do you mind if I sit down, OK?
Is that OK?"

"Sure," said the stranger.

Vins sat, heavily, lifted his frozen-sore ankle, and
picked at the dressing. He needed a new one. This
one wasn't giving him any benefit anymore. The first-
aid box would be in through the hatch and to the
left.

"You're trespassing," asked the stranger. "You've
no right to be here. This world is forbidden to you."

"Is it death?" said Vins, feeling a spurt of fear-
adrenalin, which is also recklessness-adrenalin, in his
chest at the words. Did he dare say such a thing?
What if this stranger were the King of the Land of
the Dead, and what if he, Vins, were disrespecting
him? "Are we all dead? That was one theory we had,
as to why the sun rises awry, and why the stars don't
move—and—and," he added, hurriedly, remembering
the previous day, "why the map is so wrong."

"Wrong?"

"An England-shaped sea where England-land
should be. An Atlantic-shaped landmass where the
ocean should be. *You* know what I'm talking about."

"Of course I do. This is my world. Of course I do."

"My ankle is hurting fit to scream," said Vins.

The stranger moved his arm in the darkness. "This,"
he said, "will have to go." Vins assumed he was pointing at the shuttle. "You've no right to dump this junk
here. I'll have it moved, I tell you. And you—you are
trespassing on a forbidden world. You, sir, have in-
curred the penalty for trespassing."

"You can see pretty well for such a dark night," said Vins.

"You can't?" said the stranger, and he sounded puzzled. "Old eyes, is it?"

"I'm thirty-three," said Vins, bridling.

"I didn't mean *old* in that sense."

There was a silence. The quiet between them was devoid of cricket noise; no blackbird sang. The air was blank and perfectly dark, and only the meanest dribble of starlight illuminated it. Then with a new warmth, as if he had finally understood, the stranger said, "You're a *homo neanderthalis*?"

"And I suppose," replied Vins, as if jesting, "that you're a *homo sapiens*?" But as he said it, even as he gave the words their sarcastic playground spin, he knew it was true. Of course it was true. A creature from the *spiritus mundi* and from dreams and childhood games, standing right here in front of him.

"You're from Earth, of course," the *sapiens* was saying. "You recognized the map of Europe. You steered this craft here. I don't understand why you came here. You boys aren't supposed to know this place even exists."

Vins felt a hard knot of something in his chest, like an elbow trying to come out from inside his ribs. It was intensely uncomfortable. This being from myth and legend, and the race of Homer and Shakespeare and Mohammed and Jesus, was *standing right in front of him now*. He didn't know what to say. There wasn't anything for him to say.

"You want," the human prompted, "to answer my question?"

"You're *actually* a *homo sapiens*?"

"You never met one?"

"Not in the flesh."

"I lose track of time," said the *homo sapiens*. "It's probably been, I don't know. Centuries. It's like that, out here. The time—drifts. You got a name?"

"Vins."

"Well, you're a handsome fellow, Vins. My name is Ramon Harburg Guthrie, a fine old human name, a thousand years old, like me. As I am myself. And no older." He chuckled, though Vins couldn't see what was funny.

"A thousand years?" Vins repeated.

"Give or take. It's been half that time since your lot were shaped, I'll tell you that."

"The last human removed herself four centuries ago," said Vins, feeling foolish that he had to speak such kindergarten sentences.

Ramon Harburg Guthrie laughed. "Shouldn't you be worshiping me as a god?" he asked. "Or something along those lines?"

"Worship you as a god? Why would I want to be doing a thing like that? You're species *homo* and I'm species *homo*. What's to worship?"

"We uplifted you," Ramon Harburg Guthrie pointed out. "Recombined you and backed you out of the evolutionary cul-de-sac, and primed you with—" He stopped. "Listen to *me*!" he said. "I'm probably giving entirely the wrong impression. I don't want to be worshiped as a god."

"I'm glad to hear it," said Vins. "There's nothing subcapacity about my *neanderthalis* brain pan. I speak from experience but also from scientific research into the matter, using some of the many *homo sapiens sapiens* skulls that litter the soil of the Earth. I've spent twelve years studying science."

"Our science," said Ramon Harburg Guthrie.

"Science is science, and who cares who discovered it? And if you care who discovered it, then it's not *your* science, Ramon Harburg Guthrie, it's Newton's and Einstein's."

But his tone had wandered the wrong side of angry. The *homo sapiens* lifted whatever it was he was holding in his right hand. When he spoke again, his high voice was harder-edged. "I built this place," he said. "It's mine. It's a private world, and visitors are not allowed. I don't care about your brain pan, or about my brain pan, I only care about my privacy. You—go. Are there others?"

"We crashed," said Vins, feeling a sense of panic growing now, though he wasn't sure exactly why. It was more than just the mysterious *something* the man was holding in his right hand. It was something else.

"I don't care how you came here. You're trespassing. Not welcome."

"It's hardly fair. It's not as if you put up a sign saying no entry."

He scoffed. "That'd be tantamount to shouting aloud to the whole system, *here I am*! That'd be like putting a parsec-wide neon arrow pointing at my home. And why would I want to do that? I built my world away from the ecliptic and down, it's as flat as a coin and its slender edge is angled toward Earth. You can't see me, you inheritors of that polluted old world. You *don't know* I'm here. There are similar ruses used all about this solar system. Similar eyries and haunts, radio-blanked bubbles and curves of habitable landscape tucked away. A thousand baubles and twists of landscape. Built by the old guard, the last of the *truly* wealthy and *truly* well-bred individuals. Who'd trade true breeding for a mere enhanced physical strength and endurance?" He spoke these last five words with a mocking intonation, as if the very idea were absurd. "And yes I know your brain pans are the same size. But size isn't everything, my dearie."

Vins was shivering, or perhaps trembling with fear, but he summoned his courage. "I'm no dearie of yours," he said. "What's that in your hand anyway? A weapon, is it?"

"How many were there in your crew."

Of course Vins couldn't lie, not when asked a direct question like that. He tried one more wriggle. "A severely spoken and impolite question," he said.

"How many in your *crew*?"

"Four," he said. "Including me."

"Inside?"

"Are *they* inside? The ship?"

"Are they inside, yes."

"No. They wandered off. They were seduced by this world, I think. It's a beautiful place, especially when you've been tanked up in a spaceship for three months. It's a beautiful, beautiful place"

"Thank you!" said the *homo sapiens* Ramon Harburg Guthrie. And there was genuine pleasure in his voice. He was actually flattered. "It's my big dumb object. Big and dumb but *I* like it."

The sky, minutely and almost imperceptibly, was starting to pale over to the west. The silhouette had taken on the intimations of solidity; more than just a 2D gap in the blackness, it was starting to bulk. Dark gray face propped on dark gray body, but there was a perceptible difference in tone between the two things, one smooth and one the rougher texture of fabric.

"*You* didn't build this," said Vins. "I'm not being disrespectful, but. I'm not. Only—who can build a whole world? You're not a god. Sure, the legacy of *homo sapiens* is a wonderful thing, the language and the culture and so on. But *build* a whole world?"

"Indeed, I did build it," said Ramon Harburg Guthrie levelly.

"How many trillions of tons of matter, to pull one g?" asked Vins. "And how do you hide an Earth-sized object from observation by . . ."

"You've done well," said Ramon Harburg Guthrie, "if you've taken the twentieth-century science with which we left you and built spacecraft capable of coming all the way out here." He sounded indulgent. "But that's not to say that you've caught up with us. We've been at it millennia. You've only been independent a handful of centuries. Left to your own devices for a handful of centuries."

The light was growing behind the western horizon. The human's face was still indistinct. The object he held in his right hand was still indistinct. But in a moment it would be clearer. Vins was shivering hard now. It was very cold.

"That's no explanation, if you don't mind me saying so," he said, with little heaves of misemphasis on account of his shivering chest and his chattery teeth. The human didn't seem in the least incommoded by the cold.

"It's not a globe," he said. "It's my world, and I built it as I liked. It's not for you; it's *me*-topia. You're not supposed to be here."

"It's beautiful, and its empty; it's void. There aren't even deer or antelope or cows. How is that utopia?"

He was expecting the human to say *each to his own*, or *I prefer solitude*, or something like that. But he didn't. He said, "Oh, my dearie, it's void on *this* side. I haven't gotten round to doing anything with this side. There's world enough and time for that. But on the *other* side of the coin, it's crowded with fun and interest."

"The other side," said Vins.

"It's a little over a thousand miles across," said Ramon Harburg Guthrie. "So it's pretty much the biggest coin ever minted. But it's not trillions of tons of matter; it's a thin circular sheet of dense-stuff, threaded with gravity wiring. There's some distortion; it appears to go up at the rim, highlands in all directions, and on both sides, which is odd."

"Which is odd," repeated Vins. He didn't know why it was odd.

"It's odd because it's a gravitational effect. It's not that the *rim* is any thicker than any other place on the disk. But the gravitational bias helps keep the atmosphere from spilling over the sides, I suppose. I lost interest in that a while ago. And the central territories are flat enough to preserve the landscape almost exactly."

"Preserve the landscape," chattered Vins.

"I had it pressed into the underlying matter: the

countries of my youth. Europe. That's on the other side. On *this* side is the reverse of the recto. It's the anti-Europe. But landscaped, of course. Water and biomass and air added, not just nude to space. No, no. It's ready. Sometime soon I'll live over this side for a while."

"The anti-Europe," said Vins. The cold seemed to be slowing his thought processes. He couldn't work it out.

"Stamp an R in a sheet of gold, and the other side will have a little Я standing proud," he said. "*You* know that. Stamp a valley in one side of a sheet and you get a mountain on the other side."

The light was almost strong enough to see. That gray predawn light, so cool and fine and satiny.

"Stamp a *homo neanderthalis* out of the hominid base matter," Ramon Harburg Guthrie said, as if talking to himself, "and you stamp out a backward-facing *homo sapiens* on the recto." This seemed to amuse him. He laughed, at any rate.

Vins put a knuckle to his eyes and rubbed away some of the chill of the night. The human's features were—just—visible in the gray of the predawn: a long nose, small eyes, a sawn-off forehead and eggshell-delicate cranium above it. Like a cartoon-drawing of a *sapiens*. Like a caricature from a schoolbook. A stretched-out, elfin figure. A porcelain and anorexic giant.

"You're not welcome," Guthrie said, one final time. "This world is forbidden to you and your sort. I'll find your crewmates and give them the sad news. But I'll deal with you first, and I'm sorry to say it, because I'm not a bloodthirsty sort of fellow. But what can I do? But—trespassers—will be—" and he raised his right hand.

This was the moment when Vins found out for sure what that right hand contained. It was a weapon, of course, and Vins was already ahead of the action. He pushed forward on his muscular neanderthal legs, moving straight for the human. But then he jinked as hard as his sore ankle permitted him, ninety degrees right. The lurch forward was to frighten Ramon Harburg Guthrie into firing before he was quite ready; the jink to the right was to make sure the projectile missed and give him a chance of making it to the long grass.

But Ramon Harburg Guthrie was more level-headed than that. It's true he cried out, a little yelp of fear as the bulky neanderthal loomed up at him, but he kept his aim reasonably steady. The weapon discharged with a booming noise, and Vins' head rang like a gong. There was a disorienting slash of pain across his left temple, and he spun and tumbled, his bad ankle folding underneath him. There was a great deal of pain, suddenly, out of nowhere, and his eyes weren't working. The sky had been folded up and propped on its side. It was gray, drained of life, drained of color. But it wasn't on its side; Vins was lying on the turf beside the rock, and it was the angle at which he was looking at it.

There was a throb. This was more than a mere knock; it was a powerful, skull-clenching *throb*.

Nevertheless, when Ramon Harburg Guthrie's leg appeared in Vins' line of sight, at the same right-angle as the sky, he knew what it meant. This was no time to be lying about, lounging on the floor, waiting for the coup de grâce of another projectile in the—

He was up. He put all his muscular strength into the leap, and it was certainly enough to surprise Ramon Harburg Guthrie. Vins' shoulder, coming up like a piston upstroke, caught him under the chin, or against the chest, or somewhere (it wasn't easy to see); and there was an *ooph* sound in Vins' left ear. He brought his heavy right arm around as quick as he could, and there was a soggy impact of fist on flesh. Not sure which flesh; but it was a softer flesh than Vins' thick-skinned pelt; it was a more fragile bone than the thick stuff that constituted Vins' brain pan. Although, as he had said, the thickness didn't mean that there was any compromise in size.

The next thing that happened was that Vins heard a rushing noise. He looked where Ramon Harburg Guthrie had been, and there was only a thread, a string wet and heavy with red phlegm, and it wobbled as if blown in the dawn breeze; when Vins looked up, he saw this string attached to the shape of a flying human male. The string broke, and then another spooled down, angling now because the flying man (propelled by whatever powerpack he was wearing, whatever device it was that lifted him away from the pull of the artificial gravity) was flying away to the north.

Stunned by his grazed head, it took Vins a second to figure out what he was seeing: The string was a drool of blood falling from a wound he, Vins, had inflicted on the head of Ramon Harburg Guthrie. "Clearly," he said aloud, as he put a finger to his own head wound, "clearly he's still conscious enough to be operating whatever fancy equipment is helping him fly away." His fingers came away jammy with red.

"Clearly, I didn't hit him hard enough."

The sun was up now. In the new light Vins found the gun that, in his pain and shock, and in his hurry to get away, Ramon Harburg Guthrie had dropped.

The sixth morning.

While the figure of the *sapiens* was still visible, just, in the northern sky, Vins dashed inside the shuttle; he pulled out some food, the first-aid pack, some netting. It all went into a pack, together with the gun.

When he came out the *sapiens* could no longer be seen.

His head was hurting. His ankle was hurting.

He hurried away through the long grass, following the path that Murphy had originally made. He didn't want to leave a new trail, one that would (of course!) be obvious from the air; but he didn't want to loiter

by the shuttle. Who knew what powers of explosive
destruction Ramon Harburg Guthrie could bring
screaming out of the sky. It was his world, after all.

There were a number of lone trees growing high
out of the grass before the forest proper began, and
Murphy's old track passed by one of these. Vins let
the first go and stopped at the second. He clambered
into the lower branches and shuffled along the bough
to ensure that the leaves were giving him cover. He
scanned the sky, but there was nothing.

There was time, now, to tend to himself. He pulled
a pure-pad from the first-aid box and stuck it to the
side of his head, feeling with his finger first. A hole,
elliptically shaped, like the mouth of a hollow reed
cut slantways across. Blood was pulsing out of it.
Blood had gone over the left of his face, glued itself
into his six-day-beard, made a plasticky mat over his
cheek. He must look a sight. But he was alive.

He ate some food and drank more than he wanted;
but it wouldn't do to dehydrate. Exsanguinations pro-
voke dehydration. He'd learned that.

The leaves on the tree were plump, dark-green,
cinquefoil. There were very many of them, and they
rubbed up against one another and trembled and
buzzed in the breeze. The sky was a high blue, clear
and pure.

The sixth afternoon.

He dozed. The day moved on.

He heard somebody approaching, tramping lustily
out of the forest. Presumably not Ramon Harburg
Guthrie then.

It was Murphy. He could hardly have been making
a bigger racket. Vins' strong fingers pulled up a chunk
of bark from the bough upon which he rested, and
when Murphy came underneath the tree, he threw it
down upon him.

"Quiet," he hissed. "You want to get us killed?"

"No call to throw pebbles at me," said Murphy, in a hurt voice, his head back.

"It was bark, and it was called for. Come up here and be quick and be *quiet*."

When he was up, and when Murphy had gotten past the point of repeating, "What happened to your head? What did you do to your head? There's blood all over your head," Vins explained.

Murphy thought about this. "It makes sense."

"Where did you get to, anyway?"

"I was exploring!" cried Murphy, in a large, self-justifying voice.

"Keep quiet!"

"You're not the captain, and neither you aren't," said Murphy. "You're not the one to tell me don't go exploring. Are we scientists? I've been down to the sea, to where the surf grinds thunder out of the beach. All manner of shells and . . ." He stopped. "This feller shot you?"

"It's his world."

He peered closely at Vins' head. "That's some trepanning he's worked on you. That's some hole."

"He made it, and he says we're not allowed here. He'll kill all four of us. We can't afford to be blundering about."

"He's threatening murder. That would be murder."

"It surely is."

"And is he," asked Murphy, "not *concerned* to be committing murder upon us?"

"He's *homo sapiens*," said Vins. "I told you."

"And so you did. It's hard to take in. But it explains . . ." He trailed off.

"What does it explain?"

"This is an artifact, of course it is. That'll be the strange sky, that'll explain it. The stars don't move, or hardly, because it doesn't rotate. The sun—that'll be an orbiting device, flying its way around and about.

Maybe a mirror—maybe a crystal globe refracting sunlight to produce a variety of effects." He seemed pleased with himself. "That explains a lot."

"You sound like Edwards," said Vins.

"Don't insult my family name in suchwise fashion!" growled Murphy.

"It's a thousand miles across. It's a flat disk. I don't know how he generates the gravity. It's clearly not by *mass*."

"So you met an actual breathing *homo sapiens*?" asked Murphy, as one might ask, *You met a unicorn? You met a cyclops?*

"I think," said Vins, "that he was expecting me to . . . I don't know. To worship him as a god."

Murphy whooped with laughter and then swallowed the noise before Vins could shush him. "Why on sweet wide water would he want such a thing?"

"He said that he—he said that *they*—uplifted us," said Vins. "Brought us out of the evolutionary dustbin, that sort of thing. Taught us the language. Left us their culture in the memory banks, saved us the bother of spending thousands of years making our own. He was implying, I think, that we *owed* them."

"Did you ever read Frankenstein's monster's story? That's a *homo sapiens* way of thinking," said Murphy. "There's something alien in all that duty, indebtedness, belatedness, *you-owe-me* rubbish. But what you should've said to *him*, what you *should* have said, is: My right and respectfulness, sir, didn't Shakespeare uplift *you* out of the aesthetic blankness of the Middle Ages? Didn't Newton uplift you out of the ignorance of the Dark Ages, give you the power to fly the spaceways? Do you worship Newton as a god? Course you don't—you say thank you and tap at your brow with your knuckles, and you *move on*."

"It's all a dim age," agreed Vins. He was referring to the elder age. It was something in the past, like the invention of the wheel or the smelting of iron, but only a few cranks spent too much time bothering about it. Too much to do.

"How could you fail to move on? What sort of a person would you be? An ancestor worshiper, or something like that."

"They withdrew from the world," said Vins. "It's vacant possession. It's ours, now. All the rainy, stony spaces of it."

"And I say this is the same, this place we've stumbled into. I say this Murphytopia is the same case—it's vacant possession."

He was quiet for a while. Vins was scanning the sky through the branches, looking for signs if the human.

"I say it's ours and I say the hell with him," said Murphy, rolling his fist through the air

"Here," repeated Vins. "It's forbidden us. He says it's forbidden to us."

"*He* says?" boomed Murphy, climbing up on his legs on the bough to shout the phrase at the manufactured sky. "And who's *he* to stop us?"

"Will you *hush*?" snapped Vins.

The sky was a clear watercolor wash from high dark blue to the pink of the low eastern sky. There were a few thready horizontal clouds, like loose strands of straw. The sun itself, or whatever device it was that circled the world to reflect sunlight upon it, was a small circle of chili-pepper red.

"It is beautiful here," said Murphy. Sitting down again on the turf.

"It's mild," agreed Vins.

"Does that mean that those old children's stories are true?" Murphy asked. "They, the *sapiens*, messed up the climate and then just walked away. Pumped up some *homo sapiens* bodies to *neanderthalis* endurance levels, crash-loaded their minds with English and French and Russian and whatever and just ran away."

"Who knows?"

"But this is what bugs me," said Murphy. "If they

had the—if they *have* the capacity to build whole new worlds, like this one, and provide it with a beautiful climate, you know, *why* not simply sort out the climate on Earth? Why not reach their godlike fingers into the ocean flow and the airstream and dabble a bit and return the Earth to a temperate climate?"

Vins didn't answer this at first; he didn't think it was really addressed to him. But Murphy wouldn't let it go.

"Left the mess and just ran away. Cold and snow and rain and deserts of broken rock. That's downright irresponsible. Why *not* mend the mess they'd made? Why not?"

"I suppose," said Vins, reluctantly, "it's easier to manage a model like this one. Even a rather large model, like this one. The climate of the whole Earth—that's a chaotic system, isn't it? That's not a simple circular body of air a thousand miles across, that's a three-dimensional vortex tens of thousands of miles arc by arc. Big dumb object, he called it."

"He?"

"Maybe they can't crack the problem of controlling chaotic systems any more than we can. *He* is the *homo sapiens* I met. When I said *he* called it that, I meant Ramon Harburg Guthrie called it that."

"Doesn't sound very godlike at all."

"No."

"And doesn't excuse them from fleeing their mess."

"I wasn't suggesting that it did."

"And what *were* you suggesting?"

Vins coughed. "I'll tell you—I'll say what I'm suggesting. Ramon Harburg Guthrie said that the elder *sapiens*, the wealthiest thousands, fled throughout the system. They built themselves little private utopias of all shapes and sizes. They're living there now, or their descendents are. But these should be our lands. Why would we struggle on with the wastelands and the ice—or," and he threw his hands up, "or Mars, for crying in the wilderness, Mars?" He spoke as an individual who had lived two full terms on Mars, once during his compulsory military training and once during his scientific education. He knew whereof he spoke: the extraordinary cold, the barrenness, the slow and stubborn progress of colonization. "Why would we be trying to bully a life out of Mars, of all places, if the system is littered with private paradises like this one?"

"I like the cut of your jib, the shape of your thinking, young Vins," said Murphy, saluting him and then shaking his hand. "But what of the man who scratched your head, there? What of that bold *sapiens* fellow himself?"

"He thinks he's hunting us," said Vins. There was something nearly sadness in his voice, a species of regret. "He doesn't yet realize." He pulled the gun out of the bag.

They sat for a while in silence. From time to time Murphy would go, "Remind me what we're waiting for, here?" And Vins would explain it again. "He'll come back," he said. "He'll get his skull bandaged, or get it healed-up with some high-tech magic-ray, I don't know. But he'll be back. He has to eliminate all four of us before we can put a message where others can hear it."

"And shouldn't we be doing that? Putting the message out there for others to know where we are—to know that such a place as *here* even exists?"

"That would require us to stay at . . ." prompted Vins.

"Stay in the shuttle," said Murphy. "I see. So you reckon he'll? You think he'll?"

"What would *you* do? He came before with some sort of personal flying harness, like a skyhook, and a handgun. He'll come back heavier. He'll hit the ship first, to shut that door firm."

"I guess we already tried the radio. Broadcast, I mean. But who'd be listening? Who'd be monitoring this piece of sky? Nobody." He picked some bark from the bough and crumpled it to papery shards between his strong fingers. "I suppose," he continued, "that this *homo sapiens* feller, he's not to know how long we've been here. For all he knows we just crashed here, this morning. Or we've been here a month."

"He'll have to take his chances," agreed Vins. "He'll come back and hammer the ship, smash and dint it into the dirt."

"Then what?"

"There are several ways it could go. If he's smart, if he were as smart as me, he'd lay waste to the whole area. I'd scorch the whole thousand-square-mile area."

"But he lives here!"

"He lives on the other side. He don't need here. But he won't do that. He's attached to it, he's sentimentally connected with the landscape, its beauty. With its vacuity and its possibility. He won't do that. So, *if* he's smart, he'll do the second-best option."

"Which is what?"

"He'll wait until dark and then overfly the area with the highest-power infrared detection he can muster. He'd pick out our body heat. Or, at least, it would be hard for us to disguise that."

"You think he'll do that?"

Vins bared his teeth and then sealed his lips again. "No I don't think so. He'll want to hunt us straight down. He'll blow the ship and then come galloping down these paths we've trailed through the long grass. He'll try and hunt us down. He'll have armor on, probably. Big guns. He'll have big guns with fat barrels."

"Other people? Other *sapiens*?"

"That," said Vins, "is the real question. That's the crucial thing. He called this world *me*-topia. Does that suggest to you, Murphy, a solitary individual, living perhaps with a few upgraded cats and dogs, maybe a metal mickey or two?"

"I've no notion."

"Or does it suggest a population of a thousand *sapiens*, or a hundred thousand, living in the clean open spaces on the far side of this disk—living a medieval Europe, perhaps. Riding around dressed in silk and hunting the white stag?"

"I've really no notion."

"And neither have I. That'll be what we find out."

"You're a regular strategos," said Murphy, and he whistled through his two front teeth. "A real strategic thinker. And then?"

"Then?"

"Then what?"

"Well," said Vins. "That'll depend, of course. If it's just him, I don't see why we don't take the whole place to ourselves. There's a lot of fertile ground here, a lot of settlement potential for people back home. And if it's more than just him—"

"Maybe the far side is crawling with *homo sapiens*."

"Maybe it is. But *this* side isn't. We could pile our own people onto this side of the world and see what happens. See if we can arrive at an understanding. Who knows? That's a long way in the future." He peered through the leaves at the luster of the meadows, the beaming waters, the warm blue sky.

Murphy dozed, and was not awakened by the brittle sound of something scratching along the sky. But he was awakened by the great basso profundo *whumph* of the shuttle exploding: a monstrous booming, then a squat eggshaped mass of fire that mottled and clouded almost at once with its own smoke, and pushed a stalk of black up and out in an umbrella-shape into the sky. Some moments later the tree shook heartily. After that there was the random percussion and thud of bits of wreckage slamming back to earth.

Murphy almost fell out of the tree. Vins grabbed him.

Their ship was a crater now, and a scattering pattern

of gobbets of plasmetal flowing into the sky at forty-
five degrees and crashing down again to earth at forty-
five degrees, the petal pattern all around the central
destruction.

"Look," Vins hissed.

A ship, shaped like the sleek head of a greyhound,
flew through, banked, and landed a hundred yards
from the crater. It ejected a single figure and lifted
off again.

The sound of the explosion was still rumbling in
the air.

"Was that our ship?" said Murphy, stupidly. "Did
he just destroy our—"

"Shush, now," said Vins, in a low voice. "That's
him."

"Then who's flying the ship?"

"It'll be another *sapiens* or else an automatic system; that hardly matters. The ship will circle back
there, in case Edwards or Sinclair are nearby and
come running out to see what the noise is. But *he'll*
come after us. He knows I won't be fooled by—" And
even as Vins was speaking, the figure, armored like
an inflated figure, like a man made of tires, turned its
head and selected one of the trails through the grass
and starting trotting along it.

"That's a big gun he's carrying," Murphy pointed
out. "He's coming this way with a very big gun."

"He's coming this way," said Vins, taking the gun
out of his sack and prepping it, "with his eggshell skull
and his sluggy reactions."

"What are you going to do?" asked Murphy.

"Do you think he'll look upward as he comes under
this tree?"

"*I* don't know."

"Don't you?"

"And if you kill him, what then?"

"I hope not to kill him, not straight off," said Vins,

in a scientific voice. "I'll need him to get that plane to come down so we can use it."

He was coming down the path. Vins and Murphy waited in the tree, waiting for him to pass beneath them—or for him to notice them, the two of them, in the tree and shoot them down.

He was armored of course. He came closer.

Maybe that's the way it goes. It's hard for me to be, from this perspective, sure. Indeed it's hard, sometimes, to tell the difference between the two different sorts of human. These neanderthals, after all, are not created *ex nihilo* via some genetically engineered miracle; they were ordinary *sapiens* adapted and enhanced (strengthened, given more endurance) the better to carry on living on their home world. The stay-at-homes. The ones sentimentally attached to where they happened to be. They're the same people as the *sapiens*, whom they—perhaps *surprisingly* quickly—supplanted. Does it matter if they come swarming all over Guthrie's bubble-wrapped world? Is that a better, or a worse, eventuality than that place remaining the rich man's private fiefdom?

It's all lotus.

The seventh day.

The sun rose in the west, as it did. Clouds clung about the lower reaches of the sky like the froth on the lip of a gigantic ceramic mug of cappuccino: white and frothy and stained hither and thither with touches of golden brown.

The grasslands rejoiced in the touch of the sun. I say *rejoiced* in the strong sense of the word. Light passed through reality filters. Wind passed *over* the shafts of grass, moving them, pausing, moving again; but light passed *through* them. Wind made a lullaby song of hushes and then paused to make even more eloquent moments of silence. But the light shone right through. Light passed through *two* profound reality filters. This is photons. These are photons. Photons were always already rushing faster than mass from the surface of the sun. They were passing through a hunk of crystal in the sky, modified with various other minerals and smart-patches, and were deflected onto the surface of the world. This globe served the world as its illumination. The photons passed again through the slender sheaths of green and yellow, those trillions of close-fitting rubber bricks we call cells; cells stacked multiple-layered and rippling out in all directions, gathered into superstructures of magnificent length and fragility; and in every single cell the light chanced through matter and came alive, alive, with the most vibrant and exhilarating and ecstatic thrumming of the spirit. That's where it's at. The light, the translucence of matter, the inflection of the photons, the grass singing, and just after.

Forbidden Planet

Stephen Baxter

If you have a nodding acquaintance with the long history of *Star Trek*, you'll probably know that the original 1960s series was allowed not just one but two pilot episodes before its final green light. But if you watch the classic 1956 movie *Forbidden Planet*, you might be forgiven for thinking you're viewing an even earlier *Trek* pilot. And in a sense you are.

It is the year 2257. Under the command of brave and handsome Commander Adams (Leslie Nielsen, who eventually morphed into the straight-faced hero of the *Naked Gun* comedies), United Planets space cruiser C57-D lands on the planet Altair IV, in search of the lost spacecraft *Bellerophon.* They discover obsessive scientist Dr. Morbius (Walter Pidgeon), living in an impressive home with a sophisticated robot, Robby, who speaks 187 languages and can make diamonds, and Morbius' teenage daughter, Altaira (Anne Francis). Nobody else survives.

Morbius warns Adams he must leave, before his crew are hunted down by a "planetary force" that destroyed the *Bellerophon*—a horror we come to know as the "id-monster." Adams wonders how come only Morbius, his wife (now dead), and Altaira were spared, and how philologist Morbius, a language expert, managed to build Robby. Meanwhile, the crewmen drool over Altaira. In the end Adams bags her for himself, and Morbius shows disturbing signs of jealousy.

And the crew come under attack by the monster. A spectral outline hurls itself against their perimeter shielding—but it disappears when Morbius wakes from a nightmare. . . .

At last Morbius reveals his secret. He has been exploring stunning machinery left behind by the long-dead alien Krell. In the film's finest sequence the men explore a twenty-mile-wide cubical machine buried in the ground; walkways, with ant-sized astronauts passing along them, bridge what looks like the interior of an immense valve radio.

There are headsets to boost your intelligence—which is how Morbius was able to build Robby—and the machine's purpose is to enable the materialization of thoughts: Think it, and it becomes real. But as well as crystallizing conscious ideas, the machine also unleashes the subconscious rage of your deeper mind, the id. This unfortunate side effect killed off the Krell themselves.

And as he unwisely tinkered with the machinery, Morbius' own released demons did for his crewmates: the id-monster is Morbius' other darker self. Now Morbius' unhealthy jealousy over his daughter threatens to wipe out Adams and his crew—but Morbius at last sacrifices himself, leaving Altaira in Adams' arms.

Planet, made in 1956, is distinguished from other genre movies of its time in that it is *actually quite good science fiction*. This was recognized by the field's practitioners. It is said that one master sf author (Lester Del Rey) remarked to another (Frederik Pohl), "That's the first original science fiction movie I've seen that could have made a fine novelette for *Astounding*" (the top sf magazine of its day). This was despite the fact that none of the principals involved in *Planet* had had much involvement with the genre before. Before *Planet*, director Fred McLeod Wilcox was best known for his work on *Lassie Come Home*. With a screenplay by Cyril Hume from a story by Irving Block and Allen Adler, the story was original (or at least, as Shakespeare was long dead, out of copyright—see below).

The production, filmed in Cinemascope and bright Eastman Color, took two years, costing a then-hefty $1.6 million—indeed this was the first sf film to cost in excess of $1 million. But it was money well spent. The production design was fine throughout—arguably the finest in genre movies until *2001* a decade later. The id-monster was effectively animated by Josh Meador, who had worked at the Disney studios. The planet Altair IV, around the landed spacecraft, was created on a vast set with a circular wall painting; in some sequences you can see the crewmen actually walk off into the distance, without ever colliding with the painted mountains. The soundtrack by Louis and Bebe Barron, or rather the "electronic tonalities," without a bar of melody, was created entirely electronically and cost a cool $25,000.

Planet was unusual for its time in showing a relatively positive future, of men (mostly) and technology united in a future of prosperity and peaceful exploration. In the 1950s Cold War fears shaped sf. Many of the finest genre movies dealt with the horrors of Communist invasion and nuclear war either directly, like *On the Beach* (1959), or through metaphors of alien invasion and mind control, like *The War of the Worlds* (1953) and *Invasion of the Body Snatchers* (1956). It wasn't an age of exploration and wonder but of hunkered-down fear, in which you didn't go seek out the alien, but it came to hunt you down in your home.

But that's not to say that *Planet* was escapism. *Planet* has an intellectual depth that remains impressive. This colorful genre movie, all spaceships and ray guns, is a steal from Shakespeare! The Bard's play *The Tempest* (written about 1611) is beamed up from an island on Earth to an island in space. Shakespeare's Duke Prospero becomes Morbius. The virginal Miranda is Altaira. The supernatural sprite Ariel becomes Robby, and the subhuman creature Caliban is the id-monster.

There may be cultural nods in the name of the *Bellerophon* too. In Greek myth Bellerophon stole the winged horse Pegasus and, trying to fly up to heaven, was killed. Alternatively *Bellerophon* was the ship that took Napoleon to his final exile on the island of St. Helena. Either of these sound like workable metaphors for Morbius, but the reference is never explored in the movie. In contrast to all this mythical stuff, the ship from Earth is utterly utilitarian, with no name at all but a number, and its all-male crew, dressed only in gray, have lust but no romance in their souls: "Nothing to do but throw rocks at tin cans, and we gotta bring the tin cans."

So the movie has depth. But it isn't without faults, such as the utterly leaden humor. Suffice it to say that Robby gets the best lines.

And then there is Altaira. It's not uncommon for movies of this period to make uncomfortable viewing regarding their treatment of women, but this one is particularly teeth-curling. Altaira, after all, has been effectively imprisoned by a father who, as is hinted darkly, may lust incestuously after her himself. She has grown up almost feral, never having met another adult save her father, and has a total and supposedly charming naïveté: "What's a bathing suit?" The salivating men of the C-57D ruthlessly exploit this naïveté in trying to get it on with her. Commander Adams *blames her* for provoking this behavior, before moving in for the kill himself. The movie's treatment of Altaira is both creepily exploitative and a missed imaginative opportunity.

These faults aside, the movie's dark tone, sophisticated emotional maturity, and multiple meanings have been unpacked by its audiences ever since its release.

There is humility in Morbius' encounter with the Krell. Just as conquering Anglo-Saxons once cowered in superstitious awe of ruined Roman cities, so even the starfaring humans of the future are dwarfed compared to the mighty achievements of this vanished race. You might even look for a biblical parallel. Adams is like Adam, and Altaira like Eve, in a planetary Garden of Eden whose equilibrium is ruined by their kiss.

On another level, perhaps there's a metaphor even in this expansive movie for the bombs-and-bunkers horror of the Cold War: You meddle with advanced technology at your peril. Shakespeare's Prospero was a ruler and an intellectual who gave up power but stayed in the world of knowledge. In the 1950s, however, scientists were distrusted; so Morbius' curiosity about the Krell machinery is foolish arrogance that nearly ends up killing everybody. He's not the only scientist in sf to have echoes of another literary prototype, Faustus.

In the end, however, this tale of starships and alien machinery is all about humanity. Adams' sense of duty is compromised by love, and the id-monster is an embodiment of Morbius' murky jealousy over his daughter. So it isn't the Krell machinery that threatens the humans but their own inner flaws. Many sf tales of exploration are extrapolations of the American dream of the frontier: We can put our conflicts behind us if only we can find enough room. But *Planet* tells us that no matter how far we travel, we can't leave ourselves behind.

Fifty years on, *Planet* remains influential—and not just in the borrowing of its name by Britain's leading specialist sf chain. The movie's innovative use of electronic music and striking visuals have found endless echoes; it is impossible to gaze on vistas of vast alien machinery like those in *Total Recall* (1990) or *Babylon 5*'s Epsilon 3, for instance, without recalling the chambers of the Krell. Its psychological storyline is often homaged too. The id-monster is echoed in at least one of the theories about the meaning of the current hit TV show *Lost*—set, of course, on another island.

Robby remains one of the best-loved robots ever seen in the movies. His inability to harm humans, drawing on the then well-established Laws of Robotics set out in Isaac Asimov's *I, Robot* stories, places him light-years away from the usual "kill-all-humans" idiot-robot portrayal much panned in *The Simpsons* but still, ironically, taken seriously in, for example, ironically, in the movie *I, Robot.* Robby went on to star in an unrelated kid's movie called *The Invisible Boy* (1957). The "Danger, Will Robinson!" robot of the 1960s TV hit *Lost in Space* wasn't Robby, but it wasn't terribly unlike the altruistic avatar of Altair. Robby toys are still produced, and original models are highly prized collectibles.

The movie's strongest influence is secondary, however, through *Star Trek*. Explorations in space have always been a key theme in science fiction —for instance, AE van Vogt's *The Voyage of the Space Beagle* (1950). But media folk tend to be influenced primarily by other media products, and *Trek* creator Gene Roddenberry made no secret of the fact that his thinking was heavily shaped by *Planet*.

Planet's echoes are obvious even in *Trek*'s original pilot, *The Cage*. For the United Planets read the United Federation of Planets. As Commander Adams went before him and James T. Kirk would later, brave Captain Pike leads the *Enterprise* on an adventure of interplanetary discovery. The C-57D, with the Navy-cruiser feel of the *Enterprise*, is stocked with an earthy doctor and a ship's engineer of the traditional mold ("All right, it's impossible. How long will it take?"). *Planet* has sliding doors, force-field shields, communicators (mounted on the crew's belts), and a replicator (in Robby's belly). Just like Adams, Pike finds human survivors on a remote planet. And Pike gets first dibs on the beautiful girl, just like Adams, and just as Kirk would many times.

To some extent all of *Trek*'s planetary excursions took place in the shadow of Commander Adams' sole expedition. Kirk and his successors would frequently find themselves humbled before the titanic achievements of superior races. And *Trek* often demonstrated its visual debt to the movie—for instance, the Krell underground complex is reminiscent of the interior of a Borg cube.

Even *Planet*'s nod to Shakespeare found many echoes in *Trek*, beginning with the *Original Series* episode, "Conscience of the King," which featured a production of *Hamlet*. Who could forget General Chang, in *Star Trek VI: The Undiscovered Country*, a movie which actually took its title from a Shakespeare line, taunting Kirk with quotations from the Bard, which always sounded better "in the original Klingon"? In a sense the circle was closed in the *Next Generation* episode *Emergence*, in which, in a holodeck production of *The Tempest*, the robot Data, a distant descendant of Robby, actually gets to play Prospero.

Trek emulated *Planet* in mixing interplanetary adventure with strong characterization and at least an attempt at moral complexity. Even if *Trek* rarely achieved the multilayered depth of *Planet*, without the movie's prior demonstration that at least some of the audience could accept such seriousness in sf, *Trek* would surely never have dared go where no franchise had gone before.

And, amazingly, *Forbidden Planet* itself has stayed imaginatively alive. The hilarious 1990s stage musical *Return to the Forbidden Planet* deconstructs the movie by putting Shakespeare's lines *back in*, and by camping up the cheesy 1950s skiffyness—think Troy Tempest–style peaked caps and epaulets, a roller-skating silver robot, and ray guns made from Bakelite hair dryers. This is a homage to the movie that *Planet*'s makers could barely have imagined but surely would have loved.

Forbidden Planet showed that spectacle and seriousness could combine in effective genre moviemaking, and it casts a long shadow today. But as is the fate of much of the best sf, maybe it was too smart for its cinema-going audience. While contemporary so-bad-it's-good B-movie dross like *Earth vs. The Flying Saucers* raked it in, and Roddenberry's son-of-*Planet* behemoth went on to become a multibillion-dollar franchise, *Planet* itself recouped only half its budget.

Author and Story Notes

Stephen Baxter started to read sf in the 1960s, so he was immersed in the culture of the 1950s: Asimov, Clarke, Dick, Sheckley, and the rest—and *Forbidden Planet*, regularly shown on TV all through his formative years. Not surprisingly, it's had quite an effect . . . as you can see from the Afterword to this volume.

Steve is currently working on a series of history-tampering novels called *Time's Tapestry*. In addition, he's continuing the *Time Odyssey* series in collaboration with Sir Arthur C. Clarke.

In his introduction, **Ray Bradbury** has owned up to the fact that, had the plan to have him write the screenplay for this much loved SF movie gone ahead, the first thing he would have done would have been kill off Robby the Robot (or at least severely downgrade his status in the film). The second would have been to make more of the Id. Somewhere, on one of the alleged myriad alternate Earths, that movie was made—now all we need to do is find a way to get there. . . .

Ray is currently being fêted by a number of independent specialist presses—the editor's own PS Publishing included—all of them hell-bent on reissuing those classic Bradbury story collections and novels from days gone by. Meanwhile, despite having clocked up eighty-six years, Ray is still working feverishly on a dizzying number of projects.

Peter Crowther drives his wife, Nicky, to distraction by tuning into any TV channel that's showing *Forbidden Planet*, no matter how long the movie has been running. "It's one of those films," he says, wistfully and without apology, "that I could watch over and over again. It's the whole mythos of the Krell . . . those colossal tunnels—both vertical and horizontal—of equipment and the incredible poignancy of that wonderfully superior race doomed to extinction because of its own progress. Highly relevant today, methinks. But relevance aside, it's just a marvellous movie . . . and when I realized that this year was its fiftieth anniversary, I just knew we had to commemorate that in some way. And, with this book, I think we've done exactly that . . . in spades! My thanks go to all the contributors as well as to Marty Greenberg and the gang at Tekno Books and, of course, our friends at DAW Books."

This year (2006) saw the appearance of *Dark Times*, Pete's fifth collection, with another at the planning stages. The long-awaited second part of his *Forever Twilight* cycle and a separate short SF novel, *Kings of Infinite Space* are scheduled for a spring 2007 publication, to tie in with Pete's appearance as a Guest of Honor at the World Horror Convention in Toronto.

Paul Di Filippo wanted to play with the archetypical structure of the kind of tale in which the hero dashes off on a rescue mission to a mysterious world and succeeds in toppling the hidden empire or conspiracy or potentate thereon. But the author sounds a cautionary note. "In my story, the hero is misguided, and the nexus of mystery triumphs, as it should, since it has access to a higher level of understanding than the limited protagonist."

This year sees the publication of Paul's new collection, *Shuteye for the Timebroker* and his Creature from the Black Lagoon novel, *Time's Black Lagoon*. He lives in Providence, RI, where he and his longtime partner, Deborah, occasionally take pity on visiting British writer/editors, driving them out to see Lovecraft's final resting place and taking them for burgers in aluminium diners straight out of Will Eisner's *Spirit* comic-strips.

You will easily be able to deduce the oldest possible age **Scott Edelman** could have been when he first saw *Forbidden Planet* by his admission that, at least at that initial viewing, he was far more interested in the shiny surface of Robby the Robot than in the somewhat softer surface of Anne Francis.

Being born in 1955 makes Scott one year older than *Forbidden Planet*, and he didn't actually get to see it until ten years later . . . and then the next day, and the next one, and the one after that; it was in constant rotation on something called *The Million Dollar Movie*, aired multiple times weekly by WPIX in New York. "For them, it was a money-saving operation," Scott says, "but for me, it was indoctrination. I'm sure that *Forbidden Planet*, with its robot, rocket ship, and creature from the Id was one of the reasons I fell in love with science fiction."

The novelization of the film was also meaningful to young Edelman. "I remember being in the Boy Scouts not too long after having overdosed on the film," Scott recalls, "and discovering the book as my troop paused at a newsstand just as we were about to go on a field trip. We walked across the George Washington Bridge, and as we hiked for six miles across New Jersey, and my fellow scouts learned to tie knots, reproduce bird calls, and properly identify trees, I ignored the real world for outer space, reading as I walked, constantly tripping over my feet, but never losing my place. Which I guess says as much about me as does my preference for Robby the Robot over Anne Francis."

Scott Edelman the editor currently edits both *Science Fiction Weekly*, the Internet magazine of news, reviews, and interviews, and *SCI FI*, the official print magazine of the SCI FI Channel. He was the founding editor of *Science Fiction Age*, which he edited during its entire eight-year run, and he has also edited *Sci-Fi Entertainment* for almost four years, as well as two other SF media magazines, *Sci-Fi Universe* and *Sci-Fi Flix*. He has been a four-time Hugo Award finalist for Best Editor.

Scott the writer has published more than fifty short stories in magazines such as *The Twilight Zone*, *Absolute Magnitude*, and *Science Fiction Review*, and in anthologies such as *Crossroads: Southern Tales of the Fantastic*, *Men Writing SF as Women*, and *MetaHorror*, as well as in two of *Forbidden Planets'* predecessors, *Moon Shots* and *Mars Probes*. He has twice been a Stoker Award finalist in the category of Short Story.

Matthew Hughes thinks he first saw *Forbidden Planet* on a black-and-white TV in the late fifties before he was even into double digits. "So the film might well have been my introduction to the idea that the psyche contains different levels, components, rooms to visit and maybe get stuck in," he says, "and thus has had an effect on my work that I haven't even begun to gauge."

Matt has produced four novels and a short-story collection and is currently partway through a series of novels following the career of Henghis Hapthorn, foremost freelance discriminator of the Archonate on a far-future Old Earth.

"From the initial conceit of *Forbidden Planet* to the motivating idea behind my story is a short distance,"

Alex Irvine writes. "In the movie, remnant technology brings the psychodrama to a head, while in this story the planet itself is the technology. This was interesting to me because it adds an interesting subtext to the question of the psychological effects of space exploration, which I've written about in other stories, i.e., to what extent does the pure experience of another world become its own psychological minefield? Perhaps that's enough to destabilize anyone, without the added complications of winsome refugees or arcane technologies.

"The inner space of the human mind is more interesting than the scenery of outer space for its own sake, as the makers of the film surely knew. In the film, though, the turmoil of this inner space is manifested by the device of the energy monster that assaults Dr. Morbius's compound. I wanted to see what kind of effect it was possible to achieve with a subtler, more introspective take on the same dynamic. What if the manifestation of the character's emotional imbalance were not a placeholder like the energy monster but a subtle rebellion of the planet itself against the laws of reality the other characters need to understand their phenomenal world?"

Alex also skipped the romantic interaction, which, he says, "although it was apparently inspiring to Gene Roddenberry, doesn't move me. The Shakespearean roots of the story were impossible to ignore, and although Robby the Robot is usually pegged as Ariel whenever someone bothers to draw up a schema comparing *Forbidden Planet* to *The Tempest*, I always wanted Robby to be more of a Caliban figure . . . thus my own title, and the nod to Caliban's dream soliloquy in the story."

Alex is the author of the novels *A Scattering of Jades*, *One King, One Soldier*, and *The Narrows*. Much of his published short fiction is collected in *Unintended Consequences* and the forthcoming *Pictures from an Expedition*. In addition to the Locus, Crawford, and

International Horror Guild awards for his fiction, he has won a New England Press Association award for investigative journalism. He is assistant professor of English at the University of Maine, where he teaches fiction writing.

Jay Lake grew up without television or movies, living in the Third World in the era before satellite television or VCRs. So at an age when most protowriters are staring at late night horror movies (or whatever the equivalent for their generation), he always had his nose in books. Jay's first exposure to *Forbidden Planet* was actually in the theme song to *Rocky Horror Picture Show*, to which he lost many, many evenings in college. For years Lake confused Robby the Robot with Will Robinson's robot from *Lost in Space*. So though he grew up reading science fiction, he reluctantly confesses that he'd never seen *Forbidden Planet* until he was preparing for this project. Jay knew from researching the movie that it was an adaptation of Shakespeare's *The Tempest*. He knew from hanging around art directors' offices what Robby looked like and talked like. And he certainly knew about Anne Francis.

Watching the movie, Jay realized how profound its influence was on everything from the original *Star Trek* to New British Space Opera. While this is a truism that was surely obvious to everyone else in the genre, Jay must own his naïveté with some pride. It brought him fresh at the age of forty-one to this film, which is among the great wellsprings of our fictional culture. Jay watched the movie, brushed up his Shakespeare, and decided that *King Lear* was more interesting for his purposes. The result, of course, is left to the judgment of the reader.

Jay lives in Portland, Oregon, with his books and two inept cats, where he works on numerous writing and editing projects, including the World Fantasy Award-nominated *Polyphony* anthology series from

Wheatland Press. His next novel, *Trial of Flowers*, will be available in the fall of 2006.

The creators of *Forbidden Planet* made no secret of the fact that they'd borrowed and updated the plot of Shakespeare's *The Tempest*. "In the same spirit," says **Paul McAuley**, "I hope that no one minds that my little homage to this marvelous film borrows and updates its robots, monsters, and supertechnology hidden in an underground alien city."

Paul has worked as a researcher in biology in various universities, including Oxford and UCLA, and for six years was a lecturer in botany at St. Andrews University before becoming a full-time writer. His first novel, *Four Hundred Billion Stars*, won the Philip K. Dick Memorial Award, and his sixth, *Fairyland*, won the Arthur C. Clarke and John W. Campbell Awards. His latest novel is *Mind's Eye*. He lives in North London.

" 'Kyle Meets the River' was a tricky write," says **Ian McDonald**. "The *Forbidden Planets* theme was a rich compost, and I wanted to try to plant a seed from my future India concept, but it didn't really take until I remembered J.G. Ballard's comment about Earth being an alien planet. Then the very same day, I read a newspaper article about the high-security gated enclaves for reconstruction workers in Iraq. There are forbidden worlds all around us, at every footstep, it seems.

"Looking back on the original movie now, what strikes me—apart from Leslie Nielson—is that, unusually for a fifties American film, there isn't a villain. There's no ridiculous, infantile Darth Vader . . . just monsters from the Id all the way down. And you don't beat those with a fluorescent tube and Joseph Campbell cod-mythologizing."

Ian lives just outside Belfast in Northern Ireland and has day jobs in television program development.

His most recent novel was *River of Gods*, BSFA award winner and Hugo and Clarke Award nominee. "It's set in India on the centenary of its independence," Ian explains, "and 'Kyle Meets the River' draws on the same background." Continuing this trend of trying to get the tax department to pay for his foreign holidays, Ian's latest project is *Brasyl*, unsurprisingly set in present, mid-21st- and 18th-century Brazil.

Michael Moorcock last saw *Forbidden Planet* in French. "It rather improved on the somewhat wooden acting of the majority of the cast," he says, while accepting that the movie remains an elegant piece of science fiction.

"The moral, applied to the obsessions of the day, remains a perfectly good one in the liberal humanist tradition," Mike adds. "In fact, I'm surprised there hasn't been a remake, perhaps with a better cast and less hokey comic relief. But no doubt, if there were, it would be twice the length, contain unnecessarily gruesome special effects and a far more lugubrious message. So perhaps the only improvement is to watch it in the French version."

Mike's most recently published novel, *The Vengeance of Rome*, concluded the Pyat quartet, a sequence of novels also comprising *Byzantium Endures*, *The Laughter of Carthage*, and *Jerusalem Endures*, about international events that came to permit the Nazi Holocaust.

Mike lives in France and Texas and is currently working on a memoir of Mervyn and Maeve Peake and a text accompanying Peake's *Sunday Book* illustrations, which will be first published in Paris.

Forbidden Planet loomed frustratingly large in **Alastair Reynolds**'s imagination—"Ever since it was shown on BBC2 in the mid-seventies," he says, "as part of a run of classic science fiction movies. I think they also showed *This Island Earth* in the same Wednesday evening slot. I say 'frustratingly' because I remember only seeing the film up to about the point when Robbie arrives to meet the crew—then we had to go out somewhere. I was quite impressed by what I'd seen up until then—I thought the flying saucer space cruiser was seriously cool—and also more than a little scared. It must have been a good ten years before I saw the film all the way through, and I've never looked back since. The influence of it—for better or worse—runs through almost everything I've written, and in my wildest fantasies I get to design, script, and direct the all-conquering remake. I still see the future in glorious Eastman color.

"One of my favorite bands, Pavement, once recorded a song entitled 'Krell Vid User.' " Need we say more?!

Al is the author of four novels set in the *Revelation Space* universe, plus two stand-alone books, *Century Rain* and *Pushing Ice*. A collection of stories from the RS universe is due in 2006, and he is now at work on another novel, as yet untitled, which will be a return to that universe. Al has been a full-time writer since 2004, and he and his wife live in the Netherlands.

A child of the seventies, **Chris Roberson** reckons he must have seen *Forbidden Planet* half a dozen times before he was eighteen. "The movie always seemed to me like the product of another world, a glimpse into some alternate history that almost, but didn't quite, happen. The men of United Planets Cruiser C-57D, with guns and swagger, looked like they belonged more on the deck of a WWII PT boat than walking under the green skies of Altair IV, which might have contributed to the movie's sense of verisimilitude, even in such a fantastic setting.

"I was haunted by the electric silhouette of the creature from Morbius's id, trying to claw its way through the protective field, which still seems as real to me as any high-tech CGI phantasm from a contemporary blockbuster. I still hold by my theory that the creature that attacks the crew, time and again, is the product of Altaira's id, and not Morbius's, and there's nothing anyone can say that will convince me otherwise."

Chris's short fiction can be found in the anthologies *Live Without a Net, The Many Faces of Van Helsing, Tales of the Shadowmen, Vols. 1 and 2,* and *FutureShocks,* and also in the pages of *Asimov's Postscripts,* and *Subterranean Magazine.* His novels include *Here, There & Everywhere, The Voyage of Night Shining White,* and *Paragaea: A Planetary Romance,* and he is the editor of the anthology *Adventure Vol. 1.* Roberson has been a finalist for the World Fantasy Award for Short Fiction, twice a finalist for the John W. Campbell Award for Best New Writer, and, again, twice a finalist for the Sidewise Award for Best Alternate History Short Form (winning in 2004 with his story "O One").

"I've loved that marvelous, slightly clunky, oddly affecting motion picture ever since I first saw it," says **Adam Roberts** of *Forbidden Planet,* "and my story was written in a sort of dialog with the movie. What I took from the movie (apart, obviously, from the idea of, like, a *planet* that was, well, *forbidden*) was: one, the idea of basing SF on a classic text (in my case not *The Tempest* as in the film, but, in perhaps a rather oblique way, the Island of the Lotophagoi from Homer's *Odyssey*); and two, the sense you get from the film of the forbidden planet itself as just lovely looking—not an actual slagheap or slate-mine somewhere like in *Doctor Who,* and not a real stretch of the Mojave a short drive away from the studio's backlot, like a thousand Los Angeles SF B-movies; but those gorgeously painted backdrops, those wonderfully staged sets.

"The thing about those old-style painted special effects is that they always look that little bit cleaner and nicer than modern-day photorealistic CGI. They're already halfway to being painterly art, in the same way that the melancholy of Edward Hopper's paintings looks much more beguiling than any photograph from the same era. It has close affinity to the cover art of Edmund 'Emsh' Alexander or Frank Kelly Freas or Chesley Bonestell, those superb artists that produced cover artwork for *Astounding* and *Galaxy* and all the rest in the 1940s and 1950s. There's something so wonderfully clean, fresh and attractive about those images, especially when you compare them to some of the digital art (to pluck an example from the air: *Attack of the Clones*) that has been directly inspired by them.

"To make that comparison is to realize how cluttered and offputting the latter mostly is, and to rekindle your yearning for the former. So my idea in this story was to try to hark back to that aesthetic. If it seems counterintuitive that I've written a John Campbell-ish story in the idiom of Don DeLillo, then I can only say that it makes a weird kind of sense to me. After all, part of the appeal of the film is the way it buries an oblique postmodernity ('monsters from the Id!') inside the livery of a full-blown action-adventure science-fiction narrative."

Adam is Professor of Nineteenth-Century Literature at Royal Holloway, University of London. He lives west of the capital with his wife and daughter. Adam's latest novel is *Gradisil* (2006) and his next will be *Land of the Headless*.

CJ Cherryh
Classic Series in New Omnibus Editions

Julie E. Czerneda

Web Shifters

"A great adventure following an engaging character across a divertingly varied series of worlds."—*Locus*

Esen is a shapeshifter, one of the last of an ancient race. Only one Human knows her true nature—but those who suspect are determined to destroy her!

BEHOLDER'S EYE
0-88677-818-2
CHANGING VISION
0-88677-815-8
HIDDEN IN SIGHT
0-7564-0139-9

Also by Julie E. Czerneda:
IN THE COMPANY OF OTHERS
0-88677-999-7
"An exhilarating science fiction thriller"
—*Romantic Times*

To Order Call: 1-800-788-6262

Julie E. Czerneda

THE TRADE PACT UNIVERSE

"Space adventure mixes with romance...a heck of a
lot of fun." —*Locus*

Sira holds the answer to the survival of her
species, the Clan, within the multi-species
Trade Pact. But it will take a Human's
courage to show her the way.

A THOUSAND WORDS FOR
STRANGER
0- 88677-769-0

TIES OF POWER
0-88677-850-6

TO TRADE THE STARS
0-7564-0075-9

To Order Call: 1-800-788-6262

OTHERLAND

TAD WILLIAMS

*"The Otherland books are a
major accomplishment."*
—Publishers Weekly

"It will captivate you."
—Cinescape

*In many ways it is humankind's most stunning
achievement. This most exclusive of places is also
one of the world's best-kept secrets, but somehow,
bit by bit, it is claiming Earth's most valuable
resource: its children.*

CITY OF GOLDEN SHADOW (Vol. One)
0-88677-763-1

RIVER OF BLUE FIRE (Vol. Two)
0-88677-844-1

MOUNTAIN OF BLACK GLASS (Vol. Three)
0-88677-906-5

SEA OF SILVER LIGHT (Vol. Four)
0-75640-030-9

To Order Call: 1-800-788-6262